CHICOPEE PUBLIC LIBRARY
449 Front Street
Chicopee, MA 0

W9-AVL-843

G.G.

MAY 0 4

*Other Avon Romances by*
**Karen Hawkins**

AN AFFAIR TO REMEMBER
THE SEDUCTION OF SARA
A BELATED BRIDE
THE ABDUCTION OF JULIA

# Karen Hawkins

# Confessions of a Scoundrel

*An Avon Romantic Treasure*

**AVON BOOKS**
*An Imprint of HarperCollinsPublishers*

This is a work of fiction. Names, characters, places, and incidents are products of the author's imagination or are used fictitiously and are not to be construed as real. Any resemblance to actual events, locales, organizations, or persons, living or dead, is entirely coincidental.

AVON BOOKS
*An Imprint of* HarperCollins*Publishers*
10 East 53rd Street
New York, New York 10022-5299

Copyright © 2003 by Karen Hawkins
ISBN: 0-7394-3240-0

All rights reserved. No part of this book may be used or reproduced in any manner whatsoever without written permission, except in the case of brief quotations embodied in critical articles and reviews. For information address Avon Books, an Imprint of HarperCollins Publishers.

Avon Trademark Reg. U.S. Pat. Off. and in Other Countries, Marca Registrada, Hecho en U.S.A.
HarperCollins® is a registered trademark of HarperCollins Publishers Inc.

Printed in the U.S.A.

*Many thanks to Barb Hoeter,
who designed my clever new website
(www.karenhawkins.com)
to help me launch the Talisman Ring Series.
Thanks, Barb!*

*And to my new and wonderful editor,
Lyssa Keusch,
for her endless patience and wonderful advice.*

*Did ye hear the story of the St. John talisman ring? They say 'tis magic! Whichever of the brothers holds it in his possession will meet his one true love. At this moment, the ring 'tis hangin' from a ribbon on the coat of Brandon St. John, the handsomest of all.*

The Pemberleys' new maid, Anne, to her future mistress, Miss Liza Pritchard, while the two were addressing invitations for the wedding

# Chapter 1

*Brandon St. John is a very sensual man. When-
ever he looks at me, I get the most delicious shivers right down to my toes, just as if—Oh! Sorry. I
forgot I was talking to you.*

Miss Liza Pritchard to her fiancé, Sir Royce Pemberly,
on Bond Street, while shopping for
a present for Sir Royce's sister

"**H**e's dead."
From the depths of a brandy-fumed
slumber, Brandon St. John heard every word, rec-
ognizing his younger brother's voice instantly.

*Damn it, what is Devon doing in my dreams?* Devon was an annoyance when Brandon was awake.
During sleep, he was a positive menace.

"He cannot be dead," someone else answered.
"He's too stubborn to die in such a neat fashion,
stretched out in his own bed."

Brandon groaned at the new voice—it belonged to his half-brother, Anthony Elliot, the Earl
of Greyley.

Just to make Brandon's dream a true nightmare, Marcus, his oldest brother, added in a deep
voice, "Brandon is not dead; he was snoring when
we came in."

"A pity we can't set him afire," Devon said cheerfully. "That would wake him."

Someone grabbed Brand's foot, jerking him the rest of the way into wakefulness. "Go away," he ordered, his voice muffled by his pillow.

Devon shook him again. "Rise, Brand! You've work to do."

"I've sleep to sleep, first," he muttered.

But there was no swaying Devon. "Get up!" he demanded.

Brandon started to lift his head, but the pounding behind his temples made him think better of it. "Poole!" he called in a rusty voice. Poole served as Brand's valet, butler, and general manservant. "Where is that man? I need my pistol."

"Pistol?" Anthony's voice deepened with amusement. "Are you going hunting?"

"Yes," Brand answered. "I'm going hunting for the damned rodents who've infested my chambers."

"Poole cannot fetch your weapon now," Devon said, always eager to spread bad news. "We told him we were famished and he's gone to find us some breakfast."

Bloody hell, what a horrid way to start the day. Brandon hated mornings. They were filled with annoyingly cheerful people who liked to aggravate other, more important individuals who needed extra sleep to make up for the fact that they had not slept the night before.

"Perhaps we should call for a nice cool pitcher of water," Anthony said, his deep lazy voice filtering through the air. "That should get this slug-abed on his feet."

Brand pulled the pillow over his head. His throat felt like the bottom of a salt barrel—scratchy and dry. And that was just the beginning of his complaints; his head ached, his stomach roiled, and the inside of his mouth tasted like chalk.

He had a vague memory of the night before. Of a beautiful woman with reddish gold hair and a card game where the stakes had gone from guineas to articles of clothing to other, far more stimulating wagers. Celeste was perfect for him in every way—beautiful, intelligent, talented in bed, and married to someone else. No man could ask for more. Except Brandon.

Marcus's dry voice came from the foot of the bed. "It appears our brother has had yet another difficult night."

Brandon would have shrugged if it hadn't meant he'd have to move. Marcus was wrong—it hadn't been a difficult night at all. And that was the problem. No matter how much Brandon enjoyed a dalliance, within two weeks he inevitably found himself looking for a new challenge.

The sad truth was that every amusement of late had seemed flat. Brandon was living beneath a horrible pall—a feeling that somehow, some way, he was missing out on something important.

*What maudlin nonsense.* Brandy apparently had the unfortunate side effect of making one mawkish. From now on, he'd stick to port. Brandon lifted his aching head and forced his lids to rise. Blinding light pierced his eyes. He groaned, and then groped blindly for the half-finished glass of brandy that rested beside his bed. He gulped it down, his throat stinging as he thunked the glass back on the stand.

"Hair of the dog?" Anthony said with amusement.

Brandon wiped his mouth with the back of his hand and turned to squint over his shoulder. "Just tell me what you want and then get the hell out of here."

"How rude," Devon said. "I expected a greeting, at least."

"From Brandon?" Anthony appeared astonished. "Unless you wear skirts, have a full bosom *and* a husband, Brandon will not give you the time of day."

Brandon tried to decide whether to glare or just ignore Anthony. Truthfully, of all his brothers, Brand was closest to his half-brother. Anthony's sleepy air was a hoax—he had more energy and determination than any man half his size. And he had a sharp wit that always made Brandon grin.

Not now, of course. No one could smile at this time of the morning. Brand eyed his half-brother blearily. "I thought you were still on your honeymoon."

"Anna and I returned last night, just in time for the meeting."

*Oh bloody hell, the meeting.* Brandon rubbed his temples. "I'd forgotten."

"We noticed," Marcus said, his blue gaze coolly reproachful. The oldest, he ruled the family fortune, his life and those of the younger members of the St. John family with an iron fist.

As the next oldest in line, Brandon should have been deeply involved in the family financial endeavors. But even at an early age, Marcus's unrelenting need to control everything and everyone around him—especially the family fortune—had set Brandon's teeth on edge.

Thus it was that at the genteel age of twenty-two, when most of his friends were drinking and whoring their way through London, Brandon had collected what money he could and purchased two ill-kempt estates outside of Shropeshire. That had been many years ago and the estates were now merged into one, a very productive and profitable venture providing Brandon with an astonishing income. It had been years since he'd drawn on his St. John accounts, a fact that had infuriated Marcus even more.

Not that Brandon cared. He hadn't done it for Marcus, but rather to prove something to himself. When his estate had first turned a profit, he'd been overjoyed. But now, with the work complete and his fortune even more secure, Brandon found that he was a little . . . bored, a feeling that had lingered and grown over the ensuing months and years. He sighed restlessly and glanced at Marcus.

"If you must have a meeting, then have one." Brandon rolled onto his back, the sheets tangling about his hips as he stuffed the pillow beneath his head. "We're all here, so we might as well get it over with."

Devon's humor faded. "We cannot meet in your bedchamber. It smells of a French whorehouse."

Anthony tilted his head to one side, his gaze narrowing. "I recognize that perfume. Is it—"

"Get out," Brand interrupted. He should have known they would make things difficult. He lifted himself on his elbow and pointed to the door. "Give me a few moments to dress and I'll join you."

"You'd better," Marcus said. "We're through being nice."

"Nice? Is it nice to break into someone's house and rudely awaken them?"

"We didn't break in; we knocked. Poole answered. He informed us you were asleep. We informed him that we really didn't care. Then we came here."

From now on, Brand would see to it that his valet carried a weapon whenever he answered the door before noon.

"We'll give you five minutes to dress," Marcus said.

"Five minutes?"

"That's more than I'd have given you," Anthony said. He glanced at the door. "Sorry to disappoint you, Bridgeton. I know you wished to see us set Brandon afire."

"Bridgeton?" Brand followed Anthony's gaze to the doorway. There, lounging at his ease, was Brandon's brother-in-law, Nicholas Montrose, the Earl of Bridgeton.

Nick grinned on catching Brand's bleary gaze. "Lovely morning, isn't it?"

"Go to hell," Brand growled.

It was insulting that his brothers had brought Bridgeton, whom they all detested, although "detest" was too strong a word. They'd all detested him *before* he'd married their sister, Sara, but only after he'd compromised her so badly he'd been forced to wed her. Now though, to everyone's surprise, it seemed as if it was a love match.

A rakehell of the worst sort, Bridgeton had proven to be a doting husband and devoted father. It was difficult to maintain a healthy hatred for a man who treated your sister as if she were made of glass, but Brandon did his best.

He pushed himself into a sitting position and tossed the sheet aside.

Devon shook his head. "For the love of God, put on some clothes."

Brand promptly stood. For good measure, he even stretched mightily though he had to keep one hand on the bedrail to remain upright. The whole world seemed to swirl before his eyes.

"Come, everyone," Marcus directed. "We'll wait in the outer room while Brandon dresses." Marcus strode out the door, Anthony and Nick following.

Devon trailed behind, stopping when he reached the doorway. He tilted his head to one side, his blue eyes sparkling with mischief. "Was she worth the trouble?"

"Who?" Brandon asked.

"The delightful Celeste. She has been talking quite freely you know, hinting that the two of you might become more than friends."

"She errs. We have nothing more than a brief dalliance."

Devon shrugged, a curious look in his eyes. "Brand . . . why not? Everyone knows her husband has one foot in the grave—has for years. He's at least twenty years older than Celeste and once he's gone, she'll inherit a fortune. If you play your cards right, you could—"

"—get dressed before Marcus decides to drag

me into a meeting with no clothes at all. Leave, Devon. Unless you want me lounging naked during the entire meeting."

Devon started as if to say something else, then apparently thought better of it. "Oh very well. I was just trying to help." He disappeared out the door, leaving Brand alone.

Brandon raked his hair from his face. Devon was a fool. Marriage was the furthest thing from Brand's mind—from any sane man's mind.

The St. Johns were targets for every matchmaking mama in town. Over the years, Brandon had watched as woman after woman had set their cap for either him or one of his brothers. At first, it had been an amusement. But then, after a while, it became an annoyance. Now Brandon found it a deadly bore. He wanted nothing to do with a needy woman, one who saw him merely as an end to a means. When he married, it would be to a woman of substance and breeding, one with as many funds to her name as he had to his.

That the two would come together as equals on all levels was, he'd decided, the only way such a union could work.

Poole entered the room, a letter and a tall glass with a yellow mixture resting atop a tray.

Brand eyed the glass sullenly. "I hate that stuff."

"Yes, sir." Poole removed the glass from the tray and held it out.

"I don't want it."

"Yes, sir." Poole continued to hold out the glass.

"You're incorrigible."

"Indeed, sir. It's my duty."

Brand sighed, took the glass, and threw back the

contents, fighting a shudder as the thick liquid slid down his throat. "God, what's in that?" he gasped.

Poole took the glass and replaced it on the tray. "Two raw eggs, a boiled kidn—"

"*Wait.* I don't want to know." Brand closed his eyes and tried to breathe through his nose to still the nausea.

Poole set the tray to one side and picked up the letter. "This came for you this morning, sir." He turned away to open the wardrobe.

Brandon opened the letter.

*St. John,*

*I must see you. I'll be arriving tomorrow evening. Send me word when you're free. Please. This is very important.*

*Yours,*
*Wycham*

Roger Carrington, Viscount Wycham, was an old acquaintance of Brand's. They'd known each other since Eton, and while they hadn't been close friends since, they kept in touch. "I wonder what he wants."

"Sir?"

"Nothing." Brandon folded the letter and replaced it on the tray. "I hope my brothers didn't trouble you when they came in this morning."

"Trouble me? Oh no, sir. I was already awake when they arrived. However, I am sorry you were disturbed. I tried to stop them, but it was impossible."

"You cannot stop a St. John," Brand said, his stomach settling. He took a long breath, and then said in a stronger voice, "My buff breeches and the blue coat."

He washed and dressed in less than ten minutes, a true feat considering the intricacy of his neckcloth. Poole's magical concoction had wrought its usual miracle and Brandon was feeling better by the moment.

He smoothed the sleeve of his new coat with a faint appreciation. He felt far more human now and quite capable of dealing with his brothers. "Poole, my new watch fob, if you please. And—no, wait."

Poole halted by the dresser. "Sir?"

"Today's meeting calls for something more . . ." Brand smiled. "Something that might irritate my brothers as much as they have irritated me."

Poole raised his brows.

"The St. John talisman ring."

"The ring, sir? You told me to hide it and never admit where it was."

"Just get it. Find a pin and a ribbon, too."

Poole bowed, then opened a small silver cask in the far corner of the dresser. He dug among the watch fobs a moment then withdrew a small silver circlet. He handed it to Brandon, the morning light glinting off the etched runes that decorated the band.

Brandon held it in his palm, the metal strangely warm. Mother had believed that whomever possessed the ring would find their true love. It had worked for Anthony, who had married his Anna less than six months after he'd received the ring.

But for Brandon . . . he'd had the blasted thing for almost two months and it hadn't done a damn thing.

Not that he wanted it to "work." God knew he was perfectly happy as he was, no matter what his brothers thought. No, what he really wanted to do was trick one of his brothers—perhaps Devon—into taking the ridiculous thing.

Poole handed him a short red ribbon. Brand tied the ring to the end of it, then pinned it to his coat directly above his heart. The red ribbon stood out in stark relief against his dark blue coat, the ring gleamed brightly. "There," he said with some satisfaction. "That should make them nervous."

"Indeed," Poole said, "it has the same effect on me."

Brand grinned, then left to join his brothers and brother-in-law in the small outer apartment of his lodgings.

"There you are," Anthony said from where he leaned against the mantel. "We were just—" His eyes widened. "The talisman ring."

Devon's head jerked up. Perched on the edge of Brandon's writing desk, he had been idly twirling a brass paperweight. "God, no! Brandon, don't think you can trick me into taking that blasted thing. I won't have it."

"It's in my possession. I can wear it if I want."

"You're just trying to make me nervous," Devon said.

"Am I?" Brandon walked past Bridgeton and Marcus, who were both seated in the matching chairs before the fireplace, and took a place on the settee.

"You are a devil," Devon mumbled. "I have nightmares of finding that blasted thing under my pillow."

"Don't give him any ideas," Anthony said with a twinkle.

Brand regarded his half-brother with a flat stare. "Unlike you, my dearest brother, I have no intentions of hiding the ring in someone's cake. It's a wonder I didn't break a tooth."

Anthony chuckled. "I just wanted to share the wealth."

Brandon wondered what the ring was really worth. Probably not much, though it appeared to be of some antiquity. But to the St. Johns, it was as priceless as it was annoying. None of them really wanted to keep it because of the rumors of the ring's mystical powers. Not that they believed such nonsense . . . it was just the *idea* of what it represented that made them cringe. But since it had been Mother's, it was far too dear to simply lock away.

Brandon looked at the shimmering ring and tried to remember a day when she hadn't worn it. They'd all taken turns fobbing off the blasted ring, especially his brother Chase, who always—

Brand glanced around the room. "Where is Chase? I thought we were all supposed to attend."

Marcus's frown deepened. "Chase is the reason for this little meeting."

Devon hefted the brass paperweight in one hand as if trying to ascertain its weight. "Our beloved brother left town two days ago."

Marcus nodded. "Of his own free will and in fairly good health. The problem is that I recently discovered he's been residing in the pocket of Viscountess Westforth."

Westforth. Brand tried to recall the name. "I've heard of her. A racy piece, is she not? Part of the demimonde."

Marcus nodded. "That's her."

"Where is Viscount Westforth?"

Devon polished the paperweight with his sleeve. "He died four years ago, racing his curricle to Bristol."

"A poor whipster?"

"A drunk one. He challenged young Oglethorpe on the Bristol Road. They were both deep in their cups; Westforth was a bit of a wild one." Devon tossed the paperweight into the air and stretched out his hand to catch it.

Brandon leaned out and grabbed the paperweight in midair. He then carefully placed it on the table before him, out of Devon's reach. "Let me guess the rest of the story. Since Westforth's death, his widow has been living off his largesse."

Devon shrugged. "Something like that. Westforth's father, the Earl of Rutland, believes their daughter-in-law is to blame for Westforth's death. He believes she encouraged her husband's wild ways and was glad when he died. Rutland saw to it that she didn't collect much when Westforth died, but she apparently has enough to exist. Or she did. I wonder if she's suddenly found herself short of funds."

"In a word," Marcus said, "if this history is correct, Lady Westforth may very well be a fortune hunter."

Brandon didn't like the thought of his little brother in the coils of such a woman. Chase seemed vulnerable now.

At one time, Chase had been the most light-hearted of the St. Johns—forever playing pranks on one or the other of them. All that had changed sometime last year, though no one knew exactly what had happened.

It began rather gradually. Chase had transformed, thin layers of change at a time. Now he was bitter, seemingly filled with self-loathing and frequently drunk, even before noon.

It was painful watching blithe, happy-go-lucky Chase disintegrate before their very eyes. That was the reason Brandon and his brothers had begun intervening in Chase's life—he was not himself. "How seriously is he involved?"

Marcus's expression darkened. "If we don't do something soon, he may marry the chit. He obtained a special license."

"Bloody hell! Why would the fool want to get married?"

Anthony raised a brow. "Some of us find the wedded state far from deplorable."

Brandon stifled a sigh. God save him from the cheery false happiness of a newly wedded couple. He wondered if perhaps he would ever feel that way . . . then decided it didn't matter. First he had to find a woman who managed to keep him interested longer than two weeks. "Where is Chase now?"

"Gone to make the final arrangements," Marcus said. "We should act while he is out of town."

Knowing Chase's volatile temper, that seemed

to be the best way to proceed. "Something must be done at once."

"I'm so glad you agree," Marcus said, a slight edge to his voice. "That is why I called for a meeting this morning."

Brandon met his brother's gaze without flinching. "I overslept," he said softly. "I will not apologize again."

Marcus's mouth thinned, his jaw tightening.

Brand didn't back down. He met his brother's gaze solidly.

Anthony sighed. "Enough, you two. Brandon, you should know that we held the meeting this morning."

"And we made some excellent decisions." Devon's grin glinted.

Brandon didn't like the sound of that. "What decisions?"

"Someone has to visit this woman," Marcus said, "and ascertain her intentions. Then, if necessary, buy her off."

Bloody hell, surely they hadn't—"I am *not* visiting Chase's paramour. I paid off the last actress he was involved with and he nearly took my head off for it. I won't do it again."

Marcus crossed his arms, a satisfied smile touching the hard line of his mouth. "*You* missed the meeting."

Brand leaned his aching head against the high back of the settee. "I wish I could assist you, but I'm busy today. Too busy to irk Chase into challenging me to a duel."

"If you can't go," Marcus said, "then ask someone else. I just want it taken care of and quickly."

That was a thought. Brand looked at Devon. "Can't," he said promptly. "I'm going out of town."

"When?"

"As soon as possible."

"And I," Anthony volunteered, "am to meet Anna at the modiste's."

"Your wife can surely spare you for an hour or so," Brand said in a surly tone.

"You obviously have never spoken to my wife."

Brandon had spoken to Anna many times and he had to admit that Anthony probably had a point. Anna was just like Brandon's sister, Sara—they possessed spines of pure steel. That was probably why they were such good friends.

At the thought of Sara, Brandon looked at his brother-in-law and wondered if Bridgeton might be willing to assist him. The man did seem determined to get involved in family matters.

As if he could read Brandon's mind, Bridgeton shook his head. "It would be in bad form for someone other than a member of the family to attend to such a delicate situation."

Brandon glowered. "Why did you even bother to come?"

Nick smiled gently. "To watch the festivities, of course."

Brandon decided he really, *really* disliked his brother-in-law. "Blast you to hell."

"On that note, we'll leave." Marcus stood. "Lady Westforth is not a milquetoast female like some of Chase's past acquaintances. I advise you to approach her carefully."

"She is also quite beautiful," Devon said unexpectedly. "She has violet eyes, so pure they look as if—" He flushed when he realized everyone was looking his way. "Or so I've heard."

Brandon sighed. "Actress, opera singer, or orange seller . . . what difference does it make? I will offer the chit money to leave town and she'll accept. They always do."

"It's settled, then," Anthony said. He glanced at Marcus. "Are we finished?"

"We are. Brandon, however, has just begun." Marcus's hard blue eyes gleamed with humor. "Come, everyone. Our brother has a busy day ahead of him."

"I thought you were staying for breakfast."

"We were," Marcus replied coolly, "but we don't wish to keep you from your duties. We'll eat at White's."

They filed out, all in such good spirits that Brandon was hard put not to start a brawl right on the steps of his own establishment.

For several long moments after their merriment had faded, Brandon remained on the settee, resting his head against the pillowed back and wishing he was still asleep.

What a morning. He was ill, tired, and in a horrid mood. His neck ached too, as if he'd slept in the wrong position. He suddenly remembered the letter and sighed. Oh yes, he also had to worry about his friend, Wycham. Worst of all, he now had to rescue a brother who, when he finally returned to town, would be angry enough to split Brandon on the end of his sword.

It was not a good way to start the day.

# Chapter 2

*It is one of the more unpalatable facts of life that very few women gracing the ballrooms of London possess one-tenth the beauty and wit of those found in the most common gaming hell. Which is why I prize my Liza all the more.*

Sir Royce Pemberley, trying to cheer up his friend, Mr. Scrope Davies, as that gentleman morosely examined the new crop of eligible females lined up against the wall at Almack's

"**P**lay at least one game. It will help keep your fingers nimble."

Lady Verena Westforth gazed at the cards her brother shuffled with such ease. A tiny itch rested in the palms of her hands. She curled her hand around the familiar feeling and forced her lips to curve into a faint smile. "Did you come all the way from Italy to tempt me into bad habits?"

James grinned, his golden hair glinting in the morning light. "What you have is talent, not 'bad habits.' Father says—"

"Spare me what Father says. He thinks any vice is a gift, so long as 'tis well done."

James's grin widened. "There's none like him, is there?"

"No, thank the heavens. The world would end if two such beings existed on the same planet."

"You sound like Mother." James eyed her fondly. "It's good to see you, Ver. It has been too long."

She returned his smile. There was a bond between her and James that went deeper than most. A bond that stretched across the distance she'd imposed between herself and her family.

Perhaps it was because James was her twin, though one wouldn't credit it to look at the two of them. It was true they both had blond hair, but hers was the fine gold of a new guinea, while his was dark blond streaked liberally with brown.

Even their eyes were different; Verena's were violet and James's were brown. Still, there were some similarities. They both possessed the faintly almond-shape eyes and the flyaway brows of some ancient Slavic ancestor.

Father always said they were descended from Russian royalty. But then Father would say that. She met James's quizzical gaze with a smile. "It's good to see you, too, even if you *did* arrive in the dead of night."

"It wasn't *that* late."

"It was almost dawn. And since it's been months since I last heard from you, I can't help but wonder if you're in trouble."

His expression froze, but then he grinned at her, his brown eyes crinkling at the corners. "I am always in trouble. But don't fret. The Lansdownes were born under a lucky star. No matter what, our paths are made."

Though she didn't believe his bravado for an

instant, Verena had to smile back at him. She knew his faults too well—most of them mirrored her own. Impatience, an endless thirst for excitement, and a deeply rooted dislike of being ordered about. "I wish you'd at least stay in my guest bedchamber."

"No one knows I'm your brother and I'd like to keep it that way. It's for your own good."

"If I had a reputation to protect, I might agree with you. But I don't, thanks to Andrew's father."

James's smile faded at the mention of the Earl of Rutland. "Is he still set on destroying your peace?"

"Every chance he gets," she replied lightly, though the effort cost her. She'd always known that Andrew's father hadn't liked her, but she hadn't realized the extent of the old man's feelings until after Andrew's death. Unknown to her, Andrew had been shielding her from bitter comments, vile rumors, and more.

Once he was gone, his father went unchecked, doing what he could to see to it that Verena became a social pariah, unwelcome except in the lowest levels of London society.

He'd thought to chase her from town, to remove her from Westforth House. But Verena had dug in her heels and instead of fleeing, had made a place for herself among the demimonde and turned Westforth House into the home she'd never had.

"Damn Rutland," James said. "I'd skewer his gizzard on my sword if I thought it would help." He absently dealt the cards into four hands on the small table. "Ver . . . are you happy?"

"Of course I am. Why do you ask?"

"I don't know. It just seems that you're . . . well, you're far too much alone." James sighed and set the cards on the table. "Do you still miss Andrew?"

"Every day." She said the words simply and was pleased to note that she only felt the briefest twinge of sadness. Andrew's life had been short and brilliant, a star flashing across the sky then disappearing from sight. He'd left her very little on his death except a heart full of memories and the deed to Westforth House. But those things were worth more than she could say. "I think I miss his laughter the most of all."

"That's one thing I'll give your late husband," James said, his voice touched with envy. "He enjoyed every minute of his life. I hope the same can be said about me once I'm gone."

There was something wistful about the way James said that. Verena eyed him narrowly. "That's it. Tell me what's wrong."

"Ver, don't—"

"*Now*, James. Or I'll write to Father and tell him you seem very out of sorts and could use a visit."

James's eyes flashed. "You wouldn't!"

"Try me."

He rubbed a hand over his chin, a childhood habit that usually meant he was puzzling through some thorny problem. "Perhaps I just came to see how you're getting on."

"And perhaps Father really is a Russian grand duke, as he loves to tell everyone."

"I don't have anything to tell you, thank you," James said, reaching into his pocket as if to draw out his watch. "Do we have time to play a game before the carriage—" He pulled his hand from his pocket, his brow lowering. "*Damn!*"

"What is it?"

"My watch. It's gone. I had it when I climbed from the carriage because I distinctly remember checking the time and—"

"Blast," Verena muttered. She marched to the bell pull and tugged it with more force than necessary.

"Ver, what are you—"

"Just wait." She crossed her arms and stared at the door.

Within seconds, a tall, cadaverously thin individual opened the door and peeked in. "Rang fer me, did ye?"

"Yes. Please come in."

He entered the room, his wide smile accentuated with an improbably bright gold tooth. "Whot can oiye do fer ye, m'lady?"

"Herberts, Mr. Lansdowne has lost his watch."

"Whot a pity."

James frowned. "Verena, I don't understand why you're telling this to your butler. He couldn't know—"

"Couldn't he?" She pinned a glare on Herberts. "Well?"

The butler sniffed. "Oiye moight know where the gent's ticker is. And then again, oiye moight not." He shoved his hands into his pockets and reeled back on his heels. "Mayhap the lad left it in his carriage."

"Mr. Lansdowne's watch is not in his carriage and you know it."

"M'lady," the butler said in an injured tone. "Oiye hope ye aren't implyin' anyfing unsavory about me character."

A choke of laughter erupted from James.

Verena ignored him. "Herberts," she said, only louder this time. "Return it. Now."

Herberts shook his head, his long, thin face folded in disapproval. "Ye're like a rat with a bone in yer teeth, ye are. 'Tis not a pretty way fer a lady to act."

Verena merely raised a brow and waited.

The butler sighed heavily. "Oh very well. Oiye pinched it. But the lad deserved it; he didn't hand o'er so much as a ha'penny fer openin' the door. Not a single grinder."

"What?" James exclaimed, all trace of amusement gone. "You expect a vale for merely opening a door?"

The butler cast an unimpressed eye over James's perfectly pressed eveningwear. "It's whot the *real* gentry do."

James opened his mouth as if to retort, but Verena forestalled him. "Herberts, even if Mr. Lansdowne owed you a vale—which I question—you have no right to steal from one of *my* guests." She marched to a small table by the door and pulled it out from the wall. "Empty your pockets."

The butler's face turned mournful as he slowly moved to the table. Shaking his head sadly, he reached deep into his pockets and deposited a handful of objects on the table. The items flashed as they clunked into a glittering pile.

"Good God!" James rose from his chair to see

the loot. Four rings, two watch fobs, an ornate snuffbox, one watch, and no less than seven cravat pins lay on the table.

He sent an admiring glance at Herberts. "You are quite good. Have you ever thought of—*Ow!*" James rubbed his ribs where his sister had elbowed him. "What was that for?"

"For what you were about to say." Verena turned to Herberts. "You know the rules. No stealing from my guests. For penance, polish all the silver in the pantry. Twice."

The butler blinked rapidly. "Twiced? Don't ye think once would do the trick?"

"Twice," Verena said sternly. "Or you may give your notice now and I will hire another butler in your stead."

Herberts straightened his shoulders, an expression of noble suffering flittering across his thin face. "Very well. Oiye'll polish all the silver in the bloomin' pantry. *Twiced.*"

"Thank you," Verena said. "That will be all."

"Oiye, m'lady." The butler started to turn toward the door, but then he caught himself. "Blimey! Almost fergot." He executed a nearly perfect bow, then beamed pleasantly at Verena. "Thet'll do the knacker, won't it, missus?" Chuckling pleasantly, the butler quit the room.

James waited until the door closed before he burst out laughing. "Good God, where did you get that character?"

"The Society for Wayward Women's Servant Referral Service. Viscountess Hunterston runs it and, well, the prices are very reasonable." Verena bit back a sigh. Being independent was a costly venture, one she'd welcomed from the beginning. But she had to admit that there were times when it was just the teensiest bit wearing. Times like . . . well, all of the time, if she was honest.

Despite her disapproval of Father and his schemes, she had him to thank that she was able to make it at all. Rutland had destroyed her credit with both society and the banks when she'd come to Westforth House after Andrew's death. Determined to keep the house from her, the old earl had hired an entire army of solicitors to make her life miserable.

Verena had been left with no recourse but to use the skills Father had taught her—she entered the world of the demimonde and there, across the green felt tables of London's most exclusive gambling hells, she made her living, one careful card at a time.

She was not a flamboyant player; Verena only won enough to make her way in the world. She didn't want the attention a winning spree would have caused and she had nothing to prove. Not anymore. But still, she itched to put her talents to the test.

James pocketed his watch, then examined the snuffbox with a practiced eye. "Here I was, thinking you'd turned into a saint when in reality, you've found a better game."

Verena took the snuffbox from James and placed it back on the table. "I hired Herberts to serve as a butler and nothing more. If you want to know the truth, he is all I can afford. That and Viscountess Hunterston especially asked if I could take him on since his last placement didn't take."

"I can't imagine why." James flicked an especially large ruby cravat pin on its side. "Whose are these, anyway?"

"I have no idea." She scraped all the items into a large pile. "Herberts arrived just a month ago. In time, I'm certain I will be able to break him of his bad habits."

"You can't reform a shyster."

"Yes, you can. Everyone can change." She carried Herberts's haul to her desk. Once there, she unlocked the top drawer and placed the items inside. "What a bother. I suppose I shall have to find a way to return all of this."

"If you want me to take care of it for you, I'll—"

"No." She locked the drawer and replaced the key in her pocket. "I'll see to it myself."

James grinned as he returned to his seat and picked up the deck of cards. Verena watched how his fingers flew, the cards melding, merging, flickering from one picture to the next. He met her gaze and grinned, his teeth flashing whitely. If she had not known him so well, she would have never realized that beneath his carefree air was a hint of desperation.

She took the chair across from him. "Is it a woman?"

His fingers faltered and two cards flicked from the deck to land on the floor. He reddened, then picked them up and put them back in the deck. "I never could hide anything from you."

"I know. You were silly to even try. Now out with it."

His grin faded. After a long moment, he sighed and said, "Ver, I'm being blackmailed."

"By whom?"

He sent her a grateful glance for her quickness. "I don't know. All I do know is that I made an error in Italy, one that may well cost someone their life."

"Someone?"

His cheeks darkened. "I'd rather not say."

Verena thought about this. "I take it she's married."

James's strained expression melted into genuine concern. "It's a mess, Ver. I'm at my wits' end."

"How much do they want?"

"I don't know yet. I was told to come to London and they would contact me, but I expect it will be five thousand pounds at least. Perhaps more."

"Good God! That's a fortune."

James winced. "Sabrina's husband is . . . he's very jealous."

"Apparently with good reason."

James flushed. "It wasn't like that!"

"It never is."

"That's unfair."

"Hmm. Let me guess . . . she's unhappy and lonely and her husband never pays her any heed. I daresay she told you that this was the first time she'd ever been unfaithful and you, being the quixotic, romantic fool that you are, believed her."

James rubbed a hand over his face. "At the time of the affair, I thought Sabrina was . . . well, I know now I was wrong. But I'm caught. Her husband knows something happened. If he discovers it was me, I'm doomed."

"Don't return. Stay away from Italy until it's all blown over."

"I can't. I have too much at stake. I was in the

middle of a project—" He glanced at her, then managed a smile. "I stand to lose far more than five thousand pounds if I stay away more than a few weeks."

"What exactly does this blackmailer have over you?"

"Letters. Well, not letters. Poems, really."

Verena's gaze widened. "*Love* poems?"

James managed a weak smile. "I'm quite good, you know."

She had to chuckle at that. "I daresay you are. How did this blackmailer find the letters?"

"A month ago someone broke into Sabrina's room and stole the box where she'd been keeping the verses."

"Did they steal anything else?"

He shook his head. "Not a blasted thing. Whomever it was had to know exactly what they were looking for."

"Are you sure they want money? It seems ludicrous they would send you here if that was their only objective."

James's face creased with worry. "I know. I wondered if—but no. It has to be money. What else could they want?"

He had a point. "I suppose that leaves us with the question of 'how much?' Do you think they knew you'd come here, to my house?"

"Surely not. No one knows I'm your brother."

"What a mess."

"I know. If I don't pay whatever they ask, this villain will turn everything over to Sabrina's husband. There will be nowhere to hide and all my work—" He placed his elbow on the table and rested his forehead in his hand. "Everything will be ruined. I'll be humiliated."

"Being humiliated is the least of your worries if this man is as dangerous as you think he is."

"He's killed three men for doing far less than what I have. The problem is that all of my capital is invested. Ver, if they ask for money, I'm sunk. Everything I have is tied up."

"How long before they contact you?"

"It should be any day now." He swallowed a little convulsively. "What will we do?"

"The right thing," she said with a bravado she was far from feeling. "Perhaps, if I'm very, very lucky, I can find a wealthy suitor who will marry me and hand over a large sum as a wedding gift."

She'd been joking, trying to lighten the moment, but he immediately brightened. "Perfect! Are there any wealthy men hanging about? One you could finagle into an engagement?"

Verena had to laugh. "James! I have no desire to sell my freedom for a few guineas. Not even for you."

He tried to hide his disappointment. "Oh. Of course not. Although . . . you wouldn't have to actually marry anyone, you know. Just tempt and tease. Get him excited, then tell him you need some money for a modiste's bill or some such nonsense and—"

At her lifted brows, he managed a weak grin. "I know, I know. I'm just teasing. Father always said it would take a Greek god before you married again."

That was sadly true. Though she had quite a few admirers, none were acceptable. Not even handsome, urbane Chase St. John. Within moments of meeting the young peer, it had become obvious that they shared a sense of the ridiculous. They got along famously, but only because he reminded her so much of James that she could not bring herself to completely rebuff him.

"Ver, what am I going to do? I just know they will want more money than I can gather. I'm doomed."

Verena bit her lip. How could she help James? Her coffers were rarely full. Her gaze was drawn to the table. There *was* one way to help James.

She placed her fingers on the cards and smiled as excitement trilled along her spine. She was tired of hiding, tired of barely making ends meet, tired of being careful. It was the time for bold action. Feeling more alive than she had in four years, Verena picked up the deck of cards and shuffled them, her fingers blurring with the motion.

She dealt out four hands. "Turn up the top cards."

He did as she instructed. On the top of each pile of cards lay a queen. He grinned up at her, realization dawning. "You are the best."

The words warmed her heart. She'd missed having her family nearby. Oh, she'd tried to compensate by developing friendships, but she found herself holding back from most overtures, a sad effect of her upbringing. She rather thought the family motto should not have been "Forever Intrepid," but "Trust No One."

Still . . . one had to have acquaintances, at least. So Verena began holding a dinner party the first Tuesday of every month. She invited a variety of people, most of them the wittier members of the demimonde. They ate, drank, laughed and talked, and she was always careful that the food was magnificent, the wine outstanding, and the conversation never boring. Soon, invitations to her parties were treasured items.

In fact, she'd just held her last dinner party, not two weeks ago. Among her regular guests had been Lady Jessup's new admirer, Lord Humford, who had, according to the gossips, disappeared shortly thereafter. It was rumored that he owed a great deal of money for his folly at the tables and that his options were to flee the country or be tossed into debtor's prison. Verena was quite sure she'd have chosen a life of exciting travel over prison, as well.

She caught James's gaze and patted his hand. "Don't worry about the money, however much they may ask. We will find a way to raise it. But it will be my way and by my terms or not at all."

"Ver, thank you! Are you certain this won't get you in trouble somehow?"

"Surely even a Lansdowne deserves a winning streak." Only one, of course. But one would be enough.

Smiling to herself, she sat down with James and began to play.

# Chapter 3

*There are 365 days in a year but only seven sins.
That means that one can commit each of the seven
sins a total of 51 times over the course of a year
and still have an entire week left for atonement. Of
course, that's if you commit only one sin a day; a
really determined fellow could work in a lot more.*

Mr. Scrope Davies to Edmund Valmont, while
watching a sparring match at Jackson's Salon

The black and yellow phaeton rolled to a stop
in front of the narrow lodging on Kings
Street, the matched set of grays prancing daintily.
A wizened individual dressed in the buff and blue
uniform of the St. Johns hopped down and raced
to hold the horses.

Brand glanced at the gray sky above with a
glum glare. Damned rain. That's all he needed to
make this day a complete and utter waste.

He glanced at the groom. "Walk the horses. I
shouldn't be above ten minutes."

The groom led the horses off as Brandon made
his way to the front stoop. He placed his foot on
the bottom step and paused to pull off his gloves
as the wind tugged hard on the length of his
greatcoat.

The residence appeared presentable, which was surprising considering the type of female Chase admired. Brandon could just imagine the mysterious Lady Westforth—he had little doubt that she painted her face and wore gowns cut to her navel, if she bothered even to dress at all. Chase's taste in women ran toward the obvious.

Last year, when Marcus had sent Devon to pay off one of Chase's charmers, the lady in question had held the entire interview wearing nothing more than a sheet. Devon had been thrilled.

Brand might have enjoyed this little drama himself if only his neck didn't ache and his eyes feel as if he'd rubbed them with sand. God knew it would make an amusing story to tell at White's, if nothing else.

The skies overhead rumbled threateningly. Brandon shoved his gloves into the pocket of his greatcoat. This should be relatively easy. All he had to do was convince Lady Westforth that it was in her best interests to leave Chase alone for a few weeks. His interest would wane; it always did. Brandon smiled grimly. He'd be through with this little errand before noon.

Brandon walked up the steps to the wide oak door and rapped lightly. Leaves skittered by, the wind swirling them into little whirlpools of brown and gold. He shifted from one foot to the other, the cold seeping through the soles of his boots.

The sky rumbled again and the breeze stiffened, cold fingers of air ruffling his uncovered head. Why didn't someone answer the door? He grasped the brass ring and banged it firmly.

A long moment passed. Finally, shuffling footsteps could be heard. The door opened and a tall, cadaverous individual stood in the opening, his nose suspiciously red, the faint reek of brandy sifting through the air.

The man hoisted his breeches and eyed Brand up and down before saying in an avuncular voice, "Here now, was that yew a-banging on me door?"

Brand's faint sense of irritation increased. "Yes, I knocked on the door. How else would you have known to answer it?"

The man scrunched up his nose as if considering this. "Oiye moight have known ye was here a'coss of the sound of yer carriage pullin' up." He beamed as if he'd just explained a complicated mathematical theorem. "Didn't think o' that, did ye?"

Brand took a steadying breath, his temper on the rise. "Is Lady Westforth home? I wish to speak with her *now*, please."

"Here now, guv'nor! There's no need to be ticky. Oiye can hear ye jus' fine without yer yelpin' like a scalded dog."

Good lord, it was bad enough that Brandon had to consort with women the caliber of this Westforth woman, but to be subjected to her ill-trained staff was more than Brandon could handle, especially today.

He'd be damned if he'd miss another of Marcus's meetings. Ever. Hell, he might just move into Treymount House in order to ascertain that not only did he not miss a bloody meeting, but that he was the first one present.

He rubbed a hand to his forehead where a faint echoing ache was beginning to form. "Is Lady Westforth receiving callers?"

"She moight be." The man wiped his nose with the back of his hand and gave a very wet sniff. "And then agin, she moight not. Whot's it to ye?"

If the servant was any indication of the quality of the woman of the house, then Brand's job would be quick work indeed. "Inform Lady Westforth that I am here." He reached into his coat pocket and produced a heavy vellum card. "My name is Brandon St. John. I need only two minutes of Lady Westforth's time." Not even that if she was as desperate for funds as her caliber of butler made it seem.

The butler took the card between his fingers and squinted at it. "Mr. St. John, eh? Oiye'll tell her ye're here." The butler peered over the card at Brandon and gave him one last suspicious look. Then, to Brandon's utter amazement, the man stepped back and shut the door firmly in his face.

In all of Brandon's years, he'd never been left to cool his heels on the front stoop like a tradesman who'd found his way to the wrong door. It was galling.

By God, he hadn't come here to be left on the stoop. His temper crackled into flames as he reached for the knocker. Before he could slam the brass ring into the wood, the door was yanked open yet again.

The butler gave him a sheepish grin, a single gold tooth glinting in the light. "The missus said ye wasn't to be left on the stoop." He stood to one side and waved at Brandon to enter. "Oiye'm to show ye to the sittin' room. Ain't ye a lucky bloke?"

Brandon wished he could just turn and walk

away, but that would only mean delaying the inevitable. So instead, he swallowed his ire and walked into the foyer. He waited for the butler to offer to take his coat, but the man merely stood there grinning like a fool.

"It's me first week, ye know. Oiye'm not conversant with all the rules yet."

Brand wasn't going to argue with that. He shrugged out of his greatcoat, then handed it to the butler.

"Hoo! Ye shouldn't do thet! Wish oiye could accept it but the missus'd have me hide if oiye took such a handsome gift." The butler reluctantly handed the coat back to Brand, who was too stunned to say a word.

"There ye are, guvnor! If ye wish to reward me, all oiye want is me shillin'."

"Shilling?"

"Fer openin' the door fer ye—"

"*Herberts!*" came a feminine voice from the stairs.

The butler snapped to attention. "Aye, missus?"

*It's about damned time.* Brandon followed the butler's gaze, a half smile already carefully in place. But the moment he saw the woman who stood at the bottom of the steps, his smile froze, slipped, then disappeared altogether.

Devon had been wrong; Lady Westforth wasn't beautiful at all. Her bottom lip was too short, her chin far too determined, her figure not the thin, willowy type society favored. She *was* blonde, her hair the color of ripened winter wheat, but the strands were thick and straight with no sign of curl so favored by the women of the *ton*.

Brandon's mood lifted. Perhaps Marcus had been in error. Chase could not possibly fancy himself in love with this woman. Brandon was just thinking that perhaps he was wasting his time coming here at all when the woman turned her head, her questioning gaze meeting his.

Her eyes were the deepest violet, fringed with thick lush lashes; her skin creamy white with the faintest touch of pink. But it was her smile that stole his breath.

He couldn't explain what it was, but when she looked at him like that, humor lighting her gaze, her lips curved in a smile, a deep thrum of awareness gripped him. His entire body responded as if in some way, he recognized her. Knew her . . . intimately.

She nodded gracefully. "Mr. St. John. I hope you will forgive Herberts. He's new and he doesn't yet understand all of his duties."

Brandon took firm hold of his erratic thoughts. What had been in that foul concoction Poole had fixed for him this morning? Whatever it was, it had left him befuddled as if still drunk. "Lady Westforth. I hope I'm not intruding."

"Of course not! Herberts, take Mr. St. John's coat and brush it. You may return it when he's ready to leave."

"Yes, missus," the butler said in a disconsolate voice as he took Brandon's coat. Herberts ran a hand over the fabric and brightened a bit. "Perhaps oiye'll wear it about a bit, jus' to see what it feels like to have such a fine piece o' workmanship on me back—"

"No!" Lady Westforth shook her head emphatically. "Butlers do *not* wear the coats they take to brush."

Herberts' face fell. "Ye sure 'bout thet?"

"Positive." She collected Brand with her gaze and flicked her hand toward a set of double doors. "This way, if you please. We can speak in here."

Brandon followed the lady's softly rounded figure into a sitting room. He couldn't help but watch her walk, noting the way her hips swayed beneath her silk gown. She was shorter than he'd first realized, her head only reaching his shoulder, and a bit plumper than society deemed attractive.

Of course, society was rarely right about such things. Celeste was thought to be the perfect woman—people fawned over her, women sought out her company, men wrote sonnets to her eyes. Brandon, meanwhile, could barely contain a yawn at the thought of carrying on a two-minute conversation with the chit.

Lady Westforth sank into a chair and gestured to the one opposite hers. "Pray have a seat."

Brand started to refuse, for he had no intention of staying long. But somehow, looking down into her face and noting the warmth of her expression and the way her eyes crinkled at the corners when she smiled, he found himself sitting, his lips almost curved in response.

Damn it, what was he doing? He was supposed to pay this woman to remove herself from Chase's life, not have tea with her. He cast a cursory glance about the room, surprised to discover that it was elegantly appointed, though small. The furniture was so closely placed that his knees almost touched hers.

She regarded him steadily, her gaze never wavering. "You look very much like your brother, only . . ." She tilted her head to one side, a thick lock of hair falling over her shoulder. "You're taller."

"I'm also older than Chase." *And I don't play the fool for anyone. Especially Cyprians like you.*

She colored as if she'd heard his thoughts. "He spoke of you often. I know he is quite fond of you and your brothers."

So Chase had been sharing family confidences, had he? Blast it, what was his brother thinking? This woman was everything a man of means should avoid—the only way she could support herself was to find someone willing to pay for the pleasure of her company. She was no better than the shallow females who flung themselves onto the marriage mart every year, trolling the bacheloreal waters for an unsuspecting male capable of supplying endless pin money and a house in London for the season.

Brandon knew all about the avarice of women. During his first year on the town, he'd become embroiled with a seemingly naive innocent. He'd been enthralled. She'd been equally taken, though only with his bank account and family name.

By the time Brand realized his error, she'd almost managed to capture him. Had it not been for his friend, Roger Carrington, Viscount Wycham, Brand would have ended up yoked to the girl for life. But escape he had. After that distasteful episode, he'd been cautious to eschew virgins, unmarried women, and any other female who might need funding. Which was why Celeste should have been a more amusing companion—she didn't need his name or his money. It was a pity she hadn't been interesting enough to hold his attention past their first bedding.

Lady Westforth clasped her hands in her lap. "Mr. St. John, how may I assist you?" She settled in her seat, her knees moving just out of touch of his. "I must apologize for Herberts. I hope you haven't allowed his inefficiency to put you out of sorts."

"Of course not."

"I'm glad. I think he will do well once he learns all the rules. Part of it is my fault. I didn't think to tell him not to leave someone standing outside." She shook her head ruefully, a sparkle in her violet eyes. "I have to remember that what is obvious to me, may not be so obvious to him."

Brandon answered with a faint smile, aware that he was having the oddest urge to agree with her. To agree with everything she said.

What was it about this woman that made him feel instantly at ease? Was it the intimate way she spoke—as if she already knew him well and accepted him as he was? Or was it the way she met his glance head-on, unflinching and unapologetic? Perhaps it was simply the humor that softened her expression, or the sensual line of her mouth. Whatever it was, he found it incredibly appealing and he suddenly realized the danger Chase had been in.

She possessed the kind of allure few women possessed—a natural charm that went beyond beauty. And an intangible physical presence. He could almost feel the attraction thrumming through the air between them.

No wonder Marcus had been so determined that the woman be dealt with quickly. Brandon, even with his head and neck aching, his eyes grit-filled, and pure irritation pounding through his blood, found his gaze locked on her. His heart pounded a slow, determined beat as he wondered at the fullness of her curves, at the smile that lurked in her amazing eyes.

What would she be like in bed? Would she be as uninhibited and natural as she was now? His body heated treacherously at the thought. She would be wanton between the sheets, he knew it. Knew without words, without reason, that she would give as good as she got.

For the space of an instant, Brandon envied his own brother for possessing the woman who sat across from him. The idea irked him and he scowled.

"Mr. St. John? Is something wrong?"

Yes, there was. Everything was wrong. She was wrong—wrong for Chase. And especially wrong for him.

She regarded him with a questioning lift to her brows. "Mr. St. John, is there something I—"

"I daresay you know why I've come." The sooner the interview was over, the better.

Her frown lasted only a moment, realization lighting her amazing violet eyes with hints of blue. She nodded once, firmly and without compunction. "Your brother."

"Yes."

"I hope he's well."

"He left London several days ago and has not yet returned. But then, you know that."

"I don't know any such thing; I'm not his keeper." She hesitated, then added after a moment's thought, "And neither are you."

Brandon's gaze narrowed. Surely the woman was not censuring him? But one look into her violet eyes and he realized she was doing just that. His irritation flamed into anger. He regarded her icily. "The relationships I share with my family are none of your concern."

She should have been thoroughly put in her place, but instead her gaze narrowed. "Just as the relationships *I* share with your family are no concern of *yours*."

His jaw tightened. "I beg to differ. Everything to do with my brother is very much my business."

"Mr. St. John. Let us come to the point, shall we? I have a horrid temper and I'd hate to box the ears of such an exalted personage."

He raised his brows. "Exalted personage?"

"A St. John. Society has deemed your family to be above the rest of us." A faint air of scorn rested about her, delicate yet lethal. "I would hate to disagree with society."

"Would you?" A smile tugged at his mouth. "I get the impression otherwise."

"You are very perceptive. I care naught for titles nor the prestige of birth."

"Only money," Brandon said succinctly.

Her chin lifted. "I enjoy money. Who doesn't? Life would be dreadfully dull without it. But I do not make it my main purpose. Nor does it affect my friendship with your brother."

"What *is* your main purpose, Lady Westforth? Marriage?"

"Don't be ridiculous. I have no intentions of ever marrying again."

He could almost believe her. Almost. "Never is a strong word."

"I've been married before. And while I have no complaints, I find the freedom I have now much more to my liking." She leaned forward, her dress pulling across her full breasts, her gaze direct and challenging. "But thank you for inquiring. Now, was there something else? Or did you just come to raise my hackles?"

Brandon found that his anger had heated into something more insidious. She was an interesting bundle of pride, sparkle, and self-possession. Added to that, she had a sharp wit and a lush figure. Rounded and plump, she would keep a man warm in bed for hours.

He shifted in his chair and realized that far from being offended, he wanted to taunt her all the more. It was fascinating the way her eyes sparked with heat when she was angered.

*Damn it*, he admonished himself, *make the offer and be done.* "Lady Westforth, let me be plain. Whatever your designs for my brother Chase, they are at an end. I've come to make you an offer— my brother's freedom in exchange for a certain amount of funds. A very, very generous amount of funds, if I say so myself."

She stood so quickly that he didn't have time to pull back, her legs brushing against his knees. "It is time you left."

He leaned back in his chair and crossed his arms over his chest. "I suggest you resume your seat and listen to what I have to say."

Her hands fisted at her sides. "You've said enough as it is. I will ring for Herberts. He will see you to the door."

Brandon's irritation faded as hers grew. She was no fool. She knew what he thought of her and she was ready to retaliate without hesitation. "I'll leave as soon as we've come to an understanding. How much will it take to get you to leave my brother alone?"

"Of all the—" She clamped her lips over the words. "You are attempting to purchase my cooperation."

"Yes. And I am willing to offer a considerable sum."

"Offer all you want; I won't take your money."

"No?" He did smile then . . . of course she wouldn't take the money. And tomorrow, the sun wouldn't rise. He pulled the bank draft from his pocket then reached out and captured her hand where she held it fisted against her thigh. He pried her fingers loose, noting that her skin was warm and soft, and placed the draft in her hand. "Here. Take this. It should make it worth your while." He pressed her fingers closed and looked up into her eyes. "*Very* worth your while."

He knew what she was going to do . . . she'd protest, of course. They all did, or pretended to. But soon enough they'd capitulate and take the money. All too soon, he'd be on his way, secure that Chase was once again out of harm's way.

For some reason, the thought bothered him.

There'd been a moment when he'd been certain she was different from all the others. Just a moment. But now . . . he noted how her fingers gripped the bank draft. He met her gaze with a superior smirk. "Afraid you'll lose it?"

Her gaze narrowed, became scathing. She jerked her gaze from his and glanced down at the draft crumpled between her fingers. "You have erred, Mr. St. John. Money does not make anything worth my while."

Then she did the most astonishing thing. She lifted the bank draft and held it in front of his face and ripped it into tiny pieces.

"I don't need your money, nor do I need you." To his startled chagrin, she held her hand over his head and showered him with tiny pieces of paper.

# Chapter 4

*Do you know what Hunterston says of Miss Grenville? That she is lucky enough to fancy she is beautiful and unlucky enough not to be. Took me a week to puzzle that one out, but by Jove, he's right!*

Edmund Valmont to his friend, the Duke of Wexford,
as they played a game of billiards at Wexford House

It had been many minutes since Verena had thought that Brandon St. John quite possibly the handsomest man she'd ever seen. He was tall, powerfully built, with blue eyes that contrasted devastatingly with his black hair.

Fortunately for her, that first positive impression had been far overshadowed by her realization that he was also, in addition to being incredibly handsome, a pompous jackass badly in need of a set down.

And she was just the woman to deliver it. She smiled as she watched him dust bits of paper from his shoulder. Several stubborn pieces remained lodged in his hair, giving him a much deserved horned appearance. Verena decided she couldn't be bothered to point that out. Let him go about in public with tattered bits of paper in his hair. It was just a pity she wouldn't be there when people pointed and laughed.

"What are you looking at?" he snapped, his brow lowered.

"Oh, nothing. Mr. St. John, thank you for visiting. I'll ring for Herberts to bring your coat. I daresay he's wearing it even now." She watched with satisfaction as Brandon St. John's expression went from irritation to blazing anger.

She turned toward the bell pull when St. John, still in his chair, caught her by the wrist. She glanced down at him, too amused to be vexed. "Yes?"

St. John's mouth thinned, his eyes burning even more brightly. "I am well aware of the usual machinations of your type of woman."

"Type? Just what *is* my type of woman?"

His gaze raked her up and down, insolently lingering on her breasts. It was almost as if he could see through her clothing. A faint tingle of heat sliced to her stomach, surprising her.

Finally, his gaze traveled back to her face. "Shall I speak plainly?"

"I'm not sure I can take much more plain speaking. Not without retaliating in some fashion. If you proceed much further, you might want to gather a pillow from the settee for protection."

His lips twitched, surprise softening his blue gaze for a moment. "I don't wish to insult you, but we both know what has occurred."

Her tongue curled around a hot rejoinder and it took every bit of the masterful control she'd learned over the last four years to keep from uttering the comment aloud. "Yes, you offered me money to stay away from your brother. I have never been more insulted."

His hold loosened the tiniest fraction and she became aware of the warmth of his hand against her skin, of the way his long fingers completely encircled her wrist.

"What will it take to get you to leave my brother be? Two thousand pounds?"

Verena wished he'd release her so she'd at least have the satisfaction of slapping him soundly.

His gaze narrowed. "Three thousand pounds."

Three. Thousand. Pounds. She didn't know what amount James would need, but three thousand pounds would certainly be useful. Verena wet her lips. It would be nice to have the money for her brother. Wonderful, in fact. Especially since she wouldn't have to actually do anything to earn it.

The truth was that she'd sent Chase St. John on his way two entire days ago. What would Brandon St. John do if she told him the truth—that she'd already refused his brother's offer of marriage?

She'd hated refusing Chase, for she could see that although he was sadly tipsy at the time, he'd meant every word. In reality, he'd taken it in good part and she thought that perhaps his feelings were not as deeply engaged as he thought.

Verena looked at Brandon from beneath her lashes and hid a smile. Apparently Chase had not confided in his brothers about what had occurred. They obviously thought he was still under her influence.

She smiled sweetly at her captor. "Please release my hand. You have a very heavy grasp."

His grip loosened a bit more, though not enough for her to win her freedom.

Her smile slipped. "You are being rude."

"I don't want you to toss anything else over my head. The next item might hurt."

If Verena had any say in the matter, it would hurt a lot. "You're bruising my wrist."

She was finally released, though she could tell he did not believe her for a moment. She tried to match St. John's mocking smile with one of her own, though the way her cheeks pulled, she feared it was more a baring of the teeth than a smile. "Tell me, Mr. St. John; do you believe in witchery? You make it sound as if I held your brother under a spell of some sort."

"You used your physical attractions to gain my brother's interest. We will not stand for it."

"We?"

"My brothers and I."

Good God, the entire family thought she was some sort of marry-by-morning type of woman, desperately searching for a wealthy husband. It would be a remarkably irritating idea if it were not so humorous.

And poor Chase! She'd had no idea the extent of his suffering, but now she wondered if perhaps his brothers weren't suffocating him. Had she any sense, she would tell Brandon St. John the truth and send him on his way, her foot firmly planted on his muscular rump.

Unfortunately, he had engaged her sense of the ridiculous with his pompous attitude. It was so much more amusing to taunt the man than just to blurt the colorless truth. She returned to her chair and folded her hands in her lap in a demure fashion. "Mr. St. John, I must confess to something."

He didn't look in the least impressed. In fact, he appeared to be a little annoyed. "What's that?"

"I am very fond of your brother." She looked at Brandon through her lashes. "Very, *very* fond."

His jaw tightened, his glance ice blue and as cold as the Thames in the dead of winter. "I do not take it lightly when someone tries to take advantage of a member of my family."

"Advantage? How do you know *he* hasn't been trying to take advantage of *me*?"

"Chase is not the type of man to take advantage of anyone. Besides," Brandon's gaze flickered over her with dismissive intent, "how could anyone take advantage of a woman like you?"

Verena's humor fizzled into a flash of fire. She never lost her temper, never uttered a less-than-ladylike word, and never, ever spat. But at this moment, she found that she had to fight the urge to do all three.

What Brandon St. John really needed was a good firm slap across the face followed by a sound foot stomping. And perhaps, for good measure, she might throw in a quick punch to the ribs, too.

Just one, of course. She wasn't a mean woman. Not yet, anyway.

Still, his arrogance cried out for retaliation of some sort. And in teaching Brandon St. John a lesson, Verena would be doing a favor to all of womanhood.

Heavens! If she considered it much longer, she'd feel positively noble. Perhaps she *should* take his money. Oh, not to spend—she had her own means of raising funds—but just to prove to him that she was not to be toyed with. She'd take his bank draft, yank it right from his fingers, and then wait for him to find out from Chase that he'd been duped. It was a delightful notion. And when the high and lordly Brand St. John came crawling back to retrieve his funds, she'd have him right where she wanted him. Her humor returned and she grinned.

Brandon did not seem to enjoy her display of humor. His scowl grew in matched proportion. "Lady Westforth, you will tell my brother you are not interested in him. That you wish him to leave you be. And in return, I shall pay you a goodly amount. It's a simple arrangement, one made every day."

"Oh, I'm afraid I can't do that."

"Why not?"

"Because I'm insulted."

His brows rose. "And?"

She leaned forward and said in a gentle tone, "When I feel insulted, it makes me somewhat cantankerous. And thus it is impossible for me to agree to anything. You *do* want me to agree to take your offer, don't you?"

He managed a brief nod, though it was apparent his temper was wearing thin.

She smiled beatifically. "Excellent! It might benefit us both if you would explain your meaning when you said 'a woman like you.' Perhaps I'm being a bit severe in my interpretation."

He leaned back in his chair, watching her through half-closed eyes. "A glutton for punishment, aren't you?"

"I want to know where I stand."

"Very well. You asked. How old are you?"

"How old—I don't see that that is any of your business."

"Then let me guess." He pursed his lips. "I'll say . . . thirty-t—"

"Twenty-six," she snapped. Really, there was no reason for the man to be so . . . *personal.*

He grinned—a real grin this time, one that crinkled his eyes and drew a faint dimple at one side of his mouth in the most attractive way. In the space of a second, he went from stern and unyielding to something far more palatable.

Despite her irritation, Verena caught herself wanting to respond to that smile. Her own lips quivered and a quiet laugh bubbled deep inside, though she tried to repress it. "I hope you're satisfied now, though I don't know what you expect to prove."

"Merely that you are older than Chase by almost two years."

"What's two years? I daresay there are dozens of successful couples who've got more years than that between them."

"You are also far more experienced than he."

She gave an inelegant snort, then caught herself. That's what came of being with her brother for hours on end the past two days—she'd forgotten all of her manners. She pressed her fingers to her lips and coughed politely. "Ah, I mean, that's not true."

He raised his brows, his blue eyes truly alight with laughter. "Lady Westforth, you are a woman of contradictions."

"Is that another of your objections?"

"No," he said slowly, as if the information surprised him, as well. "It was merely an observation."

Verena didn't like the rather intimate way he was now regarding her. "We aren't through cataloguing your objections to my person."

"I thought I'd said enough."

"One would think. But then I'm not your average dainty miss, who wants to hear nothing but soft words and false compliments. I'd rather know up front what problems are ahead so that I may deal with them."

"You are stubborn."

"I prefer the term 'forthright.'"

His lips twitched, but he didn't smile. "Then I shall continue. In addition to your age, there is also the matter of your reputation."

"Reputations can be misleading. For example, *you* are reputed to be a man of fashion and sophistication. A gentleman, so to speak. Yet here you are, as rude and boorish as a country squire."

Brand almost winced at that. He supposed he was being rude, though he was at a loss as to how he could accomplish his goal without offering insult of some sort. Of course, had this been an uneducated orange seller from Vauxhall Gardens, she wouldn't have realized she was being insulted.

Marcus had been right; Lady Westforth was different from Chase's usual inamoratas. She was far more intelligent and she possessed a devastating sense of humor. Brandon noted the exotic tilt of Lady Westforth's eyebrows and the way they lifted when she smiled. She was a lovely woman. What was really strange, though, was that the longer he remained with her, the more he became aware of that fact.

"Come, Lady Westforth. Enough of this. What will it take for you to leave my brother alone?"

She smiled, shaking her head. "I can't help but think you are overstepping your brotherly boundaries. What will Chase say about all this?"

"He'll be furious. He always is."

"Always? You've done this before?"

"The St. Johns take care of their own. I've already told you that."

"Yes, but—" She stopped, then waved a hand. "I daresay he will let you know his feelings on the subject when he returns."

Her cheeks were faintly flushed, her eyes sparkling as if she were trying not to burst out laughing. Brand found himself wondering what she looked like in the throes of passion. If her eyes shone the same way, if her skin would flush when she became aroused. He'd bet his last pence that her hair was a sensual experience by itself, as long and thick as it appeared.

She was well rounded, her breasts large enough to fill his hands, her hips nicely curved. He pictured her lying naked in bed, her hair unbound and falling over her bare shoulders.

The image heated him quickly and he had to rein in his untoward imagination. Intelligence, beauty, and wit. It was a heady combination. Bloody hell, poor Chase never had a chance. Not with a woman like this. Had someone told Brandon twenty minutes ago that the notorious Lady Westforth would be tossing insults at his head and that instead of being furious, he actually felt like laughing, he'd think they were crazed. But he found that he rather liked the fact that the cat had claws.

Of course, there was no surprise in that; except for Chase, the St. Johns were never drawn to milquetoast females. They needed fire to match their fire. And unless he was greatly mistaken, Lady Westforth had more than her fair share of sparks.

He leaned forward, suddenly anxious to get this over with. "I will raise my offer to five thousand pounds. And that is all I can offer."

All traces of humor fled from her face. "Surely you jest."

"I will send a draft within the hour."

Her gaze dropped to the pieces of bank draft that littered the floor. He could tell from the stiffness of her shoulders that she was at war with her decision. He supposed he understood—it must be galling to have your hand called in such a brutal fashion. But she obviously needed the money. Her expression hardened his heart once again. She was indeed the type of woman to be avoided at all costs. "Take the draft," he said softly.

At first, he thought she'd refuse. Instead, she reached over and touched his hair. Brandon could feel the heat from the palm of her hand brushing his ear. He closed his eyes, fighting a flash of lust.

She leaned back, withdrawing her hand. Between her fingers was a piece of the original draft.

She offered a smooth smile. "Five thousand pounds is a fortune. You must fear my influence a great deal."

"You must leave town long enough for Chase to forget you. I don't know what he's said, but he's not prone to serious emotions. I daresay he'll mourn for a few weeks and then be back to normal in a trice." Brandon looked her over slowly and wondered if that was entirely true. He'd known her for only fifteen minutes and already he was regretting that he wouldn't have the chance to know her more.

Damn, but Chase had all the luck.

"I shouldn't take the money . . ." She pursed her lips, her gaze measuring his.

A strange sense of hope flickered through him. He thought of the women he knew—from Celeste to the score of others he'd dallied with. Not one of them would have turned from the opportunity to gain five thousand pounds. In their own way, women were more avaricious than men. But this woman—for some reason, he wanted her to be different.

"I shouldn't take the money," she said once more. "But I will."

Brandon blinked, wondering if he'd heard aright. "I beg your pardon?"

She lifted her chin, her eyes lit as if in triumph. "I'll take the five thousand pounds. Since you are so determined that I take it, I will. Send the draft to me within the hour and I will tell Chase I think it best if we never see one another again."

He'd been wrong. She *was* like all the others. Disappointment weighed his chest. "We are decided then," he said grimly. And then he stood. Not because he wanted to go, but because there was no other reason to stay.

She smiled, a mysterious, faint curve of her lush lips that reignited his desire. "Mr. St. John, you may trust me in this—your brother is safe from my influence."

That was what he wanted to hear. But somehow, he felt . . . cheated. He'd really begun to believe that she would refuse the money and prove herself above such tawdry proceedings. That had been his error. "I'll send the draft this afternoon. But be fore-warned, if I find you contacting Chase or allowing him entrance into your house, I will demand the return of the funds. And I shall be relentless."

"I cannot imagine you being anything else." She stood and held out her hand as if to offer him a friendly shake.

It was infuriating that this woman would take such dreadful advantage of his family and then stand there with a smile as if she'd done nothing wrong. Brand took her hand, but he did not shake it. Instead he held it tightly in his, noting again how small her fingers seemed and how delicate her wrist.

The desire to shake her composure was overwhelming, though not as overwhelming as the desire to prove to himself that the attraction he felt for her was physical and nothing more.

Brand tightened his grip, his fingers firm. Her eyes widened, but she made no move to free herself. A faint color stole into her cheeks and he wondered if she felt the same draw he did.

The thought tantalized. He tugged her closer.

She took a half step, bringing herself within reach. That was all it took. Brand hauled her hard against him, her breasts pressed against his chest.

She gasped. "I—"

He kissed her, devoured her, took possession of her mouth as if he'd never before tasted a woman. All the heat of his anger, all the frustration of seeing the woman who would destroy his brother's peace, all the built-up passion that had simmered through him from the moment she'd first smiled, burned through him and sank through the kiss, scorching and searing.

She did nothing to discourage him. Indeed, she melted against him, her mouth opening beneath his, her hands clutching at his coat. He forgot his purpose, forgot who she was, forgot his responsibilities, and just kissed her. Kissed the woman who so brazenly defied him. She moaned softly and the throaty sound brought Brandon to his senses.

He broke the kiss, though he did not release her. Bloody hell, what was he doing? She stayed where she was, her chest rising and falling rapidly as she clung to him, one hand tight about his lapel, the other clutching something else. He looked down and realized that she'd unwittingly grasped the talisman ring.

The thought chilled his emotions. He pulled her hands from his chest, his body so rigid with desire that it was all he could do not to stagger. After a deep breath, he found his voice. "It was just a kiss, Lady Westforth. In your case, I'm certain it was but one of thousands."

Her face flushed and she fell back a step, her chest heaving in outrage. "You—"

"Come. We both know you are not naive. You welcomed the kiss, as did I. But now . . ." He shrugged.

She wiped her mouth with the back of her hand, her eyes flashing. "I thought you detested my 'type' of woman."

"I do. Consider the kiss a bonus of sorts. A reward for your cooperation. Now, if you will excuse me, I must go. Good day, Lady Westforth. I'll see myself to the door." He bowed and left.

Moments later, Brand climbed into the seat of his phaeton and urged the horses to a brisk trot. He felt disoriented, as if he'd been traveling too far, too fast and he wondered what had possessed him to kiss the woman.

All he knew for certain was that five thousand pounds was a bargain.

Twenty minutes later, Verena held a crisply drawn bank draft in her fingers. She eyed the scrawled signature thoughtfully. Brandon St. John. Before today, she'd known precious little of him except that he was reputed to be cutting a swath through the female population of the *ton*—the *married* female population. He was said to be a master of seduction.

Verena now knew how he'd gotten such a reputation—he was a master at making you feel unique, special. Sexuality dripped from his lips, shone in his eyes, emanated from his heated skin. One moment, they were talking and the next . . . She closed her eyes, reliving the feeling of his mouth on hers. It hadn't been a real kiss. It had been a branding.

She took a deep breath and released it, rubbing at the palm of her hand. She glanced down to where the famed talisman ring had made an imprint in her skin. The mark was gone now, but the place was still warm, tingly even. Verena curled her fingers over the spot.

James walked into the room, his brown eyes bright with curiosity. "Herberts said you had a visitor this morning."

She nodded. "Brandon St. John."

"What did he want?"

"To purchase my cooperation."

He raised his brows. "For what?"

"His brother, Mr. Chase St. John, has developed an inappropriate interest in me. Mr. St. John did not know it, but I already sent his brother on his way two days ago."

"Well!" James crossed to the window and lifted a corner of the curtain aside. "Herberts said the man possessed some fine horses and a very nice coat."

"He's wealthy beyond comprehension. Which is why he attempted to purchase my cooperation."

James's eyes brightened. "How much did he offer you?"

She held up the check. "Five thousand pounds."

James dropped the curtain, his gaze wide. "Five—good God! It's a fortune and I—" He caught sight of her face and groaned. "You aren't going to accept it. Don't say another word! I couldn't stand it. Why, oh why couldn't his brother have become enamored of *me*, instead of *you?* I would have gladly taken the money and—"

"I wouldn't touch that money with a pole. Don't you see, James? If I accept the draft, I am admitting that I can be bought. And I'm worth far more than five thousand pounds."

He moaned and dropped his face into his hands.

She had to smile. "You think I'm mad."

He removed his hands, his smile twisted. "No. Just far too pure to be a Lansdowne."

"That's not true. I want to keep the money. Really, I do. It's just that—" She waved her hands hopelessly, the draft fluttering. "I can't."

"Pride," he said, shaking his head sadly. "That's a sin, you know. One of the big seven."

"If you want to know about pride, ask the St. Johns. My teensy amount is negligible in comparison."

"I find that hard to believe," he said. She slashed a glance his way and he grinned. "Don't eat me! I'm just teasing and you know it. If you hadn't promised to win funds for me at the gaming table, I would be furious now." He came to her and linked an arm about her neck. He kissed her forehead before dropping into a chair and grinning up at her. "So stop cutting me with those vicious looks of yours and tell me about the great Brandon St. John. Is he as impressive as they say?"

Impressive? Brandon St. John was far too handsome for Verena's peace of mind. She cleared her throat. "He's quite tall, has thick black hair and very blue eyes." He could also kiss in a way that left her beyond breathless.

James's gaze narrowed. "And?"

"And what?" she asked, her cheeks suddenly hot. "That's all."

"Hm." James regarded her shrewdly. "I see. What are you going to do with that bank draft if you don't mean to make good on it?"

She tilted her head to one side and considered all the possibilities. "Perhaps I should frame it and put it on display." She walked across the room and held the draft against the corner of the glass mirror that hung over the mantel. "Right here. That way no one who comes into this room can fail to see it."

"You wouldn't!"

"Or perhaps . . ." She went to the front window. "I could have it hung here, so that the light will illuminate his signature, not to mention that it can be seen from the street below."

"You are going to cause a scandal."

She shrugged. "So? I'm not a part of polite society; what would I care?"

"But Brandon St. John is. You think to humiliate him."

"I think to teach him a lesson. A very badly needed one."

James laughed reluctantly. "Lud, Ver! I'm beginning to feel sorry for the man."

"You should. I intend to bring him to his knees." That was a pretty picture, indeed—Brandon St. John, crawling on his knees, begging her to . . . to what? To kiss him again? "Hm. Maybe I should hold a dinner party in honor of the great St. John's munificence. It would be rather humorous if one or two people knew of his visit today. It *is* an amusing tale."

He grinned. "You should be careful about teasing St. John. You will draw the ire of the entire family if you aren't careful."

"I already have. But this . . ." She pulled the check through her fingers and smiled, thinking of Brandon St. John's face when he discovered that he was being ridiculed.

There were always those among the demimonde who were marginally accepted by the *ton*. If she could invite the right people, the story would spread quickly indeed. "My next dinner party is next Tuesday. I shall invite just ten or twelve people. But ten or twelve *very* talkative people."

"A gossip fest." James sent her a shrewd glance. "Are you certain St. John didn't do something *else* to heat your temper? Something more than just offering you this money? You seem vindictive; a woman scorned."

"I've never been scorned in my life." Scoffed at, perhaps, and thought to be "that kind" of woman. But never scorned.

James raised his brows. "Remember when you were ten and you thought I was the one who'd stolen your new shoes? You snuck into my room and glued all of my shoes to the floor."

"That was years ago," Verena said loftily. She'd progressed far beyond that. Now when she wanted revenge, she made sure it poked the person in the right places.

James quirked a brow. "Do you want a more recent example? What about the day before you married Westforth? You accused me of stealing the two rather expensive bottles of wine you were saving for—"

"It wasn't wine, it was port. And you did steal them. I found the empty bottles in your room."

"You enacted the most horrible revenge."

She grinned. "Ants." That had been one of her better days.

He didn't smile. "They bite, you know."

"They do not! Not that kind, anyway. It was all your imagination." She chuckled. "You should have seen yourself! Running across the church-yard, tearing off your breeches right in front of poor Lady Birlington. She screamed loud enough to wake the dead, though I noticed she didn't bother to look away."

James gave a reluctant grin. "She still writes to me, you know."

"I'm not surprised. I thought she was going to jump into that pond after you."

"I could have drowned."

"Only if you sat down. It was so shallow it was more a puddle than anything else."

James sighed. "Father hoped that Andrew would tame that sense of humor of yours."

"Well he didn't. He merely added to it." She placed the check on the mantel and smiled. "I wonder if St. John will call on me once the story of his infamous visit gets back to him? I do hope so."

James looked at her quizzically. "Now you sound as if you rather liked him."

Liked? She didn't like Brandon St. John at all. Especially not after he had kissed her in such a . . . thorough manner.

Well, perhaps that one part was enjoyable. But she hadn't liked the way he'd treated her beforehand. "He's arrogant and overbearing. However, his concern for his brother is beyond reproach." There. That sounded fair. She was rather proud of herself.

"Perhaps. I'm not one to imagine all sorts of ill happenings, but it would still behoove you to tread carefully. Of all the St. Johns, Brandon is considered a force indeed. He goes through women the way most men go through cravats."

"I shall make sure he doesn't attempt to tie me about his throat."

"Ver, I'm not joking. He's far more dangerous than you believe."

"I'm quite capable of handling him." Verena tilted her chin to a very impertinent angle. "Besides, Brandon St. John had better hold himself at a respectable distance in this little battle."

"And if he doesn't?"

She picked up the bank draft and waved it in the air, smiling sweetly. "Then I will indeed cash this draft and the unfortunate man will find himself five thousand pounds poorer. At which point I win not just the battle, but the entire war."

# Chapter 5

*The only thing worse than a woman who cries is one who laughs.*

The Duke of Wexford to Viscount Hunterston,
while standing in the library taking port
at the Dashwood Fete

The rain came and went in the space of a day, leaving London damp and noticeably cooler. Brandon told himself that he was glad he'd sent the promised bank draft to Lady Westforth so quickly. All he had to do now was write a quick note to Marcus to confirm that all was well.

For now, Brand returned to his usual occupations. Or tried to. He found Devon at Jackson's Salon, his supposed trip miraculously cancelled. There they whiled away the rest of the afternoon, sparring in a friendly fashion that left Devon with a split lip and Brandon with a bruised cheekbone.

It would be an exaggeration to say that he thought constantly of Lady Westforth as he went through the evening. Indeed, there were long stretches of time when he didn't think of her at all—a whole hour at one point. But the meeting had colored his expectations. He found himself noticing how banal the supposed beauties of the day seemed to be—how utterly devoid of humor, how bland, how very unlike Lady Westforth they all were.

Not a one had enough wit to make him smile, even a little. And none challenged him or even threatened him, which he found insipid. Brandon found himself wondering what Lady Westforth would say if he surprised her with a visit. The idea took hold and it was with great difficulty that he reminded himself of the type of woman she was—the exact type of woman who could be bought off for a mere five thousand pounds.

Not, of course, that five thousand pounds was a small amount. Perhaps she was facing some dire circumstances that had forced her to accept the funds. He thought about this for some time, considering all the possibilities, each more dire than the first.

Most of his imaginings had to do with orphans and paying physician bills for a variety of worthy but poor individuals. As soon as he realized what he was doing, he took his unruly imagination firmly in hand and refused to allow it any more leeway.

Lady Westforth was an example of the exact type of woman he always avoided: needy, impertinent, and—to judge by the quality of servant she had answering the door—practically insolvent. She was the kind of woman who would, without compunction, attempt to trap a man into an indiscretion for her own gain.

Still . . . he couldn't help but realize that she

was something more than that. There was something about her . . . some indefinable quality that left him edgy and intrigued. So intrigued that he found he could think of little else.

But such preoccupation was exactly the thing he'd decided would never happen. It was with a surly disposition that Brandon made his way to White's to await his friend, Wycham. By half past ten, Brand realized that Roger wasn't going to appear, which was no surprise. It was just like the flighty viscount to send an urgent message and then not show. With Roger, everything was an emergency.

But waiting had made Brandon even more impatient than usual. Something stirred within him, a sense of slow desperation. The feeling ached a path between his tense jaw and his heart. Years ago, after he'd purchased his estate and turned it into such a success, he'd faced this same feeling . . . of emptiness. He'd returned to London, restless once again and ready for a new challenge. But something had changed. The old amusements had paled. So, too, had his old companions. Though young at the time, he felt like a man in his dotage as he watched his erstwhile friends run the gamut of excesses. His life, which had once seemed full of amusements, now seemed empty and dull and there wasn't a damned thing he could do about it.

Except, perhaps, start a very ill-conceived flirtation with a violet-eyed beauty who promised to be a challenge . . .

No. Never that. He already knew the outcome of such a liaison. Brand rubbed a hand along his jaw. He needed to get out of London. Away from Lady Westforth.

He had Poole pack his things and he went to spend the weekend at his sister's house just outside of Bath, where he played with his little niece and walked through the new wing with his brother-in-law, admiring all the improvements that were being implemented.

Before three days had gone by, Brand found that Sara's obvious wedded bliss was more than he could stand and he made his excuses and left, the old restive feeling returning in force. When he reached London that evening, he found a note from Marcus asking Brandon to meet him at Almack's. Brand changed into the required black coat and knee breeches, reaching Almack's at precisely eleven, when the doors were closed.

He entered the assembly room and looked for his brother, passing by a group of four or five older women standing near the door. He didn't notice them at first, for it was common practice for the chaperones to sit near the doorway so they could see who was attending and comment on the costume of whomever had the misfortune of being out of fashion.

But after a moment it became apparent that they weren't watching the door at all, but him. One of them caught his eye, turned bright red, and then clapped a hand over her mouth as if to hold in a spate of giggles.

He glanced down at his perfectly pressed breeches and cravat and shrugged. Silly chatterers. Brand returned to his quest to find his brother. Where the hell was—ah! Marcus stood in the furthest corner of the room, arms crossed as he regarded the staid dancing with the air of a man waiting his turn to be executed.

Brand made his way to his brother's side. "Having fun?"

Marcus didn't smile. "I was wondering when you'd return."

"I was rusticating. However, I found that I cannot stomach more than three days of our brother-in-law's company."

Marcus didn't even bother to agree. "I saw a friend of yours yesterday."

"Oh?"

"Your old school friend, Viscount Wycham."

"I was supposed to meet him before I left for Bath, but he never showed. The last time I saw him, he was in danger of being tossed into debtor's jail. He must have gotten his father to step in for him."

Marcus's face registered disapproval. "He's a bit old to be acting like a green one, isn't he?"

"Yes, but he is the only son and the old earl has spoiled him. Did he say where he was staying?"

"I didn't speak with him. I was returning home from a meeting at the docks with the new shipmaster we just hired. I saw Wycham coming out of a tavern on the East Side." Marcus frowned. "I don't think he was happy to see me for as soon as he caught sight of the crest on the coach, he ducked back inside. I wonder what he was doing?"

"Who knows? Wycham always walked his own path." Brand glanced at his brother. "I'm surprised you're here. I thought you'd sworn off Almack's because of the stale cake."

"Aunt Delphi came to visit and she wanted to see some of her friends." Marcus cast a jaundiced eye toward the refreshment table. "I think they have the same exact pieces of cake that they had last time, and it has been four months." He shifted his gaze back to Brandon. "Did you receive my note?"

"Of course. I assume Chase has returned and is not happy."

"He did indeed return. But as to his not being happy . . ." Marcus eyed Brand for a moment. "When you made your visit to Lady Westforth, I seemed to have been remiss in asking you for certain details."

A silent warning began to sound deep inside Brandon's head. "Details? What details?"

"Oh I don't know. Did the lady seem angry when you left?"

What was this all about? Brandon frowned. "Not angry, really. She wasn't happy I was there, but she seemed fine with our arrangement. Almost triumphant."

"Hm. So you think the interview went well."

"It went perfectly. Why? Are she and Chase still—"

"No. Nothing like that."

Brand realized that his hands were curled into fists. He relaxed them now. "Good."

"It's strange, but when I informed Chase that we had taken care of Lady Westforth and that she would no longer be bothering him, he had a most peculiar reaction." Marcus pursed his lips. "He laughed. And for a very long period of time. Apparently Lady Westforth sent him on his way a good two days before you arrived on her doorstep."

*Damn it!* She had tricked him. But despite his irritation, Brandon had to admit to a faint sense of appreciation.

Marcus's gaze narrowed. "I take it she didn't bother to inform you of that fact."

"No."

"You never mentioned how much it cost to win her cooperation. What did you pay her?"

Brandon hated to say, but Marcus pinned him with a determined stare. "Five thousand pounds."

"Five—we've never had to pay more than three before. What happened?"

"She was persuasive. Very," Brandon said. No wonder the chit had been in such high humor— she'd all but robbed him. Worse, he'd spent a good amount of time talking her into the higher amount. He'd almost insisted on it, now that he thought about it. "That little minx."

"Oh, she didn't stop there. That's why I wanted to know your version of the meeting."

"*My* version?" Brand blinked. "Then you've heard . . . *her* version?"

"Have you noticed people are staring at you?"

Brand started to say no, but then he remembered the women by the door. He glanced their way now and saw that they were still looking at him, giggling behind their gloved hands, whispering furiously.

In fact, now that he took the time to peruse the ballroom, a number of people were looking at him, amused expressions on their faces. "Bloody hell."

Marcus nodded, though a faint glimmer of a smile lit his eyes. "Lady Westforth had a little dinner party shortly after you left last week. She regaled the world with the story of how you attempted to buy her cooperation to do something she'd already done." Marcus's smile widened. "The only good thing is that she didn't execute the draft."

Brandon's heart gave an immediate leap. "She didn't . . ." Why then, had she taken the money to begin with? He wondered if she'd planned all along to use the draft to embarrass him. Part of him was furious, but a small, very quiet part was relieved. She hadn't taken the money for any reason but to mock him.

"Chase warned that she wasn't his usual fare," Marcus said after a long silence. "I'm inclined to agree with him if her dinner party was anything like rumor has it."

"What happened?"

"She had quite an interesting flower arrangement. Your bank draft was part of the ornamentation. It had been folded to look like a little frog. Your name, of course, was clearly visible."

Brand could see it now. The room packed with eager guests, all hanging on Lady Westforth's every word while she amused them with her rendition of the meeting. He could almost hear her embellishments, see the laughter in her violet eyes. "How many people know?"

"Everyone. It is the talk of the town." Marcus flicked a dark glance his way. "Did you really kiss her and tell her to consider it a bonus?"

Brand's ears burned. "That baggage!"

"Hm." Marcus regarded him coolly.

Brandon winced. "Where's Chase?"

"At his lodgings. You know, I believe he sincerely cared for Lady Westforth. Though he laughed when I told him how we'd taken care of his little problem, there was a moment when I mentioned the special license that he looked as if he was in pain."

Brand nodded shortly. "I am going to find Lady Westforth this very night and—"

"Get another kiss?" Marcus's gaze narrowed. "Don't be a fool. Avoid that woman like the plague. At least do so until this story has died down."

"I can't just stand by and—"

"You have no choice. She hasn't left you any. Give it some time and soon no one will even remember the incident."

Brand clenched his hands into fists. How the hell was he supposed to pretend that nothing was wrong when the entire *ton* was snickering behind his back? It was intolerable. Damn that woman! And damn his own stupidity for kissing her and giving her even more ammunition with which to mock him.

He slowly released his breath. Marcus was right. Brand would have nothing more to do with Lady Westforth. For now. But the moment this furor died down, he would have his revenge.

No one would be able to help Lady Westforth then.

\* \* \*

Another week passed during which Brandon put up with an onslaught of whispers followed by a maelstrom of jovial comments from those who thought they knew him well enough to tease. His brothers were the worst, Chase foremost.

Brandon suffered it all with a polite, unamused smile, whiling away the time by thinking of all the vengeance he'd soon visit on the hapless head of the notorious Lady Westforth. He began to look forward to their next meeting, imagining what he'd do to put her in her place.

Overall, it wasn't the gossip that bothered him. He didn't mind being the topic of conversation—he was a St. John and he'd always been at the center of attention. What was intolerable was that, for the first time in his life, he'd been cast in a comedic manner as if he were the key actor in a farce. But slowly, just as Marcus had predicted, society's attention was directed elsewhere, mainly the marriage of Sir Royce Pemberley to Miss Elizabeth Pritchard. It was the marriage of the season since the bride was considered a bit of an eccentric.

Miss Pritchard did not disappoint. Not only did she feature nearly every possible color in her choice of gown, shoes, gloves, jewelry and accompanying flowers, but her monkey, while hopping up the aisle performing his duties as ring bearer, took exception to Lady Birlington's rather obnoxious pug dog.

The two animals took one look at one another and, barking and shrieking, met in midair. By the time Miss Pritchard hiked up her skirts and rushed to the rescue, the pug's diamond collar had been snatched off while the monkey's little blue and orange outfit was ripped to shreds. Fortunately, other than being a bit ruffled, neither animal seemed harmed by the confrontation.

After the wedding, Brand stayed for the reception and then went on to Lady Shelbourne's ball. Lady Shelbourne was Sir Pemberley's sister and she rather enjoyed large functions, working diligently to provide the best of everything. Even Marcus could not complain of the quality of food served or the ability of the orchestra.

It was in the early hours of the morning when Brand made his way back to his lodgings. Poole met him in the hallway, an anxious expression on his face. "Mr. St. John! Someone has come to see you."

For some reason, Brand's thoughts immediately flew to Lady Westforth. "A woman?"

Poole shook his head. "No, sir. Lord Wycham."

Brand swallowed a faint sense of disappointment. "How long has he been waiting?"

"Hours, sir. I tried to tell him that you weren't in, but he insisted on waiting. Something is *very* wrong, if you'll pardon my saying so."

Brand glanced through the open door to where a red chair rested in front of the fire. Due to the high winged back and the slumped position of the person sitting, the only thing visible was a pair of spindly legs encased in blue breeches.

Empty bottles and numerous tipped-over glasses adorned the side table, testimony of how the last several hours had been spent. "You did right, Poole. Bring some tea and toast."

"At once, my lord."

"No, damn you!" came a raspy voice from the depths of the chair, the legs moving as if the owner were attempting to sit straighter but couldn't. "I won't have any toast. Nor tea. I ate pap when I was a child and b'God, I'll not eat it again."

Ah, Roger was on one of his sprees, was he? Smiling to himself, Brand waved Poole on before he entered the room and crossed to the chair. His smile faded when he caught sight of Roger's haggard face. This was something far more than a dissolute spirit. "Good God, what's happened?"

Roger blinked up at him, a faint quiver passing over his pale countenance. His cravat hung about his neck in wrinkled splendor, his shirt unbuttoned. Worse, his hair was in such disarray that two curls stuck out on either side of his head like devil's horns, a strange contrast to his angelic face. "Brand, they are going to hang me."

"You are bosky."

"Bosky." Roger tried to laugh, but his voice broke. "God, that's rich. I have had too much to drink, but that's nothing. Brandon, I've messed up in the worst way and if you can't help me—I don't know what I'll do."

"I'd be glad to assist you in any way I can."

Wycham's expression smoothed a little. "I knew you'd say that. Brandon, it's about Lady Westforth."

Brand stilled. "Do you know her?"

"Yes. Over a month ago, I attended a dinner party at Verena's. She has them the first Tuesday of each month."

Brand's jaw tightened. Wycham had called Lady Westforth by her Christian name. How well *did* his friend know the disreputable Verena? He managed to smile, though it cost him dearly. "I daresay she regaled you with some tale about me."

"You? Oh. The check." Roger waved a hand. "No, it was before that. You hadn't even met her then. Brand, I went to the dinner party to meet Humford. Did you know him?"

Humford was a minor peer of the realm, known for his shipping interests and his capacity for gossip. When tipsy, he often boasted that he dabbled in the affairs of the Home Office, though Brand found that highly unlikely. Of course, he'd since fled the continent due to his debts. He was exactly the type of person Brandon expected to meet at Verena's. "Mixing with the plebeians, were you?"

Roger flushed. "Brand, I know there is bad blood between you and Verena, but she's not what you think. She's—"

"You don't know what I think."

"I know how you treated her when you thought Chase was enamored. I've seen the draft myself." Roger flushed at Brand's hard gaze. "Just hear me out. You don't know Verena and yet—"

"Continue your story. We are not likely to agree on that subject."

Roger didn't respond, but after a moment, he sighed. "Oh, very well. The night before the dinner party, I ran into Humford at White's. He'd heard I was on my way to Devonshire and asked if I would deliver something for him, a list of some sort. I—I couldn't see what the harm would be, so . . . I agreed."

"Like that? Without asking any questions?"

"It seemed a harmless request." Roger wiped a shaky hand over his face. "We were both invited to Verena's for dinner and he asked me to meet him there. I went, fully expecting him to tell me it was all a hum, but he'd already been there and left."

Brand frowned. "He'd left?"

"Verena said he suddenly got pale and began looking through his pockets as if he'd forgotten something. He left twenty minutes before I arrived."

"I heard that he left the country shortly after that."

"No. Brandon, he didn't go anywhere. Some time after he left Verena's, someone killed him," Roger said in a strangled voice. "They found his body floating in the Thames. He was garroted, his tongue—" Roger looked as if he might be ill.

"Bloody hell. This is serious."

Roger nodded, his face pale, sweat glistening on his forehead. "He left notes in his desk that mention my name. Brandon, they think I have the list but I swear he hadn't given it to me yet and had I known—"

"Wait! 'They think?' Who are 'they'?"

Roger took a shuddering breath. "'They' are the ministry. And this list, whatever it is, is worth a fortune." Roger swallowed, the noise loud in the quiet room. "Brand, I'm not sure, but perhaps it was a coded missive, something of vast import."

Brand took the chair opposite Roger's. "If this list was so important, why would Humford give it to you in the first place?"

"I don't know. I—I just saw him in White's and

he asked—and I thought it wouldn't be much of an inconvenience. I never believed those stories of his, anyway."

"Did you know him well?"

"We've known each other forever, though we've never been close. His father and my father were friends since they were both in short pants."

"I still think it is strange that he asked you to assist him."

"Lord, you don't have to tell me. I've asked myself why he did so a thousand times and all I can think of is that he already knew he was in trouble and I happened by and he knew he could trust me."

"Did he say anything else when he asked you to meet him at Lady Westforth's? Anything of import?"

"No. He just seemed distracted. Upset." Roger squirmed in his chair. "I didn't really pay much heed."

Brand frowned. Something didn't add up about this story. Something . . . elusive. "This dinner party—the one Humford left—who was there?"

"Humford and Lady Jessup. Mr. and Mrs. Kemble. Oh, and the Oglethorpe-Whites and their daughter, Anne. And . . . well. . . ."

"Don't forget the lovely Lady Westforth."

"Leave Verena out of this."

Brand didn't think that would be possible. "Who else was there?"

Roger wiped his brow, his hand shaking. "I don't know. I—I can't remember."

"Sometime later today, when you can think clearer, I want a list of every person at the party. Every person, Roger. Do you understand?"

"Yes. It is a nightmare. I didn't even know about Humford's death until the day after the dinner party. I stopped by his lodgings and two men were waiting there, almost as if they knew I was coming. They told me what had happened and then—" Roger tugged on his cravat, his gaze wild. "It was horrible; they interrogated me like a criminal."

Brand sent the younger man a frown. "Whatever they told you, they can't hang you for just offering to deliver a note of some sort."

"They don't have to. Just being charged with such a crime will cause a huge scandal . . . Brand, it will kill my father. I've already disgraced him with my debts. He can't take much more."

Roger was right—the old earl's health was indifferent at best. Brand smoothed the sleeve of his coat thoughtfully. In order to save Roger's family the embarrassment of a public inquiry, someone had to find that damn list and quickly. Somehow, some way, the frustrating Lady Westforth was involved in this. Brand would have to visit her now, to discover more about Humford, if nothing else.

A slow sense of purpose filled Brand's veins, warming him and calming the restless feeling. "Roger, go home to Devonshire. Stay with your father until I get things worked out here."

"The ministry will come looking for me."

"Don't tell anyone you have gone—it will take them a few days just to realize you aren't in town.

All we need to do is stall them. Meanwhile, I'll do what I can to find that list."

"Do you think you can?"

"I hope so. But first, I want you to tell me something. Had Humford told anyone else about the list?"

Roger blanched, his gaze sliding away. "I—I don't know. I can't imagine—"

"This is important. *Did he tell anyone else?*"

"Yes. No. I mean, I'm not sure but I think . . . he's always been fond of Verena, you know. She never encouraged him, but he thought the world of her."

Brand's jaw tightened. "I thought so."

Roger struggled to his feet. He stood, swaying, his face drawn. "Brand, if you feel you must speak with Verena, I'll go with you and—"

"No. If you stay in town, the ministry might decide to take you into custody without any further ado. You will go to Devonshire and leave Verena to me." Brand stood and placed a hand on his friend's shoulder. "Trust me with this, Roger. I will not let you down."

Roger managed a weak smile. "Of course."

"Stay here until my carriage is brought around. You should leave right away."

"Brand, I don't know how to thank you—"

"Nonsense. I was nigh dying of ennui. You've given me a new purpose in life—to find that list." And to spend time with the woman who'd disturbed his peace more than any other. Brand was certain that if he saw Verena for more than a few moments, he'd find the flaws hidden by her violet eyes. Flaws that would end this attraction he held for her.

"What a mess," Roger said. He rubbed his eyes as if every bone in his body ached. "I deserve to be hanged."

"Horse whipped, perhaps." Brand cuffed Roger on the shoulder. "But not hanged."

"You won't . . ." Roger swallowed as if unsure how to continue. "Brand . . . no matter what, promise you won't hurt Verena."

Brand frowned. "Exactly what is your relationship with Verena?"

"I met her a year ago and we were close, after a fashion. Oh, it was never very serious, at least not on her side." Roger's smile twisted into a grimace. "I'm not her type, you know."

"What is her type?" Brandon shouldn't have asked the question, but his curiosity was piqued.

"I don't know," Roger said thoughtfully. "She's damnably independent and wants—oh, I don't know what she wants. I only know it wasn't me."

For some reason, Brand found this bit of information far more fascinating than he should have. He forced himself to shrug. "Trust me in this, at least, I will treat Verena exactly as she deserves." And oh, how he'd relish each and every second.

Roger didn't look very satisfied. "If Verena is involved, she must have a good reason." He held out his hand. "I'll give you two weeks and then I'm returning to London."

Brand shook it with a firm grip. "Fair enough. I will not fail you." He wouldn't, either. Not only would he find a way to ward off the spell Lady

Westforth had cast over him, but he'd also discover the missing list for Wycham.

And then . . . he smiled, feeling genuinely alive and excited for the first time in weeks. Lady Westforth had best beware.

# Chapter 6

*It's not that I mind losing so much. It's that I hate not winning.*

Viscount Hunterston to the Dowager Duchess of Roth, while writing a marker for his evening's losses at the annual Roth Charity Ball

**V**erena stood before the mirror in the drawing room, and adjusted the jeweled pin she'd set in her hair.

"Perfect." James stood in the doorway, watching her in the mirror's reflection. "Is that a new gown?"

"Oh, no! I've had this one for two years, though the dressmaker just changed the neckline." She turned as she spoke and faced him.

His brows went up at the sight of her décolletage. "It looks as if she left off part of it."

"Nonsense. It's the fashion." She noted that he looked handsome. His black coat fitted to perfection and his burgundy silk waistcoat made his eyes seem even darker than usual. He would break hearts tonight.

The door opened and Herberts stuck his head in. "M'lady? Oiye found something on the stoop."

"What is it?"

"A rock. And stuck beneath it was this note." He entered the room and held out a crumpled bit of paper. "It's addressed to Mr. Lansdowne."

"Bloody hell," James muttered. He reached out and took the dirty note and opened it.

"That will be all, Herberts," Verena said.

He sniffed loudly, his gaze on the note. "Are ye sure ye don't want a drink afore ye—"

"No. Thank you. You may leave now."

He slowly went to the door. "Oiye can haf cook make ye a nice pot o' tea if ye want—"

"No," Verena said. "Call for the carriage. Mr. Lansdowne and I will be leaving soon."

Herberts sighed then trudged from the room. The second the door closed, Verena turned to James.

"Well?"

"It's the blackmailers. Ver, they aren't asking for money."

Verena blinked. "*What*? What do they want if not money?"

He held out the note.

*Lansdowne,*

*Find the missing list.*
*Humford was just a warning.*

She looked up at James, her brow furrowed. "What list?"

"I don't know. Who is Humford?"

"Lord Humford is a minor lord—he is a notorious hanger-on, but he tells the most delightful stories. Or he did. He recently left the country due to his debts."

James looked at the note. "Are you certain? This is worded as if—" He bit his lip.

Alarm filtered through her. "James, do you think someone—surely not! I mean, we did think it was sudden, the way he just vanished, but—" She pressed a hand to her heart. "I cannot believe anyone would harm Lord Humford. He was a harmless old man."

"To you, perhaps. But it seems he may have been a threat to someone. Verena, we have to find him."

"Then we're going to the right place; he was well known at Hell's Door." She frowned. "What is this list? It's the strangest thing."

"Whomever sent this believes we know what they are talking about."

"We?"

"They sent it here, Ver. And not to my hotel." James's frown deepened. "I don't like this at all."

"Well, they're very wrong if they think either of us have any idea about this list. Come, we're going to be late and it looks as if we have work to do. Just promise me that you'll behave yourself this evening."

James's expression was the epitome of guileless surprise. "I promise I won't do anything Father wouldn't approve of."

"Oh no, you don't! I want more assurance than that. I have worked hard to establish myself here and I won't have you destroy it by drawing too much attention to yourself or me."

"For your information," he said in a lofty tone,

"I have no plans for this evening, but to assist you in your endeavors and now, to find this Humford fellow."

"Assist me? I don't need any help, thank you."

"No? I could cause a distraction so you can switch out your hand. I suppose I could faint. Or tip over the punch bowl." He tapped his chin thoughtfully. "I know! I'll see if I can find St. John and challenge him to a duel. That should cause a stir."

"Brandon St. John never inhabits gaming hells." Which was a pity, in its own way. She stifled a sigh; her plans for him had gone sadly awry. It really was a pity he hadn't become so infuriated with her that he'd stormed into her house and swept her into his arms for a punishing kiss.

*Oh my, that would have been something indeed.* She still tingled from his last embrace. Well, she wasn't through yet. She smoothed the bodice of her dress, enjoying the way her new necklet caught the light. Made of delicate silver wire twisted into an elegant design, the necklet framed the only scrap of St. John's draft that Verena had kept—the part with his arrogantly scrawled signature.

James groaned when he saw it. "You are determined to make him angry, aren't you?"

"The man deserves a lesson in humility, one he will not soon forget."

"He will seek revenge."

"I certainly hope so."

James lifted his brows. "You sound interested."

She shrugged. "Of course I'm not interested in Brandon St. John. I just have this overwhelming compulsion to remind him that I am not a woman to be ignored."

James snorted irreverently.

"Besides," she continued airily, "I needed more jewelry and this was amazingly inexpensive."

"Inexpensive? You're wearing five thousand pounds worth."

"Only part of five thousand pounds. Lady Farnsworth got butter on the draft and I had to rip that portion off and toss it out."

"That's what happens when you make table decorations out of an expensive item." He shook his head. "It's a good thing Father's not here. He'd have had an apoplexy by now."

"You don't think he'd like my necklet?"

"He'd hate it." James touched the heavy loop of pearls that decorated one of her wrists. "At least you have something of real value—" His smile suddenly slipped and he lifted her arm toward the light. "They're false."

She pulled her arm free. "They're paste, but they're very well done."

His lips twisted with distaste. "There's no need for you to go without necessities."

She burst out laughing. "Only a Lansdowne would think pearls a necessity. I suppose you would consider silk gowns and plum pudding necessities as well?"

"But of course." He shrugged, the graceful gesture betraying his time on the continent. "Shall we go? I've become quite thirsty, standing here, debating with you. And I need to find out about this Humford fellow and see what's toward with this list. The sooner we get that issue resolved, the better I'll like it, especially since they are involving you."

Verena took his arm and smiled. "I'm ready when you are."

Hell's Door was the newest craze of the demimonde—the discreet gaming hell run by Lady Farley, a loquacious widow with a penchant for expensive champagne and the finest quality diamonds. Located in a small, stylishly appointed street on the edge of the fashionable part of London, the gaming hell appeared much like every other house on the street—three stories of modish stonework broken by large, imposing windows. But the interior was something more.

No fewer than twenty gaming tables filled the front rooms, sporting Monaco, faro, and whist. Fortunes were made, though more often lost, across those baize-covered tables. The only real winner was Lady Farley who had, in less than two years time, made a sizeable fortune.

Tonight, as all other nights, Lady Farley's rooms sparkled with the rich gleam of silk, the flash of cravat pins and watch fobs, and the sparkle of hundreds of glasses filled with the best champagne, port, and brandy. It was, all told, a very good night to be a sinner.

As she always did, Lady Farley strolled through the rooms, making sure the refreshments never ended, the music wasn't too loud, the play satisfactory. She entered the main parlor, her calculating gaze immediately finding a tall, dark-haired man dressed in the height of fashion. Her glow of satisfaction increased tenfold.

Not only had she attracted a St. John to her

humble establishment, but she'd managed to lure Brandon St. John himself, London's undisputed leader of fashion.

It wasn't his usual fare—the demimonde represented the fringes of polite society and as a St. John, he was far too aware of his own worth to mingle with the mere "fringes." Yet here he was, sitting in *her* salon, playing faro.

Fanny tried to hide a flush of triumph, but her burning cheeks told her that she was failing miserably. One of the *ton*'s most eligible and wealthiest bachelors, a man known for his fastidious tastes . . . it was beyond even her wildly hopeful expectations. She motioned to a servant. "Jacobs, do you see the gentleman at the faro table?"

"There are two gentlemen at the—"

"The handsome one."

The servant stiffened. "Handsome? My lady, I'm not qualified to—"

"The dark-haired one. The one on the left."

"Ah. Yes, my lady."

"Keep his glass filled all night."

"Yes, my lady."

"Good! And if he seems to want something—anything—make sure that he gets it."

"Anything, my lady?"

"Anything."

"Yes, my lady." Jacobs bowed and could soon be seen hovering near St. John.

Fanny thought she would die of pride.

From where he sat at the faro table, Brandon was well aware of the scrutiny of his hostess, but he studiously ignored her. He was here for one reason and one reason only—to track a wily, if beautiful, vixen to her lair.

And a surprisingly nice lair it was, too. He'd heard of Hell's Door, but had never attended. Unlike Chase, who lived and breathed such low amusements, Brand found empty play a bore. Any fool could count the cards. Indeed, in his youth, his brothers refused to play him, saying it was no fun to lose every hand.

He allowed a servant to refill his glass. After his meeting with Wycham, Brand had spent the night going through the facts. Someone had stolen this mysterious list from Humford and then killed the man. And somehow, in some way, Lady Westforth was involved. But in what way? Did she know something about the incident, or was she in league with the murderer?

He remembered her smile, the warm way she'd spoken to him. He also remembered that though he'd given her five thousand pounds in a bank draft, she'd not exchanged it. Things simply did not add up.

It hadn't taken him long to decide what needed to be done; first, he must gain Lady Westforth's trust. Then he would find the answers to Wycham's unfortunate situation. Brand thought that it would be a fairly simple thing to pretend to become an admirer. From what he'd heard, she was usually surrounded by a swarm of them anyway, unlucky bastards.

He took a slow sip of port, thinking of his decision. It wouldn't take much to join her court. Women like Lady Westforth expected attention.

They craved it. And he would use that craving to his own benefit.

He would pursue her, woo her, win his way into her bed. Before the week was out, she'd tell him everything he wanted to know.

He smiled into his glass. Damn but he was excited at the prospect. Of course, once he had her to bed, the thrill would diminish, but until then . . . He wondered about her involvement in Humford's death. Had she known something? Brand swirled the port in his glass, watching the rich liquid circle into a funnel.

Poor Wycham. Ever since they'd been in school, Roger had fallen from one scrape into another. But this . . . Brand wondered how Roger had gotten into such a fix. It was unbelievably sad that he had no one to turn to, that he'd been forced to ask for help from an old schoolmate. Brandon couldn't imagine life without his family, without his brothers and sister who, though impossibly interfering, still cared about him and did what they could to make his life better.

Brandon's hand tightened about his glass. He would help Roger any way he could.

A slight stir arose at the door. Verena stood in the opening, dressed from head to foot in white and silver. On a normal woman, such a preponderance of brilliance would outshine any tendency toward beauty.

But on Verena, whose smile seemed to brighten the whole room, the gown seemed fitting somehow. As if she and no other woman deserved such angelic dressing.

But she was no angel. Brand owed her dearly for her tricks. And Humford, perhaps his very life.

Brandon tossed back the rest of his drink, collected his money, and stood. Somehow, some way, he'd get Lady Westforth alone.

Tonight was going to be interesting. Very interesting indeed.

# Chapter 7

*London feeds on scandal. It nourishes, sustains,
contains, and invigorates her. Not that I listen to
it, of course. I'm far, far above all that.*

The Dowager Duchess of Roth to Sir Royce Pemberley,
while meeting that handsome scamp in the park
one very damp afternoon

**B**rand waited until the crowd that had gathered to greet Verena had dispersed somewhat before he moved into her line of sight. There was a moment's hesitation, a faint coloring of her cheeks, and then she broke into that fascinating smile. Brand lifted his glass toward her in a silent toast.

A flicker of surprise showed in her face, but no embarrassment. She even returned the favor, inclining her head in his direction. He had expected that she'd avoid him, but he'd not counted on her natural brazen temperament. She soon broke away from the small group and made her way to his side.

"Mr. St. John. How delightful." Her tone dripped with ill-concealed humor.

The room seemed dressed in dark browns and reds, while Verena in her white dress drew all the light and held it. Brand couldn't help but smile—

her choice of gown was brilliant. "Lady West-forth, it is always a pleasure seeing you." He looked down into her upturned face, aware of a stirring of unmistakable lust. Her hair was pulled back, twisted in a braid and fastened around her head like a crown. She didn't try to ape fashions that wouldn't compliment her, but wore what suited her.

Brandon had to agree that she looked fresh and bright, soaking the color from every woman in the room. His gaze flickered to her shoulders where they showed above the white gauze rosettes that decorated the neckline of her gown. A silver neck-let rested against her throat and drew the eye. He saw the necklet and looked away, only to return his gaze immediately.

She placed her fingers on the silver chain and dimpled up at him. "Do you like it? I had it made just last week."

"So that's where my draft ended."

"Alas, yes. The signature was all I had left after Lady Farnsworth got butter on the rest of it." She peeped at him from beneath her lashes, a deli-cious laugh gurgling in her throat.

He should have been angry. But instead, his blood quickened. By God, he would enjoy this little contretemps. More than he'd enjoyed anything in a long, long time. "You, madam, are incorrigible."

"Only when forced."

"I'm sorry if you feel that I have forced you into anything."

"Ha! You've never been sorry for a single thing you've ever done. Have you?"

"I hate apologizing so I make it a point to always be in the right."

She tilted her head to one side and regarded him with mock seriousness. "Mr. St. John, you are certainly taking this in good part, which is most unfortunate."

"How so?"

"Because if you insist on being such a good sport, then I shall have to cease and desist in my efforts to make everyone laugh at you. I would truly hate to do that, so do you think you could work up a nice glower? Or a stern frown, like a displeased tutor? Just one will do. Then everyone who is watching to see what is going to occur between us, mortal enemies that we are, will realize that I was perfectly within my rights to mock you."

"Lady Westforth, I don't know who taught you such brutal tactics, but I applaud them." Brandon captured her hand and kissed it, brushing his lips lightly over her skin. He was aware of an instant ripple of attraction, like the hint of movement along the surface of a pond. His body heated as his attention fixed on her lower lip. God, but she was a tasty morsel. One he would enjoy devouring, one delectable inch at a time.

It was strange, but he'd never before experienced this combination of powerful physical attraction combined with an innate appreciation for a dauntless spirit. It was disconcerting, to say the least. Not that it would interfere with his plans. Will she, nil she, the luscious Verena was about to be thoroughly and completely seduced.

Some of his thoughts must have been visible,

for her fingers trembled against his. She tugged her hand free, her color high.

Her companion joined her then, a strikingly handsome man with gold coloring that strongly echoed her own. She turned to the man as if she were a drowning victim finding a rope within reach. "Ah! Mr. St. John, allow me to present Mr. Lansdowne. He is an acquaintance, recently come from Italy."

Another victim. Brand should have felt some pity for the fool, but somehow all he could think about was that the man before him was now standing beside Verena. He'd drawn her hand through his arm as if he knew her intimately.

Irritation inched along Brandon's shoulders. "Do you plan on staying in London long?"

"As long as Lady Westforth allows me to." The gentleman arched his brows toward Verena, who returned his smile.

The bounder. "I hope you conclude your business swiftly and profitably," Brand said. "In the meantime, perchance you will join me in a game. Faro, perhaps?"

Lansdowne brightened, his brown eyes alight. "Faro! I'd love to play, though I'm not very good."

"Neither, apparently, am I. I was losing just before you entered."

"A temporary lapse, I'm certain." Mr. Lansdowne was so excited by this offer that he seemed to forget Verena stood at his side. "Perhaps we can set our own terms. The house has limits, you know, but for men like you and I, there's no need to waste our time playing for so little. We can raise the wager to—Ow!" He clutched his arm where Lady Westforth had been resting her hand.

"Poor Mr. Lansdowne!" she said smoothly. "Is your arm acting up again?" She looked at Brandon, all innocent concern. "Gout, you know."

"At such a tender age? Mr. Lansdowne, I'm sorry to hear that."

The man rubbed his arm glumly. "Not as much as I am."

Lady Westforth sent him a perfunctory smile. "I suppose this means you can't play cards. Not with your arm bothering you."

"Can't play ca—Oh!" He smoothed his sleeve over his arm. "Yes, that could be difficult. Well. Mr. St. John, it was pleasant meeting you." He bowed, sent a dark glance at Lady Westforth, and then walked away.

"How long have you known him?" Brand asked as soon as the man was out of hearing.

Verena managed a shrug, though Brandon thought he detected a faint color to her cheeks. He was just going to ask her a more pointed question when an elderly gentleman appeared at Verena's elbow.

"Lady Westforth and Brandon St. John! I'd have never thought to see the two of you together, especially after—well, it doesn't matter, does it?" The old man peered from one to the other. "I take it you've cried peace?"

"Indeed we have," Brand said. "In fact, we have become so close that Lady Westforth now wears my name on her necklet."

Verena blinked, her fingers resting on the necklace. "Unfair," she murmured.

"Not in this game," he answered beneath his smile.

A reluctant smile touched her lips. "You're incorrigible. I think I like that."

Jameson leaned closer. "Since you are friends now, I hope you are up to a game. I've a table saved. Mr. Cabot-Lewes is waiting us there."

Verena looked at Brandon, that damnable smile in her eyes, and also a touch of something else . . . was it triumph? "A game of cards. I would enjoy that ever so much. Shall we?"

Brandon bowed. "Of course."

They were soon ensconced at Jameson's table, which was tucked into a corner, partially hidden by a set of large, leafy plants. Mr. Cabot-Lewes was introduced and Brandon garnered that the man was a cit who'd made a huge fortune in the tea trade. The man was short and thick and completely bald except for a thick fringe of white hair. He was also effusive in his admiration of Verena to the point of idiocy.

Brandon was beginning to realize what Marcus had meant when he suggested that Lady Westforth was the darling of the demimonde. Everyone seemed to know her, and she them.

"Shall I deal?" she was asking now. The light from a candelabrum shone directly over her head, touching her crown with silver and limning the delicate lines of her shoulders. Her silver necklet caught the light and revealed Brand's name and made him smile. She'd branded herself, whether she realized it or not.

She picked up the cards, her movements graceful and unhurried, and dealt them.

Lord Jameson watched her with an air of satisfaction. "Perhaps your beautiful hands will put some magic back in the cards. God knows they were going flat."

Mr. Cabot-Lewes nodded his approval, his fleshy chin jiggling noticeably. "Good to have you with us, Lady Westforth. And you, too, St. John. We need some fresh blood this evening."

Jameson chuckled. "Fresh money, you mean." He gathered his cards and tossed a gold coin to the center of the table.

Brandon looked at his own cards. He could feel the attention of the two men. They were like sharks circling an especially fat fish.

Jameson played a card. "It's an honor to be playing a St. John."

"Is it?" Verena said, disbelief in her voice.

Brandon grinned at her, but she pretended not to see.

Lord Jameson gestured at him. "St. John, tell Lady Westforth how you not only have the devil's own luck, but you can spot a Captain Sharp a mile away."

Verena faltered, and a card fell from her fingers to the table. Her color high, she shook her head. "I'm sorry. It slipped." She collected her card.

"Don't worry, my dear," Jameson said. "We all make mistakes. All of us, except your friend, that is. I'd sooner try to cheat the devil at cards than Brandon St. John."

The faintest hint of breathlessness touched Verena's voice as she turned to Brand. "How can you tell if someone is playing foul?"

Cabot-Lewes cackled. "The same way we all

tell when someone's playing foul—by how often they win."

"If that's the case," Jameson replied, "then you've never cheated a day in your life." He watched as Brand played his card. "What's the real pity is that no one would ever believe that I've cheated a day in my life, either."

Verena managed a faint smile for this witticism. How she wished she'd taken James's advice now. She'd taunted St. John into attending her only to discover that he possessed the one mystical penchant she'd rather he didn't—that of discerning foul play.

She glanced at him from beneath her lashes and found him watching her, his blue eyes intent. He sat slightly out of the light, as if he disliked being the center of attention, his dark hair falling over his brow in a way that made her itch to brush it back.

She fixed her gaze firmly on her cards. It was silly to think that he could spot a cheater. Lord Jameson was renowned for his teasing manner and he was not averse to making up a rumor just to amuse his listeners.

Still, it wouldn't hurt to be cautious. Especially since she'd quite decided to make St. John's purse her own. Verena lost one game. Then two. All the while, she was watching Brandon, but she could see no sign that he was more capable of spotting someone fuzzing the cards than anyone else.

If anything, he seemed far too focused on her to pay much attention to the game, often staring at her with a speculative gaze that made her frown.

Despite his earlier gallantry, he seemed very serious this evening.

She played the third game straight as well, and tried not to wince when she lost yet again. Her pile of guineas had thinned noticeably, as had the stack in front of Brandon. It almost hurt when he negligently tossed a marker onto the table when he ran out of coins.

Verena ran her fingers over her last guineas, catching James's eye from where he stood across the room. He read her expression immediately and frowned.

This really could not continue. If she was going to help her brother out of his predicament, Verena was going to have to take some chances. Risks. The very thing Father and James lived for and she avoided. Even though the blackmailer hadn't asked for money, Verena was certain she and James would need it—Father always said there were few problems a handful of gold could not fix.

James stopped a passing servant and spoke quietly. Within moments, the servant arrived at Verena's table, three bottles of port on his tray. "From Mr. Lansdowne. In celebration of Lady Westforth's beauty."

Verena sent James a grateful smile. "Oh my! How generous!"

Brand's sharp gaze raked over the bottles. "Indeed."

Lord Jameson held out his empty glass. "I don't even know the man, but I think he's a prince."

Mr. Cabot-Lewes agreed, allowing the servant to fill his cup to the rim. "If I ever meet him, remind me to thank him for his largesse. Port is my favorite."

Brandon frowned at Verena. "Shall I order you something else? Some sherry perhaps."

"Oh no! I love port." She allowed the servant to fill her glass as well.

Verena played the next two hands more aggressively, winning one and losing one. She made sure everyone's glass remained full, including her own, though she drank little. She couldn't afford to drink, not if she wanted to play this game well. When no one watched, she poured her port onto the dirt of one of the large plants that sat at the sides of their table.

Time passed and the servant, heavily bribed by James, continued to refill their glasses. Soon, Lord Jameson showed serious signs of inebriation. He caught Verena's gaze and smiled, a woozy, unfocused smile that set her nerves at rest.

She glanced next at Mr. Cabot-Lewes. He was squinting at his cards, blinking as if his eyes wouldn't focus. Verena hid a smile.

Last, she glanced at Brandon. The light from the candelabra warmed his black hair and touched his cheekbones, giving him a harsh appearance. She noticed that the glass at his elbow was almost empty—again. She nodded to the servant, who immediately refilled the glass.

Brandon looked up then, his gaze resting on hers. There was something insolently possessive about him, as if he thought he had but to crook his finger and she'd fall into his lap.

*That might be interesting, falling into his lap,* her unruly imagination told her. Or it would have been interesting, if she hadn't been so determined to show him that she was completely unaffected by his presence.

She lifted her chin and met his gaze with a challenging one of her own. He smiled, his eyes softening slightly and just as before, she felt a strange sense of connection with him. As if he knew who she was and all of her sins, and he didn't give a damn about a one.

She forced her gaze back to the stack of guineas on the table before her, her palm itching. Brandon St. John was a very dangerous man.

"Lady Westforth," Jameson slurred. "It's your deal."

Verena took the cards, her fingers sliding over the smooth surfaces. She glanced at Brandon, but he was regarding his glass with a fixed gaze. Jameson and Cabot-Lewes were so sotted they could barely sit up. The time was now.

She shuffled the cards, deftly placing the queen on the bottom. Verena won the next three hands. As she pulled in her winnings, she met James's gaze across the room and gave him an infinitesimal smile. Things were indeed going well.

"Lady Westforth, you are not drinking."

The dark voice feathered over her. Verena found Brandon's intense gaze on her. He had the most astonishing eyes, a blue so rich they appeared black in certain light. "You mistake, Mr. St. John. I've had more than my fair share."

He lifted his own glass and she noticed that his hand appeared slightly unsteady. She was almost chortling at her good luck when it became Brandon's turn to deal. She watched him fumble a little with the cards and she smiled encouragingly at him when he passed the first card her way.

His eyes narrowed and he gave her a raw look, hot and proprietory. One that sent a shiver down her back. She pulled away at the intensity of his expression. He must have realized he'd shown too much, for he immediately looked away, dealing the remaining cards.

Verena picked up her cards, more shaken than she wanted to admit. It wasn't that he'd looked at her in such a way; men tended to do that, especially after imbibing so much port. But her own reaction startled her. Her body had softened as if he'd touched her intimately, like a lover.

It was not a response Verena was used to having. Indeed, she could recall only one other time that she'd reacted that way to any man's look. And that had been with Andrew.

She looked at Brandon again. Surely not. Surely she didn't feel anything for Brandon St. John other than—

"It's your turn, Lady Westforth." Brandon's gaze slid over her again, but this time with more control. His deep voice curled about her, brushing her bared shoulders. "Do you discard?"

Verena found that her hands were trembling just the faintest bit. That would not do at all. How could she change her cards if her hands shook as if she had the palsy? She quickly discarded, then placed her cards on the table.

Brandon's attention seemed to move on to Lord Jameson. Verena almost sighed in relief. To give her something to do with her hands, she picked up her glass of port and took a sip. Everyone's glass was empty but hers. That would not do at all. She glanced around to make sure no one was looking, then reached down to pour it into the plant.

Strong fingers encircled her wrist, bearing her hand up. Up. Back to the table. Verena looked into Brandon's eyes.

He smiled, his teeth flashing in the dim light. "I do so hate to see good port go to waste."

"What's that?" Cabot-Lewes asked, straining to look over the table without getting up from his seat. His double chin quivered. "Did Lady Westforth spill her drink?"

"Not yet," Brand said. He leaned forward so that no one could hear him. "I believe the port is not to your liking. Shall I order you some lemonade instead?"

Verena pressed her lips together. "I don't know what you're talking about. I was merely looking at the plant, enjoying how very . . . green it is." She looked meaningfully at her wrist. "You can release me now."

"Take a drink."

"No."

"Verena." He leaned even closer. To anyone watching, it was a lover's intimate moment, his hand about her wrist, his lips near her ear. "Drink it or admit you were tossing it out."

It was a threat. Verena didn't like threats. But even worse, she didn't like men who tried to force her into saying things she didn't want to say. "Release my wrist."

He lifted his brows.

"I cannot drink with your hand about my wrist."

He released her hand, a challenge in his hard stare.

Something deep inside Verena quivered at his challenge. This man had insulted her, trifled with her, and now, on top of everything else, seemed determined to hold her out for mockery. Well! She would show him. Every drop of Lansdowne blood that flowed through her veins began to simmer in earnest.

Verena locked her gaze with Brandon's, lifted her glass, and drank the port. Not just a sip, either. She drank the entire glass, one burning gulp at a time. The port seared its way down and made her eyes water, but she finished the last dregs. Then she set her glass on the table with a thump.

He swore softly. "You little fool. You'd do anything other than admit the truth, wouldn't you?"

Lord Jameson chortled. "Here, here, Lady W! That's the way to show him!"

Verena blinked back the water that stung her eyes. Her whole body felt as if it was afire. "Whose turn is it?"

Brandon leaned back in his chair, a faint sense of disapproval clinging about him as Jameson continued the game.

Verena didn't care what Brandon St. John thought. She was a full-grown woman and if she wanted to drink port, then she would. Any time of the day. In fact, she just might have another glass. Or two. Maybe three.

She caught the eye of a passing servant and pointed to her glass. It was immediately filled, as were those of everyone else at the table. Verena quickly emptied that glass, as well. Why not?

She'd already won a fair amount. If she was careful, she'd still rise a winner. And that was enough. For now.

Verena allowed a servant to refill her glass yet again.

Brand's disapproval grew until it seemed to Verena that it hung over them like a cloud.

She refused to acknowledge him, but spared no pains to flirt with Lord Jameson and Mr. Cabot-Lewes. She took a deep sip of the port, finding that it wasn't nearly so bad this time. The more one had, the better it tasted. Perhaps that was the trick.

They played another round of cards and to Verena's surprise, not only was her glass empty once again, but she won. She was considering asking for more port when Brandon's voice sounded in her ear.

"Don't even think it, damn you. If you get any more, I will be the one tossing it into the plant."

She sniffed. "You are not my father."

"No," he said grimly, his gaze raking over her in a way that made her shiver.

"You aren't my brother, either."

"No, I'm not," he agreed quickly enough.

"Then you can't make suggestions about the way I live."

"I'm not making a suggestion. I'm making a statement. You've had too much to drink and I'm not going to allow you to have any more."

"Allow? Who do you think you are?" She glared at him challengingly. Strangely, his face seemed to waver in front of her. "Stop that."

"Stop what?"

"Moving. It's making me ill."

He dropped his cards onto the table. "That's it. We're leaving."

"We're not going anywhere. I came to play and I'm going to play."

He stared at her a long moment, his face as black as a thundercloud. Finally, he picked up the deck of cards. "Then we'll play. But a new game."

"I say, what's going on?" Jameson asked blurrily.

Brandon shot him an indifferent look. "Lady Westforth and I have an argument to settle. We're going to cut the cards in answer."

Cabot-Lewes waved a hand. "Carry on. I think I'm done for, anyway. Do we know who won?"

"I hope I did," Verena said, wondering why she'd eschewed port for so long. It was marvelous stuff. She lifted her glass, disappointed to find it empty but for two or three drops. "How sad." She looked at Brandon, who sat so sternly at her side. For some reason, the sight of him warmed her and she smiled. "If I win the cut, do I get more port?"

"An entire bottle."

She sighed happily. "That seems fair."

He shuffled the cards and then placed them in front of her.

Verena looked at the cards and wet her lips. She was going to go home a winner tonight. She could feel the positive hum of luck pouring through her veins. She reached for a card, then stopped, meeting St. John's gaze. "Wait. If you win the draw, what do you get?"

His gaze flickered over her, resting on the curve of her décolletage, her bared shoulders, her bottom lip. "If I win," he said, "then I earn the right to see you home."

She eyed him suspiciously. There was something wrong with this plan, she knew it. But for some reason, she couldn't fathom what it was. "Anything else?"

His gaze flickered over her. "What else could there be?"

"Well, I get a whole bottle of port if I win, but you only get to ride home with me. That doesn't seem even."

"By Jove," Jameson said. "She's right! You should get more than that if she's to win an entire bottle of port."

"How about a kiss?" Mr. Cabot-Lewes said. He beamed, his round face damp with perspiration. "I won a kiss at cards once. Best kiss I ever had."

"Seems fair to me," Jameson said. "Well, Lady W? What do you say?"

Verena put her elbow on the table and rested her chin in her hand. "I don't think I can. Mr. Lansdowne brought me. It would be rude to leave with someone else. And it would be really rude to kiss someone else, *not* that I want to kiss Mr. Lansdowne."

Brandon's mouth curved into a smile. "You don't?"

"Not at all. He's not my cup of tea," she confided easily.

Jameson chuckled. "The poor man!"

Cabot-Lewes nodded sadly. "And he sent us that lovely port, too. Shouldn't kick a man who made such a dashing gesture."

"I don't think he'll care," Brand said coolly.
"He's busy at the faro table."

Everyone turned to look. Verena blinked blurrily across the room. She could just make out the
back of James's head where he sat near Lady Farley. "I hope he had better luck than I've had this
evening." She leaned toward Brandon and said in
a conspiratorial voice, "I usually win, you know.
Only very carefully."

Brandon thought he'd never seen a more
adorably drunk woman in his life. Especially not
after only three glasses. "You don't drink often,
do you?"

"Never. Inhibits your judgment, you know."

"Inhibits? You don't appear inhibited at the
moment. Perhaps you meant to say that it *impairs*
your judgment."

"Meant what I said. Said what I meant." She
pointed a finger at him. "Do you know what my
father believes?"

"What?"

"A good card player doesn't drink."

"And are you a good card player? Or a
crooked one?"

"I don't like your tone." She tried to look offended but failed miserably.

He placed his elbows on the table and leaned
closer. "Choose your card, Verena."

She looked at the deck and wet her lips nervously. Brandon watched her tongue trace a line
over her lips and his body tightened. Bloody hell,
but she was a luscious bundle.

Finally, she reached out and flipped over a card.

A jack of clubs beamed up. "Ha!" she said triumphantly. "Beat that!"

"Bloody good one, Lady W," Jameson said, nodding sagely, his cravat askew.

Mr. Cabot-Lewes nodded enthusiastically. "Hard to beat that with one card."

Brandon turned over his card. A king of hearts beamed up at them.

Verena blinked.

"The St. John luck," Jameson crowed. "Warned you about that."

Brand stood and placed a hand on Verena's elbow. He wanted to get her out of here before Lansdowne realized she was gone. "Come, Lady Westforth. I will see you home."

She looked up at him. "Now?"

"This instant."

She sighed, then clambered to her feet, swaying a little.

Jameson and Cabot-Lewes stood as well and made effusive farewells. Brand didn't give Verena time to respond. He said their good-byes and bundled her out of the gaming hell and into his carriage before she knew what had happened.

# Chapter 8

*Kissing is an art best left to the experts as it is far more dangerous than swordplay. One injudiciously welded pair of lips can cause more harm than the sharpest blade.*

Sir Royce Pemberley to his new wife, Liza, while sitting in the Shelbourne box at the Theatre Royale

The carriage rumbled down the streets of London, the lights flickering through the windows to trace fleeting patterns. Verena settled back against the squabs, trying to ignore the fact that Brandon sat directly across from her, his knee hard against hers.

What was it about him that made her feel so nervous, as if she stood on a narrow ledge and one misstep could lead to something indecently dangerous? She clasped her damp hands together, aware that her heart thundered in her ears.

She would just look out the window and pretend she wasn't aware of him, though it was difficult. He was so large, leaning in the corner of the coach with his hands in his pockets, his eyes fixed on her.

Verena supposed she should be thankful that he wasn't taking advantage of their solitude by making improper advances. Although, to be honest, she'd welcome an improper advance or two. Especially now, the night air crisp on her bared shoulders, the motion of the carriage increasing her port-induced dizziness until she felt as if she were drifting on a cloud, free and as light as air.

There were other feelings, too. Feelings she hadn't experienced in a long, long time. Feelings of restlessness. Of wanting.

She leaned back and closed her eyes, trying to shut out the man who sat across from her. But it did no good. She could see him through her eyelids. In fact, had she pen and paper, she could have drawn him, every last line—the way his eyes crinkled when he finally smiled, the way his mouth could tighten when he didn't like something, the broad width of his shoulders, the powerful lines of his thighs . . . hmmm.

*His thighs.* She smiled to herself. How she'd like to see those thighs right now. Undressed. Right at mouth level where she could—

"You should never drink." His voice dripped amusement. "I can't believe you only had three glasses of port. My mother could drink more than that."

"Your mother was an alcoholic?" She opened her eyes and squinted in the semi-darkness. "I suppose that's only to be expected. If I had six children, I'd be fond of the bottle, too."

"She was not an alcoholic." He chuckled. "But you're right. Six children would be a good reason to become one. She had her hands full." He eyed her for a moment. "Verena. That's a very unusual name. Where did it come from?"

Verena should have objected to his use of her Christian name, but she rather liked the way it rolled off his tongue. It sounded almost French the way he said it. And everyone knew that French was the language of love.

"Well," he said, moving impatiently, his knees seeming to press further into her side of the carriage, invading her space, bringing even more disquiet. "Are you going to tell me about your name or am I to guess?"

"Guess."

His mouth curved in a smile. She really, really liked his mouth. She thought perhaps it was her favorite part, except for his thighs, of course.

"Let's see . . . Verena." The light from the street caressed a path down his jaw to his chin. "It was your grandmother's name and when she died, she left you a fortune."

That *was* a lovely story. Verena immediately dreamed up a kindly old grandmother worth more than the crown prince. "That would certainly be fortunate for me, but it's wrong. It's the name of a small town. My parents believe I was conceived there, on the banks of the river."

"How risqué. My parents were just as bad. I remember once finding them entwined in the pantry." He shifted in his seat, scooting down a bit. His legs were suddenly no longer pressing against her knees, but stretched to either side, cocooning her in warmth.

Verena wanted to move away, but there was nowhere to go. She was imprisoned between a pair of long, muscular legs. How . . . delightful.

The carriage rounded a corner, and somehow, Brandon used the motion to shift yet again and now his knee was almost against her seat, his thigh pressed firmly to hers. Verena sucked in her breath, a shiver traveling across her shoulders, down her chest. It tightened her nipples and sent a tremor of hot lust through her. Blast it, had she known that port was such an insidious drink, she'd never have touched a drop.

"Tell me about your husband. He was a sporting man, was he not?"

She blinked, trying to reel in her muddled senses. "Andrew? He liked all sports, especially those he could wager on." She scooted a little to one side, away from Brandon's dangerous legs. For they were dangerous—they made her think all sorts of improper thoughts. Like what he'd look like naked. She glanced at him from beneath her lashes. His clothes fit to perfection and she could tell that he was made with a sculptor's hand.

God was to be commended on producing such a fine specimen. In fact, just to honor the realization, Verena decided to say an extra ten Hail Marys that very night.

Feeling very pious, she smoothed her skirts over her knees, relishing the feel of the silk. She felt amazingly alive, aware of every little nuance, of the flickering light, of her gown beneath her fingertips, of the sounds of the horses as they clopped through the streets. The night was wonderfully magical.

"Did your husband want children?"

She frowned at Brandon and wished the light

were more definite. She could barely make out his face, though his eyes seemed to burn through her. "No, he didn't. Not yet anyway."

Brandon thought he could see the faintest hint of sadness in her eyes. He shifted again, bringing his leg more fully in contact with hers. She looked down, but made no move to retreat.

It was a pity he had such a large carriage. He made a mental note to order a smaller one on the morrow. "I understand Westforth died in a carriage accident shortly after your marriage. Did the horses bolt?"

"No, Andrew did." She managed a small smile. "He was racing and he took a corner too sharp. He broke his neck."

"I'm sorry."

"Don't be. It was swift and painless. And he died the same way he'd lived—free. As sad as I was, I think I knew even back then that it was meant to be."

There was a catch in her voice that made Brandon frown. "You still miss him."

She looked out the window, the dark leather that lined the walls of the carriage a perfect background for her beauty.

Beauty. It was strange, but he now thought her every bit as beautiful as Devon had described. It was more than her face or body, though those features were noteworthy in their own right. It was something more. Her spirit perhaps.

Brandon sighed impatiently. He was being ridiculous. He should be asking about Humford instead of feeding this strange curiosity he had about her—who she was and where she'd come from and all manner of things.

She chuckled suddenly, leaning back against the squabs, her teeth flashing as she smiled. "Do you know what I don't miss about being married?"

"What?"

"His snoring."

Brand grinned, wondering what she'd do if he grabbed her to him and kissed her. She needed to be kissed, he could tell. And if he was honest, he yearned to wrap his arms about her and taste her yet again, to see if his memory of their one embrace was anything near the truth, or a sad exaggeration resulting from his overactive imagination.

She pulled back, nose in the air. "You're laughing at me."

He captured her hand. "I did not laugh."

"No, but you smiled and that's close enough. How much farther is it? I want to go home."

"That's where we're going."

"It is certainly taking long enough." She eyed him suspiciously, though she made no move to free her hand from his. "Are you certain you're taking me to my house and not yours?"

"I don't have a house. I rent lodgings off St. James's Street."

"What? A St. John without a house? I thought there was a law against that. Something about 'all pompous asses shall possess their own abodes.'"

He grinned. "You know, I believe my mother would have liked you."

"I doubt it. I rarely get on well with other fe-males. I don't know why that is."

He rubbed his thumb over the back of her hand, marveling at the smoothness of her skin. "Perhaps it is because you're too forthright."

"Forthright? You mean 'honest'?"

Brandon didn't reply. He wasn't sure what he meant. All he knew was that the woman who sat so tantalizingly near wasn't sitting anywhere close enough. He wanted her beside him. On him. Under him. A growing heat filtered through him.

She sighed. "You aren't going to answer and I know why. You don't think I'm honest *or* honor-able or you'd have never offered to pay me to leave your brother alone. In fact, you think I'm a horrible person."

"I do not," he said slowly. "I am beginning to realize that I was wrong about some things, but I had good reason to think them true."

" 'Think' and 'some.' What a delightful way to make a decision."

"I admit I was somewhat hasty in my judg-ment."

" 'Somewhat hasty,' " she scoffed. "There's nothing like a partial retraction of a gross error. It's rather like being *almost* with child."

Brandon opened her hand, admiring the shape of her fingers where they were splayed across his. Long and delicate, her hands were the hands of a musician, of an artist, of a skilled lover, perhaps. The thought tantalized and Brandon lifted her hand to his mouth.

He gently ran his lips over the length of her fingers, stopping to taste the crest of each knuckle. A slow, shivery heat built, tormenting and teasing.

She watched, wide eyed, her mouth parted. "You—you shouldn't do that."

He kissed her first finger. "Why not?"

"B-because it—" She swallowed.

He ran his lips the length of her second finger. She shivered then, closing her eyes, an expression of yearning on her face.

She was so transparent, her every emotion flickering across her face. Brandon could not look away. He pressed a kiss to the sensitive place where her third finger joined her palm, his tongue flicking out to tease the delicate fold.

She jerked forward, her knees pressed together, her breathing erratic. The gesture was so primal, so pure. Brandon's control stretched to the breaking point. He pressed her fingers to his lips and closed his eyes. He dared not claim the promised kiss—he would not have the strength to stop the embrace from becoming something more.

"St. John . . ." Verena swallowed, her tongue darting out to wet her lips. Her entire body was aflame. She wanted him—now. "I will give you the kiss I owe you."

His eyes narrowed, an almost slumberous seductiveness to his voice. "You've had too much to drink."

She barely kept her smile, the pressure within her was so great. "No, I haven't. But I'm going to wish I had if you do not kiss me."

His lips quirked, his eyes gleaming hotly. "If you were to come over here . . . to my side of the carriage . . ."

Her breasts ached for his touch. "Yes?" she whispered breathlessly.

"And if you were to settle yourself in my lap and wrap your arms about my neck . . ."

"Yes?" Any moment now she would burst into flames and melt into a puddle of thwarted desire. "What would you give me?"

"I would give you an *extra* kiss, one you would never forget." His voice threaded through the night, luring her forward. "I'm saving the kiss I owe you for a time of *my* choosing."

It was wanton. Verena knew it. Yet she found herself sliding forward, to the edge of her seat. His legs were to either side of hers and it was remarkably easy to lift herself into his lap.

He engulfed her, pulling her to his chest, his mouth descending on hers. It was as it had been before—more than a kiss, it was a devouring, a branding. His mouth covered hers, his hands molded her back through her dress. She moaned beneath the onslaught, opening to him, wrapping her arms about his neck.

Waves of desire burst through her, shattering her thoughts. All she knew was what she felt—his tongue thrusting into her mouth, making her writhe against him, his hands warm and demanding, cupping her breasts. Her nipples hardened and she arched into his touch, her entire body melting against him.

The carriage rumbled to a halt and with it, Verena's senses returned. She pushed herself from him, forced her weak knees to move her back to her seat. Once there, all she could do was lay against the squabs and fight for her breath.

They sat for a moment in the stillness, looking at one another, both breathing as harshly as if they'd been running. It was an agony. Verena yearned to be back in his embrace, to feel his hands on her once more, to taste him deeply.

She pressed a hand to her forehead. "I—I didn't mean for us to—"

"I know. Verena, I—"

The door opened and the footman pulled down the steps.

Brand sighed, raking a hand through his hair. He met her gaze with a wry smile. "Come. I promised to see you home and so I shall." He stepped out, then turned and held out his hand.

She nodded mutely and allowed him to assist her from the carriage. Light from the portico shone around them in a golden pool. Brandon tucked her hand in the crook of his arm and walked her up the steps to the door. Verena put her hand to the knob, then stopped.

"What is it?"

She frowned at the knob and tried to turn it again. "It's locked."

"Do you have a key?"

"Of course not. Herberts is supposed to wait up for me."

Brandon raised his brows. "And you really believed he would?"

She didn't answer. Brandon grinned, then reached past her to swing the brass knocker.

There was a long silence, both of them aware of the gaze of the footmen.

Brandon leaned forward, his voice heavy and low. "You, madam, owe me a kiss."

"I gave you one in the carriage."

"No. That was an *extra* kiss. And you know it."

He was right. Verena bit back a sigh. She'd hoped he'd forgotten that. The port-induced fog was rapidly dissipating mainly due to the passion that had dizzied her in the carriage. Now, more than ever, she was all too aware of the dangers of being alone with a man like Brandon. He wouldn't be all pretty words and impassioned declarations. No, he was a man of action. Or rather actions, which was the problem. Verena didn't think he'd stop at one kiss and she was beginning to realize that she didn't want him to.

Perhaps if she just allowed him to kiss her here, on the stoop. His carriage sat in full view, as did his servants. Surely that would keep Brandon from doing anything more than he should. And might serve to remind her of her obligations to her own pride, as well.

She rubbed her hands on her skirts, remembering the feel of his mouth on her fingers, of his fingers on her breasts. God help her, but he was far too sensual for her comfort. "Very well, Mr. St. John. If you must have your kiss—" She closed her eyes, puckered her lips and waited.

He didn't say a word.

Verena puckered a bit harder, praying he'd just take his kiss and be gone.

The silence grew. Eventually, she opened her eyes a bit and peered at him through her lashes. He stood before her, arms crossed, a very unamused expression on his face.

She sighed and straightened. "You don't want your kiss?"

"Not like that." He turned and banged on the door again.

Verena winced. "You'll crack the wood."

"I'd like to crack something," he growled, his brows low. "Where the hell is that butler of yours? I've never seen such a lazy, untrained—"

The doorknob turned and then the door slowly creaked open. Herberts stood in the door, blinking blearily, his hair in disarray, his neckcloth untied. "Here, now. Did oiye lock the door by mistake?"

"Locking the door was no mistake," Brandon said impatiently. "You were napping."

"Me?" The butler tried to look offended, but a drool line at the corner of his mouth marred the effort. "Oiye'll have ye know oiye was sittin' roight here, the entire time."

"With your head on a table," Verena said, sailing past him. "No, no! Don't argue. Just take my cloak." She handed it to the butler. "Mr. St. John will be staying for a very short time. There is no need to bring refreshments."

Herberts nodded emphatically. "Good thing ye tol' me that, missus, else oiye'd have fetched 'em afore ye knew it."

Brandon handed Herberts his coat and Verena lost no time leading the way to the sitting room. The quicker this was over, the better.

Verena barely waited until he'd closed the door before she plastered a smile on her face. "Very well. You wanted your kiss."

"In good time," he said slowly. He gazed down at her, as if he was trying to see into her heart. "Verena, I want to ask you a question. What do you know about Lord Humford?"

Verena blinked. *Humford. Was Brandon involved in the blackmail against James?* "Why?"

"Didn't you have him to dinner a month ago?"

"I have a dinner party the first Tuesday of every month. I always invite Lady Jessup and she either brings him or her son as her escort."

Brand's gaze never left her face. "He's dead."

Verena froze, her face paling. *"What?"*

"Right after he left here."

"No!" She pressed a hand to her mouth. "How do you know? I should have thought—" She closed her eyes, her breathing shallow. "Oh my God. *No.*"

Brandon searched her face. Either she was honestly surprised or she was the best actress of his acquaintance.

"He was murdered, Verena."

Her eyes flew open. "Wh-who would do such a thing? He was a harmless old man!"

Who indeed. Looking at Verena, Brand found himself faced with a very unlikely dilemma. He believed her. Verena had not known about the murder. Her reaction was too quick, too true. He would have been able to tell if she were dissembling. Relief lightened his mood and he was pondering what to do next when the doorknocker thundered.

Herberts could be heard shuffling down the hall in answer.

Brand glanced at Verena. "Are you expecting company?"

"It's probably Mr. Lansdowne, come to make sure I arrived safely. If you want your kiss, you had best claim it now."

His time with her was at an end and he still had questions to ask. He had to see her again. The thought pleased him far more than it should have. "Lady Westforth, would you care to go for a carriage ride tomorrow? I bought a new set of grays for my phaeton and I thought you would enjoy an hour of fresh air."

"Are you certain your reputation can handle the strain of being seen with me? I'd hate for people to begin cutting your acquaintance."

He could have told her that as a St. John, he could be seen in the company of all manners of lowly born persons. But it suddenly struck him how snobbish such a sentiment would seem. Good God, when had he gotten so . . . He frowned. "If you don't wish to go riding, then perhaps we can—"

"No, no! I didn't say that. I was merely surprised at the offer. I suppose I should go. It might not do your reputation credit, but it could be of immeasurable help to mine."

Brandon had to smile at that. While Verena would not accept money from him, she obviously had no compunction about using him to better her standing in society. "It's so nice to be needed."

"Isn't it?" she said placidly.

He eyed her a moment longer, quelling a desire to laugh. "You really are a most ungracious woman."

"And you, sir, are a very rude man."

He opened his mouth, but she held up a hand. "Don't even try to deny it. You are rude and you like being rude."

Brand started to protest, then stopped. She was right. He did enjoy bypassing all the annoying civilities. "I don't like pretending I'm something I'm not. If you want gentle wooing, Chase was the man for that."

For some reason, that tiny bit of truth made Verena grin in return. "I don't want to be wooed at all. But I would love to take a ride in the park if you will promise not to claim your kiss there."

"I have the right to demand my kiss when and where I will."

"I'm asking you to be a gentleman."

Before he could answer, the door opened and Herberts announced James. Verena's brother's face was rigid with disapproval, though he managed a bow in Brandon's direction. "St. John! What a surprise—I didn't expect to find you here."

Brandon lifted his brows. "Who did you expect to find? My carriage is the only one out front."

James's mouth tightened and Verena hurried to intercede. "Mr. St. John, thank you so much for seeing me home. I look forward to our ride. Shall we say tomorrow at ten?"

James didn't look very happy to hear that, but he simply moved out of the doorway.

Brandon eyed him a moment longer, then turned to Verena and bowed. "Until tomorrow." He locked his gaze on her for one last moment, the gaze a promise and a threat. And then he was gone.

Verena sank into a chair as soon as the door closed. She felt drained, exhausted. "Blast and double blast."

"Indeed." James came to sit across from her. "You disappeared without leaving me word. Had it not been for Lady Farley, I would be playing yet, thinking you safe."

"I'm sorry. I was overcome with the heat." And two—no, three—glasses of port, though there was no need to explain that part to her brother.

James frowned. "What's this about tomorrow? You aren't going to see St. John again, are you?"

"He wishes me to go for a ride with him, that's all."

"Ha! He wants more than that."

"Nonsense."

"Verena, just look at how he stares at you. He could barely keep his eyes off of you this evening."

"That's because he was trying to ascertain if I was cheating."

"Did you?"

"I tried."

James shook his head. "I don't trust him."

Neither did she. Verena pursed her lips. What was Brandon St. John after? "James, about Humford. Someone murdered him right after he left my house."

James froze, his eyes dark. "Murdered? Who told you this?"

"St. John. This evening. He told me about it as if he thought I already knew."

"Damn." James's mouth thinned. "I don't like this one bit, Verena."

"Nor do I. I'm going riding with St. John and see what else I can discover. Something is amiss."

"It could be a trap."

"Why would someone set a trap for me? I don't have anything to hide."

He scowled. "I still don't like it. What if he is the one looking for this list? The one who murdered Humford?"

"He's not." She caught James's disbelieving gaze and flushed. "St. John had nothing to do with Humford's murder."

"I don't know how you can be so certain."

"He has nothing to gain. St. John is already abominably rich. And then there's the fact that he told me about Humford's demise."

"Yes?"

"James, everyone believes Humford fled the country. It's the perfect way to hide a murder—no one has even looked for the poor man. No murderer would point out something that increased suspicion."

"I suppose you have a point."

"Of course I do." Verena didn't let James say more. Her mind whirled. Brandon St. John may not have killed Humford, but he *was* connected to the missing list in some way. She was sure of it. All she had to do was worm the truth out of him.

For some reason, the idea didn't strike fear in her heart. All it did was send a quick trill of excitement down her back and it was with a far more cheerful demeanor that she planned her route of attack. Heaven help Brandon St. John. He was going to need it.

# Chapter 9

*Men are like large, overgrown pups. They don't know how to behave in company and have a horrible tendency to muss the rugs.*

Sir Royce Pemberley's new wife, Liza,
to Miss Devonshire, who was complaining
of her brother's sad tendency to
tromp mud into the morning room

Early the next morning—far earlier than he usually rose, Brand forced himself from bed and dressed with care. His thoughts went immediately to Verena. He would enjoy their little ride this morning. But first things first—rising at such an hour had left him with a raw hunger.

He smiled grimly as he walked down the street to White's. Once there, he selected a table in the corner and made his way to it, pausing when he caught sight of a familiar face in one corner. Chase. Brand hesitated, then turned and made his way toward his brother. "There you are," Brand said, taking a chair and looking at the dishes of eggs and ham with interest.

Chase looked anything but pleased. "What are you doing here?"

"I'm a member. I come here all the time."

"I thought you'd be out saving me from opportunistic women. Or was that just last week's task?"

Though he tried not to show it, Brandon's anger flickered. Damn it, he'd worked hard not to be Marcus's puppet. But then, this was Chase. He had a gift for spotting weaknesses and, when cornered, he never failed to attack them.

Brandon motioned for a servant to bring him a plate. "I'm glad I found you."

Chase picked up his glass and took a deep drink.

Brandon frowned at the unmistakable scent of brandy. "Bit early for that, isn't it?"

"It's not early; it's late. Unlike you, I have yet to sleep." The gentle light of the club softened the lines about Chase's mouth, marks of dissipation usually found in a much older man.

Brand had to bite back the desire to say anything; Chase did not take chastisement well. A servant set a place setting before Brandon and he busied himself with filling his plate. Brandon waited for the servant to leave and then he said, "I need to speak with you about something of great import."

"I have nothing to say to you."

"Ah, but this is about Lady Westforth."

Chase's gaze met Brand's, curiosity warring with the desire to appear uninterested. Curiosity won. "Is she still tormenting you by flaunting your bank draft? Perhaps you'd like me to see if I can buy her off." Chase leaned back in his chair, and waved his glass. "No, wait. That would only give her more St. John drafts to make her little paper animals out of, wouldn't it? If we continue, she could end up with a menagerie."

Brand took a bite of ham. "I believe she's moved on from there. Now she's making jewelry with my name prominently displayed. Last night, she had a necklet that contained my signature."

Chase threw back his head and laughed. Brand wondered how long it had been since he'd heard that sound.

"Brand, you're going to find out that there's only one Verena. I could have told you about her, but you didn't see fit to ask." His amusement faded a little. "In fact, no one conferred with me at all. When will you realize that I'm no longer nineteen years of age?"

"When you cease to act it. Look, Chase, I'm sorry if you feel we overstepped our bounds. Perhaps we did. But your behavior has not encouraged us to do anything else." He looked pointedly at the glass that rested at Chase's elbow.

"I don't need you or Marcus," Chase sneered, taking a defiant drink. "Stop breathing over my shoulder every time you think I might do something to disgrace the blessed St. John name, will you? I'm tired of it."

Brand almost winced at such obvious bitterness. What had happened to his younger brother? "Did you really ask Verena to marry you?"

Chase stared into his glass. "What has she said?"

"Not a word. And I wasn't going to ask her." Brandon helped himself to more eggs and eyed his brother thoughtfully. "Well?"

"I don't have to answer that."

"I know."

Chase sighed and set his glass on the table. "I asked her to marry me but she refused."

"Do you . . . do you care for her?" The bite of ham Brand had just eaten seemed to stick in his throat.

"Of course not."

Brand swallowed. "She's remarkably personable."

"She's more than that. Verena is special, Brand. She's honest and to the point and—"

"She cheats at cards. I saw her do it last night."

Chase grinned. "So do we."

"Only when we play one another."

"How else do you think she affords her house?" Brand lifted his brows. "She does it for a living?"

"Only when necessary."

"Did she tell you all this?"

"No. I just watched."

"That's not what I'd call honesty."

"No one is perfect. Not even you."

Brand set his fork and knife on his plate and pushed it back. "Not even I." At one time, he and Chase had been close, almost inseparable. That had been years ago, of course. Sometimes Brand missed the old Chase, the one who laughed without rancor coloring his tone, the one who teased and enjoyed life so much.

But that had all changed now. And so had Chase.

Perhaps there was something in what his brother said. Brand frowned down at his napkin, toying with the edge of it. Finally, he looked up.

"Chase, something has happened, something that involves Verena."

"What?"

"I will tell you, but you cannot tell a soul."

"Not even Marcus?"

"No. Not yet. Not until I've figured it out myself."

Chase eyed Brandon warily. "What's happened?"

Brandon related to Chase all the events that had led up to the day, though he omitted the kiss he'd won from Verena in the game last night.

In fact, he omitted quite a few things.

Chase shook his head. "Verena would never be involved in something as horrible as a murder."

"Not even for the money?"

"She didn't cash your bloody bank draft, did she?" Chase waved a hand. "If Verena needs money, all she has to do is win it."

Chase had a point. And after Brandon had seen the two drunken sots they'd played with last night, he didn't think it would be all that difficult.

"Besides," Chase continued, "if she'd been really strapped for funds, she could have married me."

Brandon tossed his napkin onto the plate before him. "You are right."

Chase tapped his fingers on the table, his brow folded in thought. "Brandon, have you asked Verena about this lost list?"

"No. I just mentioned Humford."

"Did she know about that?"

"I don't think so. From her expression, she seemed stunned to discover that he'd been murdered."

Chase looked at Brandon thoughtfully. "You seem to be reading a lot out of her expressions, especially for someone who loathes her."

"I don't loathe her; I disapprove of her."

"Then you like her."

"I didn't say that."

"Then you *dislike* her."

He didn't dislike her, either. In fact, as much as he hated to admit it, he was beginning to develop a strong admiration for Verena, one entirely inappropriate to someone in his circumstances.

Brandon caught Chase's amused gaze and frowned. "Damn it, Chase, what in the hell do you want from me?"

"Admit you are wrong about Verena. She is not what you thought."

"You don't know what I thought."

"Everyone knows what you thought. It shows in the way you treated her, the way you marched into her house and waved your money in her face."

"You're exaggerating."

"Am I?" Chase placed his elbows on the table and leaned forward. "You want to know what *I* think?"

"No."

"I think you are attracted to her. I think you've been attracted to her since the beginning and *that* is why you feel you have to be such an abominable bore—to remind yourself constantly that you, a St. John, are above the lowly Lady Westforth."

"I am not such a pompous ass as that."

Chase leaned back in his chair, an expression of disbelief on his face.

The words rankled. Verena had said almost the exact thing. "I am *not* pompous. I've never been pompous about anything."

Chase gave a choked laugh. "Brand, you've spent your whole life being so bloody perfect that the rest of us feel like toadstools."

"Nonsense. I am not perfect and I'd be the first to admit it. Why, I have a horrible temper. I'm always late, no matter how I try to be on time. I cannot seem to remain interested in a woman past the second week of bedding. And I cannot for the life of me tie my cravat into a mathematical." He touched his cravat ruefully. "If you knew the times I'd tried that, you wouldn't be sitting here telling me I'm anything close to being perfect."

"Just listen to you. Even your category of faults is laughable. You're so perfect you make my teeth hurt." The sneer returned. "You don't even know how perfect you are, which is why people still like you even though they shouldn't."

"Chase, we were talking about Verena."

Chase picked up his glass and examined it in the light. "I've already told you what I think about Verena. Like it or not, she's not capable of such deception as you describe. If I were you, I'd tell her everything. Perhaps with her help, you can figure out a way to assist your friend."

Brand wished it would be that easy. "Chase, I may be guilty of thinking Verena less than acceptable, but you must admit that you are guilty of the opposite fault—you think she is a guileless innocent."

"I think she is a woman. A genuine, gentle, considerate woman who showed me compassion at a time when I—" Chase clamped his mouth closed.

Brandon reached across the table and gripped Chase's wrist. "When what? Chase, what happened to make you so bitter?"

For an instant, he thought his brother would tell him. But then Chase shoved himself from the table. The demons were back, his eyes shadowed.

"Damn it, Chase. You have to tell me. You have to tell someone."

Their gazes locked for a fleeting second and Brand almost flinched at the pain he saw there. But then it was gone, hidden behind the twisted smile.

Chase pulled his arm free. "It's something only I can face. I made a mistake, Brand. The worst one you can make. And I have to pay for it."

"Just tell me—"

"No. Because then you'd try to fix everything and you can't. Not this time."

"Try me."

Chase's gaze fixed on Brandon's face. "If I tell you my sins, will you promise to leave them alone? It's my duty to repair the harm I've done."

"Harm? Chase, what—"

"Promise."

The quiet word filled the space between them. Brandon took a slow breath. If he didn't promise, Chase would never tell him what had occurred. But if he did promise, his hands were as good as tied—he couldn't help Chase no matter how much he needed it.

After a long moment, Brandon shook his head. "I can't promise that. You know I can't."

Chase's gaze seemed to burn into his. After a

long moment, he looked away. "I didn't think you could."

"You knew I couldn't. Chase, whatever has happened, you have to tell someone."

"I know." Chase sighed heavily, then managed a twisted smile. "I'd love to stay and chat, but I must be off. I'm a St. John, you know. I've brandy to drink, cards to play, women to bed. That sort of thing."

"Whatever is bothering you, drinking and whoring will not help."

"No, but it might pass the time until I grow enough courage to do what I must." He gave Brand a mocking salute and walked away.

Brand watched him go. Whatever was wrong with Chase, no one could help him until he was ready. It was painful to admit.

In the meantime, Brandon *could* help Wycham, who must be pulling out his hair while waiting for news. It was imperative that he let Roger know what was occurring. And then, once that was accomplished, Brand would visit Verena and take her for the promised ride through the park. He'd have her alone then, with no interruptions.

Impatient to be on his way, Brand called for pen and paper and hurriedly composed a letter to his friend.

"Please pass the butter."

Verena handed her brother the butter dish, watching morosely as he prepared his toast. "I don't know how you can eat at a time like this."

"Eating helps me think."

She eyed his trim figure. "Apparently you don't do much thinking."

"Only when forced by necessity." He took a bite of toast, his gaze already unfocused.

She had to smile, even though it was the last thing she felt like doing. Memories from last night burned in her mind. Had she really sat in St. John's lap and kissed him with such wanton abandon?

Verena pressed her fingertips to her lips. How . . . thrilling. She hadn't felt so free since Andrew had been alive. It was a pity she felt that way about Brandon St. John. Any relationship she may have with him would not be of the long-standing variety. Their lives were too disparate, too different to allow such luxury of thought. Besides, Verena had been shunned once by the *ton*, she'd be damned if she'd open the door to allow such a thing to happen again.

The door opened and Herberts entered. "Halloo, m'lady! Yer lordship."

"Herberts, Mr. Lansdowne is not a lord. You should address him as 'sir.' "

"Sir, eh? Oiye'll try and 'member that, oiye will."

"Thank you. Did you want something?"

"Yer mail arrived." Herberts picked up a letter from the top of the pile and held it toward the light streaming from the front window. "Looks as if Lady Burton's havin' another ball. Didn't she have one not a week ago? Seems as if she's got nothin' better to do than have parties."

"Herberts," Verena said in a voice of long suffering. "You are not to read my mail, nor attempt to read my mail at any time."

"Whot if it falls open in me hands?"

"*Especially* not then."

Herberts sighed as he set the tray beside Verena. "Gor! Ye've a rule fer everything, don't ye?" Sighing heavily, he wandered out of the room.

James chuckled as the door shut. "I do hope you'll see your way to letting him go with me when I return to Italy. He would be so much more fun than the man I have working for me now. Roberts is dreadfully correct. Almost dull."

Verena rested her chin in her hand as she flipped through her correspondence. "You may have him with my blessing. I've thought about telling Viscountess Hunterston that while he is a dear old man, he's just too—" She picked up a letter and stared at it, then held it out to James. "It's for you."

James's expression froze. He reached for the letter and ripped it open. His face paled as he read.

"What is it?"

He handed her the letter.

Though poorly written, the handwriting matched the first note.

*Lansdowne,*

*You have one week to find the missing paper. Don't do anything stupid. We will be watching. And if you fail, both you and Lady Westforth will pay the price.*

Verena silently handed the letter back to James. His brows lowered. "Bloody hell."

She stood then, too impatient to remain seated.

"Think, James. We have to figure this out. It's almost as if they believe . . ." She took a quick turn about the room. "James, we know Humford was a part of this, right?"

"Yes." He nodded slowly. "Which means we should start there."

"Correct. He was in this house the night before he was murdered, less than a month ago. It was the week before you arrived."

"Did you know him well?"

"Not really. He frequently accompanied Lady Jessup. I invited him because of her."

"That evening, did he seem unusual to you?"

"He was distracted, but other than that . . . well . . . he *did* leave early."

James blinked. "Why?"

She frowned, trying to remember. "We were all sitting in the dining room, waiting on the second course. We were late starting, because of Viscount Wycham. He didn't arrive until we were almost through with the meal."

Verena paced back and forth, wracking her brains. "I finally gave up on Wycham and seated the guests. We were all sitting there, waiting on the second course when suddenly, Humford bolted out of his chair and ran out. It was very strange, though I—" She bit her lip. "Wait. I remember something. He patted his pockets as he went. As if he'd—"

"—lost something." James eyes gleamed. "Verena, do you think your butler could have stolen this list from him?"

Verena went to the door. "Herberts!"

He appeared almost immediately, his head covered by an old rag, a polishing cloth in one hand, a silver spoon in the other. "Aye, missus?"

Verena tore her gaze from his headwear. "I have some questions to ask."

Herberts saluted with the spoon. "Ask away!"

Where to start? Her gaze fell on the letter in James's hand. "The letter, the one Mr. Lansdowne is reading, did it come with the rest of the mail?"

Herberts shook his head. "No, missus. Oiye found thet letter on the stoop this mornin'. It's a wonder it didn't blow away."

"Did you see who delivered it?"

"No. There was no one there, though oiye went to the door as soon as someone knocked."

Verena took a calming breath. "There may be more letters like this coming. I want you to watch for me. If you see who brings them, come and tell me at once."

"Very well, missus. Anythin' else?"

"Yes, I need you to empty your pockets."

"Now?"

"Now."

Herberts groaned. "M'lady, oiye think I should return to rubbin' the silver, if ye don't mind. Oiye can empty me own pockets and—"

"Herberts." She pointed to the breakfast table.

He blew out his breath in a huge gust, set the spoon on the table and began to dig through his pockets.

James leaned forward, his eyes widening. "Good God!"

Verena looked at the glittering largesse. Four

watch fobs, three rings, two cravat pins, a large gold watch, and seventeen brass buttons winked at her from the table. "Herberts!"

"Oiye'm sorry, m'lady. They jus' fell into me pockets, they did."

She picked up a button. "Fell?"

"Well, those oiye had to cut off, but the rest of 'em were jus' lying around."

"In someone's pocket," James said, trying to control his laughter. "Herberts, you are a nonpareil."

The butler adjusted his headpiece. "Oiye'm sorry, missus. Oiye won't do it again."

"That's what you said last time."

"This time oiye mean it."

James leaned forward as Verena peered through the stolen items. "Do you see anything suspicious?"

Verena shook her head.

"Bloody hell."

Bloody hell, indeed. Verena managed to smile at Herberts. "Thank you. That will be all. And . . . wait."

She marched to her desk and opened a drawer where Herberts's previous ill-gotten gains lay. She unceremoniously dumped the new loot on top of the old and then stirred a bit. Verena selected a few choice items before handing them to the astonished butler. "Here, Herberts. Take these with you." She closed the drawer and locked it.

He brightened. "Take it wif me? Then oiye can keep all of it?"

"No. You will return them . . . eventually. For now, if I keep your pockets full, perhaps you won't attempt to filch anything else."

The butler slid the items in his pockets, nodding wisely. "Thet's the knacker, missus! You'll outsmart me yet." He picked up his serving spoon and beamed pleasantly. "Oiye'll finish the silver if ye don't need anything else."

"One more thing," James said. "While you were going about your duties within these last few weeks, did you happen to find a list of some sort?"

"No. Can't say as oiye did."

"I see," Verena said, her heart sinking. "Thank you, Herberts. That will be all."

The butler left and Verena sank back into her chair. "It was a long shot."

"But a good one." James tapped the letter with one finger, trying to clear his thoughts. "What do we know, Ver? Father always said for us to think it through. One minute at a time."

Verena watched him closely. Her brother's gifts were not as temporal as her own. He was a strategist. A planner. Father often called him "the general" and with reason. James never did anything without thought. From the lay of his cravat to the cut of his boots, he was a planned production, perfectly turned and ready for anything.

He rubbed his chin thoughtfully. "If it was a gem or some gold they were after, I'd understand it. Instead, they send us this silly letter, everything couched in veiled terms, almost as if it's written in co—" He lifted a brow. "Damn. It couldn't be . . ."

She leaned forward. "What is it? What are you thinking?"

James's brow lowered in thought. "Do you know where he lived?"

"No," Verena said, "but Lady Jessup would."

James pursed his lips. Father had always held that it was fine to be whatever one wished, so long as one was superior at it. He then proceeded to teach his children superior skills— gambling, the rudiments of the wager, betting strategies, how to dress and talk like the best of the *ton*.

To his credit, James knew how to ride, dance, fence, exchange witticisms with princes and paupers alike. He knew how much to pay in vales at posting inns, how to find the cleanest beds and the cheapest rates among the many hotels in town. He knew how to dress fashionably even when his pockets were to let. And he knew, without thinking, that this situation required far more duplicity than Verena was capable of.

At one time, she'd been Father's chosen. He'd called her his masterpiece, for she'd inherited Mother's fair countenance coupled with Father's nimble fingers. It was, Father had said, an unbeatable combination.

But Verena hadn't been like the rest of them. Her heart had never been in the game. Then, Verena had met Viscount Westforth and she'd promptly married, much to Father's chagrin. He'd thought her capable of catching an earl, at the least. But Verena would not be gainsaid and she'd had her way in the end, marrying her precious Andrew and forever turning her back on Father's way of life.

Which was a bloody good thing, to James's way of thinking. She'd been protected, or she had been until he'd arrived in her life. A line of irritation tightened across his shoulders.

He stood and tossed his napkin to the table. "I'm going to take the note and see what I can discover. Don't go anywhere until I return."

"But St. John—"

"Is the one who told you about Humford to begin with. He's onto something, Ver. And I don't trust him."

She was silent a moment, but then she lifted her head and sighed. "Very well. I'll stay away from him. But I'm not going to sit tamely at home while you jaunt about town."

He tucked the letter in his pocket. "Go and visit Lady Jessup and find out where Humford lived. When I return, we'll go to his lodgings together and see what's to be found."

She followed him to the door. "Be careful. You're the only brother I have."

He grinned and bent to press a kiss to her forehead. "You be careful, too. If I'm not back by midnight, lock all the doors. I'll come as soon as I can."

James gave her a last, quick wink and then he was gone. Verena heard him ask for his greatcoat, followed by Herberts's muffled reply.

The clock on the mantel chimed the hour and Verena realized that Brandon would soon arrive. She didn't have time for such nonsense now, though in her heart she knew it wasn't nonsense.

She wanted to go on that ride so badly, it frightened her. He would have to be satisfied with a note of apology.

Leaving the rest of her mail scattered on the table, she swept from the room, ordering her carriage as she went.

# Chapter 10

*His Grace? I would rather call him His DisGrace.*
*It would be far more fitting.*

Miss Devonshire to her friend, Miss Mitford,
commenting on the scandalous behavior of the
Duke of Clarence in fathering a number of
illegitimate children

**M**uch later in the day, Verena returned from
Lady Jessup's. The poor woman had been
horrified to hear of Humford's death. Horrified,
but not so distraught that she couldn't take the
time to garner every available detail.

Unfortunately, Verena had no real information
to share, a fact Lady Jessup took as a challenge.
She plainly thought Verena was holding back the
juicier tidbits, hoarding them as if they were gold
nuggets and nothing Verena did or said could
make her change her opinion. Verena was forced
to sit through what seemed like a horrid interro-
gation, interspersed by maudlin remembrances of
Humford's many kindnesses and a litany of recalled conversations, none of which seemed to
have the least purpose.

By the time Verena made good her escape, she

was exhausted. Her carriage pulled up to the front stoop just in time to see James on the steps.

He stopped on the lower stair and waited for her to join him. "Well?"

"Number 12, Dray Street."

"Excellent. We'll take my carriage. I've ordered a change of horses and then we'll be off." He took her arm and walked up the steps beside her.

"What did you find out?"

He gave a secretive smile and rapped the brass knocker sharply on the door. "Not as much as I'd hoped, but—"

The door opened and Herberts beamed at them pleasantly. "There ye be, m'lady and m'lord! Ah, I mean 'sir.' " He took Verena's cloak while a rather rough-looking man with shaggy blond hair and an astonishing number of freckles took James's coat and hat.

"Who's this?" Verena asked.

The man bowed, flashing a wide smile that revealed crooked teeth and a cleft in his chin.

Herberts cleared his throat. "He don't speak much, which oiye think is a benefit. But his name is Peters. He's the new footman."

Verena frowned. "I didn't hire a new—"

"Weel there, missus. Thet's whot oiye told him, oiye did, when he walked up and begged fer a position. 'Peters,' oiye said, 'oiye'm not the one as hires footmen. But oiye can tell ye thet we needs ye in a very bad way.' Isn't that right, Peters?"

Peters nodded his head emphatically.

"He's in trainin', he is," Herberts said, casting a critical eye at the man. "Oiye think he can be a good 'un with a little practice."

James snorted.

Herberts leaned toward Verena and said in a conspiratorial voice, "An' he don't cost hardly at all."

"Oh. Really? Perhaps, I—but no. Herberts, you can't just hire—"

"Here now, Peters!" Herberts said sternly. "Don't be holdin' his lordship's coat so that it trails the ground! Do ye want to spend the rest o' the afternoon brushin' it?"

"Aye, sir!" Peters's good-natured grin never faded, though he did lift the coat a bit higher.

"That's the natter! Now off with ye," Herberts said, shooing the man away. "Take it to the kitchen and spread it afore the fire, just like I tol' ye."

Peters obediently marched down the hallway.

"And see that ye don't wears it, neither," Herberts yelled after him. "Thet's agin the rules."

James had stopped trying to withhold his laughter.

Verena sighed. "Herberts, I cannot afford another—"

"Shush, now, missus. Oiye know how things is. Thet's why Peters will work out wonderfully. You see, oiye tol' him a little fib. Oiye tol' him that most footmen don't get paid until they've served fer a half a year at least. A trainin' period, as it were."

"A half a—Herberts! The man will starve."

"Nonsense. He gets room and board, jus' no more. Whot more can a feller want than that, oiye ask ye? An' if ye're worried 'bout his trainin', oiye'll do it meself, oiye will."

"That," James declared, "I must see."

"I don't like this," Verena said.

"Oh come on, Ver. You've a new footman and it will barely cost you a pence. Come, let's retire to the morning room. I want to know what Lady Jessup had to say."

Verena sighed and pushed her hair from her neck. She supposed there wasn't any harm in trying Peters out. After all, she'd already hired a thief for a butler. "Very well. Herberts, let us know when Mr. Lansdowne's carriage arrives."

"Yes, ma'am! Oh, and whilst ye were gone, ye had a gentleman caller." Herberts began to dig in his pocket. "A real nice gent it was, too. Same one from the other day, it were. Tall and black-haired, though he seemed a might upset ye weren't in and—Ah! Here 'tis." The butler produced a bent and crumpled card. "He said to give this to ye."

Verena took the card. The St. John crest rode high on the heavy vellum, a single phrase scrawled below Brandon St. John's name. *Six o'clock.*

James plucked the card from her hand.

"James, really! Give that back. It's just—"

"I can see what it is. I don't like that bounder—" He glanced at Herberts, who stood listening, nodding his agreement.

James scowled and then grabbed her elbow and pulled her into the morning room. "That will be all, Herberts. Thank you." He shut the door and looked at the card one last time before tossing it onto a small table by the settee.

Verena picked up the card, noting how forcefully the words "six o'clock" were written. Brandon must have been in quite a temper. That was yet another reason she should end this little flirtation. She had a horrid enough temper herself without complicating her life with his.

James turned to face her. "Ver, I've been thinking. We have to find that list."

"But we don't even know what this list looks like!"

"Bloody hell," he said, his face falling. Then, because it wasn't strong enough, he followed with a worse curse in Italian, then French, and last German.

Verena eyed him with a lifted brow. "Are you through?"

"Not yet." He added a curse in Russian. "There. *Now* I'm done."

"Wonderful." Verena set Brandon's card on the table before her. "What did *you* find out?"

He was silent a moment, then he sighed. "I thought to see what I could discover about Humford. I made a guess at one thing . . . that since he was a bit of a gambler, I thought Lady Farley might know him."

"Did you discover anything interesting?"

"Yes. He'd been playing at Hell's Door quite frequently in the weeks before his death. Or he was until she refused him entrance."

"Debts?"

"Over ten thousand pounds."

Verena gave a silent whistle. "That's interesting. So he needed money and badly."

"Which brings me to my other conclusion. You said that he was always bragging about his connections to the Home Office."

"Oh, he always said that. He'd been mocked quite heavily for it, too."

"I think he was telling the truth."

She frowned. "Humford? Working for the Home Office? Don't be silly. The man was a very nice person, but hardly what I'd call well informed."

James shook his head. "I don't think he was doing anything of import. But perhaps he was doing enough that he managed to get his hands on something of value." He rocked back on his heels. "A list, for example."

Verena tilted her head to one side, considering this. After a moment, she nodded. That *was* a possibility. "If that's true then this is serious, indeed."

James nodded grimly. "That's what I fear. If the list came from the Home Office, then there may be foreign elements involved. And someone thinks that Humford left that list here."

"Oh my God. James, you are right. We do have to find this list." She pressed her fingertips to her temples. "But . . . how big is this thing? And how long? And what's on it? Are there ten names? Or a hundred buildings? It could even be in code so that it looks like a laundry list. Or the contents of the prince's cravat drawer, for that matter. Or even—"

"Easy!" James gave a wry smile. "Don't let your imagination get carried away. Our situation is difficult enough."

"We must try and find it." She looked around the room. "I suppose we should start here."

"My thinking exactly."

"I'll tell Herberts to have your carriage returned to the stables for now."

"Very well. I'll start in the front hall."

"I'll start in the dining room. That's where he was when he realized this list was gone."

James went to the door and held it open. "After you."

Two hours later, they were back in the sitting room, this time Verena sat on the chair near the fire while James lay on the settee. They'd searched the house top to bottom, even peering into the attic. They were both disheveled, dust on their shoulders. A cobweb hung from James's left ear. They'd combed the house as thoroughly as possible. They'd even involved the servants, though Verena hadn't been able to tell them more than she'd lost a piece of paper.

She sighed wearily and stretched her feet before her, noting that her left slipper was scuffed. A loud knock heralded the entrance of Herberts who carried a tray containing scones and a gently steaming pot of tea.

Verena straightened thankfully. "Lovely! I am so hungry."

"So oiye thought, m'lady," Herberts said setting the tray on the small table. "Oiye said to Cook, 'None o' us know whot they're lookin' fer, but take me word, they're workin' up a hunger.'"

"Well, you were quite right," Verena said.

Herberts nodded, watching as she poured two cups of tea. He leaned toward James and said in a confidential voice, "There's brandy in the top right-hand drawer o' the desk. Not much, mind ye, but enough to put some flavor in that dishwater her ladyship favors."

James grinned and got up from the settee. "Herberts, you're worth your weight in gold."

The butler's thin cheeks stained a pleased pink and he puffed out his narrow chest. "Weel now, oiye tries me best, oiye do." He beamed pleasantly. "Did ye find what ye were lookin' fer, m'lady?"

"No, I'm afraid not."

"Can oiye ask whot it is thet ye're missin'? Bein' a collector o' sorts, there's little thet gets by me eye."

Verena sent a glance at James. Should she tell the butler? James answered with a faint shrug. She looked down at the gently steaming cup and sighed. What could be the harm? "We've lost something very important. It's a list."

"A list, eh? Of whot?"

"I don't know." At his confused glance, she hurried to add, "It's not my list, it belongs to someone else. But they lost it here and I cannot find it."

"Oiye take it thet this list is valuable?"

"Very. More than I can say."

"Never fear, m'lady. Oiye'll find yer list or me name ain't Henry Harold Henry Herberts."

James, who was in the middle of sipping his doctored tea, choked.

The butler nodded sagely. " 'Tis a muddled name, isn't it guv'nor? 'Tis why oiye wanted to become a butler. No one cares 'bout me Christian name—everyone jus' calls me Herberts. 'Tis a relief in a way." He made sure Verena had enough crème for her scone and then he went back to the door. "Call if ye needs me. Oiye'll be in the hallway with Peters, trainin' him on the correct way to open the door."

James chuckled as the butler left. "I wish Father could meet your Herberts."

"I don't. Father might corrupt him." She sank her teeth into a buttered scone, sighing with pleasure as the cake filled her mouth. It was some few moments before she could speak again. "I wonder if there aren't some other clues to be found."

"Where?"

"I don't know . . . somewhere. Maybe at the dinner party."

James finished his scone, nodding thoughtfully. "Do you have a guest list for the night of the dinner party?"

"Certainly." She rose and went to the escritoire that rested in one corner of the room and opened it to reveal a messy pile of papers. She fished for a moment, then held up a much crossed piece of foolscap. "Here it is."

James took the paper and read through the names. He raised his brows. "Impressive. You move in exalted company."

She curled her nose. "Tell Mr. Brandon St. John that, will you? He thinks me little better than a common doxy."

James frowned. "What are you going to do about him and the kiss you owe him?"

Verena choked. "Good God, how did you come to hear—" She clamped her mouth closed.

"Lady Farley," he said succinctly.

"I should have known. That woman is a horrid gossip."

"Ver, what were you thinking? I cannot believe you were so naive as to wager a kiss."

"I know, I know. I was a little—" She bit her lip. She was not about to admit to James that she'd had too much port. Especially not after she'd warned him so many times to be on his best behavior.

James shook his head, a frown on his brow. "I hate to admit it, but you don't have a choice now. St. John is the type of man that the more you thwart him, the more determined he'll be to have you."

"I don't want to kiss him." She'd already done that. What she really wanted was for *him* to kiss *her*. But James wouldn't understand that any better than she understood it herself.

James regarded her for a moment, his gaze examining her narrowly. "Are you certain?"

"Of course. Although we must discover what he knows about this. There has to be a reason he mentioned Humford's death in such a way. It was almost as if it was a test of some sort."

James rubbed his chin. "You're right. Meet with him then, but wait until I'm present."

"Very well. It doesn't matter to me if, or when, I ever see him again," Verena lied. She was fascinated and she knew it. "I have to wonder what he really wants."

James snorted. "I can tell you that."

Verena's cheeks heated. "Nonsense. He has access to far too many women to be interested in me. No, I think he has another reason. I wonder if he suspects us of being involved in Humford's death." Which was a very lowering thought indeed.

"Nonsense. He just wants an excuse to be with you. You underestimate your attractiveness, Verena. You always have. You look just like Mother."

"Thank you. There's no greater compliment."

He smiled quizzically. "Do you miss them?"

"Our parents? Of course. But I wanted a different way of life and Father—" She shook her head. "He never approved of my marriage to Westforth."

"He has high expectations. I don't think he's approved of my way of life, either."

"That's not true. He's always said you were merely looking for the right enterprise and that once you found it, you'd excel as no one has ever excelled before."

"I certainly hope he's right about that." James tucked the guest list in his pocket. "I should be on my way. Humford's lodgings may yield more clues."

"I'll go with you."

James glanced at St. John's calling card, which she still held in her hand. "What about your meeting at six? We may not be back by then."

"That's quite all right. I want to meet with him again, but on my terms." She smiled to think of his irritation on returning to her house and finding that she'd just left yet again. Whatever the outcome, she was enjoying this little game. She caught James's worried expression and grinned. "Never fear. I may have married Westforth, but I was born a Lansdowne."

"Don't make St. John wait too long. He is not the kind of man to take such maneuvering kindly. But one kiss, Verena . . . one *very* short kiss."

Verena looked down at Brandon's calling card,

the smooth texture delightful on her fingertips. His signature was very like the kiss he'd given her—bold and sweeping. She wondered idly if he was even capable of something less . . . a warm, gentle kiss perhaps. Feathery light and—She almost smiled. She couldn't imagine Brandon St. John doing anything so tame.

She caught James's curious stare and blushed. "I suppose I could give him a very short kiss, though I fear it will make him angry. Although since people tend to blurt out the first thing on their minds when they're angry, this could work to my benefit. If he's primed just right, he'll tell us how he's involved with this mess, and then I can send him on his way."

His brow cleared. "You remind me of mother when you talk like that."

"Father doesn't call her his Bastion of Logic for nothing."

James put his arm about her and gave her a hug. "You're just like her. I'd kiss your cheek but you've a smudge."

"And you've a cobweb on your left ear."

He wiped his ear and grinned. "I'll comb my hair if you will comb yours."

"Done."

Within moments, they had cleaned the cobwebs and dust the best they could.

Then they called for a carriage and embarked for Humford's lodgings, leaving Herberts and Peters to keep all intruders at bay.

At exactly six o'clock, Brandon St. John presented himself at the front door of the Westforth residence. He was already in a foul mood—not only had Verena not appeared this morning, but he'd had no luck in discovering anything more about Wycham's situation. He'd gone over every scrap of information Wycham had given him. He'd even attempted to contact Sir Colburn, a gentleman Devon knew from the Home Office.

Brand glanced up at the silent house before him and frowned. It seemed quiet—almost too quiet. He sent his groom to walk the horses and then ran up the stairs. Once he reached the landing, he tucked his gloves into his pockets and rapped the knocker.

To his surprise, the door was opened before the first rap had even faded into silence. Herberts didn't answer the door, but a rather freckle-faced behemoth with a gap-toothed smile. He straightened importantly and cleared his throat. "Here, now. Whatcha wantin'?"

Brand paused. "Where's Herberts?"

"Roight here, oiye am," Herberts replied, beaming around the giant's shoulder. "Oiye'm trainin' the new footman. Here now, Peters, stand back a bit so as oiye can see the gent."

The footman stepped back and Herberts smiled benignly. "How're ye doin', Mr. St. John? Weather's a bit dicey, ain't it?"

The weather was no more uncertain than Brandon's temper. "I've come to see Lady Westforth."

"Did ye now? Whot a pity."

"A pity? Why's that?"

"She ain't here, not properly speakin'."

Brandon's foul mood soured even more. "Did you give her my card as I requested?"

"O' course oiye did! Handed it roight to her when she and Mr. Lansdowne come home."

Mr. Lansdowne. Brandon decided that he hated that name. Hated it with a passion. "I take it that Lady Westforth left after Mr. Lansdowne."

"Oh no! They went together, they did. They've important business to attend to, ye know. Horrible business."

Brandon frowned. "What are you talking about? What horrible business? Has something happened or—"

"Oops!" The butler bit his lip. "Oiye don't think oiye was a'posed to say anything about thet, so let's jus' pretend oiye didn't." He looked over his shoulder at Peters, who still hovered in the background. "Ye see how oiye did thet? Oiye let some of Lady Westforth's private business out in public? Don't ever do thet. It's agin the rules."

Herberts turned back to Brandon. "Oiye'll tell Lady W ye was here. Ye'd best get on yer way." He peered over Brandon's shoulder at the sky and shook his head. "It do look like rain, don't it?"

Brandon followed the man's gaze to the darkening sky. "I doubt—"

*Thud!* The door closed firmly, leaving Brandon standing on the landing.

By God! He was a St. John. People did *not* treat him this way.

He sucked in his breath, raked a hand through his hair. Damn it, he'd discover whatever secrets Verena was hiding, claim his bloody kiss, and show her that he was not a man to be trifled with.

Verena was about to discover the price of playing with a man born with an ill temper. He was certain it was far higher than she was willing to pay. Far, far higher.

# Chapter 11

*In my first season, I wanted a man of wit and grace—the first son of an earl would have done. Last season I lowered my sights to the second or third son of a viscount. Now I'd settle for a man more plump in the pocket than he is in the waist.*

Miss Mitford to her mama, Mrs. Mitford, while the two were making a list of "possible suitors" for Miss Mitford's (regrettably) third season

The rain came with a vengeance. It slashed, thrashed, poured and pelted. Though Brandon had his hat firmly on his head, the collar of his greatcoat pulled up about his ears, cold water seeped through the heavy wool, weighting his shoulders and soaking through to his shirt.

Brand ignored it all. Every hour, on the hour, he came to the Westforth townhouse. And every hour, on the hour, Herberts trudged to the door to tell him that Verena had not yet returned.

But at eleven, something changed. Lights were on in parts of the house. Brand squinted through the rain for a long moment. Finally, he turned to his footman. "Take the carriage home."

The man blinked, water dripping from his hat brim in a steady stream. "Home, sir?"

"Home." With that, Brandon strode to the front door, grabbed the brass knocker and pounded on the door. After a long moment, it opened.

Herberts stood in the doorway, Peters nowhere in sight. "Bloody 'ell, guv'nor! Ye're too fine of a gent to be standin' in the rain. What do ye want now?"

"For you to open the bloody door," Brand snapped.

"Here now, there's no need to get in a huff. Oiye came as soon as oiye could. Me room is below stairs, ye know. And 'tis a bit o' a walk."

Rain dripped off the eaves and found Brand's collar. He swallowed, trying to control his temper. "I want to speak to Lady Westforth. Now. And don't try and tell me she's not in."

The butler scratched his nose. "It's late, ye know. Very late. And ye're as wet as them cobblestones in the street. Ye might muss me rugs."

Brand rubbed a wet hand over his wetter face. "I don't give a damn about your rugs."

"If ye gets the rugs wet, ye know who'll be dryin' em out, don't ye? Me, thet's who."

"She's in, isn't she?"

Herberts grinned, his gold tooth shining. "Aye. But now she's not receivin' company, it bein' so late and all."

Brandon lifted his hat and raked his hair back from his face. It was a mistake, for immediately a thick stream of cold water oozed down his collar. He slapped his hat back into place. "That does it. I am no longer asking."

"No?" Herberts glanced over his shoulder. "Oiye wonder where Peters has wondered off to?"

"Stand aside, Herberts, or I'll knock out every

tooth you have left in that empty gourd you call a head." The butler hesitated and Brand pushed his way past the man. "I need to speak with Lady Westforth, rugs be damned."

Herberts sighed. "Ye're askin' fer it, ye know." At Brand's furious glare, he held up a hand. "Not from me! From Lady W. She don't go with bad manners. Hates 'em, she does."

Brand shoved out of his coat and handed the dripping mass of wool to the butler, placing his soggy hat on top of the pile. "Tell Lady Westforth that I'm here."

The butler laid the hat and coat on a side table where they dripped a steady stream of water on the marble floor, seeping onto the edge of the red rug that lined the hall. He shook his head disgustedly. "Oh, very weel. I'll tell her. What's yer title?"

"You know my name and title. I'm Mr. Brandon St. John."

"Well ye act like a bloody earl, ye do. Ye burst in here like ye was born to the purple."

Brandon's shoulders and neck were completely wet, as was most of his back. His shirt stuck to him beneath his evening coat, and he could no longer feel his feet in his wet boots. "Either you tell Lady Westforth that I have come to call or I will personally search the house for her." Brand leaned closer and said through his clenched teeth, "Dripping water the entire way."

"Ugly when ye're irritated, ain't ye? Oiye suppose there's naught fer it, but to fetch m'lady." The man's hand slid out, as stealthy as a snake.

Brand reached into his pocket and fished out a coin and then tossed it to the butler.

The man eyed the coin for a long moment, then sighed. "Very well. This way, guv'nor." He led the way to the sitting room where he tossed open the door and said in a grand voice, "Lady Westforth, oiye fink ye've got a visitor—"

"Herberts," Verena's exasperated voice lifted through the doorway. "I specifically told you not to allow anyone—"

Brand stepped inside.

Verena sat at a small escritoire, a quill in her hand. As soon as she saw Brand, she replaced the quill in the holder with a hard jab. She stood, her face pink. "I thought I said no visitors."

"I didn't give him a chance." Brandon strolled to the fire that burned merrily in the grate and held his hands to the welcome warmth.

"Oiye couldn't keep him out, missus," Herberts said with a shake of his head. "He seems determined to see ye."

"I am even more determined *not* to see him. Show him out." Her eyes snapped fire at Brand. "I do not appreciate you forcing your way into my house."

"I've thought you many things, Lady Westforth," Brand said, noting grimly the steam rising from his clothing. "But I never thought you a welch."

"A-a-" She couldn't even seem to say the word.

"Now jus' wait a minute," the butler said, huffing and puffing as if someone had insulted his honor and not just his mistress's.

But Lady Westforth's reaction far surpassed his. Once she regained her breath, her mouth thinned to a single line. "A welch? I've never welched on anything in my life."

"You will be welching if you send me away,"
Brand said, "for I've come to collect my debt." His
gaze narrowed on her thoughtfully. "You do remember our wager, don't you?"

Color heated her cheeks, the sudden red making her creamy skin appear even more pale. "You
wish to collect your debt now? In the middle of
the night?"

"It's not that late. Only eleven, I believe. Lady
Westforth, are you a woman of your word? Or
not?"

Her proud chin lifted in the air and Brand felt
an unusual stirring of appreciation. She was not
only beautiful, but she was fiery, awash in passion. With her gold curls and wide violet eyes, she
carried innocence like a fragrance. It wafted about
her and soaked into the consciousness of her fol-
lowers without their even being aware of it.

But Brandon was more discriminating than
most of Lady Westforth's admirers and he would
resist her particular brand of charm. Resist it to
the death. So though he felt far from it, he grinned.
"I want my kiss and I want it now."

"That's a pity for I'm not in the mood to hand
out kisses to men with no manners. It is rude of
you to barge in here, unwelcome and uninvited."
She swept to her feet and walked past Herberts to
the door. "Mr. St. John, it is time you left."

"No."

She looked at him a moment more and to his
chagrin, he thought he detected a sudden hint of
laughter in her eyes. All of his frustration and
anger slipped away and he found himself smiling
in return.

Her lips curved in response, and their anger dissipated as one. They remained that way, smiling at one another, gazes locked, for a long moment. Then, to Brand's surprise, Verena winked at him, whirled on her heel and left.

"Herberts," her voice floated in the room after her, "would you and Peters escort Mr. St. John to the door?"

The little minx! Brand heard the fall of her footsteps on the stairs and he bolted from the room. He'd just set foot back in the foyer when a steel hand closed over his arm.

He turned around to face the new footman. "Look, Peters. I'm not in the mood to play."

" 'Ere now, guv'nor," Herberts said from where he stood well behind the footman. "Oiye can't let ye up those steps."

"Tell this philistine to remove his hand."

"Oiye wishes oiye could," the butler said honestly. He leaned forward and said in a confidential tone, "Whot's this wager ye're nappin' about?"

"A kiss."

"Ah! And she won't pay, eh? Ain't thet just like a woman?" Herberts sighed heavily. "Ye know, if ye weren't talkin' 'bout m'lady, oiye wouldn't mind ye askin' fer a good buss on the smacker."

Brandon looked at Herberts with a slight sense of astonishment. "You believe I'm in the right?"

"If ye won thet kiss fair and square, whot more is there to say?" Herberts rocked back on his heels a bit. "O' course, since the missus is a woman, oiye'm certain it ain't quite as simple as thet."

Brand stood still a moment longer, considering his options, aware of the footman's steely grasp. It wasn't just that damned kiss. That wasn't what drove him to such lengths. No, he told himself, it was for Wycham. His friend was depending on him to find that blasted list. If Brand didn't find a way into the house and soon, Wycham might grow impatient and return to town. He'd be in jail before Brand could help him.

Fortunately, there were more ways to gain entrance to a house than through the front door. Brandon yanked his arm free from Peters's hold, walked to the door, collecting his coat and hat as he went. As he opened the door, he turned and said in a voice loud enough to carry up the stairs, "I will be back."

From where she sat, hidden around the curve of the top steps, a shiver traced through Verena. He'd been furious at her dismissal, she could see it in the hard blue blaze of his eyes, in the way his broad shoulders sat so rigid and straight. She held her breath until the door slammed shut, then she walked back down the stairs.

"Whew!" Herberts called up the stairs. "He's a very angry man, m'lady. Whatever ye done to piss him off, oiye'd be rethinkin' it. He'll not be gone long."

Peters nodded in agreement.

Verena managed a smile. "Hopefully, I will have time to figure out how to deal with him before he returns." Outside, the rain lashed against the windowpanes and rattled the shutters. Verena leaned against the bottom stair railing. "Herberts, I believe I'll finish the letter to my parents and then retire. It has been a long, long day."

"Aye, m'lady. Would ye like a wee dram to

ward off the chill? Some brandy to warm yer bones."

"No, thank you." Verena wearily made her way to the sitting room. As rough as the butler was, he had a caring streak that greatly reconciled her to his presence in her house.

She paused by the desk. "Close and lock the doors. You needn't wait up on me."

"Very well," the butler said. "Oiye hopes ye don't gets too angry 'bout the mess the gentleman left in the foyer. He was drippin' like a sieve. Oiye warned him not to come in, but he wouldn't listen. He's left a trail o' water wider than me arm."

"I'm sure it will dry by morning," Verena said absently, looking through her note to see where she'd left off. She barely noticed the sound of the door closing or the retreating tread of the butler's footsteps. The rain tattooed against the window, pouring so hard now that it trickled down the chimney and sputtered the fire.

Verena dipped her pen into the ink and started writing again, but it was no good—her mind was too full of James's lost letters, the missing list, and worst of all, Brandon St. John. She wished she hadn't promised James that she wouldn't see St. John alone. Though after she'd seen him, wet and furious, she had to admit that it was probably safer.

She sighed wearily and replaced the pen in the holder. Nothing had gone well today. Even the visit to Humford's lodgings had been a wasted few hours. The man had lived like a monk, fastidiously clean, every shirt drawer organized. It was so neat that the entire apartment had an unlived-in feel to it. She and James had searched every nook and cranny, but had found nothing.

Verena leaned back in her chair and stretched her legs before her, mulling over the day's events. Minutes stretched and faded. Somewhere behind her, a faint creak sounded. She tilted her head to one side and frowned. The creak sounded again, only louder this time. What was that?

A waft of fresh air chilled her and the sound of the rain suddenly got louder. The lamp flickered as if a faint wind had tickled the flame and then went out.

Total darkness filled the room. Verena stood, heart pounding, the hair on the back of her neck prickling with urgency. She wasn't alone. She whirled and took a step toward the door when two huge arms wrapped about her, a large hand clapping across her mouth. Verena only managed a horrified gasp before the fingers tightened.

"I told you I'd be back," came a deep masculine voice.

# Chapter 12

*If I cannot be young and pretty, then I will at least be old and bejeweled.*

Mrs. Mitford to herself, as she was clasping the famous Mitford rubies about her neck

**V**erena recognized Brandon's voice instantly. She also recognized the fury in his tone. Without another thought, she bit his hand, nipping forcefully on the pad of his thumb.

"Damn!" He yanked his hand free and shook it in the air as if trying to shake off the pain like so much dust, leaving only one arm imprisoning her.

Verena lifted her foot and slammed it down on his instep. Thank heavens she was wearing her good French heels.

"Argh!"

She was released instantly. Verena could have made her way to the door. She could have screamed, too, and brought Herberts and the rest of her scanty staff to the rescue. She could have, she told herself as she relit the lamp.

The sight that met her eyes was infinitely gratifying. Brandon St. John was hopping up and down, waving his hand like a child who had mashed his thumb in a doorway.

She bit her lip. It was sad that they were at such loggerheads, for she recognized in him a kindred spirit. Life came easy to Brandon St. John, just as it came easy to Verena. It made them both a little too confident, a little short-tempered with others, and a little arrogant.

"Oh, it's not that bad," she said, as he fell to the settee and grabbed his foot with his uninjured hand.

"What kind of shoes do you have on?" he demanded, looking at his own leather boots.

She knew him to be an honorable man. So honorable he squeaked with it. So honorable that as he looked down his aristocratic nose at her, she couldn't help but realize that he had a point. She wasn't his equal in any sense of the word. She'd never admit it, of course, but she knew that she was in no position to argue about virtue and honor. "I cannot believe you broke into my house like a common criminal."

He sucked on the pad of his thumb, his blue eyes blazing. "You have the sharpest teeth. Like a bloody ferret!"

"Are they? I've never had to resort to such physical expressions to make myself clear. I told you I had no wish to kiss you tonight."

His eyes blazed. "You weren't going to kiss me at all, were you?"

She looked at the fire, wondering how he'd guessed. "Perhaps."

His gaze narrowed. "Liar."

"I am not a liar. I'm a prevaricator. There's a difference, you know."

To her chagrin, he smiled. She tried not to return it and failed miserably. He really was charming in a gruff way, sitting on her settee and making it appear absurdly small. The rain had wet him through and through, his hair slicked back from his forehead, making his blue eyes all the brighter.

The door opened and Herberts stood in the opening. "M'lady, oiye thought oiye heard voices and—what the he—"

"Herberts!" Verena said, frowning.

He reddened. "Sorry, m'lady. Oiye was jus' shocked to see the gentleman still in the house." The butler settled his shoulders and then made a show of cracking his knuckles. "Shall oiye fetch Peters and toss the bloke out the door?"

Verena looked at Brandon. He was so wet that his clothing stuck to him like a second skin. He had to be miserable. And she *did* owe him a kiss. Her gaze flickered over his mouth and she found that it was really quite difficult to swallow. "No, thank you, Herberts. That will be all."

The butler's mouth opened and closed twice before he managed to stutter, "Ye want me to leave ye? Alone? Wif *him*?"

"Leave, Herberts. I can handle Mr. St. John."

"Are ye sure, m'lady? Oiye kin stay if'n ye want me to. And Peters can come an—"

"I'll be fine. Please leave."

Herberts backed slowly to the door. "Perhaps I should jus' stay a mite and see if ye needs some refreshment. Do ye wants me to bring ye something to wet yer whistlers?"

"That won't be necessary," Verena said. "Close the door."

He sighed and pulled the door to. It had barely settled in place before he yanked it back open and stuck in just his head. " 'Ere now, what was I thinkin'? Oiye fergot to mention that Mr. St. John is a wee bit damp. Perhaps oiye should bring him a cloth to dry—"

"Herberts." The "s" lingered an unconscionable time.

He sighed. "Very well." He shut the door with a disapproving *bang*.

Brandon stood and limped to the fireplace. "That is the most deplorably trained servant I've ever seen."

"You haven't met my upstairs maid."

"Your *upstairs* maid?" he said blandly, steam rising from his clothing. "I look forward to it. Perhaps we should retire there now and you can introduce me—"

"Just stop it!" A smile trembled on her lips. "You are incorrigible."

"I'm determined."

"In this instance, it's the same thing." She shook her head. It was late at night, the rain creating a cozy feeling. It had been a long time since she'd shared a late-night conversation with a man. She crossed her arms, suddenly aware of how lonely she had been. Until now. "I don't know why you persist in this. You don't like me. You never have."

"I want what is owed me."

She eyed him for a long moment. "No. I don't think that is it at all. If you wanted your kiss, you would have already taken it. I think you want something else."

Brand turned back to the fire, noting the faint steam curling from his sleeves. She was far more intelligent than he liked. "I've never said that I don't like you." She started to respond and he held up a hand. "Trust . . . that is another thing."

"What have I ever done to give you reason not to trust me? Ask your brother. Had I been of a different nature . . ." She shrugged. "But that is neither here nor there. I am not a woman who uses other people. I take care of me and my own. And that's all I have ever been guilty of."

"Is that why you cheat at cards?"

Her color rose. "Who said I cheated?"

"Are you denying it?"

"No. But I'm not confirming it, either."

He watched her with narrowed eyes. "I didn't come to argue with you, you know. I came to collect what's mine." And she was right—he did want more than a kiss. She owed him far, far more than a simple embrace. She owed him for every cold, miserable minute he'd spent outside her house.

She sighed, frustration evident in every line of her body. "You, sir, are abominable."

"And you, my dear Lady Westforth, are delectable." He slowly crossed the room to her side. At least in that, there was some truth. She was beautiful, and the memory of her lush curves haunted him still.

He stopped in front of her and lifted a curl from her shoulder. The silken strands slid between his fingers. Her hair was thick and heavy, surprisingly so.

"What are you doing?" Her voice was breathless.

"You have the most beautiful hair. It's the color of ripe wheat."

She jerked away. "I refuse to believe that you broke into my house so that you could pay me compliments."

He dropped his hand back to his side. "You are right; I'm not here to compliment you. And not just for the kiss, either. I'm here because I want to know—"

Her gaze darkened. "Know what?"

"All of your secrets."

"Secrets? Why on earth would you think I have any secrets?" She opened her arms and gestured about the room. "Look about you, Mr. St. John. I am a simple woman. I love simple things. What could I possibly have to hide?"

She was good, he had to admit. There was something direct and guileless about the way she spoke. He was not fooled, but he *was* tired and wet and miserable, chilled through and through. And beneath that weariness was a slow burn of lust, brought on from her kiss last night and kept to life by her refusal to see him. That was why he was so determined to have her. She'd thwarted him and it was not a feeling he liked.

His gaze fell on a silver tray by the window, a bottle of amber liquid arranged with some glasses. He gestured toward it. "May I?"

"Of course. I apologize for not asking you sooner. It's not my habit to offer refreshments to housebreakers."

Brand poured himself a drink. "Would you like some?"

"I don't drink."

He grinned. "Not well, anyway."

She hunched a shoulder in his direction and turned away.

Brandon carried his drink to a chair in front of the fire. "Come and join me, Lady Westforth."

She made no motion to join him. "I'd rather you leave."

"In this rain?" He made himself comfortable in one of the chairs.

"Afraid you'll melt?"

"No, but it's very unhealthy for devils to be cold. You might say it is against our nature."

Her lips quivered. "At least you admit that much."

"I will admit much more if you join me." He took a sip of the liquid, sighing when it warmed a path down his throat to his chest.

Verena walked slowly toward him, her gaze considering. "Why are you here, Mr. St. John?"

"Right this moment, I'm enjoying my glass of brandy and the company of a beautiful woman. Later on . . ." He shrugged, watching her over the rim of his glass.

"You make me nervous when you compliment me. It doesn't ring true."

"What do you expect? Incriminations?"

"No. Nothing so pleasant."

He smiled. "Have just one drink with me."

"I don't drink," she repeated, though more softly this time.

"Except when playing cards?"

"I allowed my pride to choke my good sense. Normally, I only drink a glass of wine with my evening meal. It muddles the brain."

"Which would be fatal in a woman who uses her brain so much."

She sank into the chair opposite his, eying him warily. "You are determined not to like me, aren't you? I wonder why. Do I remind you of some other woman, one who has wronged you?"

He frowned at her over his glass. "I am not so silly as to punish you for something someone else did."

"Then why do you seek to punish me at all?"

"I don't. I have no desire to hurt you."

"Then what do you want?"

Brandon looked down into his glass. The fire reflected in the drink like red sparks in amber velvet. What *did* he want? He should be interested in one thing and one thing only—the truth. But if he were entirely honest, he would admit that he wanted—*her*. All of her. "I want the kiss you owe me."

"Just that one, simple kiss?"

He nodded, meeting her gaze. Heat flared between them. It would not be only one kiss and there would be nothing simple to it. Brand's gaze dipped to her mouth and he marveled at the soft pink of her lips.

"If that's all you want, then take your bloody kiss and be gone." Her nose curled in a way that looked more like she'd tasted something sour than a woman about to be thoroughly seduced.

Brandon decided that it was a good thing that somewhere along the way, he'd made the decision that a kiss wasn't enough. The kiss itself was merely the opening shot in the battle to come. For that was what a kiss was—a weapon. A stealthily employed weapon that could, when yielded in the right circumstances, produce effects not unlike an explosion.

Brandon's body tightened at the thought of that explosion, of Verena's lips beneath his, of her body against his own. "You're right. I should just take my kiss and be gone."

She folded her hands in her lap, pursed her lips, and closed her eyes.

Brand almost choked on a laugh. "What's that?"

She opened one eye. "A kiss." The words were muffled since she didn't unpucker.

He chuckled then. "Stop that. I'm not even sure . . ." He looked about the room and shook his head. "No, not here."

She opened both eyes, the pucker disappearing. "What do you mean 'not here'?"

"It's too bright."

"Bright? What difference does that make?"

He waved a hand. "I want the mood to be right. The ambiance of a romantic moment is a delicate thing."

"Romantic? Who said our kiss had to be romantic?"

He cocked a brow at her. "I believe the conditions of the kiss were 'when and where' I required it."

She frowned and he could see that she was trying to recall the wording of their wager. "I
think . . . perhaps we—"

"You may ask Jameson the next time you see
him. Meanwhile, I require my kiss now and I want
it . . ." He eyed her for a moment. "I want it in
your bedchamber."

She shot out of her chair like cannonfire, almost
stumbling as she did so. "*What?*"

"You heard me. I want the kiss in your bedchamber."

"You are not going to my bedchamber."

"Reneging on your bet, aren't you? Why am I
not surprised?"

"I am not reneging. You are taking unfair advantage of me."

"No one forced you to accept that wager. Do you
refuse to honor it?" He shrugged. "Of course, if
you don't wish to do as you promised, I'm certain
Lady Farley, the proprietress of that gaming hell
you so love to frequent, would be glad to know of
your tendency to back out of your obligations."

Verena's jaw tightened. She plopped her hands
on her hips and jutted out her chin. "No. I will not
have you brandishing it about that I refused to
honor my word, but . . ."

Brandon could see the struggle behind her serious gaze. If she was indeed making her living
from the cards, she could not afford to have her
name besmirched in such a way as to ruin her
credit at the gaming hells. She knew that his word,
as a St. John, would have a very powerful effect.

She sighed, annoyance in every line of her
body. "Very well, St. John. Have it your way. *How-*

*ever*, you will not tell a soul that I allowed you in my bedchamber. If I agree to this, it has to remain between us."

He set his glass on a table and stood. "I am a gentleman."

She made a very unladylike snort, one that made him grin. "Follow me, St. John. And you are not to repeat one single word of this to anyone." She went to the door and yanked it open.

Herberts fell forward and landed face first on the rug.

Verena glared. "Herberts! No eavesdropping!"

The butler struggled to his feet. "Me? Listenin' in? No, m'lady. Oiye, ah, was just washin' the door."

"With your ear? How odd. Now step aside."

Herberts crossed his arms over his chest. "Ye aren't really goin' to take that blighter to yer chambers, are ye?"

"I made a wager."

"And oiye'll make a wisty caster o' his face, see if oiye don't. Oiye can't stand aside and jus' let ye ruin yerself. Oiye've principles, oiye do."

Brandon doubted that, but he wisely didn't say a thing.

"Herberts, you are not to get involved in my affairs." Verena went out the door to the hallway, both men following her. The butler rushed to get in front of her, stopping her on the bottom step.

"For the love of—" she began, exasperation heavy in her voice. "Am I to be plagued with stubborn men all evening? I made a wager, Herberts."

"Oiye heard already. Oiye just wish ye'd made a better one."

Verena sighed. "Me, too. However . . ." She lifted her head, her eyes alight. "Ah!"

Brandon frowned. "What?"

"I just thought of something." She pinned him with a triumphant gaze. "No one said that the kiss had to be made in private. If I want, I may have a chaperone with me."

Brand scowled. "I don't recall anything about allowing you to have a chaperone—"

"Nor will you recall saying that I could not have one, either. Therefore, I may have one if I wish. Herberts, you may serve as chaperone."

The rustle of silk whisked past Brand and up the stairs, Verena's blond hair passing just below his nose. "Are you coming, Mr. St. John? I haven't all night."

He watched her climb the stairs, certain that every saucy twitch and sway was purposefully done to taunt him.

Herberts stood beside him, watching as well. After a moment, the butler sighed. "Oiye hopes ye aren't mad, guv'nor. Didn't mean to interfere. It's not that oiye thinks ye aren't a good man, ye didn't lay a finger on her all evenin' and ye was alone with her fer some time. Thet says a lot, it do."

"Thank you."

"And oiye don't blame ye one bit fer wantin' yer kiss. It's just that the missus . . . she done good by me and oiye ain't a bloke as what'll ferget it. So come along now. Ye'd best get yer kiss quick-like afore she asks Cook and Peters to watch, as well."

Brandon had the distinct impression that the butler would have slung an arm about his shoulder if he'd thought for one moment that the gesture would be welcomed.

Brand sighed and put his foot on the bottom step. Suddenly, he stopped. "Herberts, do you like my watch?"

The butler raised his hands. "Oiye didn't take yer ticker, oiye didn't!"

"I know that. It's right here." Brand reached into his pocket and pulled out his new watch. "How would you like to have it?"

The butler blinked. "Whot's this?"

"I'll give it to you. Right now."

Herberts's gaze fastened on the watch, a strange hunger gleaming in his eyes. "What'll oiye haf to do?"

"Just take your time climbing those stairs."

Herberts looked at the watch, then back at the stairs. "How much time? Oiye don't want the missus mad at me. She can cast a powerful evil eye when she's o' the mind."

"Five minutes."

"Five—oh no, guv'nor. Oiye know what can happen in five minutes."

"Two minutes, then. I just want the kiss to be . . . memorable." Brandon could see that the man was wavering. "I'll give you my word as a gentleman that I won't do anything to cause her to protest."

Brandon took the watch and held it up to eye level, the silver case flashing in the light. "What do you say?"

The butler swallowed, his gaze glued to the swinging watch. "Oiye shouldn't."

"Herberts, I promise I will not hurt her. I'm here because I merely want the kiss that is due me."

Herberts looked Brand right in the eye, studying him for all he was worth. Whatever he saw there seemed to satisfy him, for he gave a brief nod and said, "It *is* a long stairwell."

"Yes."

"And oiye do haf a bad knee."

Brand dropped the watch into the butler's outstretched hand. It disappeared much as his coin had earlier.

"Two minutes and not a bloomin' second more," Herberts said.

Brandon didn't wait. He bounded up the stairs, wincing as he landed on his bruised foot. He reached the landing in record time, but found himself faced with an impossibly long row of doors. Damn it! Which one—

"Are you coming?" Verena stood in the last door on the left.

Brand closed the distance between them.

Verena leaned to one side and looked past him. Surely Herberts was close behind. "Where's Herbe—"

Strong, warm hands closed about her arms and before she could say a word, she was whisked into the room. Brandon closed the door, turned the key in the lock, then leaned against it, his arms folded across his broad chest.

Verena found it difficult to swallow. He was still wet from the rain, his shirt glued to him, outlining every muscle. "Wh-where's my butler?"

"Coming up the steps as we speak. We haven't

much time." He shoved himself from the door and strode forward. "I want my kiss."

"Wait until Herberts—"

"Do you really want one of your servants to see this?"

"I don't want anyone to see," she said hotly. "Not even me. In fact, I don't want to be kissed at all."

"Then you shouldn't have wagered."

"I didn't want to, but you *challenged* me and that is just as bad."

He caught her arms and pulled her forward. "No more talking."

"But I have a lot more to say—"

He buried his face in her neck, his lips trailing a heated path to her left ear, sending shivers of delight up her spine. "You have more to say now?" he murmured against her skin. "After all our delightful double talk? I fear my brain would explode with the strain."

She tried to control the wash of hot lust that threatened to consume her. "If you think your brain in danger of exploding, then please let me know so that I may ring for a rag to stuff in your ears. I cannot have what little brain you possess leaking on my new rug."

He lifted his head and looked down at her, his hands splayed on her waist. "You're a hardhearted woman, did you know that?"

She returned his look with a frank one of her own, an unbidden smile lifting the corners of her lips. Brandon's breath caught in his chest. In the glow of the lamp downstairs, she had appeared perfect—her golden hair curled about her face, flawless skin, straight nose—but here, in his arms, he could plainly see the faint scattering of pale freckles on the bridge of her nose. Better yet, he could see that her lower row of teeth were slightly uneven. For some reason, those slight imperfections made her all the more attractive.

"Ow!" Herberts said from the top of the stairway, his voice theatrically loud. "Oiye stubbed me toe."

Brand was out of time. "My kiss." He lowered his mouth and took what belonged to him. This was what he'd wanted since the first moment he'd seen her, when she'd turned and smiled at him— to have her here, inside his arms, her body against his. His lips covered hers, his tongue stroking hers. She opened for him, moaning softly, the sound a torment in itself.

Heat exploded through him, sizzling, searing, imprinting the taste of her on him forever. Never had he felt this for any woman.

A knock sounded on the door.

Verena ignored it, pulling Brandon closer, her hands twined in the loose folds of his shirt. He kissed with a fervor that matched her own, his hands moving possessively over her, cupping her body, holding her against his hardness. The wetness of his shirt soaked through her dress, sending shivers of delight across her skin.

"M'lady?" Herberts's voice echoed his alarm. He knocked on the door. "Are ye well?"

Was she well? She was on fire, her body quivering with heat, with passion. She wanted Brandon St. John in her bed. She wanted to feel him inside her, filling her, as she knew he would. It had been so long since anyone had touched her. So long since she'd allowed a man close enough for even this, a simple kiss.

But not a simple kiss, she realized, reluctantly pulling away. Though her entire body ached with need, she knew she had to stop it. "I-I think you've gotten your kiss."

His lips traced a line across her cheek, to her neck. "Did I?" he murmured, his voice vibrating against her.

She closed her eyes, her arms still about his neck. "Yes."

"M'lady?" The door shook as if someone was trying to pull it open. "Can ye hear me?"

"Answer him," Brandon said, his delightful mouth now near her ear. "Tell him to go away."

She should tell Brandon to go away, not Herberts, her logical brain told her. But her treacherous body disagreed. Heaven was so close, within a fingertip's touch away. Still, she couldn't—She pushed him away. "No."

"No?"

"Not . . . I can't. I don't know you or why you came here or what you want or—"

He placed a finger over her lips. "I have questions for you, too. Are you brave enough to answer them?"

She jutted out her chin. "Are you brave enough to ask?"

Brandon's mouth curved into a smile, his eyes warm with laughter. "Tell Herberts to leave. You and I can settle this ourselves."

He was right. They could settle this themselves. "Herberts?"

The rattling at the door stopped. "Aye?"

"Mr. St. John isn't here."

There was a long pause. "Where'd he go then?"

"I don't know. But he never came in here. Perhaps he left while you were locking the front door."

Again a long pause. "Perhaps he did, missus. Oiye suppose he could have slipped down the stairs."

"Perhaps."

"Or out the chimney," Herberts continued in a sarcastic voice.

"Herberts?"

"Aye?"

"Good night."

There was a loud sigh. "Very well, missus. Good night, missus. Good night, Mr. St. John." And then Herberts left, his boots trudging loudly down the stairs, a complaint in each step.

# Chapter 13

*If you believe Lady Caro Lamb's novel,* GLENAR-
VON, *the entire world revolves around rapturous
joys, passionate embraces, and unrequited loves.
I, for one, would rather the world embraced more
common concerns such as the cost of a good pair
of half boots and the quality of the new bonnets
being shipped from France.*

Mrs. Mitford, to her maid, Lucy, while allowing that
long-suffering individual to fix her coiffure

**B**randon looked down into Verena's eyes.
"Herberts is gone. That leaves you and me."
"So it does." She stepped out of his arms and attempted to straighten her gown. She pulled at the
skirts, tugging them back into place, but there was
no helping it—the entire front was soaked from
where he'd held her, the material clinging to her
awkwardly.

The sight was even more disturbing for Brand.
He could see through her dress, easily making out
the outline of her chemise, the thin ribbon that
tied in the center of her cleavage, the full round-
ness of each breast. He'd thought he couldn't possibly get more aroused than he had been.

He was wrong.

She sighed her exasperation, then abandoned her attempts to straighten her gown. Verena clasped her hands together in front of her, her cheeks pink. "I suppose in sending Herberts away, I have made a decision of sorts."

"Decision?" Brandon said somewhat dazedly. "What decision?"

"I thought you could stay here . . . with me." When he looked at her in amazement, she colored and added in a hasty voice, "Not forever, or anything like that. I just thought we might be together without—Not that I don't want to, but we shouldn't think too much about—" She pressed her hands to her hot cheeks. "Do you know what I'm saying?"

He almost choked. She was saying exactly what he'd said in one way or another to every woman he'd ever seduced. "Verena, perhaps it would be better if we just think of this as . . ." Good God, this was difficult. He raked a hand through his hair, then winced when a flurry of water dripped down his neck. "I don't think we need to qualify anything."

Her brows lowered, the flyaway corners giving her a delicate fairy look. "I suppose you are right. It's not that important."

Normally, Brandon would have found such a qualification reassuring—even though he was usually the one making minute differentiations on terminology and not his partner. But her protestations were having an odd effect on him. They weren't lessening his desire one jot. By God, he would regain some control of this seduction if it killed him.

The fact that Verena was taking such pains to place him at a distance, even as she admitted she wanted more physical contact, made him all the more determined to gain concessions from her—to prove that he was indeed in charge. That she wanted him in more than just her bed. "Verena, this . . . attraction. It's been there from the first day we met. There's nothing wrong with our acting on it."

"If I thought there was anything wrong, I would never have suggested it. I was only pointing out that physical . . ." her face flushed before she continued, ". . . consummation does not necessarily mean that we will change our behavior toward one another. We are adults. We've both been about the world some. And there's no reason we should expect more."

Bloody hell, but she was adorable. He wanted her. Wanted her now. Beneath him. Held without mercy so that he could prove to her how wrong her cool, logical ideas were. Their mating would be fiercely passionate, deeply sensual, and rich with feeling. This was no causal meeting of two equals. It was much, much more. He could feel it, taste it.

He knew it the same way he knew that though she tried to appear unaffected, her body tingled with yearning for his touch. "I disagree, sweet. I think by morning you'll find that we've far more of a relationship than you realize."

The words hung hazily between them. Brandon wondered if perhaps he'd gone mad—surely *he* wasn't the one who'd just suggested that his liaison with this lush woman was something more.

But he *had* said it. Aloud, too, which was even more shocking. *Damn it, what am I thinking?*

That was the problem—he wasn't thinking at all. She was who she was. An adventurer. A card turner. She was not the type of woman with whom one bothered to develop a lasting relationship. Perhaps he was merely reacting to the fact that she was attempting to diminish their affair.

His brow cleared. It was his pride, and nothing else. Relieved, he managed a grin.

She didn't seem to notice. She gave an absent wave of her hand and said, "I doubt it. But that's neither here nor there. Before we begin . . ." she gestured vaguely, "this . . . there are some things I want to ask you."

*This.* Never had one word held so much promise. A thin shiver crawled over his skin and he realized how chilled he was. She was stalling, but that was fine. He'd let her stall if only for a short time . . . it would make her burn all the more hotly when they finally came together.

He wiped a hand over his eyes. They stung as if on fire. A slow, heavy lethargy seemed to be creeping over him, fueled by the flashes of lust Verena was causing by her very nearness. "We can discuss whatever you want," he said hoarsely, "but first I must remove these wet clothes."

Her eyes widened. "Remove your clothes? Now?"

"When should I remove them? During our discussion? That would be very rude."

Her lips quivered and to his immense delight, she reached out and undid the top button of his waistcoat. "I rather thought we'd undress together—after we talked, of course."

Together. The two of them. Removing their clothes. God, but she was a brassy piece. He found that he rather liked that. Liked it and wondered how far it went. "What would you like to talk about *before* we remove our clothes?"

"There are some questions I want to ask you." Her violet gaze met his steadily. "Several."

He rubbed his throat, though it itched deep inside. "Fair enough. I have some questions I want to ask you, too. Who goes first?"

She pursed her lips, an innocent gesture that nearly offset him. Her lips were the plump pink of a newly budded rose—sweet, curved, lush.

"You may go first," she said finally.

Wonderful. Every fiber in his body yearned for her and she wanted to play Can You Guess. "May we at least sit?" He gestured toward the fireplace where one lone chair graced the room. He was certain he'd fall over if she continued to torment him so sweetly.

She glanced at the chair dubiously. "I suppose so. Shall I call for another chair?"

"Hell, no. I've had enough of Herberts for one day." He caught her hand and pulled her toward the chair with him.

She followed willingly enough, though she said in an exasperated voice, "Mr. St. John—Brandon, it will only take a moment to have another chair brought—"

He sat, his hand still about her wrist, and pulled her down onto his lap. He settled her there, her legs over the arm of the chair, her bottom firmly settled over his lap, her head tucked beneath his chin. She fit perfectly, as if she'd been made for him.

She sat for a stunned moment, then wiggled, trying to get up. He tightened his hold, though he let her squirm all she wished.

After a moment, he murmured, "You really shouldn't do that."

"Why not—" She stilled, her eyes widening as she felt his erection against her bottom, muffled by her skirts. Her mouth made a perfect "o." "I'm sorry. I hadn't thought of that."

"Normally I wouldn't complain." He rubbed her arm slowly, savoring the feel of her beneath his fingertips. Silky. Soft. Smooth. Everything a woman should be and more. "Are you certain you want to talk first?"

She didn't answer for a moment, but looked at him, her desire plain in her eyes.

He captured her chin. "Verena," he whispered.

Her hand closed over his wrist. "Don't."

"Don't what?"

"Don't tempt me. I'm not as strong as I thought."

"Is it weak to want someone?"

"No. But it is weak if I forget that I'm here because—" She clamped her lips together.

Ah-ha. "Because?" He waited, but he could see that she was not going to answer. "Let me guess. You think it is weak if you forget that you are here for no other reason than I am the most virile man you've ever met."

Her smile broke through once more, sunshine

on a dappled stream, lighting up the room and, in some strange way, his very heart.

"You, sir, are insufferable. Whether you believe it or not, you are not the topic of every conversation."

"I may be insufferable, but you, madam, are a spoiled, willful woman."

"Spoiled? By whom?"

"By your servants, and that blond Viking you lead around by the nose." Just the thought of the man made Brandon growl. He didn't like the way Lansdowne looked at Verena, as if he knew her better than everyone else in the room, as if they shared secrets.

"Blond Viking?" She frowned for a moment, then suddenly chuckled. "You mean James!"

"Whatever his name is." Brand had a few names he used to refer to the cretin, but he didn't think Verena would be amused.

"I shall have to use that the next time I see him—Blond Viking. I rather like that."

Brandon scowled. "You are not to call him your blond anything."

"Why not? It would embarrass him to death and that is one of my few pleasures."

Brandon wished he'd bitten his own tongue off rather than give her a pet name for her latest amor. "Blast it to hell, I thought of the name and therefore it is mine to give to whomever I will. And I will not give it to you to use on that preening peacock that you like to have hanging about."

Verena looked at him with suddenly wide eyes, a dawning expression on her face. "Brandon . . . you are jealous."

"Of him? Don't make me laugh."

Verena didn't feel the least like laughing. She felt every other emotion—excitement, fear, uncertainty, and lust—especially lust.

She eyed her captor narrowly, then shook her head. "You're jealous," she repeated loftily. "I recognize the signs."

His arm tightened and he slowly drew her against him until her chest was pressed to his. His face was only a few inches from hers, his blue eyes brilliant. "What is Lansdowne to you?"

She wasn't going to answer, but there was something sweetly possessive in the way Brandon's arm tightened, in the expression in his blue eyes. "James is a relative."

"That's a damnably vague answer." He leaned his forehead against hers, his skin hot to the touch. "Don't play games with me. I asked you an honest question; I expect an honest answer."

She bit her lip. He had a point. She wasn't really sure why she was hiding the answer. Part of it came from years of conditioning—of never revealing more than absolutely necessary.

It was the way the Lansdownes lived; the way they still did. Still, her instincts bade her to count the cost . . . what would happen if Brandon knew her relationship with James? She tried to think of the negative possibilities and could not think of a one. "James is my brother."

Brandon's brows lifted. "Your brother?"

"My one and only brother."

To her surprise, it seemed as if Brandon's face relaxed, as if he was genuinely relieved. "Ah," he said. "That explains a lot." He eyed her consideringly. "You know, I hadn't thought of it, but now . . . I do see some similarities." He lifted a finger and traced one of her brows. "Do you have any sisters?"

She placed her fingers over his lips. "It's not fair if you get to ask all the questions. I have some of my own, you know. I believe it is my turn now."

His lips quirked. "Very well. What do you want to know?"

She wanted to ask him all sorts of things—did he like blond hair? Did he enjoy shorter women, or taller ones? What was his favorite color? Did he like butter on his toast—oh a thousand things. It was a pity she was held to one question at a time.

Verena toyed with his top button, feeling the heat radiate from his skin. She pushed away all the frivolous questions that were clamoring for answers and forced herself to focus on the problems at hand. "Why did you tell me about Humford? You said it as if you meant to shock me."

A flicker of regret deepened his blue eyes to black. "I threw the information at you to see your reaction; I thought you already knew of his death."

"I was horrified. How was Humford ki—"

Brandon placed his fingers over her lips. "It's my turn."

The devil. He was remarkably good at making one play one's own games, a talent she used to relish, but now found irksome. She raised her brows and waited.

His gaze darkened, the levity slipping away. "Verena, what do you know of Humford's list? Have you found it?"

Her heart contracted. Dear God, he knew about

that, too. Did he also know about the indiscreet letters James was attempting to collect? The thought sent her heart pounding crazily in her chest and she pushed away, trying to get up.

But he held her firm, a frown between his brows. "Answer, Verena. Do you know where it is?"

She stopped struggling and gave him a considering look. Should she answer? Should she tell the truth? She knew how James would react in this situation—he wouldn't volunteer the least tidbit.

But then James still lived as Father had taught them, trusting no one, hiding who and what they were. Or he had until he'd fallen for a married woman with a careless pen and an eye for handsome young rakes.

Verena tried to sort out all the facts as dispassionately as she could, considering that she was sitting in Brandon St. John's lap, his deliciously warm body encircling hers. "I suppose it won't hurt to tell you what I know, which isn't a lot. I know that a list of some kind is missing. James and I, we've been looking for it, but it's not here."

"Are you certain?"

"We've looked everywhere."

His gaze met hers for the space of a second, then he sighed and rested his head against the high back of the chair, his arms loosening. A deep weariness seemed to cross over his face. "I was afraid of that. Verena, I must find that blasted list. I have to."

What did he mean by that? What could possibly be in the list that the whole world was after it? Even the people holding those damning letters of James's were in on it now.

Of course, Brandon's admission was, in a way, reassuring. If he'd been the one to hold James's letters, he wouldn't have so quickly accepted her answer.

Whoever held James's letters believed that Humford's list was still in Westforth House. "Brandon, why do *you* need the list? Why is it so important?"

He looked at her from beneath his lashes for a long moment as if weighing his response. "Which question do you want answered first? Then it's my turn again." He lifted a finger and traced the line of her cheek to the corner of her mouth. "Only I think my next question is going to have to do with how you look without all those clothes on."

God, but he was delectable, especially like this, playful and seductive at the same time. He was mussed by the storm, thoroughly wet, his clothes hugging his body like a second skin, his blue gaze hot and possessive. *Blast it, this is not fair.*

She had to swallow twice before she could answer. "I want an answer for both."

His eyes narrowed. After a moment, he gave a short nod. "Very well, but then you'll owe. A lot." He leaned forward to whisper softly, "And you will pay dearly."

She supposed a sedate, prim sort of woman might find sitting in the lap of a man who was not her husband or her fiancé, somewhat . . . indiscreet. Chancy. Risque, even.

Verena found it exhilarating. She placed her hands to either side of his face. "If you answer those two questions, then in the morning I will answer *every* question you ask."

He raised his brows. "In the morning?"

She pressed her lips to his forehead and then punctuated her words with soft, sensual kisses on his lips. "In. The. Morning."

Brandon had to fight the urge to bury his face in her neck, to taste her skin, and kiss her with all the passion that was building inside him. Good God, but she was a work of contradictions, bold and brazen yet soft and feminine.

Most women he knew—even those as experienced as the never-missed Celeste—didn't excite him the way Verena did. She promised, teased, tormented, all in the same breath.

But she was also vibrantly real. She didn't attempt to be some pure icon of womanhood, but was rich, and warm, and utterly in possession of herself and her body.

It was intoxicating.

He placed his hand over one of hers where it lay against his cheek, his fingers laced through hers. "Very well—since we're sharing everything. I don't know exactly what is in Humford's list. Whatever it is, it has something to do with the Home Office."

"James guessed something like that." She smiled then, her teeth white and even. "He's very good at figuring things out."

"You're fairly decent at it yourself."

"I try," she said simply. "I'm surprised you're going to such lengths to procure this list if the Home Office wants it. I wonder why . . ." She looked at him through her lashes and waited.

The little devil was trying to worm extra information out of him. He rubbed his thumb the length of hers, sliding the pad of his thumb over her polished nail. "I want that blasted list because someone at the Home Office believes a friend of mine took it. If I don't recover it, he could face dire consequences."

Her expression froze and something flickered deep in her eyes, but she said nothing.

Something was happening here, he could tell. But what? Was she hiding something? He shifted so that he could see her face in the firelight. "Verena, this is important."

Her smile was strained. "I am beginning to realize that."

"Why have *you* been trying to find that damned list?"

Her gaze turned secretive. "I have reasons— just as good as yours. Brandon . . ." She paused. "If your friend didn't take this list, then surely he is in no true danger."

"There still would be a huge scandal. The strain on his father could be fatal." He cupped her face firmly, forcing her to meet his gaze. "Do you understand, Verena? Whatever the cost, I *must* find that list."

She placed her hands on his wrists, her gaze meeting his levelly. "That is a problem. You see, Brandon, I must find it, too. We are at loggerheads once again."

# Chapter 14

⟨~~∽⟩⟨ ⟩

*Miss Mitford has been told that men like a bidda-
ble woman. So now all she does is bleat "Why yes,
Mr. Fonternoy!" and "Why of course, Mr.
Fonternoy!" As far as I can tell, all she's got to
show for such nonsense is a sore throat and the
imminent loss of her virtue.*

The Mitfords' maid, Lucy, to her brother, John, the
Duke of Devonshire's new head groom, on meeting
him outside a butcher shop on Bake Street

**T**hat was just her luck . . . for the first time in
four years—four *long* years, Verena met a
man who'd excited and thrilled her as much as
Andrew and what happened? They were both on
the trail of a ridiculous list . . . well, not too ridiculous considering that both Brandon's friend and
James stood to lose quite a lot without it.

Life was never fair, but this seemed inordi-
nately harsh—to flash such a delectable man before her and then ruthlessly steal him away. She
felt as if she'd just found out her favorite scones
would never again be served for tea.

Brandon, however, didn't seem the least upset.
"Verena, we'll look for the list together. And we'll
find it, too."

"And then what?" Verena brushed her fingers over Brandon's cheek, marveling at the intoxicating feel of a man's rough skin beneath her fingertips, the soft prickle of stubble under her palm.

How long had it been since she'd felt that exact sensation? Four years? Almost five? *Andrew*. She closed her eyes and snuggled down until her forehead rested against Brandon's cheek. A twinge of guilt flickered through her. *Stop it*, she told herself. Andrew would have never questioned her right to continue living her life after he'd died. He believed in living in the present, in tasting everything there was to taste, in reaching out and taking all that life had to give and reveling in each and every moment.

Somewhere, deep in her mind, she could almost hear his voice, encouraging her to take chances. To live, once again.

"Verena?" Brandon's warm voice slid about her.

She shivered and wrapped her arms more tightly about him. "Brandon, no more questions." She couldn't stand it for another minute. She needed him, wanted him—feelings she'd thought were dead stirred to life and required immediate attention.

Brandon's mouth tightened as if he'd argue, but then his gaze met hers, hot and demanding. "We will finish this conversation in the morning."

"The very first thing," she agreed, sliding her hands over his shoulders to his arms. It wasn't enough. She placed her lips on his temple and traced a line to his cheek. Heat built within her, swirling through her and sending shivers down her spine.

He lifted his mouth to hers, capturing her lips. He kissed her deeply, parting her lips with his tongue. She shivered beneath the onslaught, his tongue stroking the edge of hers. It was erotic, the mimicry he committed on her mouth. Her body softened, melted, heated. She moaned against him, opening her mouth wider, her arms going around his neck, holding him closer, pressing herself against him, moving restlessly in his lap, her thighs damp with desire.

His hands spanned her back, cupped her bottom, held her closer. Every touch sent a burst of fire through her, tightening her breasts, shivering down her stomach, coming to rest between her thighs where a dull ache grew.

She threaded her fingers through his thick, damp hair where it curled over his ears. God, but she wanted him. Desired him. Burned for him.

He broke the kiss, his breathing harsh in the silence. "Verena, are you certain—" He couldn't seem to form the rest of the sentence.

But she knew he was giving her one last chance to regain control.

But did she want control? She wanted him. And she knew that tonight would be a night she'd never forget. Verena caught his hand, lifting it to her lips. She loved his hands. Long and strongly formed, she was certain they were made for touching a woman, for bringing her to a world of pleasure. Locking his gaze with hers, she pressed a kiss between each finger, letting her tongue flick out and taste the delicate webbing between.

His breath grew harsher. She'd almost reached his last finger, when he curled his hand into a fist.

"For the love of God, stop!" he said hoarsely. "I won't be able to—"

She kissed his lips, gently. "It's time we took off our clothes. Together."

That word had a delicious feel to it—*together*. Verena sat up in his lap and untied the ribbon that held her gown. The strip of pink silk slid through the gathers and pulled free. Her gown gaped at the neck. Verena held the ribbon at arm's length and let it slither to the ground, a puddle of lush pink on the red carpet.

Then she placed her hands on the loose neck of her gown and pushed the material down, over her shoulders, to her waist. All she wore was her chemise, thin and damp from his embrace. It showed far more than it should have, her nipples clearly evident through the thin material.

Brandon watched, his eyes unusually bright, as if he suffered a slight fever.

Verena leaned closer to him and whispered against his ear. "I have taken my gown half off. It's your turn now."

He rested his head against the high back of the chair and glinted a smile, his blue eyes vivid in the glow of the firelight. "You believe in fair play."

"Always."

He tugged on his cravat. His fingers fumbled over the knot, but he persisted. She watched him, her eagerness building with each passing second. The moment seemed interminable.

Finally, just as her impatience was at the breaking point, the knot slipped free. Brandon yanked off his cravat and then leaned forward to do the same with his shirt. One right after the other, his cravat and shirt fell to the ground.

The sight of his bared chest caused her to shiver in delight. Broad and sculpted, he was as finely made as a statue, his chest muscles magnificent, his stomach ribbed and tightly drawn. She splayed her hands over him, running her fingers over every rich inch, lingering over the sprinkling of hair that covered his chest and narrowed to a tantalizing line that trailed all the way to the fastening of his pants.

He caught her hands and held them tight. "Not yet. Your gown first."

There was a hint of an order in his tone. But though he was issuing commands, she felt in control—almost powerful. It was a heady experience, to be wanted so much, to be desired by such a tantalizing man. She stood then, pulling her hands free. Facing him, she allowed her gown to fall from her hips to the floor where it pooled about her feet on the rug, white froth on a sea of red.

Brandon caught his breath harshly, his gaze traveling over her. Her chemise was made of the finest lawn. The white flimsy material hugged every curve she possessed, outlining her full breasts in mouth-watering detail, clinging to the slope of her stomach, draping her rounded hips.

He grasped the arms of the chair tightly to keep himself from yanking her to him. It was almost too much to be borne.

Her eyes gleamed softly, as if she delighted in tormenting him. She leaned forward and placed a hand on each of his knees and pushed them aside

so that she could stand between them, his powerful thighs against the outsides of her legs.

Her stomach was directly before him and he
could see the outline of her navel and, by just dip-
ping his chin the slightest bit, the faint tangle of
hair at the juncture of her legs. Faint tremors
wracked him. God, but she was beautiful. Beautiful and standing within arm's length.

He found her gaze on him. He loved the way
her eyes shone; she knew she was teasing him
mercilessly and she reveled in the power of it. She
sank to her knees before him and gently pushed
him back in the chair. He allowed her to direct
him, though he kept his hands locked about the
arms of the chair—he didn't trust himself to let go.

She leaned forward to place a kiss on his stomach. Then her tongue, wet and hot, flickered over
his ribs. She traced a path over his stomach and
up. He sucked in his breath, his eyes half closing
as he watched her. She locked his gaze with hers
as she gently kissed his nipple.

Brandon almost bolted from the chair. "Verena," he whispered, his voice rough.

She nipped his skin, letting her teeth abrade his
puckered nipple. He released the arms of the chair
and sank his hands into her hair, scattering the
pins and loosening the mass until it tumbled over
her shoulders.

He ran his hands through her long tresses, the
strands clinging to his fingers. "I've dreamed of
this."

"And I've dreamed of this." She placed her lips
over his nipple and sucked.

Lightning-quick stabs of pure pleasure bolted through him. "Verena!" he gasped, his hands closing over her shoulders. He held her roughly, his breath harsh, his manhood rigid against her stomach. Verena's own excitement rose to match his. She moved restlessly, pressing herself closer.

Brandon thought he would explode from desire. She was a wraith, a magical breath that brushed him with an exquisite combination of wantonness and pure desire. She wanted him and somehow, through that wanting, made his desire all the stronger.

Never had he been more taken with any woman. He couldn't stand another moment without feeling her naked beneath him. He stood, lifting her to her feet at the same time. "It's my turn," he growled, undoing his breeches with more force than necessary, struggling briefly with the wet material. But he was determined and within seconds he was bare before her.

She watched as if fascinated, her hands touching here, lingering there. It was as if she couldn't help herself. Her fingertips stroked heat everywhere they touched and he had to bite back a groan.

"Your chemise," he ordered. "Take it off."

Verena's gaze softened, her amazing violet eyes shadowed by the length of her lashes. She removed her hands from his hips and ran them lightly over her own body, lingering on her breasts as if she knew Brandon's every thought. "Now?" she whispered, her lips glistening from his kisses.

He had to curl his hands into fists to keep from

grabbing her and ripping the chemise from her body.

She must have seen his desire, for she laughed softly, the sound running through Brandon like liquid fire. She had the most sensual laugh, husky and unrestrained.

Her fingers lingered at the chemise's ribbon. "Should I—"

Brandon untied the ribbon and pulled her chemise from her shoulders, the delicate material ripping as he did so, but he didn't care. He was too taken by the expanse of creamy white skin that was bared to his gaze.

The remnants of the chemise joined Verena's gown on the floor. Brandon placed his hands on her shoulders and stood back to look at her. She was beautiful when fully clothed, but naked, she was a goddess. Every inch of her was curved, from her calves to the gently rounded contours of her stomach, to her full breasts. And every curve proved that she was a woman. Lush. Inviting. And all his.

He wasn't sure afterwards how they made it to the bed. One moment they were standing, luxuriating in each other and the next, they were on the soft mattress, chest to chest, his thigh pressed between her legs, her moisture driving him mad.

He captured her mouth with his and tasted her, luxuriated in the feel of her. Like a trace of sugar, she was sweet on his tongue and left him wanting for more.

He placed his hand on her breast, her nipple between two fingers. She arched at the touch, her midriff lifting from the bed, her breast thrust further into his palm. He gently kneaded her flesh, admiring the perfection of her breast, the womanly curve of her stomach, the incredibly sensual line of her shoulders and throat. She was art, made by a master hand, touched with a beauty of soul he was only beginning to realize.

She moaned deep in her throat, her hands resting on his wrists as if to guide his wandering fingers to other, secret places.

"You're so warm," she murmured, her hands feathering over his arms and back. "It's like there's a fire inside you."

He had a fever, he knew. But he couldn't tell if it was from standing in the rain or from the sensations caused by her fingers as they brushed and stroked and tormented.

He could take no more. He moved his thigh to one side, pressing her knees apart.

She didn't resist, but lifted her knees and opened for him. She was thoroughly wanton, as shameless as any man could ever dream. He doubted she knew how much her bold actions fueled his desire, but they did. Fanned him to a flame he'd never found before.

"I want to taste you," he murmured fiercely. "All of you."

The words sent a pleasurable shiver through Verena. He was the most sensuous man she'd ever known—every touch elicited a response, every word drove her closer to madness.

He lifted his head, his eyes narrowed to slits. "Are you afraid?"

*Was* she afraid? Her heart was certainly thundering against her ribs and she felt breathless, as if she'd been running. But she wasn't afraid. She was excited, thrilled; her whole body burned with a passion she'd never before experienced. Dare she tell him such a thing?

He captured her face between his hands, the gesture both rough and yet oddly gentle, as if he were restraining himself with only the greatest effort. "Do you want me to continue? This is your last chance, Verena. Your last chance for salvation from whatever consumes us."

She didn't want any more chances. She wanted him between her thighs, filling her up, pleasing her, reminding what it was to be a woman. But somehow she couldn't form the words.

Instead, she gripped his wrists as she planted her heels on the mattress. Then she lifted her hips to brush his, her hands sliding up his arms to his shoulders.

Every finely muscled inch fueled her desire all the more. She locked one arm about his neck and pulled his mouth to hers to kiss him boldly, recklessly, plunging her tongue in and out of his mouth.

He moaned into her mouth, his hands sliding over her waist, her hips, cupping her intimately. Verena reached between them and found his manhood. She stroked and slid her hands over his velvet hardness.

His breath hissed through his lips and he closed his eyes, his body rigid. His skin was damp, his breathing harsh against her ear. "Let go, sweet, or neither of us will get what we want."

Verena reluctantly did as he asked. She loved

the feel of him, of the smoothness of his skin over his hard muscles. The contrast was fascinating. His body lost some of its tension and he laughed softly, gently rubbing his forehead against hers. "You're beautiful, did you know that?" She wasn't beautiful. She was short, had a sad tendency to freckle at the first hint of sunlight, and possessed hips that obviously belonged to a much taller woman. But lying here before Brand's hot gaze, she realized that she *felt* beautiful, the sensation intoxicating.

He pressed her back against the pillows and placed his hand on her inner thigh. He lightly trailed his fingers up her thigh, to the damp tangle of curls. He paused for the briefest moment, then contined on, his fingers tracing a course across her slick folds. She gasped and arched into his hand.

"I want to taste you," he growled again into her ear, his fingers stroking, sliding back and forth, driving her mad.

She ran her hands through his hair and pushed his head down, past her breasts, opening for him even as she gasped his name.

Brand accepted her gift, drank of her, suckling her soft feminine folds and tormenting her flesh with his tongue and teeth. Her movements grew more frantic and he increased his efforts, cupping her bottom and pressing her up. She grew slick with need. Her hands rippled through his hair, pressing him onward, encouraging him to continue.

He found the core, raking his teeth over the delicate spot. She gasped and then held still . . . frozen in place. Brandon intensified his efforts, worshipping her in a way he'd never before worshipped any woman. With a frenzied jerk of her hips, she arched wildly, calling out his name. He closed his eyes at the sound, suckling her deeply, urging her on and on.

Finally she collapsed, spent and drained, her hand still threaded through his hair.

Brand's own body was rock hard, rigid with the effort to stay in control. While her breathing returned to normal, he sucked in slow breaths of air, willing his turgid flesh to give him more time to savor, more time to torment. If it killed him, he vowed that she would never forget this night.

Verena sighed deeply, then moved as if to close her legs.

"Don't," he said, holding her knees apart. He bent to taste her one last time, reveling in her pleasure. "I love the way you feel beneath my mouth." He placed kisses along her thighs and lower, where he stopped to place a kiss on the sensitive skin behind her knees. She moaned and moved restlessly.

Verena shivered, her skin flushed and glowing in the firelight. "You are going to kill me."

"Ah, but what a lovely way to die," he murmured. "Did you know that your toes curl when you're excited? Arched as if they, themselves, were having the ultimate pleasure."

She lifted herself on her elbows and watched him, her lips parted, her thick blond hair falling over her brow and shoulders. She looked flushed and sinful, her lips swollen from his kisses, her entire body aglow from his caresses. He grew harder just looking at her.

He moved back to her side so that he could look her directly in the eyes. Such beautiful eyes, the lashes long and lush, the color startling—a pure violet, like a flower drenched in rain.

He traced her brows with his finger, then tipped up her chin. She threw her arms about his neck and pulled his mouth to hers, kissing him with every bit of her soul, her passion.

His control began to shred. His hands wandered feverishly, his body aching for release. "I must have you."

Verena didn't think there were any more beautiful words in the entire English language. She followed his lead, letting her hands wander where they would. When they found his manhood, she wrapped her hands around his length, marveling in the velvet hardness. Heat seemed to radiate from his skin, through her fingertips, trailing through her like tendrils of delicate fire. She opened for him, rubbing the tip of him against herself.

He gasped. "Verena, please—"

"Take me," she whispered, delighting in the torment on his face. She opened her legs beneath him, her hands on his hips, pulling him forward, toward her. She pressed herself against him, wrapping her legs about his hips.

He entered her, his fullness sending deep tremors through hers. Verena gasped, feeling herself stretch and wrap about him, her flesh yielding before his.

She burned beneath him and with him and for him, their movements increasing, growing more frantic. Verena felt him grow harder, thicker, his manhood on the brink. She put her hands to his stomach and halted his motions.

He lifted himself on his elbow, poised above her, his face rigid as if he were in pain. "God, Verena," he rasped. "What—"

She put her arms about his shoulders, lifting her leg over his hip. "Lay back, Brandon. Let me do it."

Verena lifted herself up, pushing him back against the pillows and raising herself until she sat astride him, her knees on either side of his hips.

"Don't move," she ordered, then boldly settled upon him, pressing downward, his flesh joining hers. It was heaven. Slowly, she began to move. Back and forth, each stroke pleasure and pain.

"Verena," he gasped, his hands about her waist. "Don't—"

She stopped, leaning over him so that her hair brushed his broad chest. "What's wrong, St. John? Afraid? Because if you are, I'll stop." She made as if to climb off, but he gripped her waist and held her there.

"I'm not afraid of anything." His gaze burned into hers. "Especially not you. Never you."

She closed her eyes, lifting her head, her hair falling down her back. His hands molded her hips, sliding up to her breasts. He pressed and kneaded, tormenting her nipples until she writhed on him. The feeling of being filled, of completion, of being joined—she gasped as a wave of bliss rippled through her, her body enveloping his, intimately holding him, squeezing him.

Brand's hands tightened on her waist and he held her firm, his own pleasure increased, compounded. He exploded in a surge just as she collapsed across him.

Moments later . . . or maybe it was hours . . . he realized she was still lying upon him, his arms tight about her as if he was afraid to loosen his grip. He smiled at the thought, rubbing his cheek against the satiny softness of her hair. "That was beautiful."

She shifted as if to move, but he held her tight. "No," he whispered. "I want to sleep like this."

She chuckled against his chest and he smiled, relishing the feeling. He'd never felt this sort of peace. Never felt so comfortable, so . . . sated.

God, but she was wonderful. He found the blanket where it had been shoved to one side of the huge bed and he pulled it across her shoulders, tucking it about them both. "I don't want you to get cold," he said, his own voice still raspy.

She snuggled against him. "It sounds as if you are the one catching cold."

"Me? I'm never sick."

"Don't tempt the fates, St. John," she said, her yawn warming his skin. "They will get you every time."

Brandon rubbed his cheek against her hair. She was pert. Saucy. Well read. Annoyingly right. And the most perfect woman he'd ever met. He could understand why Chase thought this woman might be able to hold his demons at bay. Brand was beginning to believe that Verena could do anything she wanted to.

He pressed a kiss to her forehead and snuggled deeper into the soft bedding. She had a wonderful bed—the sheets crisp and smooth, enough pillows for twenty people, and an astonishingly thick down counterpane. The best part was that the entire bed smelled faintly of lavender.

He sighed contentedly. "I like your bed."

"I like you in my bed," she responded sleepily. "In fact, I'm almost certain that I like *you*. At times, anyway."

"You should. I've had the devil of a time trying to get close to you."

She lifted her head then, her eyes half closed with sleep, yet a faint spark of curiosity in their depths. "Why have you been trying to get close to me?"

Brandon realized that he didn't have an answer. At first he'd wanted nothing more than the whereabouts of Humford's list. But that was no longer true. Now he wanted more of *her*.

What he felt for Verena was fondness, admiration, and a hot lust. Especially hot lust. And for now, that was enough.

He grinned at her, cupping her chin and running his thumb over her kiss-swollen lips. "I wanted to get close to you because I was fairly certain you would kiss like an angel. I was right."

Her disbelief was plain. She lifted a brow, and he marveled at the way her brows curved up at the ends.

"Is that all?" she asked, a stubborn note in her voice.

He held her chin between thumb and forefinger and tipped her head back so that she had to meet his gaze. "Do you want to know all my secrets, Verena? Everything?"

She looked at him for a long moment. Slowly, she nodded.

"Then tell me *your* secrets," he whispered. "All of them."

Her gaze darkened. She bit her lip, her lashes shadowing her eyes. He could see her considering, wondering, weighing the cost. Finally, she shook her head, her hair falling across her cheek as she reached up to kiss him, her lips brushing softly over his.

"Perhaps later on, when this hand is played out," she murmured. "But not now." She snuggled back against him, pulling the covers firmly about them both.

Brandon tried to control his disappointment. Whether Verena realized it or not, they were through with deceptions. Her head rested against his shoulder, her legs entwined with his, Verena's breathing slowed. Her breath stirred the hairs on his chest and he found himself relaxing, snuggling deeper into the softness of the mattress.

He would discover why she wanted Humford's list in the morning—that, and every other secret she harbored. Even if he had to kiss each and every undisclosed thought from her lush lips.

Ah, it was a painful job, but he was willing to apply himself to it. Smiling to himself, Brandon smoothed her hair from her temples until he, too, drifted off to sleep.

# Chapter 15

*I'm not one as rails against fate. But if I'd been born to be a groom and naught else, you'd think I'd like horses more and money less.*

The Duke of Devonshire's new head groom, John, to Dawson, the head footman, while the two servants descended the stairs for dinner

**V**erena awoke the next morning to the feel of a man's muscular leg thrown over hers. She was held, imprisoned against her own feather mattress: warm, naked, and completely sated. It was, she decided with a sleepy smile, a very good day to be a Lansdowne.

It was heavenly. She kept her eyes closed against the light streaming through the cracks in the curtains and savored the feel of being held, of being cherished and cuddled.

At her side, Brandon's steady breathing sifted through the air, the faint scent of his cologne tickling her nose. It was an arousing sensation, awakening with such a large, muscular man naked in her bed, his warm skin—she opened her eyes and frowned. His *very* warm skin.

Verena lifted herself up on an elbow and looked at his sleeping face. His black hair was tousled, his cheeks covered with stubble, his skin flushed. She placed her hand on his brow, heat seeping through to the tips of her fingers.

Heavens, the poor man had a fever. It must have come from the drenching he took last night. He had been soaked to the skin.

She traced her fingers through his hair, marveling at the length of his lashes. How long had he waited outside in that atrocious weather? She rather liked feeling as if she were worth standing in the rain for. Had it been anyone other than Brandon St. John, she would have thought the gesture romantic.

But from him, it was merely a sign of stubbornness. The man hated to lose; that one trait colored his every action.

She moved her fingers across his forehead, smoothing back his hair. There was something endearing about the fact that he had a touch of the ague. It made him seem less St. John, and more Brandon.

He stirred, turning toward her as he opened his eyes. His gaze focused and a slow smile tickled the corner of his mouth.

Verena smoothed back his hair. "You have a fever."

"*For you.*" Only he didn't really say the words. He mouthed them, no sound coming from his dry throat.

He frowned, rubbing his throat.

Verena blinked. Good heavens, had he lost his voice?

He opened his mouth again, this time his lips forming a much longer sentence. But no matter how many words he attempted, nothing came forth but raspy one-syllable croaks.

Verena couldn't help it—she giggled.

Brandon clamped his mouth closed and placed a hand to his throat.

"Don't try to speak, you'll strain your throat even more."

Brandon slanted a cutting glance her way.

Perhaps it was the fact that he looked adorable sitting in the middle of her pink bed surrounded with mounds of lace pillows, his broad bare chest uncovered, his face a thundercloud. Or perhaps it was just the fact that for the first time since forever, Verena didn't feel alone. Or perhaps it was simply the liberating effects of deep, satisfying, soul-quaking sex.

Verena wasn't sure. But whatever it was, she suddenly felt invincible. Free. As strong as a mountain. She launched herself on him, pushing him back to the mattress and straddling him boldly. She chuckled at his amazed expression as she leaned over him, letting her hair trail across his muscled arms. "You know what this means, don't you?"

He shook his head, a wary expression in his eyes.

She ran the tip of her finger over his mouth and to his chin. "If you can't speak, then you can't ask me any questions."

She'd expected a reaction. A frown, perhaps. Or maybe a thin-lipped snarl. After all, he was Brandon St. John the mighty and no one dared defy him.

But since he was a St. John, she should have realized that his reaction would be a bit stronger than the average man's. His hands clamped over her wrists and he swung her down onto the mattress, moving so quickly that Verena was lying amid her pillows, her hair over her face, before she even knew what had happened.

She felt the bed give as he stood. She shoved back her hair. "What was that for?"

Brand held his two fists end to end and acted as if he were breaking a stick in half, then stabbed a finger in her direction.

"Wha—oh! I see. But you're wrong; I did not break my word. I told you that in the morning I would answer any question you *asked*. It's morning and . . ." She cupped a hand to her ear ". . . I don't hear you *asking* anything."

He glowered, his arms crossed over his broad chest.

"It may not be fair, but that's not my fault. You are plenty old enough to know the dangers of getting wet and cold."

Brandon gave her one last warning glare, then turned toward the nightstand. The morning sun filtered across him, limning his hips and thighs with delicious golden bands of light. Verena's breath caught. She especially liked the little dips and hollows on his spectacularly muscled ass.

God, but he was magnificent. And for the moment, all hers.

She rolled to her side, resting her head on her hand as she watched him walk to the stand and pour water from the pitcher into one of the glasses. He took a careful drink, grimacing as he did so.

"Perhaps I should ring for some tea—"

"No." Raspy and uncertain, his voice creaked out. He took another sip of the water. She watched him, somehow jealous of the glass he held in his large, warm hand.

Soon he would be dressed and on his way. She forced her smile to remain in place. Of course he would leave. And that was a good thing. It was, in fact, exactly what she wanted.

She had her freedom, a fairly steady income—or at least enough money that she didn't want for anything, and she had her family. What else could she want?

*To have Brandon St. John in my bed every night for the rest of my life.* Good heavens, where had that thought come from? She eyed his taut stomach for a long moment and found that her fingers itched, but not for cards. She wanted to touch him once more.

If she were honest, she'd admit that it would be lovely to have him in her bed—now and forever. What bothered her was the thought of having him in her life. He wasn't just a St. John, he was *the* St. John. The most arrogant, controlling, forceful one of the lot.

Verena tried to picture Brandon visiting a gaming hell, lounging in the small sitting room with the *Morning Post*, sitting at the table in the dining room while Herberts dished out the soup—but no picture would form. None at all.

And that, she decided reluctantly, was because she knew it could never happen. Brandon St. John came from a different place than she did—he had been raised to accept position and power, just as she'd been raised to pretend. To pretend who she was, what she wanted . . . her whole life was based on fraud, on pretending and not being.

She was better off alone. Away from both her family and anyone else who might judge or otherwise attempt to manipulate her. Thus she could continue to live her life *her* way.

Which could possibly mean spending a little more time in bed with the man before her. Surely she could allow him a few moments of rest. After all, Brandon was ill and she did have a large enough bed to accommodate both her and—

*Stop it, Verena*, she told herself sternly. Calm. Reasonable. Detached. That's how she needed to remain, no matter how handsome Brandon's face, or how taut his perfectly formed rump.

Lust was one thing. She'd give herself permission to feel every level of lust there was. But any stronger emotion, and *she*'d be the one at a disadvantage.

Brandon set down the water glass and placed his hands on the corners of the stand. He leaned forward, his head bowed.

"Should I . . . do you need anything?"

He shook his head.

He looked so bleak, as if he regretted everything. Her heart quavered at the thought. Was he regretting last night? Was he wishing he'd never returned to Westforth house, that he'd never—

He rubbed irritably at his throat, glowering.

"It's just a putrid throat. I'm sure you'll feel better by tomorrow."

"I doubt it." His voice faded on the last word, but she knew what he'd said all the same.

"I hate to say that I told you so, but . . ." Grinning, she climbed to her knees and placed her fist on her hips and said in as deep a voice as she could utter, " 'I am Brandon St. John and I never take cold. I never get ill. I never—' "

In two strides he was back at her side, grabbing her arms and hauling her out of bed. He allowed her feet to rest firmly on the floor, but held her against him, skin to skin, her breasts pressed against his chest, his hands holding her bottom intimately. He glinted down at her, a warning in his gaze.

"I was only teasing."

He didn't look pleased. But he also didn't look quite so annoyed.

Well. She supposed she should remember that not everyone was brought up in a household where wit and amusement were carried as far as they could go. And he *was* ill, which probably accounted for a great deal of his ill humor. "I am sorry that you feel poorly."

He arched a brow, but didn't answer.

"You can let me go now."

His gaze narrowed on her face, then dropped to her shoulders and beyond. He shook his head.

Her gaze narrowed. "Let me go, *now*."

Again he shook his head, only this time he snaked an arm about her waist and lifted her fully into his arms. To Verena's chagrin, he then nuzzled her neck, his hot breath sending shivers of delight through her.

Her body responded immediately, her breasts tightening, her breath catching in her throat. "You—you should stop that."

He nipped at her ear and she looped her arms

about his neck. "Really," she murmured, though she moved her head back to give him better access, "it's time you went home. Surely Chase or one of your brothers will be worried about you and—"

He stopped her with a hard kiss that sent her senses reeling. Verena forgot everything but the feel of his mouth over hers.

She kissed him back just as fervently as before, gasping when he broke the contact.

She struggled to regain her breath. Brandon's hair was mussed, a faint shadow dusted his jaw, and his left cheek showed a crease left by one of her pillows. There was no way he should have been attractive. But he was— devastatingly so. Damn it, why did men look better when they looked worse? It simply was not fair.

Brandon carefully set her back on her feet and tried to clear his throat, then winced. "Damn." The word swung in the silence like a creaky tavern sign.

"I'll call Herberts for some hot tea. That should help."

She reached down and picked up Brandon's breeches and tossed them to him. He caught them with one hand, but instead of tugging them on, he dropped them across the back of a chair.

Verena watched carefully, trying not to appear too interested in the perfect curl of hair that spread across his chest, then trickled to a thin line that went all the way to his—she shut her eyes a moment before taking a deep breath.

"Verena."

She opened her eyes and met his gaze.

"The list. Did you look for it here?"

Oh. They were back to that. Her chest almost ached with her disappointment. "James and I combed the entire house. Several times, in fact."

He placed his hand beneath her chin and turned her face to his. One of his brows lifted. "We searched everywhere."

Disappointment clouded his eyes. He nodded once and released her chin.

Verena felt strangely bereft. There was nothing wrong with being alone, she told herself. She was used to it. In fact, she usually enjoyed being alone. It could be quite pleasant at times. But for some reason, the thought made her throat tighten painfully.

Blast it, what was wrong with her this morning? She was a bundle of exposed nerves.

"I'm going to get dressed," she announced. Mainly because the silence and her wayward thoughts were beginning to tick far too loudly in her head.

She tried to walk with dignity to her dressing room. It was difficult considering she was naked and was growing more and more conscious of it by the moment.

It was one thing to be naked when romping in bed, and something entirely different when morning light streamed through the curtains and made the entire room seem painfully bright and exposed somehow.

Verena was only two steps away from the wardrobe when Brandon's arms closed about her. He scooped her up, took four strides, and set her back into bed.

"*Oh!*" She scrambled to her knees. "What was *that* for?"

He crossed his arms over his chest and stood smiling down at her, daring her without words to attempt to get off the bed.

Her own lips quivered in answer and suddenly, it seemed the most normal thing in the world to be naked in front of Brandon. "You can't keep me here forever."

"I can try," he said, only the first word audible. "Besides, you owe me some answers." He really needed some tea, she decided. She'd order some as soon as she figured out a way to get to the door.

Verena scooted toward the edge of the bed. He took a menacing step forward, his brows raised, a smile on his lips.

She chuckled. He grinned and took another step, then halted, glancing down at where his boots rested in front of him. The second his gaze left her, Verena lunged for the other side of the bed.

He beat her to it, blocking her way easily.

Verena flopped onto her bottom and yanked a sheet over her. "This is not fair! I have things to do today."

He nodded, a faint smile touching his mouth, his blue eyes agleam. "So do I. But this is far more important."

Verena bit her lip. He was so appealing, but she really needed to get up. Get out of the room. Anything to break the spell he seemed to have cast on her. "If you don't let me out of bed, I will scream. Herberts will come. And Peters with him." If anyone could stop Brand, it would be the hulking footman.

Brandon bunched his right hand into a fist and

smacked it into his left palm, a smile still on his face.

Verena had a sudden vision of that fist striking poor Herberts in the jaw. Ow. That would hurt. As annoying as her butler was, he really didn't deserve to be attacked by a six-foot-three warrior, for that was exactly what St. John looked like as he stood by her bed.

She eyed him covertly. Gone was the perfectly pressed cravat, the form-fitting coat, the flashing watch fob, the knitted trousers . . . nothing was left but the man. Bold and naked and mouth-wateringly male.

That was the problem; Verena was finding Brandon the man a little too attractive. Every finely muscled inch of him. Which normally wouldn't be a problem since she was a woman of the world.

Wasn't she?

It was just that right now, with James's life on the line because of those damn love letters—Verena's thoughts caught. What time was it? She and James were supposed to meet this morning.

He wanted to visit every guest from the dinner party. James was certain one of them held the key to Humford's lost list.

She whirled in the bed, frowning at the face of the clock over the mantel. Ah, it was only nine-thirty; she still had a half an hour. She suddenly became aware of St. John's steady gaze.

He glanced from her to the clock and back, his brows lowered. "Expecting someone?" he asked in a hoarse whisper.

"James," she said as airily as she could. "He'll be here any moment now."

Brandon crossed his arms over his chest and rocked back on his heels. He seemed unable to look away from where she sat in the middle of the bed, sheets tangled about her.

"Brandon, you cannot just keep me here. It's . . . barbaric."

He flicked a glance over her, his lips curving in amusement. Verena's cheeks heated. She pulled the sheet tighter about her.

This was an excellent example of why she could never have Brandon in her life. She had allowed him into only one small area, yet he had set up camp and was now planning ways to invade and conquer every other aspect of her existence. She could see it in his eyes.

She climbed back to her knees and pulled the sheet completely free from the bed then wrapped it about her. Trying to stay somewhat modest, she tied the ends in a fat knot at her shoulder.

Verena rather fancied she looked like a Grecian maiden. She peeked at Brandon, but he appeared singularly unimpressed with her ability to make her own clothing out of practically nothing.

The beast. "I want up."

He shook his head.

"*Now.*"

A faint grin curved his mouth.

That was it. She held her head high as she walked on her knees to the edge of the bed, her gesture edged with irritation. "Don't push me, St. John. I'm in no mood."

His grinned widened and suddenly, Verena's

irritation erupted. She placed two fingers to her lips, kissed them, then placed them on her ass.

The gesture, one as old as time, drew an immediate response. Before she could lift her hand from her rump, Verena found herself pinned to the mattress, his body completely covering hers.

She was a captive in her own bed, Brandon's delectable mouth only inches from hers. The only question was—did she really want to escape?

# Chapter 16

*The problem with the gentry is that they don't have no outlet fer their baser instincts. All that angst collects in their liver and there it sits, spoilin' away, causin' all manner of sour looks and bad dispositions.*

Dawson, the Duke of Devonshire's head footman, to Belvins, His Grace's valet, as the two stood in line in the front hall awaiting His Grace's arrival

**V**erena struggled. "Let me up!"

Brand caught her chin and turned her face to his. His touch was amazingly gentle, a definite question darkening his gaze.

Verena swallowed. His fingers were so warm. And he was ill; she could see by the glitter of his eyes that he still had a bit of fever.

He seemed to sense her softening, for his lips curved into the faintest hint of a smile as he gently brushed her hair from her forehead.

She was proof against anything but his tenderness. It made her all the more determined to get free. "Brandon, let me up. *Please.*"

For a long moment, he stared at her as if assessing her thoughts. Then, to her surprise, he rolled off and grabbed his pants. He jerked them on in a matter of seconds.

She lifted herself on her elbows, faintly aware of a sense of disappointment. Of course he'd finally been forced to agree with her—what else could he do?

Still . . . it might have been interesting if he'd tried other, more persuasive ways of getting her to agree with him. It was rather disheartening to see him give up so quickly.

In fact, she felt a little insulted. "You're leaving. Good. I want you to leave. In fact, I want you to—"

He opened the door. All he had on were his pants, which could only mean he wasn't leaving her house, but was just going to search her house by himself, the braggart. Hadn't she already told him that she and James had searched—

*Good God, James.* As if to verify her fears, the clock chimed the hour—he was due at any second. And when he arrived, he'd find Brandon stalking about the house wearing nothing but his breeches.

Verena didn't need to imagine James's reaction—she knew exactly what he'd do. There would be bloodshed—either fisticuffs or even worse . . . a duel perhaps. She gulped at the thought. James was Father's son—he handled a pistol with an accuracy that defied description. As for a small sword, there was no equal. Verena scrambled from the bed. She *had* to stop Brandon.

"*Wait!*" The sheets fell off her shoulder and tangled about her knees. She stumbled, catching the bedpost just in time. "Blasted sheets." She kicked them away and hurried to the door. She was almost there when she realized that she was naked. "Damn!" Verena dashed to her wardrobe just long enough to yank out a frilly pink robe. She pulled it on as she flew out the door.

Brand heard the desperate slap of her bare feet on the wood floor behind him, but he didn't pause. By God, he'd get her brother to answer his questions about that damned list.

He made his way to the stairs, his stride eating up the distance. He'd just reached the end of the hall when his heel came down on something sharp.

He winced, then paused to look and see what it was. As he bent to pick up a small stone that must have been carried in from the street, Verena's voice sounded in his ear, low and threatening.

"If you go downstairs dressed like that, I will personally render you limb from limb."

He glanced down at her. She was no longer clothed in just a sheet, which was a relief in itself. He'd been hard pressed not to take her again, especially after she'd had the audacity to walk about the bed dressed in that wildly indecent toga.

Of course, now that he looked at it, the pink robe wasn't much better. A froth of ruffles framed her neckline and drew attention to her lush curves, the material amazingly sheer. So sheer that he could make out her nipples through the front of the gown. Nipples that he'd tasted and teased only hours ago. Nipples that peeked as if eager to be cupped in his hand yet again and—

She crossed her arms over her chest. Brandon lifted his gaze to find her eyeing him with a disgusted look.

"Must you do that?" she asked.

"Yes." He didn't think he could help it, even if he had wanted to try.

She shifted her arms so that they covered her entire chest. "You cannot walk about the house dressed like that." She glanced down at her own dress and grimaced. "And neither can I."

"I want answers."

"You'll get them. It's just that—" She sighed. "That blasted list is not here. Or if it is, we cannot find it."

"What do we do?" His voice broke completely on the last word, but he didn't care.

"James and I are going to visit all the guests from the dinner party. We're hoping one of them will remember something—anything."

That made sense. It made a lot of sense, now that he thought about it. He nodded. "Very well."

She tilted her head to one side. "And you? What will you do?"

"I will visit the Home Office."

Her gaze widened. "Do you think that's wise? I'd be afraid they'd—"

Someone knocked on the front door, the rap of the brass knocker echoing in the foyer.

Verena whirled to face the top of the steps. "Oh no!" She grabbed Brandon's arm and tried to tug him back down the hallway. "That's James. Hurry!"

Brandon took a step back, grinning down at her bent head. He couldn't help it—she was taking him back to her room, back to her bed. Back to the place where he'd made her his. Now that he thought about it, why would he complain about *that*?

She really was the most delectable woman of his acquaintance. Especially now. Her face was flushed, her hair streaming wildly, gold curls clinging to her shoulders and arms, and her pink robe gaping in a most intriguing way.

His interest piqued, he let her push him all the way into her room. Herberts's voice echoed up the stairs as he greeted Verena's brother. Lansdowne's deeper answers were equally audible.

Verena shut the door on their voices and leaned against it. She pressed her hands to either side of her as if to further barricade him in. "You have no idea how close of an escape that was."

Escape? From what? Lansdowne might be Verena's brother, but he was not an overly large man. Brandon could have taken the brute on without the least problem. "Why are we hiding?"

"James would take exception to seeing a man walking through my house half naked. He's deadly with both pistol and sword and he has a temper that is unsteady, at best. You wouldn't stand a chance."

Brandon almost laughed. He wasn't afraid of Lansdowne, though perhaps it was to his benefit if Verena didn't realize that.

She seemed genuinely concerned for him. To Brandon's surprise, he found the thought . . . appealing. And very convenient. "Tell me why you and James are looking for the list."

"Brandon, someone has something of James's . . . some letters written to a woman with a very powerful husband."

"He is being blackmailed?"

She moved to the bedpost and rested her cheek against the curtained hanging. "I fear for his life."

"Is it that serious?"

"Yes. The tone of the notes they have been sending . . . they are very threatening."

Brandon frowned. He could see the fear in her eyes. "What a coil."

"I know. James always falls in love with the most unsuitable women. Father despaired of him for this one reason."

"Do you know who has these letters?"

"No. But whoever it is will exchange them for only one thing."

Brandon closed his eyes. The list. God, this was getting more complicated by the moment.

Verena picked up her discarded sheet and sat on the edge of the bed, pleating and unpleating the linen. "We have searched the whole house for that stupid thing and we cannot find it. I don't think it's here."

Where could it be, then? Brand's gaze narrowed thoughtfully on Verena. The morning sun was now well up, sending bright beams through the cracks in the curtain. One especially brave beam of light was now resting on Verena's feet, striping each of her toes with a band of gold.

Brandon found he couldn't look away from her small feet. For all her bravado, she was alone in the world, a fact she seemed to ignore. She seemed so strong, so capable, that it was easy to forget she wasn't like the other women of his acquaintance, all of whom had family nearby.

Brandon rubbed his neck wearily. *What the hell*

*am I supposed to do now?* They both needed that blasted list and neither of them knew where it was. Whatever happened, he knew he couldn't just leave this situation to unfold on its own. He crossed to the bed and pulled her to her feet. He placed his finger beneath her chin and brought her gaze to his. "We'll find this list, Verena. I promise."

Her gaze never wavered. "And then what?"

Brand mimed tearing it in half.

She managed a faint smile. "I wish it was that easy." She sighed, then leaned against him.

He held her to him and then stood, his chin against her forehead, his breath stirring her hair.

What *would* they do when they found Humford's list? Brandon closed his eyes, aware of a dull ache behind his temples.

He was aware of every nuance of the moment. Of the way her head fit against his shoulder. Of her heavenly scent—one of soap and lavender and crisp linens. Of the slight weight of her body against his. Having her in his arms was a natural gesture, one that felt as comforting as if they'd stood this way a thousand times.

He supposed they should move now. She needed to dress and he—he needed to get away. To think about how best to deal with this problem.

But the moment seemed too delicate—as if the slightest movement would break the accord they'd reached. He found that he didn't want to move. Ever.

The peace stretched and embraced. It was with a disappointed sigh that Brand heard Herberts's boots clambering up the steps to the door. A loud knock sounded.

Verena lifted her head. "I forgot to lo—"

The door opened and the butler stomped in, coming to an abrupt halt when he saw his mistress in Brand's arms. " 'Ere now!"

Verena started, trying to pull free of Brand's grip.

He held her tightly, though, challenging the butler with a look.

Herberts's cheeks colored. "Ah, pardon me, m'lady, but yer brother's come to visit wif ye. He's waitin' downstairs, he is."

Verena nodded. "Thank you, Herberts. I'll be right down."

The butler *tsked* loudly. "Oiye hopes ye come downstairs quick like. Oiye don't like to see ye cavortin' in such a way."

"Then don't look," Brandon said brutally.

Herberts rubbed a hand on his chin. "Oiye suppose oiye could do that."

"Herberts," Verena said with a sigh. "Have some tea sent to the sitting room once I leave. Mr. St. John has a rough throat from being in the rain yesterday."

"He does, does he?" The butler wiped his nose on his sleeve. "Oiye suppose oiye can have some tea brought to the sittin' room fer him. But not here." He gave Verena and Brandon a last, unhappy look, then he turned and trudged out of the room.

Verena gave Brand a watery smile. "He's just being protective."

"I know." Brandon wouldn't have stood for such insubordination otherwise.

She turned in his arms and he reluctantly let

her go. She walked to her dressing room, halting on the threshold as if struggling with something. Finally, she turned to face him. "Humford. You told me he had been murdered. Was it . . . was it very brutal? I wouldn't ask, but if the people who have James's letters are the same ones who killed Humford . . ."

Brandon saw it then, saw the fear in her violet eyes. Fear she kept hidden away, perhaps even from herself. But this was not something that should be withheld. "He was garroted, his body tossed into the Thames."

She paled, her hands gripping the doorframe until her fingers turned white. "I see," she whispered. She took a deep breath and released it, dropping her hands to her sides. "Thank you," she said softly. "I needed to know."

Brandon took a step forward, more alarmed than he cared to admit. "Verena—" His voice still creaked like a rusted gate, but she seemed to understand.

"I'll be careful. I have to be; James needs me." She straightened her shoulders, seeming to grow taller. "I must dress. You may wait here if you'd like. James and I will be leaving almost immediately." She offered him one last, polite smile, then she disappeared into her dressing room, the door closing behind her.

Brand took two steps towards the door, then stopped. She'd dismissed him. Coolly and without the slightest trace of emotion.

He knew all about politely dismissing someone. After all, he'd done it most of his adult life. It would never do to be the one who cared more.

Brandon knew all the rules and he lived by them. But this was the first time a woman had actually dismissed *him*.

Bloody hell, what was he supposed to do now? His jaw tight, he collected his things and began to dress. Both he and Verena needed that list—and badly. What would happen when they did find it? Verena would fight to the death to protect her brother and frankly, Brandon couldn't fault her for that. He would do the same had it been his brother.

But how was Brandon to fulfill his promise to Wycham? It seemed an impossible knot, so tightly tied that nothing could loosen it. But even if he and Verena managed to solve their differences over Humford's list, it would not help their other problems.

Brandon wanted Verena. And not just for a few hours. He wanted her in his bed, morning, noon, and night. The feeling would pall, it always did. But in the meantime . . . he'd never felt such a strong pull before. Had never experienced such blinding passion mixed with something else . . . a tenderness perhaps.

He shook his head ruefully as he put the finishing touches on his cravat. The door to the adjoining chamber opened and then closed and he heard Verena's footsteps down the hall. She walked past the door and descended the stairs, her skirts rustling as she went, her footsteps muffled on the heavy carpet runner.

Brandon listened to the murmur of voices as she and James spoke briefly in the hallway, followed by the firm thud of the door as they left.

Brandon stopped by the bed to gather his boots. The sheets and counterpane were tumbled in a large ball, the pillows scattered hither and yon. He touched the pillow where he'd held Verena to the bed and smiled when he thought of her mischievous expression.

His mood lightened. No sense in getting upset about a future that had not yet arrived. Surely he and Verena would find the list and do what must be done. And that alone would take a week or two. Suddenly feeling more hopeful, Brandon peeked out into the hallway to make certain that Herberts was not about. Then he left Verena's bedchamber and quietly let himself out of the house.

The sun had broken through the clouds and now warmed the air. Brandon paused on the bottom step, looking around the street. Everything seemed new. Fresh, somehow. He smiled to himself and tossed a coin to an urchin in a tattered blue coat who stood near his carriage.

The boy bit the edge of the coin, then pocketed it with a muffled "thankee guv'nor" and off he went.

Brandon climbed into his carriage. There was one thing he did know . . . so long as James was in London, Verena was in growing danger. She might not know it, but Brandon was about to become an even greater presence in her life.

Come what may, the St. Johns always took care of their own. And for this time, however brief it might be, Verena was his, every delightful inch of her.

# Chapter 17

*I wouldn't live much differently if I were a rich man. I've simple tastes. All I'd want is a large house, fine carriages, perfectly matched horses, an elegant wardrobe, an opera-box near the prince's, a master cook, pocket money, and a fancy piece or two. That's all.*

Blevins, the Duke of Devonshire's valet, to his master, while assisting that worthy individual into his coat

**B**rand went home where Poole, on discerning that his master's voice was not up to full strength, immediately set about making Brand's existence even more miserable by attempting to convince him to accept a mustard plaster to his chest. Brand protested as best as he could without raising his voice, though it took a good amount of growling to get Poole to leave him be.

Brandon finally escaped to White's. Once he arrived in that hallowed hall, he took up a newspaper and retired to the corner. He didn't read it, of course. His mind was too busy sifting through the situation at hand to allow for such luxury.

But the newspaper barrier protected him from the dangers of inconsequential chatter and having to deal with all the revelry that would take place had anyone discovered his rusty voice.

After an hour of sitting and sipping tea liberally laced with brandy, Brand found that his voice had made a very minor recovery. He could at least speak a few short, pithy phrases—two or three words, providing he rested his voice between times.

That was all well and good, though it did little to assuage the feeling that he had to take some action and quick. Brand rustled the paper and stared blindly at an advertisement for shoe blacking.

Suddenly restless, Brand tossed the paper aside and stretched his legs before him. He had to find that damned list. For Verena's sake as well as Wycham's. But what to do once he had it? He frowned. Perhaps they could make a copy and—

"Brandon?"

Brand recognized Wycham's voice instantly. "Roger!" he croaked, then rubbed his throat. It was far too early for exclamations.

Roger stood before him, looking pale and wan, his cravat hastily knotted, his coat wrinkled. He raked a hand through his hair and offered Brandon a sick smile. "I know you said to stay away, but I had to come."

Concerned, Brandon gestured to the chair opposite his.

Roger dropped into the chair then glanced around nervously. He pulled his chair further behind a plant that shadowed the table. "I just arrived in town and stopped by your lodgings. Your man said you were feeling a trifle off." He peered anxiously at Brand. "Are you ill?"

Brandon shook his head. "Just my throat. Why are you here?"

"I couldn't stand not knowing what was happening another minute." Roger leaned forward to say urgently, "Brand, Colburn sent a letter to my father. If I hadn't been on the lookout for it, my father might have gotten it and—"

"Colburn?"

"He's with the Home Office. He's the one who met me at Humford's. He and some other man, Farraday or Farraway or something like that. God, I don't remember!" Roger huddled forward, wetting his lips nervously, his gaze strained as he searched Brandon's face. "Have you found it yet? Do you know where it is?"

Everyone seemed to believe that it was in the Westforth townhouse, though Brand had his doubts. Verena and James had searched . . . but where could that damned list be if not there?

Brand pushed the thought away—he didn't want to draw more attention to Verena than necessary. She had enough problems of her own. "Need more information," he croaked.

"More? I've already told you everything I know." Wycham slumped miserably. "Brandon, things have gotten worse."

Brand lifted his brows.

"I'm sorry. I don't mean to be melodramatic." Roger rubbed his face with both hands. Though he was appropriately dressed for the club, his neckcloth was mussed, his waistcoat buttoned crooked, his hair twisted in the front as if he'd been clutching it. "The letter from the Home Office to my father—the one I intercepted. Colburn is giving me one week to return the lost list or he is coming to arrest me."

A week. Bloody hell. "Roger, did Humford tell you what was on this list?"

"Names, I suspect. Ten, maybe twelve. I don't know." A shadow flittered over his face and for a second, he looked older than his twenty-odd years. "I must thank you for your help. You've been everything kind while I—" He managed a twisted smile. "I haven't always been what I should have been, you know. I've frittered away my life; my father is right about that. But once this is over, I will change."

"We've all done things we've thought better of after the fact."

Wycham wiped his hands on his breeches. "I will never again wager or touch a card. And I will visit my father more often, too. He knows something is amiss, but he hasn't said a word."

Brand could feel the pain in Wycham's voice and he wished he knew of a way to alleviate it. "I will do what I can, Roger. We will find the list. I promise." Every word pronounced. Thank God for hot tea. Brand's throat felt better by the second.

Roger's smile became more genuine. "You will succeed, Brandon. You always do."

A member of the club came by and murmured a greeting to Brand, glancing curiously at Wycham.

Wycham put a self-conscious hand to his neck-cloth. "I must go. If Colburn finds that I'm in town—Brand, please keep me informed. I'm going mad not knowing what's happening. Just send word to my lodgings. My manservant can get it to me quicker than the post."

Brand nodded. "I will let you know the instant I find something."

Wycham grabbed his hand with both of his and squeezed. "Thank you! You know I wouldn't have come except for that damned letter from Colburn to my father. I don't mean to rush you, but I'm not the one bringing everything to a point."

Perhaps the time had come to meet this Colburn and face the Home Office officials who had the audacity to threaten the son of an earl. "Where is Colburn?"

Wycham paled. "No! You don't want to—stay away from him, Brand. He's not a nice man."

Neither was Brand when it came to protecting his friends and family. Besides, there was a possibility that Colburn might be able to assist Verena. Whoever was blackmailing James knew all about Humford and the list. There was a connection somewhere and it was possible the Home Office already knew what it was.

It was a very slight possibility, but at this point, Brand was willing to do whatever he had to. He was still haunted by the sight of Verena's face when he told her about Humford's death.

"I must go," Roger said. "They might send another letter to my father and I have to be there to intercept it. I think they hope to badger me into giving them what they want. But I don't have that damned list! And even if I did—" Wycham gulped, his eyes panic-filled. "Brand, did you . . . were you able to gain entrance into Lady Westforth's house?"

Brand nodded.

"Good, I—be careful, will you? At first, I

thought Verena was innocent, caught in the middle of this affair by the unfortunate circumstances of her dinner party and Humford's death. Now . . ." Wycham gave a shaky laugh. "I don't know who or what to believe anymore."

Brand felt a surge of irritation, but he quickly suppressed it. "All will be well."

Wycham looked grateful. "You are a far better friend than I deserve. And I'm fully aware of the debt I will owe you once this incident is over."

"Port," Brandon said. "Cases of it."

Wycham managed a grin. "It's yours. Now I must go. It will take me the better part of the day to get back home. Take care, Brand. Remember what happened to Humford."

Brand was not likely to forget—every time he thought about it, he pictured Verena's wide violet eyes. He watched as Roger quickly strode away, his head bowed, his shoulders hunched. Wycham was a fool to come to town.

Brand ordered another cup of tea laced with brandy, rubbing his throat as he did so. If he was going to face the lion in the lion's den, he would need every drop of his voice that he could find.

Several hours and several pots of tea later, Brandon felt much better. He grimaced to hear his own voice—it was deeper and rougher sounding, as if he'd been to sea for years on end. But it had lost its tendency to waver, so he couldn't really complain.

He entered a small office located off Timms Street and took off his greatcoat and hat. "Good day. Mr. St. John to see Sir Colburn."

A narrow-faced young man with protuberant eyes jumped up from his desk. "Yes, sir! We received your note an hour ago. Sir Colburn has been waiting." He escorted Brand down a high, drafty hall and stopped before a door, knocked, then opened it.

Brand entered. The room before him was cozily furnished—a faded rug softened the wood floors, the walls lined with overflowing bookshelves, books and papers stacked here and there. A large oak desk sat at the far end while several chairs were scattered about the length of the narrow office, seemingly at random.

For all that the day was overcast, the room was warmed by the yellow pool of light thrown by a bright lantern that sat on the corner of the large desk. Two men sat in the center of the room, one at the desk and one further away, hidden almost in the shadows. They both climbed to their feet on Brand's entrance.

Sir Colburn had the appearance of a benevolent grandfather. His white hair gleamed softly in the gloom, his eyes crinkling into an instant smile. "Mr. St. John. I hope you don't mind, but when I received your request for a meeting, I asked Farragut to join us. He has a special interest in the matter you wished to discuss."

Mr. Farragut bowed. He was a shorter, balding man with piercing dark eyes and a thick neck. "St. John."

Brand inclined his head. "Farragut. Sir Colburn. I hope you will forgive my voice."

"Bit scratchy, eh? Had the same problem myself about a month ago. Perhaps you would like some brandy for your throat? Or some hot tea? I have tea every day at four sharp. Does the constitution wonders."

Brand thought he'd float away if he had to drink one more cup of tea, but it was possible he'd need it before the meeting was over. "Tea would be fine."

Colburn immediately went to a tea set that sat on the large desk. He poured two cups, adding a dash of brandy before he brought them back to the table, setting one in front of Brandon and the other in front of a large winged back chair that headed the table.

"Thank you," Brandon murmured. He had just picked up the cup when he caught Farragut's gaze on him, a condescending look on the man's rather square face. "You don't drink tea, Mr. Farragut?"

A faint sneer touched his thick face. "Tea is fer women and nabobs as walk around with their noses in the air."

Colburn winced a bit, then cast a deprecating glance at Brand. "Though Mr. Farragut lacks certain social skills, he is one of my best agents, which is why I've had him on this case."

"Case?"

The old man set down his cup and sighed heavily. "Yes. It has become that, I'm afraid. Let's get to business, shall we? Mr. St. John, I was surprised to receive your request for this meeting. I probably should have known you'd ask for it— the St. Johns are not known to be cowardly and a frontal attack is always the most successful."

"You know why I'm here."

"Your friend, Viscount Wycham."

Brand set down his cup. "Roger is not involved in this business. I fear you've made an error."

"An error?" Farragut said. He gave a short, ugly laugh. "We don't make errors, St. John. Wycham is as guilty as—"

"Arthur." Colburn shook his head.

Farragut's mouth worked as if he would argue, but he subsided, satisfying himself by glaring at Brandon.

Colburn sighed. "It's a sad business. I know you come in an effort to clear your friend's name, but things are desperate. We've lost something. Something worth a lot of money to the right people, though we want it for another reason—to save lives."

"Whose lives?"

Colburn's mouth lifted in a faint smile. "The lives of some very important people are at risk. The list we've lost is of some of our top agents in various ports about the continent. We must recover it. If it falls into the wrong hands, our people will die." He shook his head, his blue eyes genuinely troubled.

"I thought it was something serious, but this . . ."

"It gets worse. We are not the only ones after it. Someone else has been pursuing it, someone willing to kill if necessary."

Brand took a drink. "Like they killed Humford?"

Colburn hesitated, then nodded. "We didn't foresee that. Of course, it's partly his fault this entire situation came into being."

"He worked for you?"

Colburn and Farragut exchanged glances. Colburn placed the tips of his fingers together. "Occasionally, when we had minor issues, we'd use Humford as a courier—"

"Only when forced," Farragut added, a curl to his lip. It was obvious he thought very little of Humford. In fact, Brand was beginning to believe the man thought very little of everyone.

"We gave him only very unimportant errands," Colburn said, then gave a deprecating smile. "We wouldn't have used him at all, but his uncle is a man of some influence in the House of Lords. Our funding is dependent on such connections."

"What happened to Humford?"

"He made a very foolish error. Two weeks ago, one of our regular operatives disappeared. We were astounded, for the woman in question had served us for years. Out of desperation, we used Humford. We did not tell him how serious a job he was given. We thought that if he didn't know, he wouldn't make any errors." Colburn shook his head. "I'm afraid our thinking worked a little too well."

Farragut snorted. "The man was a fool. Whoever garrotted him wasted their time—he was almost too drunk to stand. A good shove into the Thames would have served just as well, and been neater, to boot."

Colburn cast a severe glance at Farragut. "Whatever Humford's personal problems, we are indeed sorry that he was killed."

"I'm not," Farragut growled. "Good riddance, I say."

Colburn ignored him. "We think Humford told someone about his mission. Someone who realized the value of what he carried." The old gentleman paused. "We believe this person laid in wait for him outside of Lady Westforth's house, then they dragged him into an alley, and did the deed there."

*Waited outside Lady Westforth's house.* Brand dropped his gaze to the teacup on the table before him, the words thrumming through his head. "Why do you think Wycham was involved in any of this? He is not capable of such a crime."

Farragut gave a wide grin. "Ye don't know yer friend as well as ye think. He had both the motive and the opportunity."

"What motive?"

Colburn answered. "Forty thousand pounds in gambling debts. Wycham is desperate. Desperate men do not always act in ways they normally would."

Good God. Brandon wondered how Roger was going to tell his father. "I didn't know he owed that much, but he is not the type of man to murder someone."

Farragut snorted. "Then why is he hidin' behind his father's coattails if he's so innocent?"

"He's waiting to see if I can find this list and prove his innocence."

Colburn took a sip of tea, setting the delicate china back into the plate with a faint click. "If Wycham didn't do it himself, then it is possible that he hired someone."

"Impossible."

"He has been seen with some questionable men.

Men whom we have reason to suspect are attempting to do what they can to harm our country."

"He owes money and he talks to malcontents."
Brand shrugged. "If that's all it takes to become a
suspect, then you'll be interviewing at least half
the *ton*."

"Mr. St. John," Colburn said with a frown. "I
don't think you understand how serious this is. I
agreed to meet you for two reasons. One, because
I thought you might be able to assist us in what is
a most crucial matter. And two, there is every like-
lihood that you, Lady Westforth, and even
Wycham, if he is indeed innocent as you believe,
are all in dire danger."

Thank God Wycham was on his way back to
Devonshire. But Verena . . . Brand thought of her,
alone at Westforth House with nothing but a few
servants to protect her. Brand remembered how
remarkably easy it had been to enter her house
undetected the night before. The shutters on the
house were old and easily maneuvered.

He stirred impatiently. "What evidence do you
have?"

Farragut blew out his breath, his ears red.
"Against yer friend Wycham? Not as much as
we'd like, but enough to lock him up until he co-
operates."

Brand fixed him with a cold gaze. "Enough to
justify ruining his life?"

"Ruin?" Farragut's mouth twisted in disgust.
"Ask Humford what it's like to be really ruined,
him with his throat sliced open and the fish eatin'
his eyes—"

"Farragut!" Colburn's voice turned brittle. "I

warned you about your manners. Perhaps you should leave us."

The man's face grew red to match his ears. He stared challengingly at Colburn, but after a moment, he shoved back his chair and stood. "Very well. I'll go. But the gent should know we will find that list, one way or t'other." He gave Brand a last warning look, then turned and stalked out the door, slamming it in his wake.

"You will have to forgive Farragut. He discovered Humford's body. It greatly upset him."

Brand finished his tea. "Mr. Farragut does not approve of me."

"Arthur?" Colburn gave Brandon a rueful smile. "He dislikes anyone who is not in the service. You should see him sneer at the prince."

"At least I'm in good company."

"Indeed." Colburn's smile faded, an anxious expression entered his eyes. "Mr. St. John, I hesitate to ask you for a favor when your own position is so difficult. You are close to Wycham. I believe the two of you attended Eton together?"

Brandon nodded.

Sir Colburn ran his finger around the rim of his teacup. "I hesitate to say anything because of the delicacy of the subject. But we've noticed that you've also become close to Lady Westforth."

Brandon nodded slowly. They must be watching her house. The thought was far from reassuring.

Damn it, this was worse than he'd realized. He wished he had the ability to spirit Verena away, to hide her until he could figure out a way to control the ugliness that was brewing. But he knew she'd never allow such a thing. "What a coil."

A flicker of amusement brightened Colburn's faded eyes. He picked up his cup, his large, veined hand contrasting with the delicate china. "Yes, it is. A very large, sticky coil. Mr. St. John, do *you* perchance know who has the list?"

"No. No, I don't."

Colburn's gaze never wavered. After a moment he sighed. "I didn't think you did, but I had hoped . . ."

"Are you certain that Humford had this list with him when he went to Lady Westforth's? Perhaps he left it somewhere else."

"No, he had it when he entered her house. We know that much for certain."

"How?"

Colburn smiled. "Trust me. We know for a fact he had the list on him when he entered Westforth House. After that . . ." He shrugged. "Our only consolation in this whole business is that apparently whomever killed Humford did not find what they were looking for, either."

"I don't like this business."

"Neither do we." Colburn sighed. "I wish you would step down and let us take it from here. We could offer Lady Westforth protection, you know."

"Like you protected Humford."

"That was an error." Colburn pressed his hands together, steepling his fingers. "Lady Westforth is indeed a lovely woman. No one would argue that point. But she's not all she seems. It's only fair that I warn you. She and her brother—" Colburn clicked his tongue. "An unfortunate business, that."

Brand said nothing. He wasn't surprised to find that there were secrets in Verena's life—he'd guessed as much already. She wasn't a simple miss straight from the schoolroom and she'd never pretended to be otherwise. She was a wildly passionate, intensely feminine woman. And behind her outwardly quiet life were all manner of untold secrets.

One day, Brandon would know them all.

Colburn leaned back, pushing his chair from the table. "I can see you're set on this course, foolish as it is. As much as I hate to say this, if the list is not found immediately, we will have to take steps."

"Such as?"

"If necessary, we will take both Viscount Wycham *and* Lady Westforth into custody and hold them until we discover where that blasted list has gone."

"How do you know it hasn't been . . . dispersed."

"Because we know the parties interested in purchasing this list. They all wait. Since none of them have yet to leave the country, we must assume the list is still here."

Brandon pushed back his chair and stood. "Thank you for speaking with me. You've told me far more than I'd hoped you would."

Colburn stood as well. "We are an open book, Mr. St. John. If you have a question, call again. If it is at all possible, I will answer it."

Brandon looked down at his empty cup, a thought dawning. "Sir Colburn, just how large is this list?"

"Large? Oh it's quite small." He held up his

hands to indicate a very small square the size of a miniature blotter.

Brand nodded. "Thank you. I will be in touch."

"Excellent. And Mr. St. John, if you find the list, I do hope you return it to us here."

Brandon's jaw tightened. Finally, he sighed. "Yes. I will bring it directly to you."

"That's all I ask." Colburn pursed his lips, a faint frown flittering between his brows. "It would take a clever person to orchestrate this scheme. Between your friend Wycham and Lady Westforth, I believe the lady is the more clever."

Brandon couldn't argue with that. He held out his hand.

"Best of luck, St. John," Colburn said, shaking Brandon's hand. "I hope, for your sake, that you prove us wrong—on all accounts."

# Chapter 18

*I'd prefer to have a new horse to a mistress. It is always so gratifying to be welcomed at the price of a carrot rather than a ruby necklace.*

His Grace, the Duke of Devonshire,
to his friend, Sir Robert Daltry,
while bidding on a horse at Tattersall's

**V**erena dropped onto the settee in the sitting room, her white organdy skirts billowing about her. "I am too tired to visit anyone else. My feet hurt and my hair is falling down because of this horrid rain. If you want to see Lady Bessington, you'll have to go there by yourself."

It had been an agonizing day spent visiting every person who'd attended that fateful dinner party. And it had all been for naught. All they'd really learned was that word of Lord Humford's death was spreading among the *ton* and everyone had a sudden memory of the man, most much kinder than the reality.

It was fortunate that current gossip hadn't also included the manner of his death, just that he was found floating in the Thames, an apparent victim of a robbery. Verena repressed a shudder. What a horrible way to die.

James paced in front of the fireplace, his hands clasped behind his back. "I'll visit Lady Bessington later this evening at the theatre. She's the last person from that damned dinner party that we have to visit. Except, of course, Viscount Wycham."

That was strange, Wycham out of town during the season. Verena had met Wycham at a gaming hell almost two years ago and he was notoriously personable.

She wondered if Brandon knew where the young peer was. They were rumored to have been friends. She tried to picture the rather immature Wycham with Brandon, but could not quite picture it.

James rubbed a hand over his face. "We've spent the whole day searching for clues and found nothing."

"Perhaps Lady Bessington will be the answer. Someone has to have heard Humford say something irregular."

"I hope you're right," James said. "I hate the theatre, but they say she never misses a performance."

"I dislike it, myself. Father can outact any thespian to trod the boards."

"So he can. If I can catch Lady B before the production begins, I shall make my escape forthwith."

Verena kicked off her shoes. They'd visited no fewer than nine people today. That was nine houses, nine long inane conversations all leading back to the night of their dinner party and Lord Humford's mysterious death, and numerous glasses of tepid tea and stale cakes.

She never wanted to see another teacup for the rest of her life.

James's pacing slowed, his brow furrowed. "We must think this through. What exactly have we discovered so far?"

"That Lady Jessup is in dire need of a housekeeper and that Mr. Sinclair has the best scones. I really must get that recipe for Cook."

He regarded her with a flat stare. "You've been in rare form today."

She bit her lip. She had been a little flippant. It was just that she feared that if she stopped to think, then her fears for her brother would freeze her into a block of pulsing indecision.

Verena glanced at James from beneath her lashes. He was a little pale today and she suspected he was feeling a bit frantic.

So was she. Which was why she'd spent the entire day trying to stay focused on more pleasant thoughts. Like last night . . . the feel of Brandon's possessive hands as they'd roamed over her . . . the scent of his cologne on her sheets . . . the way his eyes gleamed when she'd pressed him to the mattress.

A pleasurable shiver traced through her. He was an amazing man; a pity he was so overbearing. Of course in bed, being overbearing could add to a talent already strong, rather than detract from it. But at the dinner table and in daily life, such a propensity would cause nothing but discord.

Discord and disappointment. Brandon St. John was made for the silks and satins of the *ton*—a place Verena had never been made welcome.

She pushed her shoes further away. It didn't really matter what the *ton* thought of her. Neither she nor Brandon had any intentions of allowing their relationship to progress past the "pleasant" stage.

And that was as it should be, she told herself severely. She adjusted the pretty garnet bracelet on her wrist in an attempt to hold a swelter of emotion at bay.

"Did you even hear me?" James asked.

She blinked at him, suddenly aware that he was speaking, and had been speaking, for some time now. "I . . . oh, were you talking?"

"To myself, apparently. What is wrong? You seem out of sorts. In fact," James continued, looking at her with narrowed eyes, "you've been acting very differently today. What have you—"

A sharp rap sounded and Herberts stuck his head around the door. His gold tooth caught the light. "There ye be, missus! Ye've a visitor. Shall oiye show him in?"

"Herberts, please do not stick your head around the door like that. You look like a disembodied specter. Just come inside and say what you have to say."

He brightened, but stayed where he was. "A specter, eh? Perhaps oiye should yell 'Boo!' the next time oiye comes to announce a guest." He made a horrid face, rolling his eyes back in his head. "Ooooooh!"

Verena had to swallow a grin, relieved that she could at least still smile. "Who is our guest?"

The butler's spectral mime disappeared before an arch look. "Oh, oiye thinks ye know who 'tis, missus. Ye knows him *very* well."

Verena's heart quickened. Blast it, why did she react this way just on thinking of his name? "Mr. St. John."

"In all his bloomin' glory. Oiye must say, 'tis refreshin' to see the man wif his shirt on."

Verena's cheeks heated. She cast a swift glance at her brother and found him staring at the butler as if he'd suffered a severe shock.

"Show Mr. St. John in," she said, hoping James wouldn't find his voice before Herberts could escape.

"Very well, missus. Oiye'll show him in, though oiye daresay he knows the way." The butler winked broadly and disappeared.

"What," James said in a voice that sounded remarkably like Father's, "was *that* all about?"

"It's Herberts, James. Who knows what he's thinking? Oh, dear! Where are my shoes?" She made a great show of finding her discarded slippers and putting them back on, tucking her toes in and bending way over to fit them over her heels. This kept James from seeing her face, which was every bit as red as the pillows on the settee.

Just as she finished, the door opened. Suddenly, Brandon was there, bowing over her hand, his blue eyes meeting hers with an intimate look that stole her breath.

He looked wonderful. Beyond wonderful. Tall and handsome, his black hair falling over his brow, his black coat fitted to perfection. "Lady Westforth," he said, his breath brushing over her fingers as he kissed her hand.

Her entire body shivered in response. "Y-your voice is back." Or part of it, at least. His normally deep voice was even deeper than usual, whiskey-rough and seductively rich. Just the sound made Verena sit a little closer to the edge of her seat.

He continued to hold her hand, his thumb trailing a path over her knuckles that made her thighs quiver as if they had been stroked and not her fingers. "I can speak a little," he said softly, "though I'm not yet up to singing."

"Then we won't make you do so. Would you like some refreshments? I can ring for tea and cakes."

"No, thank you. I've been drinking tea all day in an effort to keep my throat soothed. Any more and I fear my eyes will turn brown."

She realized that his thumb was still tracing that mesmerizing path over the delicate skin on the back of her hand. His fingers still clung to hers, his skin warm.

The touch ignited a welter of feelings, none of which Verena wanted to parade before her sharp-eyed brother. James was already watching her with narrowed eyes, a frown on his face.

Blast. She really didn't need her brother to become involved in her intimate affairs. In any of her affairs, for that matter, intimate or not.

Feigning an indifference she was far from feeling, she removed her hand from Brandon's and gestured to the chair opposite the settee. "Won't you have a seat, Mr. St. John? Mr. Lansdowne and I—"

"You mean James, don't you?" Brandon took the seat offered, his broad shoulders obscuring the back of the chair from sight. "Or don't you call your brother by his Christian name?"

Verena sucked in her breath. What was he doing? James locked a glare on Verena. "You told him." Wonderful. Verena felt as if she were transparent, her emotions plain for the world to see. She'd wager that even now, James was looking into her soul, seeing all the sparkling glory of her late-night tryst. No doubt he was itching to get back to his lodgings so he could write Father a long, long *detailed* letter.

Blast, blast and double blast. That was the last thing she needed—Father riding up on a white horse, breathing fire and demanding justice— which is exactly what he'd do once he discovered Brandon's worth. Only Father's white horse would not be a knight's steed, but the white horse of the Apocalypse, she thought glumly. "James, I told Mr. St. John that you are my brother because he assumed that we were—" She made a vague gesture.

James glowered, but said nothing.

Brandon stretched his legs before him. "She also told me about your missing love letters. I have a few questions about that."

Verena almost moaned aloud. What was Brandon trying to do?

James had gone rigid, his glance daggerlike. "I don't see how this is any of your concern, St. John."

Perhaps he was trying to embarrass her. Trying to wear her down with humiliation. First, he'd embarrass her before her own brother, and then the whole town. Before long, she'd be the laughingstock of all of London.

The thought took hold and grew. Verena's back

stiffened and she wondered if James would think anything amiss if she hiked up her skirts, pounced on St. John the braggart, and pummeled him into a mass of unrecognizable arrogance with her bared fists.

The nerve of the man, coming into *her* house and then spreading all of her secrets.

"I need a drink," James said abruptly, glaring at Brandon before marching across the room and sloshing a very generous portion of brandy into a glass.

Verena leaned toward Brandon and said in a low voice, "What are you doing?"

"I've decided we should have no more secrets."

"Well that's lovely for you. But I like my secrets, thank you very much."

He grinned, his teeth flashing white.

Verena narrowed her gaze. "If you continue on this course, I will never again talk to you while in bed."

His lips quirked. "That's fine with me. Talking is the last thing I'd want to do in bed with you, anyway."

"*Oh!*" How . . . intriguing. Insulting, too, in a way. But if she was honest, she could think of a lot of things she'd rather do in bed with him than talk.

In fact, now that she thought about it, talking did seem to get in the way of things. "Are you trying to embarrass me?"

"Embarr—" He frowned. "Of course not! Why would you think that? I'm merely trying to get all of our information out in the open. My father always said that a shared burden was half a burden."

James returned with a glass of amber liquid. He glanced from Verena, to Brandon, and back. "I beg your pardon? What were you saying?"

"Nothing," Verena said, her cheeks heating. "We were just discussing the need for discretion."

"That's rich," James said in a sarcastic tone. "The next time I give you a secret, I have no doubt you'll just paint it onto a sign and hang it on the front door."

"I only told him because he—"

"Because he's fooled you into thinking he has your best interests at heart. He doesn't, you know. He has something else of yours in mind."

"Oh, he's not that bad," Verena said grudgingly. Not any worse than she was. If she was honest, she'd been just as much the aggressor last night. And she'd practically thrown herself on him this morning, too, though that had had quite a different outcome.

She eyed Brandon speculatively and wondered what the outcome would be if she asserted herself yet again tonight. The idea was tantalizing, but better left alone. Whatever she did now would only complicate matters, make her think even more about a relationship that was already impossible.

James eyed Brandon narrowly. "St. John, if you use my sister badly, I will have your blood."

To Verena's dismay, Brandon looked almost pleased at the thought.

"James," Verena said hastily, "you have it all wrong. Except for our first meeting when Mr. St. John kissed me, he has behaved fairly gentlemanly."

James's head jerked toward her. "Kissed? When the hell did that happen?"

"Several weeks ago," Brandon said. "Your sister kisses divinely."

She sniffed. "I said *fairly* gentlemanly. James, he didn't come here to tease me; he came because he wants to join forces."

"We don't need him," James snapped.

Verena opened her mouth to agree, but stopped. Didn't they need him? They themselves were *point non plus*—there were no more clues to be had. "Perhaps. Perhaps not. He already knows everything."

"Not quite," Brandon said mildly. He looked at James with a curious air. "How do you hear from your blackmailers? Do they send you notes? Or does one of them visit you face-to-face?"

James's face darkened. "I'm not telling you a thing."

Verena swallowed a sharp sigh. Lansdownes never allowed outside parties to become involved in their contretemps. But this. . . . She thought once again of Humford, floating facedown in the Thames. "James, let him help us. We've looked everywhere for that ridiculous list and we cannot find it."

"We don't need any help," James said stubbornly.

"I do," Brandon said. "I need that bloody list, too. I've a friend who could hang for treason if I do not find it."

"And I could wake up dead if I don't find it and turn it over to those blasted blackmailers."

"How do you know *they* won't kill you? Or just

hold onto your letters for another payment of some sort?"

James slammed his glass on the small table by the settee before he planted himself before Brandon. "That's it! I don't know what you mean to accomplish here, St. John, but you are *not* welcome."

Brand didn't seem the least concerned. "That's a pity as I believe I have some information that might make your search more fruitful."

Verena leaned around James so that she could see Brandon. "What have you discovered?"

He leaned over so that he could see her better as well, a glint in his smile. "I met with a man by the name of Colburn. He's with the Home Office. This list you're looking for, it's about this size." He made a square with his hands.

"That small? I've been looking for something more the size of—James, will you please move to one side? It's very difficult to hold a decent conversation with you standing in the middle."

After a frustrating moment, James did as he was told, though he looked none too pleased. "I cannot believe you trust this braggart."

Verena paused. Did she trust Brandon? Strangely, she supposed she did. "Father always said to follow your instincts. Well, this is one of my instincts."

"Yes, well *my* instincts tell me *your* instincts are wrong." His frown deepened. "Wait a minute. What did you mean about St. John's voice *returning*? When did he lose it? And how would you even know about it? And what did Herberts mean when he—"

"James, please," Verena said hastily. "That discussion is for another time. Right now, Mr. St. John has come to tell us what he has found out about the missing list."

"Don't believe a word of it. He just wants to get his friend, Wycham, out from under suspicion from the Home Office."

Verena looked at Brandon. "Wycham?"

James hooked his thumbs in his waistcoat. "Who do you think the Home Office believes responsible for Humford's death?"

"He didn't do it—he couldn't have." Brandon crossed one ankle over the other, his legs stretched beneath the small table. He was completely at ease, as if he belonged in her sitting room. "Would you like to hear what else I've discovered about our situation?"

Verena nodded mutely. She noticed that James didn't bother to protest.

"The Home Office was using Lord Humford to deliver something. This list."

"What's on this list?" James asked.

Brandon frowned. "I believe it contained the names of operatives on the continent. Humford wasn't aware of the importance of his assigned duty."

"I can't believe they'd trust him with something of such import," Verena said. "He was not the brightest of men."

"Perhaps they thought that made him less suspect. And had he not opened his mouth. . . . Apparently Humford liked the attention his little favors for the Home Office got him. He bragged about his new mission to someone."

"And that 'someone' killed him," James said.

"As he was leaving Westforth House. Apparently the list wasn't on him when he died, though the killer expected it to be."

"Which explains why they think the list is here."

Brand nodded. "I've been thinking. It also explains why you, James, were brought to London."

James stiffened. "You think the letters—"

"They had to find a way to get your sister's attention. They found those love letters and used them to get you to come to England. They knew you'd come to Verena and then they'd be able to get her cooperation."

James didn't say anything for a long while. Finally, he sighed. "That makes sense."

Brandon nodded. "According to Wycham, the night before Verena's dinner party, Humford asked him to take the list and deliver it for him. Wycham was to get the list here, at Westforth House."

James let out his breath. "Bloody hell! If the person who is after this list killed Humford and also stole my letters, then I—"

"—must be on the lookout for a very brutal individual," Brand finished.

Verena swallowed hard. James was in danger—they all were. Her heart thumped fearfully.

James resumed his pacing, his head bowed, his hands clasped behind him. "I don't like this."

"You shouldn't. There are two factions after the list—the government and this . . . other person."

"Or persons," Verena said.

"That's a possibility," James said.

"I'd call it more a probability," Brandon interjected.

James let out a sigh. "This is impossible! We must—" He stopped and cut a dark glance at Brandon. "St. John, why are you sharing this information? What do you have at stake?"

Brandon met James's look levelly. He could leave now if he wanted to. He could rise from his chair and walk out the door and never look back. He could use other means to help Wycham. Perhaps Marcus had some influence.

But somehow the stakes were different now. It had become more important to discover the person or persons who were playing havoc with so many people's lives.

His gaze flickered to Verena, who sat watching him with a concerned expression on her face. He wasn't going to leave, not until they'd solved this mystery.

He had far too much at stake to just walk away. He had a very tender, succulent five-foot-two stake, with long, thick blond hair, engaging violet eyes, and the lushest curves ever to grace a woman.

It was becoming clearer day-by-day that Wycham's danger was peripheral compared to Verena's. *She* was the one closest to the missing list.

Whether she knew it or not, she was not safe and hadn't been since Humford, in all his glorious ignorance, had waltzed in her door and seated himself at her dinner table.

"I'm staying," Brandon said. He eyed James evenly. "For as long as it takes."

James's jaw jutted pugnaciously. "And if I make you leave?"

"If you *could* make me leave, then I'd just come back. Over and over. St. Johns never quit."

"And Lansdownes never allow outsiders to interfere in their efforts."

"Good Lord!" Verena threw herself back in her chair, her arms limp at her sides. "What is this? A spitting contest? You two are like a couple of roosters posturing for a gaggle of geese."

Brand had to grin; even James appeared confused. "Verena, I believe you've mixed your metaphors."

"And you've lost all your common sense." She looked at her brother. "*Both* of you. James, we've looked everywhere for that blasted list. We need help. And I'd rather it be Brandon St. John than anyone else."

Brand lifted his brows. It wasn't a declaration, but it was fairly close considering how protective Verena was.

She caught his gaze and colored. "I've already made the error of telling you everything. We might as well take advantage of that."

Wonderful. She didn't want his assistance because she believed he could help. No, she wanted his assistance because she was too bloody stubborn to share her secrets with anyone else.

Verena looked at James. "Well? Do we work together? Or shall I call Herberts to escort Mr. St. John to the door?"

Brand waited. He didn't really care what James thought. He was here to stay.

# Chapter 19

*I love women. Tall ones. Short ones. Round ones.
But especially the saucy ones. They never bore,
rarely snore, and are oft witty enough to stave off
the ennui of the second week of acquaintance.*

Sir Robert Daltry to the Duke of Wexford,
while enjoying a hand of whist at Boodle's

**J**ames fixed his gaze on Brandon with unwavering regard. "Before this goes any further, I want to know what you expect from this partnership."

Brandon smoothed his cuff. He supposed he could understand Lansdowne's distrust. It was not a situation that gave itself to fostering a sense of faith in human nature. "Since we are on a parallel journey as it were, it would be more enjoyable—and more prudent—to travel the distance together."

"You expect me to believe that you're here, sharing your information for no other reason than because you think it might be more 'enjoyable'?"

Brandon had to force himself not to look at Verena. There were a lot of different ways one could use the word "enjoyable," and they all applied to Verena. "Lansdowne, I understand why you don't trust me, or anyone for that matter. But I'm not here to cause you any distress."

"You want to be partners, then? Share information, clues?"

"Why not?" Brandon asked. "We come from a greater position of strength if we fight together."

"And when we find the list?"

"Then we find it."

"Ah, but you want it for one thing, we want it for something else. What then?"

Brand shrugged. "We cross that bridge when we get to it. But whatever we decide, we decide together."

James still looked unconvinced. "This seems very unusual to me."

"The whole bloody mess is unusual."

"Hm." James eyed Brandon thoughtfully. "What reason do you have for trusting *us*? How do you know it wasn't Verena or I who killed Humford and then stole the list? How do you know we didn't fabricate those love letters, the blackmail, all of it—just to hide our real purpose?"

"James!" Verena exclaimed.

"It's a valid question," James returned brutally. "Humford *was* here immediately before he was killed. And as much as I hate to admit it, you and I would both make good candidates for suspicion." His lips twisted. "Part of our Lansdowne legacy."

Verena colored. "That hurt."

"Only because it is true," James returned, meeting her gaze levelly. Something passed between them, a unspoken comment that made Verena's lips tighten.

Brandon watched them, his interest growing.

Perhaps this was what Colburn had meant when he'd hinted that Verena had secrets. "What exactly *is* a Lansdowne?"

James lifted a brow at his sister. "Shall I tell him? Or will you?"

She tilted her chin into the air. "I don't think he needs to know."

Oh, but he did. And very, very badly. But before she could voice her protest, James spoke.

"You've already told our darkest secrets. Why stop now?"

Brand grinned a little when Verena favored her brother with a hot glare.

"Don't look at me like that," James said. "If you trust him enough to tell him about my stupid mistakes and our subsequent predicament, then you might as well come all the way clean."

Almost as an afterthought, he added, "I don't want anything to turn up later that might plague our little partnership."

Verena stared down at her shoes, her color high. Finally, after what seemed an interminable length of time, she said, "Oh very well. But I think it's ill advised."

Brand waited.

She turned a little in her chair until she faced him, though she was careful not to look directly at him. In fact, she very deliberately clasped her hands together and stared at her interlocked fingers. "This is very difficult, but I—well, I suppose you should hear it from us. My family . . . the Lansdownes . . ."

The ornate mantel clock ticked away the seconds. Brandon waited.

She sighed and began again. "As you know, some people live by their wits. Well, my father is considered *very* witty."

James shook his head ruefully. "Ver! Do you want me to tell him?"

"I'm telling him," she said testily.

"No, you're not. You're hinting. Just spit it out. If you don't, the Home Office will."

"The Home—do you think they know?"

"Of course they do."

"Wonderful." She took a deep gulp and then finally met Brandon's gaze. "My father is a French count."

That was it? Brandon frowned.

He said, "My grandfather held an Irish title. He bred horses and was very—"

"No, no," Verena said, twisting her hands. "You don't understand. *Sometimes* my father is a French count."

Brandon paused. "Sometimes?"

"And *sometimes* he is a Russian nobleman, displaced by Unfortunate Events."

"He was an Italian prince once, too," James added helpfully. "That was one of his better ones."

"He always did look good in red," Verena said absently. She didn't dare look at Brand again.

James had been right—it was time everything was brought out into the open. And better now, before she'd come to care overly much, than later, when she was lost.

She knew what to expect of course. Disbelief, followed by distrust. The thought tightened her throat.

Brand's husky voice cut through her thoughts. "I see. Your father is—" He rubbed his forehead as if to clear it. "Good God."

"Our father is whatever he needs to be," James said brutally. "And he's damned good at it, too."

Brand nodded slowly. He looked first at James, then at Verena, a question in his gaze. "What about the two of you?"

Verena frowned. "What about the two of us?"

"Are either of you a count or countess of varying degrees? Or a Russian prince or princess?"

"Of course not," Verena said hotly.

James chuckled. "Verena's too stiff-necked to do anything so outrageous while I've never aspired to the heights my father reached. I'm content living within my trade."

"Trade?"

James hesitated just an instant. "Cards."

"Ah," Brandon said. "A family trait, that."

She caught her breath. It seemed as though a thread of humor laced his voice. Surely not. Surely his pride was already recoiling at the thought of being in league with such charlatans.

But when she stole a look at him, he was regarding her with warm humor, his eyes gleaming softly. "You haven't really surprised me, you know. I've mentioned your talent with cards before."

"You don't mind?"

"Why should I?"

Why should he, indeed, she thought dismally. It wasn't as if they were engaged in a relationship. He could afford to enjoy her low connections since none of them were his. Verena took a slow breath. "Now you know all there is to know."

"Do I?"

What else could there be to tell? Before she could ask what he meant, James interrupted. "You'd like the old man. He's a genius."

"Really?"

"Yes. And if you saw him in action, you'd think it, too."

"I don't doubt that," Brandon said. "Am I soon to have the pleasure?"

"Lord, no. They're in France right now. Making the most of the chaos, no doubt."

"Now you know all of our secrets," Verena said. In the four years she'd lived here on Kings Street in her little house, she'd never told a soul the things she'd told Brandon.

She hadn't told anyone because she knew the way of the Lansdownes. Once the cat was out of the bag, it was time to move on. A Lansdowne came, they saw, they conquered, and then slipped away before everything unraveled and came falling down around their ears.

It was a sad state of affairs when telling someone about your family could be equated with a confession. And as usual, only the Lansdownes had anything to "confess."

But perhaps she was being overly sensitive. Perhaps *everyone* had confessions to make. She eyed Brandon speculatively. What could he possibly have to confess? That he was madly and passionately in love with her?

*That would be nice.* The thought startled her. Would it be nice? Or would it be heart-wrenchingly sad? From the pain that settled in her heart, she thought she knew the answer.

"Well?" James said, looking at Brandon. "Has our confession changed your mind? Still wish to throw your future in with ours?"

"Even more so. I'm anxious to begin." His smile glinted, his blue eyes softening. "I need some excitement in my life. Things were getting tedious."

"Excitement?" Verena frowned. "You don't know what you're saying. There are times when I've thought a little boredom would be a good thing."

"Boredom is good when it's yours by choice," Brandon agreed. "But when it's forced on you, you find you'd do anything to break the chains."

James looked as if he understood completely. " 'Tis done, then. What do we do about this mess we find ourselves in?"

"The first thing we need to do is get Verena to safety," Brandon said smoothly.

She stiffened. "*What?*"

James hid a grin. "You are wasting your time, St. John."

"I don't want her here," he said with even more determination. "It could become dangerous. Especially now that the Home Office has gotten involved."

"And they know we're here," James said.

"They mentioned Verena. I'm not certain they know about you."

"They will," Verena said shortly. Who in Hades did he think he was to demand such a thing? "I assume they are watching the house."

Brand nodded.

Her heart sank. God, how she hated this. It was

far too similar to when she'd lived with her parents—always on the verge of being discovered, always planning to flee into the night.

Years of conditioning had taught her that this moment was inevitable. She still left her packed portmanteau in the bottom of her wardrobe in case she had to leave in the middle of the night.

It hadn't been used in four years and Verena wasn't even sure what was in it, but the sight of that neatly locked portmanteau made her feel safer, more confident.

And now she knew why. Once a Lansdowne, always a Lansdowne.

"That is the one problem I have with Father's career," James said. "It puts one in a damnable spot if there's ever an honest run-in with the law."

Brandon nodded. "That may be true. At first, they thought to blame Wycham for their laxity in losing the list. Then, once they discovered Verena's history, they seemed to be switching their attentions to her."

"Yes," James said, "and if they've lost something of importance, they will be looking for a scapegoat."

"Unless we find the villain first," Verena interjected.

"Which brings us back to the list," Brandon said. He paused. Verena was right. They had to find a way to draw the villain out in the open. If only they had that damned list.

Brandon raked his hair from his eyes. "James, as soon as we've gotten Verena to safety, you and I will—"

Verena stood, her eyes flashing. "*You* and James? Look, St. John, we are in this together. Wherever you go, I go."

"You don't have a say in this. It's not safe and that's all there is to it."

James regarded Brand with approval. "Two minutes into our partnership and already you are issuing orders. I like that."

"You would," Verena snapped, "especially since he is not issuing any orders to you."

"Ver, be reasonable." James protested. "Don't start getting all missish on us."

"I'm not being missish." She crossed her arms over her chest. "I am a part of this venture, whether St. John likes it or not. Unless he has plans to tie me up and keep me under lock and key, there is nothing he can do about it."

Brand rubbed his jaw where it ached. She was right. As much as he would like to lock her away, if she didn't cooperate . . . He sighed. "Will you at least promise to stay out of harm's way?"

"No." Verena paced away, then returned, her steps pulling Brand's gaze. She was innately graceful, her stride smooth. Brand decided he had never before met a woman so worth watching.

She tapped a finger on her chin. "What we need is a plan. Something to—" She stopped so suddenly, her skirts swung forward, outlining her hips before setting back about her feet.

James straightened. "What?"

Verena tilted her head to one side. "What if . . ." Her lips parted, her gaze softening as if she saw something in the distance.

Brand frowned. "Wha—"

"Sh!" James said, waving a hand in his direction. "Let her think."

Verena pressed her hand to her forehead. "What if we—" She turned and began to pace. In that instant, she reminded Brand of his own mother. She'd always paced when upset. Strange how he hadn't thought of that until now.

He wondered what Mother would have thought of Verena. He touched the talisman ring where it hung from his pocket and was a little surprised to find it warm beneath his fingers. ·

"What if," Verena said, "what if we *pretend* we've found the list?"

James frowned. "What good would that do?"

Brandon's mind raced. "Wait, James. She makes sense. If we can convince this villain that we've found the list, then all we have to do is sit back and wait. He'll be forced to act, especially . . ." His gaze met Verena's.

She nodded. "Especially if he believes we might turn it over to the Home Office."

"Check," Brandon said.

"No," Verena said, a gleam in her violet eyes. "Checkmate."

"I see!" James exclaimed. "That's brilliant."

She rewarded her brother with a wry look. "Don't act so surprised."

He chuckled. "Sorry."

"It shouldn't be difficult. We know the size of the list. Besides, the villain thinks we already have it—he *expects* us to have it."

Brandon nodded thoughtfully. "We can make

something fairly close in size—no one will need to see it except from a distance. All we have to do is wave it around a bit."

James rubbed his hands together gleefully. "We'll demand to exchange it for the letters—at *our* preferred location. That way we can control the situation, gain back those blasted letters *and* discover who is after that list in the first place."

It was a daring plan. But a good one, providing Verena stayed far away from the exchange. Brand began to feel a little more hopeful.

James paced rapidly in front of the fireplace. "We'll need a coach and some fast horses. I brought my best pistols, but Ver, you'll need two for the carriage."

"Of course," she said coolly as if being told she'd need to arm herself was something she heard every day.

"Hold on a minute," Brand said. "It's one thing for James and I to draw out the villain, and an entirely different issue for you to involve yourself in a face-to-face meeting."

Verena frowned. "I don't see that."

"You should. This person has killed before and will kill again. I won't allow you to take such a chance."

Verena blinked as if amazed. She turned wide eyes his way, and Brandon could almost hear what she was thinking. Surely he hadn't forbidden her to do something. Forbidden her as if he had some sort of say in her life.

Well he did have a say in her life, damn it. "Verena, I cannot allow it."

"That's not your decision to make."

"Like hell. James, you tell her."

James held up his hands. "I'm not saying a word. I've seen her temper far too often to offer my opinion."

Bloody hell. Brandon sliced a glance at Verena where she stood in rigid disbelief. "It's dangerous."

"It's been dangerous since Humford was given that damnable list and I, believing him to be nothing but a genial old man who told amusing stories and liked to pretend he was a government saboteur, invited him to my house for dinner."

Brand's jaw tightened. Damn it, how could he make her see reason? He eyed James with a gloomy stare. "I take it you aren't going to help. You'd just let your sister walk into danger without saying a thing."

James shrugged. "She's spent her entire life ignoring my advice. She's not going to start listening to me now."

"Exactly," Verena said with a triumphant lift of her chin. "If my involvement bothers you, St. John, then feel free to leave. James and I can carry on quite well without you."

Brandon was trapped. If he didn't join in and help, Verena would be left to her own devices, doing God knew what, and without assistance. "Very well," he said heavily. "I suppose we should start now."

"What do we do?" James asked.

"Act as if we just found that bloody list."

Verena nodded. "Since we don't know the culprit, we have to convince everyone we meet that it's real. The servants, our relatives, passersby."

It seemed simple enough, Brandon decided. "What about the Home Office? Do we tell them the truth?"

"No," Verena said. "Tell them that you believe I have the list, but will not tell you where."

"I don't like deceiving them."

Verena locked gazes with him, her brows lowered. "Who killed Humford?"

Brandon shrugged. "We don't know."

"Exactly. But who *did* know that Humford had that list in his possession?"

*The Home Office.* Brandon rubbed his forehead. Good God, the web became more tangled each day.

James cursed. "I hadn't thought of that. We have to proceed *exactly* as Verena says. We have to look excited, walk with purpose, act as if we really had that scrap of paper in our pocket."

"We'll need a hiding place, too," Verena said, looking at her desk. "Perhaps I shall keep it hidden in there."

Brandon frowned. "Why do you need a hiding place for a piece of paper that doesn't exist? We'll just pretend we've got a hiding place."

Verena barely gifted him with a glance. "If we veer from the course even a little, they will realize we are shamming."

And someone could get killed. They were playing with fire and they all knew it. Brand caught her gaze and held it, a shivery hot hum of attraction sparking between them. He thought of her in bed, her creamy skin flushed with passion, her eyes half closed as she breathed his name in her release. His body tightened instantly.

Damn it, what was wrong with him?

*Think of something else.* An image came to his mind of Humford. Of a slit throat and the drip of blood on the cobblestones. Right outside this very house. Near Verena. Brandon had to curl his hands about the arms of his chair to remain seated. "Verena, don't—"

"Brandon." She didn't move toward him. She didn't raise her voice, or gesture threateningly. But he heard the warning nonetheless.

"I can't," he said. "I can't assist this plot if you are going to put yourself in danger."

Her eyes flashed, but before she could speak, James cleared his throat. "Pardon me, you two. You both seem to have forgotten one thing: there are only three of us involved. It will take all three of us working together if we're to expose whoever killed Humford."

Brand tore his gaze from Verena. "Exactly my point. If you want my help, you will promise to keep your sister away from harm. I will drive the coach and you can be inside. There's no need for her to even go with us."

James hesitated, clearly divided between his masculine inclinations and his knowledge of his sister. After a long moment, he looked at Verena with an apologetic smile. "Ver, he makes good sense. You would just be a distraction."

"Oh!" Verena plopped her fists on her hips. "I can't decide which of you vex me the most. I am perfectly capable of helping and you know it. I'm a dead-on shot and I know how to handle the horses, too!"

"I know, but I'll be worried about you and—"

"Father would let me go. He would never suggest that I be left behind."

James stiffened at that. "Yes, well, I'm not Father."

Brandon cleared his throat. "Verena, we only want to protect you."

Her eyes flashed contempt. "I don't need protecting. I will go on this venture, either with you or without you."

Brandon sighed. "We'll discuss it later. In the meantime, we all have things to do."

She crossed her arms beneath her breasts, her jaw tight.

James cleared his throat, his gaze moving between Verena and Brandon. "Ah, pardon me for intruding, but . . . should we continue looking for that bloody list?"

Verena shrugged. "Why bother?"

"Because once our little contretemps is over, the Home Office will expect to get that list. I don't believe they'll accept that we were merely pretending to have it."

She bit her lip. "You're right. We'll deal with that later. Although, it might not be a problem once—" Verena hesitated, glancing at James.

Something passed between them. Brandon sat up in his chair, frowning. What was behind that calm, almost sad look?

Whatever it was, after a moment, Verena continued smoothly, "Once we have captured the villain."

James rubbed his hands together. "You know, Ver, I think this will work very well indeed."

Brandon rose from his chair. He'd question Verena about it later. Right now, he had things to do. "We're agreed then. We proceed from here on out as if we have the list."

Verena nodded. "How long will it take the villain to make his move?"

James frowned. "I'd give him two or three days. He will be cautious now. He can't afford to take any chances."

"I hope to God you are right," Brandon said. There was more to be said, but now was not the time. He gave James one last nod, sent a hot, telling look to Verena, then turned on his heel and left.

Once in the foyer, he paused. Damn it, he didn't like this plan one bit.

But what could he do but support it? If he didn't, Verena and James would go on without him, and he'd be damned if he'd leave Verena alone to face this mess.

"'Ere now," Herberts said brightly, coming down the hallway, Brandon's coat over his arm. "Is ye leavin' already? Oiye was jus' brushin' yer coat, oiye was."

Brandon took his coat from Herberts and pulled it on.

The butler scurried to open the door, standing to one side, his hand held out.

Brand stepped out the door, then stopped. He reached into his pocket and pulled out a coin, then turned and tossed it to the butler.

Herberts instinctively caught it, his eyes widening appreciatively. "A monkey! What'd ye give me that fer?"

"To keep an eye on your mistress. A very close, accurate eye."

"Ye wants me t' put me eyes against the peephole? Oiye suppose oiye can, o' course, though there'd not be much to see since Mr. Lansdowne is Lady Westforth's brother and all they'll be doin' is talkin' 'bout the weather or som—"

"For the love of—" Brand didn't know whether to laugh or black the man's eye. "I don't want you spying on her, you lummox. I want you to keep an eye out for anything . . . unusual. If you find anything amiss, send word to me at once." He pulled out one of his cards and handed it to the butler. "Do you understand?"

Herberts took the card, squinting at it with one eye. "Oiye suppose it wouldn't hurt to keep me blinkers peeled, seein' how 'tis me dooty anyway." His smile suddenly sank. "Wait a moment, guv'nor! Do ye think something moight happen? Something bad?"

Brandon nodded. And no one would dare harm a hair on Verena's head. She might be prickly as hell and an adventuress to boot, but she was his whether she knew it or not. And the St. Johns always took care of their own, even when that someone was a beautiful, highly accomplished member of the Lansdowne family.

Brandon frowned. He was beginning to think it was imperative that he meet Verena's family. All of them, if possible. He wondered if he should look for them at Tyburn, or if they were abroad at this time of year, residing in the Bastille. "Your mistress is a very unusual woman."

" 'Deed she is." The butler touched a finger to

the side of his nose and winked. "Haf no fear, oiye'll watch her day in and day out, oiye will. Like a hawk."

That was all Brand needed. He gave a brief wave and was soon climbing into his phaeton.

Silence filled the sitting room. Verena found that she couldn't look at the door without her eyes watering and her throat tightening in a painful knot.

James took the chair Brandon had recently left. After a moment, he said quietly, "I'm sorry."

Verena nodded mutely. They had no choice. Once they recovered James's letters, they would leave London. They would have to. She placed a hand on the embroidered cover of the settee and looked about her. This was her home. The only one she'd really ever had. "I suppose you are going back to Italy?"

He nodded. "Long enough to finish my investments. You will come with me."

She didn't really care where she went. "I suppose we should write Father and tell him—" Her voice broke and she pressed her lips together in a vain effort to stop the tears.

James leaned forward and took her hand in his. "I wish there was some other way."

So did she. God, so did she. She disengaged her hand and wiped her eyes. "What else can we do? The Home Office knows I'm a Lansdowne and will soon realize you are here as well, if they don't already. And we don't have the missing list, though they would never believe us."

"Especially once we pretend we *do* have it. St.

John is right," James said with a heavy sigh. "Someone will pay for that blasted list and it will be one of us."

"Brandon thinks he can protect us."

"To protect you." James's frown deepened. "Ver, what's St. John to you?"

What was he? He was kind and concerned, his gruffness hiding a soul as large as any she'd ever seen. She found him irresistible and impossibly stubborn.

And she wasn't sure but that she could be beginning to care about him. Far, far more than was safe.

For a short period of time, she'd allowed herself to forget who she was. Who he was. She'd not make that mistake again.

She disengaged her hand from James's and gave her brother a smile, forced as it was. "Brandon St. John is nothing to me. A friend, perhaps. But that is all."

And that's the way she'd keep it. There was no future for a man like him in her life. None at all.

Verena pushed away the unwelcome thoughts. She couldn't think about that now or she'd be reduced to a quavering mass of tears and recriminations. She had to focus her efforts on helping James. James and no one else.

"Come," Verena said, rubbing her hands together with as much enthusiasm as she could muster. "There's work to be done."

# Chapter 20

*It is quite strange how one little incident can stick in your mind, no matter what you do. Take me, for instance. I've never forgotten the day I lost 50 pounds on a horse named Unlucky. Mainly because my wife reminds me of it at least three times a week.*

The Duke of Wexford to the Earl of Greyley,
while waiting for their wives outside of a
modiste's on Bond Street

**H**ours after Brandon left the Westforth residence, he found himself still mulling over their plan. He hated it, even though he could think of no alternative. They had to draw the blackmailer out. And quickly, before someone else got hurt.

But he'd be damned if he left Verena alone in that blasted house with no one but a half-cocked butler and a freckled footman to act as guards. Brandon St. John was about to become a guest at Westforth House.

He returned home to find Poole waiting anxiously. The butler peered closely at him. "Sir, how are you feeling? Your voice—"

"Has returned." Brandon lifted his nose. Cinnamon and lemon and all sorts of delightful scents drifted from the front room. "Hmm."

Poole helped Brandon remove his coat. "I hope you don't mind, but I knew you wouldn't have a mustard plaster. So instead I made a nice batch of rum punch. A hot rum punch can do wonders for a putrid throat."

Brand hoped it would help with a soured disposition, as well. "I shall have two glasses, then." In truth, his throat was still a bit strained. The exertions of his conversation with Verena and that young hothead she had for a brother had left him more hoarse than before.

"Mr. Chase and Mr. Devon St. John called while you were out," Poole said, smoothing Brand's coat over his arm. "They asked that you meet them for a late dinner at White's at half past ten. Shall I—Heavens! What happened?"

Brand turned to catch the butler's astounded gaze fixed on his coat. "What?"

"Your buttons, sir! They are gone."

Brand grabbed his coat. A multi-caped overcoat of fine Shetland wool, it was an expensive trifle. At one time, the garment had been made all the more attractive by a double row of large, expensively set brass buttons. Not a one was in evidence now. "That blasted thief! I'll strangle Herberts the next time I see him."

"Sir?"

"The Westforths' butler, Herberts. He tends to fancy shiny objects."

Poole's eyes seemed in eminent danger of popping from his head. "Sh-shiny objects? Like a black bird, sir?"

"Only larger. And infinitely more cunning."

"A butler who steals!" Poole seemed to be having trouble swallowing. "Surely you jest."

"I wish I was." He tossed his coat back to Poole. "There's nothing for it now. Hang it up and I'll retrieve the buttons later."

Poole looked at the coat, his entire body stiff with outrage. "Perhaps it might be more beneficial if *I* were to fetch your buttons. I have a few words I'd like to share with this individual. Some hints to the profession, as it were."

Brandon wondered if they would come to fisticuffs. That might be an enjoyment in itself. After all, Poole had a good two stones on Herberts.

Reluctantly, Brandon shook his head. "No thank you, Poole. Though I appreciate your willingness to address this issue." He could only imagine Verena's reaction if his butler were to attack hers. He had a sneaking suspicion that she was rather fond of the disreputable Herberts.

"Very well, sir. If you don't wish me to meet this individual, then I shall remain here." Poole repositioned the coat over his arm. "Please do try some of the rum punch. It's my own special recipe."

Brand nodded. The scent was mouthwatering and he didn't need to be reminded twice. He entered the front room where a fire burned comfortingly in the grate, the spiced punch hanging above in a kettle. Brandon ladled some into a metal mug, cinnamony steam curling from the rim.

He took a careful sip, careful not to burn his tongue. The mixture slid down his throat and curled into a warm ball in his stomach. Bloody hell, but it felt good.

He plopped into an overstuffed chair and placed his booted feet on the low table before him. Brandon drank his punch, ruminating on the hazards of becoming involved with an independent woman. And not your ordinary independent woman, either—Verena had an edge to her, a self-confidence he'd never before seen in anyone, male or female.

Of course, he was beginning to realize that her strength might not have come from simply living alone these last four years. It was possible that it came from her upbringing, whatever that had entailed.

He thought about her closed expression when James had mentioned their parents and her stammered explanation afterwards. What *had* it been like to have such a colorful childhood?

He thought of his own youth, of the love and warmth and security. He'd had the best of everything, while Verena . . . she'd had love. He could see it in the way she and James watched out for one another. But she'd had none of the security.

He leaned back in his chair, aware of a very unusual desire. For the first time in his life, he wanted to protect someone, make them feel safe and cherished . . . it was painfully obvious she'd had neither.

Her childhood had left scars while the little he knew of Westforth didn't lead Brandon to suppose her first marriage had been a haven of any sort. What she needed, he decided, was someone who knew how to overcome the rigid barrier she'd placed about herself. Someone who demanded that she let them in her life so they could take care of her and—

Brand's feet hit the floor as he lurched upright. Good God, what was he thinking? The only way he could make Verena feel as secure as he desired was . . . His jaw tightened. Was to marry her. And he was not the type of man to marry anyone. Hell, he wasn't able to stay interested long enough to make it down the aisle.

Of course, he'd known Verena for over two weeks now, he told himself. And he had been spending hours in her company. It was also true that his interest hadn't waned one iota. If anything, it was stronger than ever.

*Wait a moment. That is only because Verena and I have been involved in this intriguing search for Humford's list. And nothing else.* Yes, that must be it. Once the list was recovered, Brand was sure that whatever feelings he thought he was having would go away—as they always did.

For some reason, the thought was not reassuring. It made him feel a little . . . sad. Verena was a delight. She was lush and sensual, intelligent and capable. In fact, she was everything he'd ever desired in a lover.

And that was all he'd ever wanted. A lover. Oh one day, he supposed he'd be forced to marry someone. But it would be someone circumspect. Someone quiet and sedate—someone like his own mother, for instance. The jumbled feelings he harbored for Verena stemmed from the fact that she was in danger. He, like all the St. Johns, had an innate desire to protect.

He was suffering from a horrid case of chivalry and nothing more. Feeling more reassured by the moment, Brand leaned back in his seat and replaced his booted feet on the low table. It was his duty to protect Verena. And protect her, he would.

He would move his things to Westforth House tonight—right into the master chamber. No matter what Verena said, he'd not leave until the issue of the missing list was settled.

*Act as if we already have the list in our possession.* Brandon sighed. What *would* he do if he'd really discovered something about that damned list? He mulled it over, his gaze drawn to his desk.

He would immediately write to Wycham.

Now he was deceiving his friend. "Blast it, but I don't like this," he muttered as he carried his mug to the desk, pulled out some paper, and dipped his pen into the ink.

*Wycham,*

*I haven't much time, but I know you're anxious to hear how things stand. I believe I know where the list is hidden. In fact, I'm sure of it.*

He hesitated. Should he mention Verena? Yes. Wouldn't that be the same as begging the killer to show up on her stoop? Of course, James was there, though not all the time. And no matter how resourceful Herberts was at sniffing any small item he might find, he was no match for someone intent on causing harm. As for Peters . . . Brand should have taken some comfort there, for the man was certainly formidable. But Peters also seemed naive and quite unable to handle a criminal of such cunning as Humford's murderer.

The thought was chilling. It was a damn good thing that Brandon was going to be installed in Westforth House this very evening. He dipped the tip of his quill back into the inkwell.

*You were right in your suspicions about Lady Westforth—she has the list. I hope to have it in my possession shortly. In the meantime, pray take care of yourself and set your father's mind at ease.*

Brandon signed the letter, sanded and sealed it, then called for Poole.

The butler came into the room, looking pleased to see the mug by Brand's elbow.

Brandon handed him the note. "Send it this evening."

"Yes, sir. Anything else?"

"Yes. Pack my bags. I'm leaving in an hour."

Poole blinked his surprise, but bowed. "Of course, sir. Shall I pack evening clothes?"

"Pack everything. I'll be gone a week or two. Hopefully no longer." He began to rise when another thought caught him. *Act as if we really have it.*

He had one more letter to write. Brandon pulled out another sheet of paper, and quickly dashed off a note. "Here," he said, sanding the note and folding it. "Have this taken to Number Two Timms Street. In care of Sir Colburn of the Home Office."

That done, Brand rose and went to dress for dinner.

The moon shone brightly through the window at Westforth House. Verena sighed and turned to her side, wondering when sleep would come. She hugged the blankets closer, watching the long, pale fingers of moonlight that had slipped through the crack in the window shades trace a lacy pattern across her wall.

This is what she got for going to bed early. She and James had passed the rest of the afternoon and early evening in preparations. They had ordered all the trunks from the attic and sent the entire household into a frenzy of packing. James reasoned that if they had indeed found the list, this would be their natural reaction—to flee once they had the letters.

There was much left to do. Their staff had buzzed with the news that their mistress was soon to leave. Verena was certain that by morning the entire street would be talking of her eminent departure. Within two days, all of London would be conjecturing on the possible causes of her precipitate flight.

"I'm scurrying off like a rat from a sinking ship." Verena hugged her pillow tighter. Once again, she was a Lansdowne, without a home and on the run.

James had stayed long enough to eat dinner, then he'd left to change for the theatre, where he planned to spread the news of her flight even further.

She kicked at the covers. How she hated sleepless nights. In the long, lonely weeks after Andrew's death, she'd laid awake night after night. At first, it had been the shock—she'd been so unprepared for the loss. But later it had been the realization that, for the first time in her life, she was alone. Completely and utterly alone. It had been frightening in a way . . . freeing in another.

Just as being with Brandon was both frightening and freeing. He challenged her, pushed her to become more. Be stronger. Verena flopped her arm over her eyes. In all the years since Andrew's death, no one had stirred her to life the way Brandon had. Verena was beginning to realize that since her husband's death, she'd been stagnating, hiding from life. Somehow, she'd gotten stability confused with safety.

It wasn't until Brandon had burst onto her horizon and shaken her from her complacency that she realized what she'd become. In her efforts to avoid becoming yet another larger-than-life Lansdowne, she'd become the opposite—a shell of a person, scarcely breathing for fear of causing a reaction of some type. She'd tried to blend in, disappear from sight. She'd almost succeeded until Brandon had ridden posthaste to save Chase from her evil clutches.

She had to grin when she thought of that first meeting, of Brandon's expression when she'd ripped his bank draft to shreds and showered him with the pieces.

From that first meeting, there had been a connection between them. Almost as if they recognized each other on some level. It was a delicious feeling, one she'd come to cherish, even as she acknowledged that it wasn't enough.

She wondered if Brandon would ever think of her after she left—worry about her safety with the same intensity he worried about his brothers. She blinked back the wetness in her eyes. She felt hollow, empty. And she had the depressing fear that it was a feeling she would just have to live with.

"Stop it," she muttered. They still had a few days left. A few days to enjoy each other before the inevitable happened. Perhaps Brandon would steal in the house tonight as he had done before. A pleasurable tremor rustled through her at the thought. She'd been burning for his touch ever since that one night of passion.

She stirred restlessly and kicked at her gown where it tangled about her legs. She needed a nice hot bath and a cup of steaming chocolate, rich and strong enough to curl her toes. Perhaps that would direct her mind from other, more lascivious thoughts.

Verena sat up, shoving her mound of pillows to one side. Yes, a large cup of rich chocolate, steaming ever so gently. If she—

A creak filtered through the house. Verena knew that sound—it was the window in the sitting room. The hinges desperately needed oil. Someone crawling through her window—

*Brandon!* She hopped out of bed and smoothed her gown, almost trembling in her excitement. Brandon was like an orange, all hard and rough on the outside, but soft and sweet on the inside. At least she *thought* he was soft and sweet on the inside. Perhaps she should peel him to be certain. She chuckled at her thoughts even as she grabbed her dressing gown and thrust her arms into it, then rammed her feet into her red velvet slippers. The door swung open silently and she made her way down the hall, stepping over the boards she thought might make a noise.

She hesitated on the crest of the stairs, peering down into the gloom below and wondering how best to put Mr. St. John in his place—right on his behind. She could barely make out a faint rustle in the recesses of the sitting room. A creak sounded as if someone had rested a foot on a loose board and then hastily removed it.

Ah-ha! There he was. She lifted the front of her robe and crept down the stairs, staying to one side to avoid making any noise. A clock struck in the background. Ten chimes. It was indeed late.

She reached the door to the sitting room and stopped to listen once more. More noises were audible here—the scrap of metal on wood, the clink of a vase on the mantel, then the sound of the drawer being opened in her escritoire.

A drawer? What was he into now? She put her hand on the knob and pushed the door open slowly. The room, like the hallway behind her, was in total darkness. She crept stealthily in, staying near the wall.

She must have made some noise, for the entire room was suddenly bathed in silence. Verena crouched low, pressing a hand over her mouth to stifle a very unadult urge to giggle.

The quiet grew and stretched. Verena's legs began to ache even though her excitement increased as the moments slid by. Finally, just as she was about to say something, the rustle of clothing to her immediate right made her turn.

A frontal attack was her only hope. She stood. "Ah-ha! I caught you now—"

Something whooshed by her face. A blinding pain exploded. She was falling. Then she saw nothing, felt nothing, but blackness.

Brand walked down St. James Street toward White's. Though well after dark, the street bustled as members of the *ton* strolled here and there, climbed in and out of carriages, and pulled up beside one another to talk.

He pulled out his new watch and checked the time. A quarter after ten. He was a bit early.

Brandon tucked the watch back in his coat pocket and strode on. White's had just come into sight down the street when someone grasped his arm. He turned. "Lansdowne!" He frowned. "Is something wrong?"

"I wanted to talk to you." James gestured toward White's. "I take it you are going to the club. May I walk with you?"

"Of course." He waited for James to fall in beside him and then they began walking. "Are you a member?"

A wry grin flickered over James's face. "I don't believe they usually allow penniless charlatans entrance into that hallowed abode."

"You aren't a penniless charlatan. Your father is a Russian nobleman."

"Today. But tomorrow . . ." James shrugged.

Brand dug his hands into his pocket. "What was it like? Living like that?"

"Exciting. Uncertain. Sometimes frightening. But it was never boring."

"Verena seems a little resentful of her childhood."

James came to a halt, his brown eyes fixed on Brand with unwavering regard. "My sister doesn't always know what's best for her."

It was a warning, that much was obvious. Brandon wasn't sure how to respond.

But before he could say anything, James turned and continued to walk. "I'm glad I caught up with you. I found Lady Bessington this evening, and she remembered something. She sat beside Humford at Verena's dinner party the night he was killed."

"What did she say?"

"That Humford drank like a fish all evening. Seemed nervous, too. Kept looking at the clock, though she said they were all doing the same thing since Viscount Wycham was late. She said Verena finally gave up on Wycham and just as they all sat down to dinner, Humford patted his coat pocket, then turned pale."

"That's when he realized he'd lost the list."

James nodded, his golden hair glinting in the gaslight. "I think so."

"Did Lady Bessington remember anything else?"

"Just that he rambled on and on about how he'd just bought a new coat and new snuffbox. Seems he'd come into some money recently. She rather thought he'd had a run of luck at the tables."

"Not according to Lady Farley," Brand said. "He owed her establishment quite a bit of money."

They walked in silence a moment.

"Have you put the plan in action?" Brand asked.

"All business, aren't you?"

"This is a serious matter."

"Yes. Yes, it is. And yes, I've put the plan in action. As soon as you left, Verena and I ordered the trunks from the attic."

He frowned. "Why did you do that?"

"Because it's what we'd do if we really did find the note." He met Brandon's gaze head-on. "We couldn't stay, you know."

A chill settled over Brandon's heart. "Why not?"

James glinted a smile that held a touch of sadness. "We're Lansdownes, St. John. We never stay where we're not wanted. Once we pretend we've found that blasted list, the Home Office would never believe we were merely play-acting. We'd have to leave."

"Of course." Brandon turned back down the street, vaguely aware of a stir in the street behind him. If what James said was true, then after this coup, Verena would be gone. The thought settled behind his heart and made his entire chest ache. Good God, what would he do when—

A horse protested, its voice strident, followed by a dismayed shout. A man on the street in front of Brand glanced back over his shoulder, his gaze moving to Brandon and James, then beyond. The man's eyes widened, his expression one of frozen fear.

Brandon whirled. A carriage ran out of control, jumping the curb and heading straight for them. The horse strained, his eyes wild, his neck lathered. He ran as if pursued by the hounds of hell. It took Brand only a second to realize that the driver was hunched down, his hands still on the reins, his face obscured by a faded black hat.

*He's going to kill us!* Brand grabbed James by the arm and yanked him, but he was too late.

The next moment passed in a hazed blur. The carriage bounded onto the sidewalk, but then just as suddenly veered away. The edge of the traces caught James and spun him backward. He went down in the street with a sharp cry.

The coach thundered on, people scrambling to get out of the way. The street was filled with angry shouts as Brandon knelt by James.

"My leg." He groaned, both hands wrapped about his knee. Blood seeped through his fingers and soaked the leg of his breeches.

Brandon cursed long and low, his heart thundering in his ears. "Wait here and—"

"Brand!" It was Devon, concern etched on his face.

Chase appeared as well. "I called for a physician."

"Thank you." Sweat beaded Brandon's brow, his fear melting into anger. "James, we must get you out of the street. Can you move?"

James's eyes were closed, his brows lowered over the bridge of his nose. "Just . . . give me a moment."

Brandon nodded. He turned to look down the street after the runaway carriage when his gaze fell on a small urchin standing at the end of St. James's Street. It was the boy in a blue tattered coat that Brand had seen outside of Verena's only two days ago.

The boy was listening to a burly man dressed in a faded black coat and outmoded hat. The man was talking, gesticulating wildly. He turned his head just the slightest bit and Brand recognized him—it was Farragut.

Farragut pressed a coin into the child's hand, then turned to look in Brandon's direction. For one moment, their eyes met. Then Farragut yanked his hat further down over his eyes and marched off. The boy melted into the crowd.

Bloody hell, what was that all about?

"Brandon?" Chase stooped beside him.

Brand said in a low voice, "Did you see what happened?"

"Yes. Through the window at White's, but I couldn't get to the door."

Devon nodded. "Every blasted person was crowded about, trying to see." He gestured at the wake of destruction left behind by the carriage. "It drove right up on the sidewalk as if the bloody driver aimed for you two. My heart about stopped. If he hadn't veered at that last moment I don't think—"

"I know." Brand's own heart was still galloping wildly, but he wasn't about to admit such a thing. "It was an unfortunate accident."

"Accident?" Chase frowned. "I wouldn't call it—"

"Pardon me." A thin individual in a frock coat

stood behind them. "I'm Doctor Lindson. May I examine the young man?"

"Of course," Brandon said. He went to stand up, but James's hand clamped about his wrist.

James swallowed, obviously fighting an enormous amount of pain. "It . . . worked."

Worked? What—Brand's breath froze in his throat. The plan had worked. But . . . so soon? How could it have—Brand closed his eyes. *My God. Verena.* His chest tightened until he could barely breathe. He stood, James's hand dropping away. He looked at Devon. "See to Mr. Lansdowne. I have to go."

"But why? What's happening? Should I—"

But Brandon didn't answer. He was gone, racing madly down the street, his booted feet ringing loudly. *Please God, let her be safe.*

# Chapter 21

*My brother Brandon? He's quite well, thank you. The last time I saw him, he was resting. Life can be quite exhausting when one has nothing to do.*

The Earl of Greyley to Lady Birlington, sitting outside the maze at Vauxhall Gardens

**B**randon raced up the steps of Westforth House. No light shone inside except for the sitting room, which was ablaze. Stifling his disquiet, he banged the brass knocker sharply.

As usual, no one appeared. Brandon knocked again, this time so loudly that the sound echoed. When no response was forthcoming, he cupped his hands about his mouth. *"Herberts! Answer the damn door!"*

The curtain in the sitting room flickered a moment before the door finally opened. Herberts stood in the opening.

"Bloody hell," Brandon said. "Didn't you hear—"

The butler's nose and eyes were red as if he'd been crying, his lips quivering piteously.

Brandon's heart thumped to a halt. "Verena—"

Herberts wiped his nose with the back of his

hand. "Th—the sittin' room." His voice warbled, a fat tear rolling down his cheek.

Blood roared in Brandon's ears. He shoved past the butler and raced toward the sitting room, his breath caught in his chest. Dear God, was he too late?

The door to the sitting room was open, light spilling into the hallway. Brand stepped into the room and came to a halt.

Verena lay on the settee, her head wrapped in a white bandage. Brand went to her side and gazed down at her, his throat peculiarly tight.

He just stood, thankful beyond words to see her chest rising and falling, to see her hand clenched about a handkerchief. Even the frown on her lips sent a tremor of gladness through him.

Brandon glanced over his shoulder at Herberts, who stood behind him. "What happened?"

The butler gave a wet sniff. " 'Twas horrible, it was. Oiye heard a noise downstairs here in the sittin' room. When oiye opened the door, oiye found the missus on the floor, crumpled like a rag."

"Did you send for a physician?"

Verena opened her eyes into twin slits of ill humor. "I don't want a doctor. I just have a little headache, that's all."

Though she was pale, her voice was even. The tightness about Brand's chest eased somewhat.

He knelt by the settee and took her hand in his, linking his fingers with hers. "Are you well?" He lifted the edge of the cloth and viewed the angry bruise on her forehead.

She winced. "No, I'm not well. My head hurts,

my teeth ache and my neck is stiff. How can you even ask such a question?"

Brand replaced the cloth. Damn it, this wasn't supposed to happen. They were supposed to pretend they'd found the list and the blackmailer would press for an earlier meeting. That was all.

He glanced at Herberts. "Were the door and windows locked?"

" 'Deed they were! Peters and oiye checked 'em all afore bed."

"Have you checked them since? It would be easy enough to break a window and climb in."

Herberts shook his head, his lips quivering. "Oiye should have stayed awake. Ye tol' me something might happen." He pulled out a handkerchief and blew his nose. As he went to stuff the handkerchief back in his pocket, Brandon caught sight of a familiar monogram—his own.

The butler caught his gaze, then looked down at the kerchief, the monogram still visible. His cheeks reddened to match his nose. "Sorry 'bout thet, guv'nor. Ye must have dropped it in the foyer." He shook out the handkerchief and held it out to Brandon. " 'Ere ye go."

Brandon looked at the none-too-clean crumpled bit of linen. "Er, no thank you. You can keep it."

"Thank ye, guv'nor." Herberts wiped his nose once more and then crammed the kerchief back in his pocket. " 'Tis the worst day o' me life. Oiye've failed in me dooty."

"You didn't fail. We didn't have any way of realizing that this would happen." Not this quickly, anyway. "Where is Peters?"

"Oiye sent him to fetch ye and then go on to find Mr. Lansdowne."

*James.* Brandon looked down at Verena's pale face. He couldn't tell her about her brother, not yet. "Once Peters returns, send him to me. Mr. Lansdowne will be coming soon. He will need a chamber prepared."

Verena's eyes opened once again. "James is staying here? I asked him and he said he thought it would be best if he remained at the inn."

"He changed his mind." Brandon rubbed his thumb over the back of Verena's hand. Her eyes slid closed once again, her brows drawn, though her lashes rose just a bit when he pressed his lips to her fingers.

Slowly, her lashes lifted. Their eyes met, a wave of heat shimmering through Brand. Only this time it wasn't anger, but pure lust. Startled at the strength of the feeling, he released her. The second he did so, though, her lips began to quiver, her violet eyes filling with tears.

Brandon caught up her hand again. "Easy, sweet."

A single tear leaked from beneath her lashes. "I don't know why I'm—my head hurts. Yes, it hurts and I'm—" She gulped a sob. "Oh, blast!"

"Herberts, is there any laudanum in the house?"

"Oiye already brought it but the missus wouldn't touch it." Herberts shook his head. "She's a stubborn wench."

"I still don't want it," she said, though her voice seemed weaker.

Herberts picked up a small brown bottle and a spoon that rested on a nearby table and handed them to Brand. "Mayhap ye can get her to take a good dose. There's no reason fer her to be a hurtin' so."

"Fetch some water."

The butler immediately scurried off. He returned almost immediately, a glass in his hand. Brand pulled the cork from the bottle and poured some of the thick brown liquid into a spoon.

He held it before Verena. "Open."

"No." She turned away a little, one hand pressed to the cloth on her head, the other balled into a fist on her stomach.

"It will make your head feel better."

"So would dying, but I don't want to try that, either."

Brand quirked a brow. "Don't make me pour this down your throat."

Her eyes flew open. "You wouldn't da—"

Brandon slipped the spoon between her parted lips. She choked, pressed a hand to her mouth, then swallowed, glaring at him the whole time.

Brandon placed the glass of water in her hand and then gave the bottle and spoon to Herberts. "That should do the trick."

"I wish you would go away," Verena snapped. She gulped the water, her mouth still twisted in disgust. "That is the most vile stuff."

"I am not leaving you alone." Ever. Brandon

wanted her safe. Warm. In his arms. Where she belonged.

"Lud, guv'nor. Oiye cannot believe someone would hurt a fine lady like the missus. 'Tis a crime."

Verena wrinkled her nose, an accusing note in her voice as she peered up at Brandon. "I need a cup of chocolate. Something to get this foul taste from my mouth."

Herberts looked skeptical. "Do ye think chocolate is a good idea after ye've knocked yer noggin? Oiye think perhaps some nice cabbage soup moight be more the thing."

Even with a bandage on her head, Verena managed a very quelling look at her butler. "I don't want cabbage soup, thank you. But I *do* want chocolate. Now, if you please."

Brandon thought he'd never seen a more adorably ill-tempered patient. He pressed her fingers to his mouth, her fingertips trembling against his lips. She was so damnably brave. Most women he knew would be bawling, sobbing hysterically. Verena merely used her injury as an excuse to procure hot chocolate.

He glanced at Herberts. "Hot chocolate, Herberts. Now."

The butler stuffed his handkerchief into his pocket. "Won't cure her head pain none."

"That's for her to decide. Now fetch some chocolate and be quick about it."

"Very well." He straightened his shoulders and marched from the room.

As soon as the door closed, Brandon released her hand and stood. "I'm going to carry you to your room. You'll be more comfortable in bed."

She lifted up on her elbows. "I can walk, thank you very much."

"Really?" He scooped Verena into his arms. "Not while I'm carrying you."

"You're despicable."

"And you need to be in bed." He didn't wait another moment, but carried her upstairs.

The bed was mussed. Brand set her on the edge of the mattress while he straightened the sheets. She waited patiently, her eyes never leaving him.

When he had everything ready, he slid his arms beneath her and laid her gently on her pillows. "There," he said, wondering why he felt so helpless. His heart was doing strange things, aching as if he'd already lost something.

"Don't move." Brand went to the door and yelled for Herberts.

The butler pounded up the stairs almost immediately. "Sir?"

"Bring some cold water and some fresh cloths."

Herberts nodded. "The chocolate's almost ready, too." He turned and clomped back down the steps.

Brand returned to Verena. She had closed her eyes and a slow tear trickled down her cheek. He sighed and sat on the edge of the bed. "Verena. It's all right. I think I'd be crying, too."

She looked at him, her violet eyes dark as if they, too, were bruised. Brandon'd had only one sister. But that one sister had taught him many things. He reached out and gathered Verena to him. "Easy, sweetheart. Easy."

The tears came and he held her, rubbing his cheek against her hair, stroking her back. But even as he comforted her, he thought of all the ways he wanted to kill the man who had harmed her.

Moments later, Herberts entered the room carrying a bowl of water, a pitcher, and a cup of steaming chocolate. He paused on seeing Verena in Brand's arms, but only for a minute. " 'Ere now, a good cry is jus' what ye need, missus. Oiye brought ye some extra cloths, too, so ye can wash yer face when yer finished. Ye don't want a red nose, do ye?"

Verena didn't think she really cared what color her nose was, so long as Brandon didn't release her. It was heavenly, being held, nothing expected, nothing given. Just shared. Perhaps it was the laudanum, but she didn't want to feel anything beyond this moment.

Herberts clumped about a bit more, rambling about how he'd been searching the downstairs windows for signs of entry. A yell from Peters sent him out the door.

The instant he was gone, Brandon chuckled, the sound rumbling beneath Verena's ear in a comforting manner. "You should see what he's done to your night table."

Verena risked a peek. Herberts, in his desire to be of service, had folded all the extra cloths into large, sloppy, flower-shaped bundles. "Where did he learn that?" she asked, amazed.

"I don't know, but you should have seen him. He had to do each one four or five times before he was satisfied." Brand brushed the hair back from her face. "We need to wash your bruise. Think we can manage it ourselves?"

Verena nodded. She wasn't better at all, though that no longer seemed to matter. Thank heavens for the laudanum. The pleasantly numbing sensation was slowly spreading through her and in a moment, she wouldn't even be able to feel her tongue.

She cast about for something bright and witty to say—something to offset her horribly red nose. "I suppose our plan is working."

Brand's mouth thinned. "Don't get me started. Can you sit on your own?"

She nodded once, then winced. Her head still ached, but from a distance now. She allowed Brandon to arrange her pillows into a huge wall of comfort. Then he gently undid the bandage around her forehead.

She watched him as he worked. He was the most handsome man in the world. And he was sitting on the edge of *her* bed. She wished she had a whole group of friends to whom she could brag. It was rather sad that she didn't. Not even one, really. Oh, she *knew* a lot of people, of course. But not well enough to confide in any of them.

Verena supposed that was yet another sign that she'd forgotten how to live.

Brandon set the bandage aside, his gaze fastened on her forehead, his mouth thinned.

"What's it look like?"

"Blue. Very blue."

She put her fingertips to the bump. "Ouch!"

His face softened. "Don't touch it if it hurts."

Verena giggled. "I shan't touch it at all. *You* can touch it. In fact," she made a huge gesture that almost sent her tumbling to one side, "*you* may touch all of me."

A glimmer lit his eyes. "You're laudanum-drunk." But he smiled and ran his thumb over her chin. "Let me get some cold cloths on your head."

She caught his hand and pressed it to her cheek, looking at him with all the longing she felt inside. "You aren't going to leave me?"

He cupped her cheek. "Never."

"Ever?"

He bent until his face was even with hers, his blue eyes seeming to burn. "Verena, I promise to stay as long as you'll have me plus one day."

"One day?"

"A very, very long day." He straightened. "Let me get the cloth."

She reluctantly released his hand. The second he stepped from the bed, she felt alone again. Alone and uncertain, afraid. But not of being hurt or meeting up with her attacker. Her fear had to do with Brandon. With losing him. Losing herself.

He returned to the bed with some cool cloths and carefully bathed her forehead. Only once did it cause her any pain, and he immediately stopped. When he finished, he said quietly, "There. That should do it."

Brandon returned the cloth to the bowl and came back to the bed with the cup of chocolate. "I believe this will cure any further ills you may have."

Verena took the cup in both hands and inhaled deeply. The heavenly aroma sent a pleasurable shiver down her spine. She put the cup to her lips and let the creamy liquid slide down her throat. It was heavenly. She closed her eyes and let the bittersweet taste fill her with a delicious peacefulness.

Suddenly, she realized how ridiculous she must look to Brandon, getting blissful over a cup of chocolate. She peeped at him. "Sorry," she said, with an uncertain laugh. "I didn't ask if you wanted any. I could pour half of this into another cup, if you'd like."

"No, thank you. I don't need my own cup. I can taste it from your expression." He pushed a strand of her hair from her face, his fingers gentle. "Finish that. It will help you sleep."

She did as he suggested though she was aware of his gaze the entire time. He watched her hungrily, as if afraid she would disappear if he looked away too long. She took the last sip and then handed him the empty cup.

He set it aside. "It's time you went to sleep."

The laudanum had taken hold now. Her nose and chin were numb and she thought perhaps the room was tilting ever so slightly to the left.

She sighed happily as she looked about her familiar room. She'd spent as much money on her bed and bed linens as she had for every stick of furniture in the sitting room. The bed represented her home. Her haven. But for the first time in four years, she didn't want to be here—not alone.

She leaned forward and put her head against Brandon's shoulder. "Stay with me?"

He stilled, a flicker of tension on his face. "That would not be wise."

"It would be heavenly." She found that somehow her fingers were now twined in Brandon's coat. She frowned. "You still have on your coat."

"I didn't have time to remove it."

There was something wrong about his coat. What was it? She squinted at it again, then smiled. Damn, but she was intelligent—far more intelligent than anyone had ever imagined. "I know what it is! You've no buttons."

"Herberts."

"Ah." It took a little concentration, but she forced her fingers to loosen from his coat. But as soon as she let go of him, he rose. A faint sense of panic gripped her.

Brandon must have read her gaze. "I'm not going anywhere." He pulled off his coat and tossed it over the chair.

Ah, her chair. Her lovely, lovely chair. She remembered the last time Brandon had been in her room, how he'd held her in his lap. The chair would always be special to her. One to be cherished. Especially once this ordeal was over and she had left England and Brandon forever.

The thought of leaving sent her mood spiraling to black. Oh God, she was going to leave. Leave her home, her beloved bed, and Brandon. Her chest ached from unshed tears.

"Here, now. Don't start that."

She looked up at him, her lips quivering. "Can't help it."

"It's the laudanum. You need to go to sleep, Verena." Brand sat back on the edge of the bed and brushed her cheek with the back of his finger, the movement hypnotic. "Close your eyes. I'll be here when you wake up."

The sadness abated as a heavy lassitude weighed her down. Her head still hurt, but only from far, far away.

It was lovely lying here, all snuggled in her bed, Brandon gently smoothing her face, her hair. She imagined him whispering nonsensical words, words of comfort and joy and love. But not love—not from Brandon.

She smiled woozily and placed her hand on his, loving his gentle touch, as if he feared to hurt her. After a moment, she said into the silence, "My head feels better."

He glinted a smile. "Good. Now sleep."

"Don't want to sleep," she said, though her eyes slid closed.

"Hm." He continued to trail his fingers through her hair.

It was almost hypnotic and she smiled her contentment. "My mother used to do that, whenever I was ill."

"Then she was a good mother. Mine did the same."

"I miss my mother." She opened her eyes to look at him. "Do you miss yours?"

"Every day. Tell me about your family, Verena. What are they like?"

Her family. How lovely that Brandon wanted to know about her family. He was such a kind man. She nestled her cheek against his palm. "I have a brother."

"I know that. I've met him. He looks very much like you."

Good old James. Always there when she needed him. She wondered where he was right now. He'd said he'd only be gone a short time, yet that had been hours ago. "I wonder where James has gone—"

"Do you have any other brothers or sisters?" Brandon asked.

"Two sisters. They are younger. I'm the oldest of us all, though by only two minutes."

"You and James are twins?"

"Yup." She sighed happily. Laudanum was a delightful drug, she decided. "I have a lovely family. My father thinks I am the best card turner he's ever come across. Except, of course, when I drink port."

"Ah yes. Our little game. That seems years ago." He cupped her face, his palm warm. "Why didn't you join your family once Westforth died?"

"Because I wanted to have my own bed." She chuckled softly. "That sounds strange, doesn't it? I love my parents, but they are sadly addicted to excitement."

"Unlike you."

"I want peace. Home. My very own bed with plump pillows and crisp linen sheets."

Brandon brushed his thumb over her cheek, enjoying the warm silk of her skin. "Was it very difficult, wandering so much?"

The smile faltered, then disappeared. Her eyes slowly came open, the violet drowning as if in a rain. "At times," she whispered. "At times it was very difficult. Every time I found a friend, we would have to leave." Her voice quavered. "Like now."

Leave. Never had Brandon disliked a word so much. He realized with a shock that he didn't want Verena to leave. What he really wanted was—he closed his eyes. What *did* he want?

Verena must have noted his pained expression for she placed her hand along his cheek. "It wasn't all bad. Some parts of living with my parents were marvelous."

"Marvelous?"

"They were not monsters. Just . . . opportunists."

"You mean scoundrels?"

"That and other things. But they loved us. And they cherished us."

Not enough, Brand thought. He wondered if anyone had cared for Verena the way she deserved. "What did Westforth think of your parents?"

"Andrew?" She smiled, a slow lazy smile. Her voice was growing more indistinct and he knew she was about to fall asleep. But after a pause, she managed to murmur, "Andrew was amused. I think he cared more for my parents than his own." Her voice faded with each word.

Brandon pulled the covers up and tucked them about her. "Go to sleep, Verena. I'll be here when you wake up." And he would, he decided. That day and the next, and possibly the one after that. However long it took to make certain she was safe and cared for.

She snuggled deeper into the mound of pillows, her hand curled to her cheek, and was soon fast asleep. Brandon watched her for a long time afterwards. Then, moving quietly, he pulled the covers more neatly about her and then settled into the chair by the fireplace and waited for dawn.

# Chapter 22

*There's one thing you can say about a St. John—
they never know when to quit. I rather like that in
a man.*

Lady Birlington to Lady Jersey, after witnessing
Mr. Chase St. John imbibe more than his fair share
of brandy at the Wexford musicale

**B**randon slowly came awake the next morning, aware first of the chill of the room and then of the ache in his neck. He was far too large to sleep in a chair, he decided glumly. And far too old.

He pushed himself upright and glanced at the bed. Verena was gone.

Brandon stumbled to his feet. Bloody hell, where was she? He ran to the door and threw it open, almost falling over Herberts.

"There ye be, guv'nor! Oiye came to see if ye wanted to join the missus fer some breakfast."

Brandon pressed a hand to his heart. "Yes. Yes, of course."

"Oiye'll tell her ye're on yer way." Herberts eyed Brandon's hair. "There's a comb on the missus's dresser. Ye moight want to give it a swipe."

With that sage piece of advice, he turned and left.

Brandon returned to the room and straightened his clothing and hair. He was just getting ready to leave when his gaze fell on a small writing desk, fresh paper tucked into the front pocket. Brandon stood, looking down at the paper for some time. Then he opened the ink and began to write.

A short time later, he went downstairs. Verena was sitting at the table, a plate of toast before her. She looked calm and composed though her eyes were shadowed, the bruise on her forehead stark against her white skin.

She met his gaze when he entered, a faint blush touching her cheeks. "How are you this morning?"

Every bone in his body ached, probably because of his fall when he'd tried to save James. "I'm fine. Verena, I meant to tell you last night. James—"

"Is in the guest chamber. I just left him."

"How is he?"

"In pain. More from the fact that he knows he cannot help us."

"Help us?"

A strained smile touched her lips. "We received another letter." She reached over her plate to where a single piece of paper rested.

Brandon opened it.

*Lady Westforth,*

*The King's Deer Inn in Little Sutton at noon.*
*Bring the list and come alone.*

Brandon looked up. "When did this arrive?"

"The physician found it on the stoop when he came to see James this morning."

Brandon folded the note and placed it on the table. "It's addressed to you."

"Yes. The others were addressed to James. They must know he is injured, which is no surprise considering they probably arranged it." She stood and he saw that she wore a plain traveling gown. "I'm leaving in an hour."

"Verena, you cannot—"

"I have to. This must end. Brandon, my brother is lying in a bed, his leg broken. Next time it will be much, much worse."

"How do you know these men won't kill you the second you show yourself?"

"Because I have the list. They don't dare lose it."

Brand rubbed his forehead. "Damn, damn, damn. I don't like this."

"Neither do I." She placed her hands flat on the table. "Are you coming with me?"

The door opened and Herberts entered with a plate of steaming ham. "Here ye go!"

Brand ignored him, his gaze still on Verena. "The letter said they wanted you to come alone."

Her lips curved into a smile. "I will be alone. Just me and my coachman."

Brandon stilled. As coachman, he'd be up high, overlooking it all, which would give him a unique vantage point from which to protect her. It was possible . . . he caught Verena's calm gaze, read her intentions in that second.

He nodded. "Very well. I'll be the coachman. What's your plan?"

"We will take the carriage to the King's Deer Inn. Once there, I will make a great scene, weeping and crying and acting frightened. If they think me frozen with fear, they will not expect much in the way of resistance."

"That is a good plan." At her surprised glance, he added, "It will also explain why you won't be getting out of the coach."

Herberts clucked his tongue knowingly. "Thet makes good sense, missus. Ye should listen to the guv'nor."

Verena looked down at where her hands were clasped in her lap. "Brand, we don't have the list. My only hope is to get my hands on James's letters and get out of there before they realize they have been tricked."

Brandon nodded. "I suppose it's the only way."

Herberts straightened his thin shoulders. "Oiye, fer one, am ready and willin' to help ye, missus."

Verena shook her head. "No, no! I don't think that's necessary. But thank you for offering."

"Oh, 'tis no problem. Peters can stay here and watch the door fer me and oiye'll just—"

"Herberts!" Brandon lifted a brow. "We need you here to watch over Mr. Lansdowne."

"But oiye—"

"It's important."

Herberts's shoulders slumped. "Oh, very well. Oiye suppose oiye'll be here a-polishin' the silver."

"Correct," Verena said.

The butler cocked a brow. "Oiye'm a good shot, oiye am."

"So is Mr. St. John."

"An' oiye've a way wid horses."

Verena patted Herberts's hand. "I'm sure you

do, but we need you here to watch over Mr. Lansdowne."

Herberts sighed. "Very well, but oiye think ye're makin' a big mistake not takin' me wif ye."

Brandon glanced at Verena. "He certainly knows a lot about what is going on."

"He reads my mail."

"Here now," Herberts protested. "Not all of it."

She sent him a quelling glance. "You aren't supposed to read any of it. Well, St. John, what do you think of our little plan?"

"It will have to do." He eyed her for a long moment, noting how the blue lump that marred her brow made her eyes appear even more violet than before. "Whatever you do, do not leave the carriage. Just get them to hand the letters through the window. The second you've handed them the list, I'll get us out of there."

He spoke with such confidence that Verena's heart lifted. It was a simple plan. It involved only two people. And it had the advantage of surprise. Father would be so proud. "We're settled then. We can leave within the half hour."

"Herberts." Brandon reached into his coat pocket and pulled out a letter. He handed it to the butler. "See to it that this is delivered this morning. It's to my sister, the Countess of Bridgeton."

Verena wondered what on earth had prompted Brandon to send a letter at a time like this. Unless, of course ... "You aren't divulging anything, are you?"

"Of course not. It's a personal message for my sister, asking for a favor."

Herberts sighed. "Deliverin' a note is an especially important duty. Do ye think ye can trust me? Oiye moight ferget to deliver it and—"

Brandon slipped a coin into Herberts's palm.

The butler brightened considerably. "Weel, then! Oiye moight jus' 'member it after all."

Verena lifted her chin in an effort to see the address on the letter, but found Brandon conveniently in the way. "As I said before, it's for Sara, my sister."

"Oh." Verena wondered if she could bribe Herberts into accidentally opening the missive. Perhaps she could—

"Oiye'll be off to see to Mr. Lansdowne," Herberts said. He shambled out the door.

The door closed and she was alone with Brandon. This was it. After today, she'd never see him again. In the interim, she had to hope and pray that he wasn't injured while helping her. God how she hated this. She hated waiting, hated wondering what horrible thing would next occur, hated everything about this. "I—I hope everything goes well."

"It will. If you will be careful, that is. No theatrics, if you please."

Verena nodded mutely. She wanted to run to him, to be enfolded in his arms, to feel his crisp linen shirt beneath her fingers, to smell his wonderful cologne. But something held her back. She felt as shy and awkward as a fifteen-year-old.

"Verena."

He was beside her, so close she could feel the edge of his coat brushing against her back.

"There is one more thing we must say." He'd regained most of his voice, but a husky edge lingered.

"What?"

"Look at me."

She turned, then wished she hadn't. He was so large, so powerful, so Brandon. She wanted to slip her hands beneath his coat and burrow to safety. She wanted to hold him and taste him and never, ever let him go.

But that was not to be. "Brandon, I—"

He engulfed her in a hug, holding her so tightly she had to fight to breathe. God, but she was going to miss him. Her heart stumbled at the thought and she pressed her cheek against his shirt.

In less than an hour, they'd be on their way. His crisp linen shirt rubbed her cheek, the scent of his cologne lulling her senses. "You'll have to change your clothing if you're going to look like a groom."

"I know. Perhaps Peters will lend me something."

"Won't you look fashionable," she murmured. This was what happened to people in her life. Brandon St. John, society's darling, would then truly be a Lansdowne.

The thought did more to harden her heart than anything else could have. "We must go. James will be waiting."

Brandon's smile faded, his blue gaze narrowed. "Verena, what's wrong?"

"Nothing. But you'd better do something about those hands, too. My father said you can always tell a man by his hands."

He looked at his perfectly clean hands. "You're right. I'll get some soot from the fireplace. Give me a moment."

Smiling, he walked to the door and held it open, bowing in the most servile manner. "After ye, missus!" he said in a tolerable imitation of Herberts.

Verena managed a faint smile. As she walked past him, he stopped her, placing an arm between her and the door.

She blinked up at him, her throat so tight it ached. "This is not the way a servant would act."

"It is if I were an impertinent servant." His blue eyes shimmered with humor and . . . something else. Something that sent a tremor down Verena's spine.

*No.* She would not allow this to happen. It hurt enough to know that she was leaving. "We should go."

"Not until you've kissed me." He bent forward, his lips within a breath of touching hers. "Verena, there is something between us. When we return, I intend on settling it."

*When we return* . . . There would be no returning. Ever. The second she and James had those letters, they would ride like the wind to Dover where a packet awaited them. She wet her dry lips. "We'll talk about this later, after everything is resolved."

"Then kiss me and we'll be on our way."

"We don't have time to—"

He gripped the other doorframe, moving so that she was trapped between his arms. "Verena, one kiss."

It was the last time she would ever be able to touch him in this way. Within hours, she would be on her way to Italy, and behind her, still in England, would be her heart, resting in the palm of London's most dashing rake.

He bent his head, his lips brushing softly over hers. That one touch, so gentle, so hesitant, ignited an instant response. She threw her arms about his neck and pressed herself to him, deepening the kiss and opening her mouth to him. Ripples of awareness tingled through her, but she was caught in a whorl of emotion, unable to do more than cling to him, yearning for him even as she possessed him.

It wasn't enough, this one kiss, no matter how hot, how passionate. It would never be enough.

Verena pressed against him, her breasts flattening against his broad chest. She was being shameless, unprincipled, but she no longer cared. This was the memory she'd always hold dearest.

Brandon felt her desperation and it ignited his senses like a wildfire. He craved this woman, his entire body ached for her, his first thought in the morning and his last thought as he slipped into slumber, was of Verena. Of her violet eyes, of the hint of a dimple that teased her cheek when she smiled, of just . . . her.

He wanted, no, he *needed* Verena. Needed her because he—

She broke the kiss and pressed back against the door facing him, her cheeks flushed. "W—we must go."

"Not yet," he said, his voice deep.

There was something about the way he said it that made her gasp as if she'd suddenly lost her breath. The air between them was always fraught with tension, but now it grew so thick, she wondered that he couldn't see it.

He turned to the door, closed it, and to her astonishment, he turned the lock.

"Brandon?"

He faced her and there was no mistaking the look on his face. She swallowed, backing away. Something touched the back of her legs, and suddenly she was no longer standing, but sitting on the edge of the settee, her knees unable to hold her upright.

Brandon stood before her. He stopped down and put his arms about her, gently turning her face to his. "For one moment, don't think about what happened last night. Or what might happen this afternoon. We are here, this second. Just us." His voice ran along her senses like a fire, melting everything in its path. "Kiss me, Verena."

She shook her head.

"Then let me kiss you." He brushed the tips of his fingers along her cheek, leaving a trail of delicate sensation.

She swallowed, aware that he was deliberately seducing her. *And what would be wrong with that?* she asked herself. Why not give in to passion? This was the last time she might ever have this chance.

Damn it, she deserved some happiness. She deserved to spend her last day in England in the arms of the man she—Verena caught herself a moment before she committed the worst sin of all, believing herself in love with Brandon St. John.

"Verena," he murmured. He took her hand and placed a delicate kiss in her palm, feathering her skin with his hot breath. Jolts of shocked desire went up her arm and traveled across her breasts and lower.

Locking her gaze with his, she touched him, sliding her fingers over his mouth. She inserted the tip of her forefinger between his lips. He bit her gently and heat built inside her as his tongue stroked her flesh. God, but he was the most sensual man she knew. Need pooled between her thighs and she clenched them together to still the ache.

He withdrew her finger and trailed his lips over her hand, to her wrist. "I want you with me, beneath me," he whispered. "Do you want me, Verena?"

In answer, Verena twined her arms about his neck and pulled his mouth to hers. His lips were hot and demanding, his hands cupping, stroking, exploring her as if he'd never before touched her— never before made her his. He groaned as she raked a hand through his hair, holding him to her.

She was never aware of how they undressed. One moment, they were fully clothed, hands desperately seeking buttons and ties, and the next they were naked, their bare skin holding their souls at bay, their clothes pooled on the floor about them.

Verena lifted her arms to twine them about Brandon's neck, brushing her bared breasts along his chest. Suddenly, touching him was not enough. She wanted to taste him, to fill her senses until there was nothing but Brandon. A wave of longing slammed into her heart and the walls she'd built to protect herself began to crack. She pressed herself to him, rubbing her hips against his, feeling his excitement. She lost herself in the feel of him, his mouth possessing hers, the hot thrust of his tongue inside her mouth, the sensuous feel of his hardened manhood against her stomach.

The edge of the settee pressed against the back of her legs. "Mine," he whispered hoarsely into her ear. "All mine."

A flush of power surged through her, making her more wanton, stirring her to new improprieties. With trembling fingers, she reached between them and placed her hand about his manhood. Velvet hard and warm, it sent a pleasurable shiver through her.

"Verena," he breathed, his face a mask of torment. She reveled in it, stroking him with a featherlight touch.

Brandon moaned. "I can't take this much longer."

Neither could she. Her whole body throbbed with desire and if he didn't touch her soon, she would explode in a whoosh of heat. Brandon slid down until his knees rested on the floor, his mouth even with her chest. The sight of his sensuous mouth so near her nipples caused them to pucker as if he had touched them. He lowered his hands and placed them on her calves. Slowly, ever so slowly, he pushed her knees apart. With hands that trembled ever so slightly, he positioned himself between her thighs.

He leaned forward to kiss her breasts, his tongue leaving a heated path. She tangled her fingers in his thick hair, pulling him closer. Her senses stretched, expanded until she was aware of every feeling, every nuance in the room. The flicker of heat from the fire. The edge of the settee against the back of her thighs. Of Brandon's hands on her knees. Of his mouth on her breasts. Every cadence burned itself into her memory and added to the ripples of passion that built within.

Verena writhed against him, her hands moving wildly over his neck and shoulders. Brandon fought for control. She was so beautiful, so brazen. She reclined before him, her thighs surrounding his hips, her skin pink and passion-kissed.

Like a man starved, he positioned himself against her. He wanted to take her gently. But she was beyond gentle. Verena threw her arms about his neck, pressing against him, enfolding him into her warm body until they were one. His breath tore from his lips as he sank into her, reveling in the feel of her, the beauty of her that captivated him so completely.

Her fingers curled, her nails biting into his arms. "More," she whispered hoarsely. "More—"

He thrust home. She gave a startled cry, her head thrown back, her hips arching to meet his. Again and again, he thrust. She clasped his hips tightly with her legs, her body writhing a sensuous dance beneath his. She arched into him, her passions rising, building. He could barely keep his own emotions under control, his body aching with the torture. But Brandon fought against it.

Just as he thought he could withhold no more, she stiffened beneath him, her body arching so wildly that Brandon had to wrap his arms about her to hold her on the settee. Brandon followed her over the edge of passion, his body exploding with a flash of heat before he collapsed against her, cradling her to him.

God how he loved her. Loved her as he could love no other. The realization echoed in his soul. "Verena," he said into the softness of her hair. "I—"

"No. Brandon, don't—" She pushed herself upright. "We have to go."

He leaned away, frowning. "Verena, we—"

"No." Her smile quavered the faintest bit. "Brandon, we cannot . . . now is not the time."

He hated to admit it, but she was right. The clock was ticking and they had much to do. Brandon nodded mutely, dropping his arms and moving away, trying to cool his ardor.

Silently they dressed. Verena's face was tense, her eyes shadowed. Brandon tried to say something several times, but the haunted look in her eyes made him fall silent.

Finally, she smoothed her hair and managed a wobbly smile. "I—We will talk about this later. After . . ."

He tilted her face to his. "When you are ready." He bent and kissed her cheek.

At first, she held herself back, but then, just as he went to move away, she pressed against him, her head nestled to his neck. His arms encircled her and there they remained until the clock chimed.

She stepped away, her color high. She went to the small desk and pulled out a small square of paper and placed it into her reticule. "We must go."

He nodded. "I'll borrow a coat and hat from Peters." She nodded, then left the room, unlocking the door, her soft voice calling for Herberts.

Moments later, dressed in an old coat, a battered felt hat on his head, Brandon helped Verena into the carriage. As he closed the door, he caught sight of a boy in a blue tattered coat, who took off running the instant Brandon whipped the horses to life.

Smiling grimly, Brandon pulled his collar up about his ears and made his way from London.

On a normal day, Verena would have been glad for Brandon's well-sprung carriage. It was far better equipped for the trip than her own, which had weak springs and an unfortunate tendency to sway around each corner. But nothing could make the long, arduous journey to Little Sutton any more palatable.

She was so nervous her stomach ached. And the fact that Brandon was so close yet so far away did not make things easier.

They reached Little Sutton at one and stopped to ask directions to the inn. Another note awaited them there, delivered by an urchin with a dirty face and directing them to a clearing half a mile from town.

Per their plan, she made sure that everyone within earshot knew she was there, that she was tired and famished, that she wanted nothing more than to return home to London. She complained and whined, then burst into tears and allowed a chambermaid to lead her back to her coach.

Brandon never dismounted, watching it all from his position on the coach.

It appalled her how easily the tears came and it

took her several minutes to stop crying once the coach was underway. Thus it was that at the appointed time, the carriage pulled into the clearing.

She patted her reticule, the faint outline of a pistol visible. She pulled it out and checked to be sure it was loaded before she leaned out the window.

Thick brush encircled them, dotted here and there with flowers. Tall trees waved overhead.

Verena scanned her surroundings anxiously. She could not see Brandon, but she was agonizingly aware of his presence. He was vulnerable sitting in the open, and she could only pray the villains did not suspect him.

Verena waited. All she could hear were the sounds of birds twittering and the wind rustling the trees. The coach rocked as Brandon climbed down. He walked forward as if checking the horses.

After several moments, she said, "No one's here."

"Wait," Brandon ordered softly.

"I want to get out." It was tortuous sitting inside the carriage while he was in the line of danger.

"No. You have on skirts. If something goes wrong, you won't be able to run back to the carriage."

"You don't know me well if you think that."

His gaze ran over her, hot and possessive. "I know you too well to let you out of that coach."

She curled her hands more tightly about her reticule. "I wonder where—"

"Hold it right there," came a voice from the edge of the clearing.

Verena's heart stumbled, her gaze meeting Brandon's. They knew that voice. Knew it because—she closed her eyes.

When she opened them, there, standing in the clearing, stood Roger Carrington, Viscount Wycham. And in his hand was a pistol, pointed directly at Verena.

# Chapter 23

*Men never understand that all a woman truly wants is a man who will listen. Understand. Pay her bills. And, of course, love her madly even when her hips widen due to an unfortunate addiction to bon bons.*

Lady Jersey to Mrs. Cowper, as the two watched the dancers waltz at Almack's

**B**rand struggled to believe the scene before him. Wycham—the traitor. Anger simmered, deep and bitter.

Roger cocked the gun, the click loud in the clearing. "Don't even think it, Brand."

Brand's jaw tightened. "What the hell do you think you're doing, Roger? This is ludicrous!"

"No, it's not. It's survival. I have no choice." He glanced toward the carriage. "Verena, pray join us."

Verena opened the door of the carriage and climbed down.

"Wait!" Brand took a step forward, stopping when Roger's gun swung his way. "You don't need her out here."

"Oh yes, I do. I want both of you where I can see your hands. And do not think of using that blunderbuss you have hidden on the coach. I will shoot the lady if I must."

Brand's hands curled into fists.

"Roger Carrington," Verena said, scorn thick in her voice. "I should have guessed."

His cheeks reddened. "You don't understand what's occurred."

"I know you've been blackmailing my brother."

Wycham reached into his pocket and pulled a crumpled packet of letters from his pocket. He threw them to the ground. "They're all yours. Where's the list?"

Brand started to turn toward the carriage, but stopped, a thoughtful expression on his face. "May I ask how you got Lansdowne's letters? It was damnably convenient that you should end up with them just as that list disappeared."

"Wasn't it? Actually, though, I had to manipulate the fates a bit."

Verena frowned. "Manipulate?"

"I knew you wouldn't just hand over the list. Especially not once you realized it might hold some worth. Therefore, I schemed a bit."

"How did you know about James?"

"I met the redoubtable Mr. Lansdowne several months ago, in France. And when I met him, I was struck by the resemblance."

"You knew of his dalliance."

Wycham shrugged. "A little money in the hands of a poorly paid servant will yield far more information than one needs. Once I heard about the letters . . . it wasn't difficult."

"That is despicable," Brand snapped. How had he been so wrong?

"No, that is good planning."

Brandon simmered and he had to force his mind to calmness. Verena needed him.

Roger gestured with his gun. "Now Verena, I want that bloody list."

"As soon as you take this list, you will be committing treason."

"I don't care."

"Roger," Brand said. "I don't know what you're doing, but—"

"Don't know—do you realize what my debts are?"

"Your father—"

"Has no money. None, Brandon." Roger gave a sharp laugh. "Oh yes, I was surprised, too. He's lost it all on the market, investing in the most ridiculous things—there's nothing left." Sweat beaded on Roger's brow. "My whole life was based on the fact that one day I would be the next earl. I was raised to be wealthy and powerful and not poor, dammit! I—I can't be poor." He swallowed hard. "So I will have that list. It's worth a fortune."

Verena shook her head. "There are worse things than poverty. Surely you can—"

"Get that bloody list!" Roger snapped.

"Roger," Brandon said, stepping forward. "If you need money that badly, I will gladly—"

"No! I don't want your money. I want my own. And I'm getting my own."

There was a cry in his voice that reminded Brandon of when they were children. "Roger, I don't know what's wrong, but you are making things worse. Just put down the gun and we'll—"

"*Give me that damn list!*"

Verena stood. "You want your list?" She reached into her reticule and pulled a small slip of paper from inside. "Here."

Roger took an eager step forward, his free hand outstretched.

Verena leaned forward, the slip of paper in her fingers, though she made no move to get closer to Roger.

He didn't notice; his eyes were on the paper. He took the two steps to reach her fingers when she let go. The breeze grabbed the curl of paper and tumbled it across the ground.

"Get that damn paper!"

Verena bent to reach it, covertly scraping up a handful of silt. As she straightened, she threw the dirt right into Roger's eyes.

"Ahhh!" Roger staggered back, clutching at his face.

Brandon grabbed the blunderbuss and turned toward Roger. But before he could aim, a loud retort rang from the woods. Brandon's gun went flying from his hands.

There, standing behind Roger, was Farragut. His brown eyes blazed angrily.

"Damn it," Brand muttered.

"Come, now. Ye didn't think Wycham capable of planning such a pretty cast, did ye?"

Verena looked at Brandon. "Who is this?"

Wycham swiped at his red eyes, blinking rapidly. "Let me introduce you. This is Farragut. He works for the Home Office."

"Aye, that I do. I've forty years in this business. Forty bloody years. And fer what? Fer nothing! So I decided to turn my knowledge into gold."

"The list," Verena said softly.

"Aye. It's of every operative we have in all of Europe. France alone was willin' to pay over a hundred thousand pounds fer it."

Verena pressed a hand to her forehead as if her head hurt. "You—you gave the list to Humford."

"And me lad, Wycham here, was going to pinch it the night of yer dinner party. Humford was to take the fall fer the whole mess."

"But then Humford lost it," Brandon said, seeing exactly what happened.

Farragut scowled. "Bloody fool. I warned him this was important, I did. And what did he do, but lose the blasted list afore a day went by."

Brand looked at Roger. "Where do you come into this?"

Farragut chuckled. "Ye'd best let me explain it. I needed someone to cover my tracks. Roger here was perfect—a desperate young nabob. And willing to do almost anything to get out from under his debts, even off Humford."

Brandon turned to Wycham, whose eyes were red-rimmed and watering furiously. "*You* killed Humford?"

"I—I hit him on the head. I only wanted to stun him, but he wouldn't be quiet. I was afraid he'd call attention and—"

"My God," Verena said, "you killed him outside of my house. You must have tossed his body in the Thames, then returned for dinner."

"No," Brandon said. "Wycham said he hit

Humford on the head. Who cut Humford's throat?"

Wycham glanced at Farragut, who met his gaze with a look of contempt. The older man's lips curled derisively. "I'm the one as took the body and got rid of it. Wycham was too ill to do more than stagger to yer house. He's no stomach fer thet sort of thing."

Roger's face paled, though his jaw was set with determination. "Not this time. This time I will do what I must."

"Roger," Brandon said in a low voice. "You can't kill someone in cold blood. It's not in you. You'd never be able to live with yourself."

A quiver passed over Roger's face. He seemed to be holding his breath. Suddenly, he gasped. "Brandon, why did you come—"

"Roger!" Brandon snapped. "Take control! Be a man for once."

Farragut laughed harshly. "Roger Carrington, a man? I'd like to see that. Fortunately, once't he's wealthy, no one will ask him to prove his manhood."

"I am a man," Roger said, his face pale. He leveled his gun at Brandon.

Brandon was conscious of the blunderbuss lying in the dirt at his feet. If only he could reach it without causing Roger to shoot wildly. Good God, what should he do?

*Pretend like we already have it.* Of course.

He looked at Roger. "I'm sorry."

Roger's brow lowered in confusion. "For what?"

"For killing you."

"But . . . you haven't—"

Brandon grabbed the weapon, lifted it and fired—but not at Roger. Farragut staggered back and fell into the shrubbery with a crash, his gun spinning through the air before falling into the bushes.

Roger's mouth opened and closed, but no sound came out.

Brandon was aware that Verena had come to stand beside him, a small pistol in her hand. "Roger, put down your weapon."

Roger's lips trembled. He looked at where Farragut lay in the dirt, blood seeping from his mouth. Without another word, Roger closed his eyes and let his pistol fall harmlessly to the ground. "I'm sorry," he whispered. "I'm so sorry."

# Chapter 24

*Pardon me. Is Lady Westforth in? I'm here to—*
*Oh dear! I seem to have lost my bracelet.*

Mrs. Cowper to Herberts, on coming to visit
Lady Westforth following the announcement
of the Joyous News

**V**erena opened the door to James's room and peered in.

He immediately pushed himself to a sitting position. "Ver!"

She went in and perched on the edge of his bed. "You look better. What did the physician say?"

"That I shall be up and about on crutches within the next few days. The timing's perfect, for our ship sails Saturday."

The news should have made her happy. Instead her eyes sprang a horrid leak. "I—I'm glad."

He took her hand, a wry smile on his face. "No, you're not. Where's St. John?"

"He was here all morning but I didn't see him." She couldn't. Ever since yesterday's horrible experience, she'd avoided Brandon, refusing to see him simply because she couldn't. Her heart was almost breaking now.

James sighed. "Are you certain this is what you want to do? Leave London?"

She didn't want to leave at all. "You know what would happen if we stayed." The suspicions would begin, and the whispers. "We don't have that blasted list."

James rubbed his chin, his brow creased. "I suppose so. I just—Verena, we only get so many chances at happiness. Don't waste this one."

Her throat tightened, her eyes burned. She wasn't wasting anything. She stood, patting his hand softly. "The only thing I'm wasting is time. I've packing to do."

She gave him an encouraging smile and left, stopping outside to rest her head against the cool wooden door. As soon as James's leg healed, they would leave and everything would be as it should be. She should be happy. After all, she would be with her family soon. And James was well.

"There you are," came a voice at her ear.

She gasped, then pressed a hand to her thudding heart. "Brandon! For the love of—you scared me!"

"I didn't mean to," he said, stepping out of the shadows. He filled the narrow hallway, made it seem darker and intimate. "How is your brother?"

"Better." Verena turned toward the stairs, anxious to get somewhere where there was more light. Why did her heart lurch every time Brandon was near? "The doctor said he should be up in a few days."

Brandon followed her down the steps. "That isn't that long. And we can all use a little rest."

Verena paused at the door of the sitting room. "How did you get in?"

Brandon shrugged. "I have my ways."

"You bribed Herberts, didn't you?"

He opened the door and stood to one side. "I'll never tell."

She paused, remembering suddenly the last time they'd been in this room. Her skin heated at the thought. A glance at Brandon told her that he was thinking the same thing, his gaze on the settee, a faint smile on his lips.

Blast, blast and double blast. She hated farewells. Back stiff, she walked into the sitting room. All too soon, she'd never see this room again. For some reason, it looked dreadfully dear. She blinked back tears when she realized that in a week, she'd be saying good-bye again.

Good-bye. That had to be the most horrible word ever written into a language. Her eyes stung and she went to the window overlooking the street to hide her tears. There was so much she wanted to say—so much she *needed* to say, but couldn't.

Brandon came to stand beside her, his leg brushing her skirts. "When we were last in this room, I started to tell you something, but you told me to wait."

"Yes, well, there's no need to—"

"I've a question or two. If you don't mind, of course."

She should tell him to leave. This very instant. But somehow, the words changed in her throat. "You may ask me anything you wish."

"How come your trunks are still in the front hallway?"

Verena stiffened. "Trunks?"

"Yes. I looked in them while I was waiting. You've clean shirts, nightgowns, that sort of thing. I know you were going to pretend to be leaving when we used the fake note, but now . . . now I have to wonder if perhaps you aren't pretending anymore."

"Oh."

He moved so that as he leaned against the window frame, his shoulder came in contact with hers. "You've planned on fleeing the country."

Verena wet her lips. It sounded cowardly when he said it like that. She turned to face him. "Brandon, we have no choice. We don't know where that list is and until we find it—"

"It's time you stopped running." His eyes burned brightly. "Forever, Verena. Have you ever used that word? Forever. It's a beautiful word."

"I am not running. For your information, I stopped running four years ago," she said stiffly.

"Did you? Or did you exchange running for hiding?" He smoothed a curl that lay on her shoulder, his voice low, intimate. "When I first met you, there were some things about you that didn't make sense. Little things. But significant for all that."

"Like what?"

"That you were known in the demimonde as a seductress." He leaned forward and rubbed his cheek along hers, the touch sparking a heat in her stomach and lower. "Yet I could find no one who recalled you ever having a lover. Not one."

She shivered. Her entire body was awash with the feel of him. "Perhaps I kept my lovers well hidden."

"And perhaps you never took one because it would mean revealing yourself."

"Brandon, there is no need for this conversation."

"Oh but there is. You see, it has been several days since I realized that I cannot live without you."

She looked down at her hands. Strange how one could see one's hands every day but never really *see* them. They were long and elegant, though she deplored how wide her thumbnail appeared to be. "Brandon, you don't know—"

"Verena, will you marry me?"

It was just like when Andrew had asked her. But unlike Andrew, Brandon had much, much more to lose. Worse, she had much, much more to lose.

"No," she whispered. "I cannot."

"Why can't you? Don't you love me?"

Did she love him. God help her, but she was awash in love. Every thought, every feeling, every sinew of her body was of him and for him and by him.

And that was why she had to send him away. "Brandon, you must think this through. I am not just a nobody. I am a Lansdowne. My family is a family of charlatans. We answer to no one and we are very, very good at deception."

"So is my brother Devon. He would have been an incredible actor."

"Would have been, if he hadn't been a St. John."

He frowned. "You are the most obstinate female. Verena, I don't care—"

"But you will. You will care when your brothers turn their backs on you. When your family refuses to say your name ever again. When people you thought were friends cut you at every opportunity, refusing to recognize you, mocking you at every turn." She lifted her gaze to his. "Do you know what that feels like? Do you have any idea? It hurts, Brandon. It stings like a cut but it's oh so much deeper. I will never go through that again."

"Good God, is that what happened when you married Westforth?"

"That and more."

Brandon looked at her for a long moment, watching her from beneath his lashes. Finally he sighed.

The sound ripped through Verena like a knife. That was it. He would leave. She would follow James to Italy and then on to France. But her heart . . . where would it be?

She closed her eyes, and made to turn away, but Brandon's hands closed over her arms. "I suppose you are right—our marriage would indeed cause a scandal. Just as your other marriage caused a scandal."

"Yes," she whispered. "After Andrew died . . . it was horrible."

His hands moved up and down her arms, rubbing, smoothing. It was as if a heavy net entwined them. Brandon pressed his lips to her temple and murmured against her skin, "But there's a difference this time. Whatever happens to us, it will happen to us together. I will never ever leave you alone. Do you understand that? No one will cut you without facing me first."

"Brand, you can't face down that sort of thing."

"Can't you?" He tilted her face to his. "Watch me."

"I can't—I won't go through that again."

He frowned. "What about me, Verena? What about the fact that I love you? That I can't live without you? You think there will be a scandal if you marry me? What if you *don't* marry me?"

She frowned. "I don't see—"

"I'll die."

"No, you won't."

"Part of me will." His hands cupped her face warmly. "You are a part of me, Verena, whether you want to be or not. I cannot live without you. If you go to Italy, then so shall I go."

"B-but your family—"

"Will understand." He took her hand and placed it over his pocket, over the ring that hung suspended on a ribbon. "You belong to me."

Her fingers closed about the metal circlet, the warmth tingling beneath her fingers. "I—I don't know what to say."

"Say you'll marry me and keep me from living a horrible nomad's existence. And if you won't marry me . . . that would be an even larger pity. Because you see, I wrote to your parents and invited them to our wedding."

Verena lost the ability to speak and breathe. She blinked up at him. "You did what?"

He smiled smugly. "You heard me. I wrote and asked your parents to come to the wedding. They should be on their way now. I do hope they make it before Saturday next."

"Why?"

"Because that's when we're getting married. I've already procured a special license."

"Brandon, how can—"

"And that's another thing. I've already sent the invitations."

"You—you did?"

"Well, no. I didn't do it myself. I'm not much in the way of organizing things. But my sister is. As is my sister-in-law. Between Sara and Anna, I believe they've taken care of the entire event, or so they assure me. I hope you will be pleased."

"But—surely you can cancel—"

"Two hundred invitations?"

Her lips moved faintly.

He shook his head. "I don't think so. I mean, we could try. But I'm certain we'd miss a few, which could cause all sorts of problems." He sighed. "And then there is the orchestra, the cake, the ball—"

"What ball?"

"To welcome you to the family. My brother Marcus is determined to stare down anyone who might offer either of us insult. So they're having a grand ball to introduce you as Mrs. Brandon St. John."

"How—when—" Verena pressed her fingers to her forehead. "Brandon, I can't let you—"

He pressed his fingers against her lips. "You don't have to let me do anything. If you don't want to marry me, then I'll just have to deal with the scandal on my own."

"What scandal?"

"Of being stood up. Left at the altar. A laughingstock of the entire *ton*. If you don't show up at the wedding after we've already invited all those people . . . well, everyone will know that you've walked out on me. Because I will be there."

It was blackmail. Rich, delicious blackmail. Her lips quivered ever so slightly. "You will, hm?"

"Oh yes. And people will talk, you know."

"I imagine they might."

"It will take forever to live it down. This sort of thing . . ." He sighed dramatically. "I am considered quite a catch and that will make it all the worse."

She had to bite her lip to keep from smiling. "I can see where it might cause all sorts of problems, especially since you are so handsome."

"Exactly my point." He traced his fingers along her cheek, the touch feather light, his gaze intense. "Verena, if you do not marry me and quickly, I will never be happy again. I love you."

She just stared at him, her heart quivering. "Brandon, I can't—"

He kissed her. Kissed her so thoroughly that she had to cling to him when he finished. "Well?" he said roughly. "Will you marry me and save me from my mistakes? Save me from dying old and alone, for I will, you know."

He looked down at his pocket and undid the ribbon. "Verena, will you please marry me?" He slid the ring over her finger.

The ring seemed to glow, the metal warm against her skin. He did have a point . . . there would be a scandal no matter what she did. Only if she stayed and married him, they wouldn't have to face it, or anything else, alone.

"Yes, Brandon," she said, her heart full. "I will marry you."

And she did.

# Epilogue

*Love is a grand thing, 'tis. An' the best parts of all is the kissin'.*

Herberts to the Pemberleys' new maid, Anne,
while trying to convince the pert wench
to ah, "honor his suit"

The wedding was the talk of the season, but Brandon and Verena were too happy to care. Brandon could not believe his good fortune—everything he wanted, everything he'd dreamed about, stood at his side. He placed his arm about Verena as they stood in the receiving line at the grand ball Marcus had hosted for them, thinking of the carriage that waited just outside.

As pleasant as the wedding had been, he was even more anxious to begin the honeymoon. He wanted Verena alone, all to himself. His interfering sister, Sara, had managed to convince Verena to move in with her during the week before the wedding, ostensibly to assist with the preparations. Brandon knew Sara was really attempting to protect his lovely bride from his attentions.

Fortunately for all concerned, Verena's room was directly over the veranda and the trellis led right to her window. Brandon found that there was a certain piquancy to stealing into his betrothed's bedchamber each and every night.

She caught his gaze and grinned, causing him to pull her to him for yet another kiss. He simply could not get enough of her. And he realized with deep gratification that it would always be that way . . . the more they had of each other, the more they needed.

Verena slipped her arm about his waist and rested her fair head on his shoulder, the faint scent of lavender rising. It was the end of a long and exciting week. Her parents had indeed arrived, claiming to be relatives of a long-deposed Russian archduke. Brandon had to give them credit—they had the looks and manners of royalty. No one suspected a thing.

James came out of the ballroom, resplendent in black coat and breeches, his crutches adorned with colorful ribbons.

Verena smiled at him. "I see that our sister Charlotte has been at you."

He regarded the ribbons with something akin to loathing. "Lud, yes. If I had been a horse, she'd have attempted to plait my tail. I'm lucky she just twined those things about my crutches and not my leg."

Brand chuckled. Verena's family was charming. After a momentary hesitation, the *ton* had become taken with them and the invitations were already pouring in.

Of course, the Lansdownes would not be staying long enough for anyone to discover their deception. Verena's father already had plans for visiting Italy, only this time as a deposed English duke. Brand made certain that the family had plenty of funds for their travels and he promised to take Verena once a year for a nice, lengthy visit, an arrangement that suited everyone to perfection.

A new guest walked through the line. Slightly stooped, with white hair and bushy brows—Brandon recognized him immediately. "Sir Colburn!"

The old man smiled. "Didn't think I'd come, did you?" He shook Brandon's hand and then gave the bride a gallant kiss. "I apologize for being late. I had an altercation with some chap driving a carriage in your front drive. Rudest man I ever met and I—" Sir Colburn waved a hand and chuckled. "Sorry. Rambling on like a fool. Comes with age, you know."

"Sir Colburn," Verena said, "have you found the missing list?"

James leaned forward eagerly. "I certainly hope you have."

Colburn shook his head. "I'm afraid not, though you were certainly kind to allow us to search your house so thoroughly."

"I just wish you'd found it," Verena said with a frown. "I fear we will never hear the end of it unless you do."

Brandon slid his hand from her waist, up her back, and then beneath the thick fall of her hair. "I'm certain it will turn up in good time."

She turned and smiled at him, her violet eyes warm with love. God, he loved her so much. Heedless of their surroundings, he bent to kiss her—

"Here now, guv'nor! Shouldn't ye save thet fer yer honeymoon?"

Brandon sighed. "Herberts."

"Good God," James exclaimed. "What are you doing here?"

The man, splendidly adorned in a new blue and buff coat complete with shiny brass buttons, his thinning hair slicked to one side, hooked his thumbs in his waistcoat and rocked back on his heels. "Mayhap ye should ask the missus about thet."

Sir Colburn frowned. "Do you know this man? He's the one who attempted to cut off my coachman as we turned into the drive!"

"Thet's because oiye was in a bit of a hurry." Herberts leaned forward to say in a confidential tone. "Ye really needs some new horses, guv'nor. The ones ye has now are slugs, the both o' them."

Brandon looked down at Verena. "Well?"

She dimpled mischievously. "It seemed to me that Herberts wasn't really . . . happy as a butler."

"Ye had the roight o' it, missus. Oiye was near to miserable."

"Poor man!" James said, though he didn't look in the least concerned.

"And," Verena added swiftly, "he has such significant talents in other areas."

"Thet's roight. Oiye can drive a coach to an inch, oiye can."

Verena smiled up at Brandon. "I thought perhaps he might enjoy being our coachman now that you've brought Poole to us."

"Poole seems t' like bein' a butler," Herberts said, his thin chest puffed out. "Meanwhile, oiye'm a dandy coachman. Bet ye're surprised to find thet out, ain't ye, guv'nor?"

"Brandon!" Devon stalked in, his brows lowered, Chase hard on his heels. "I was standing in the front lawn, bidding Lady Tarleton good-bye when someone took my new watch."

Chase nodded glumly. "I've lost my gold cravat pin, too."

Brandon looked at Herberts.

"Wasn't me!" the coachman said, holding his hands in the air.

"*Herberts*," Verena said.

The man shook his head sadly. "Oh, all roight. 'Tis supposed to be a joyous occasion, after all." He dug into his pockets and began to produce his loot. With a regretful sigh, he dropped it in a shimmering pile on a long marble table.

"Good God," Sir Colburn said, bending to look at the collection of rings, watch fobs, watches, cravat pins, an enameled snuffbox, and other glittering items. "That's quite a collection."

"There's my watch," Devon said. He polished it with his palm, then tucked it away.

"And my cravat pin," Chase said.

James winked at Herberts. "Bloody good job, old fellow."

Herberts preened. "Weel, now. Thank ye, Mr. Lansdowne. Oiye trys to keep up wif me hobbies."

Sir Colburn picked up the enameled snuffbox. "This looks familiar. I wonder if—My God!"

"What?" Brandon asked.

"I know where I've seen this. It belonged to Humford! He had it the last time I saw him. The day we gave him the list."

Verena frowned. "I didn't think he took snuff."

"He didn't," Colburn said slowly. "I wonder if . . ." With a flick of his thumb, Colburn undid the tiny catch and then opened the box. A small piece of paper fell out onto the floor. Colburn stooped to retrieve it.

"The list," James exclaimed. "Herberts must have stolen the snuffbox from Humford while he was at Verena's dinner party."

Brandon chuckled. "Which explains why he began searching for it in the middle of dinner—he knew he'd just had it and all of the sudden it was gone. I daresay he panicked."

"I can't believe you found it!" Verena said, giving a little hop. "Thank God."

Sir Colburn beamed. "Thank God indeed. Mr. and Mrs. St. John, I hope you'll excuse me, but I must go."

"Of course," Brandon said. He watched as Sir Colburn strode out of the house, almost prancing in excitement.

Verena leaned her head against Brandon's shoulder and sighed happily.

Brandon looked down into his wife's shining eyes and was suddenly overcome with the need to go on his honeymoon. And not in thirty or forty minutes, but now. This very instant. Before he took her in his arms and embarrassed them both before the whole world.

He took her hand and drew it through his. "Herberts, do you think you can extract the carriage from that mess out there?"

"Lord love ye, o' course oiye can. Are ye ready to go?"

"Already?" Devon frowned. "Aren't you going to say good-bye to Marcus and Sara?"

"Why should he bother?" Chase said. "Marcus won't care and Sara will think it vastly romantic."

"Which it is," Verena said happily. "Vastly romantic." The whole world seemed to shimmer before her, full of promise and love.

He took her hand and placed a kiss in her palm. "Shall we go, then?"

She answered him with a look that caused him to suck in his breath and bustle her outside. Moments later, Verena was sitting in her new carriage, Herberts climbing onto the box. Brandon halted just outside the door, looking so mischievous that Verena had to restrain herself from throwing her arms about his neck.

"One moment, love," he said. "I've an errand."

From where he and Chase stood on the porch, Devon squinted across the lawn. "Looks as if Brandon's coming back. He must have decided to say farewell to Marcus after all."

Chase followed Devon's gaze to find Brandon strolling across the lawn, his hands in his pockets. "I wouldn't have returned."

"No? Not even to say good-bye?"

"Not even to say hello."

Halfway up the lawn, Brandon stopped. "*Chase!*" he yelled.

Chase's brows rose and he stepped forward. "*What?*"

"*Take care of this.*" Brand threw something.

Chase didn't even think. He reached out and caught the small object. It was the talisman ring.

"*Bloody hell!*" Chase roared. "Take this back!"

"Hell, no. It's yours. It just may save you." With a wave, Brandon turned and dashed back across the lawn to his carriage.

Chase whirled to Devon, who held up his hands. "Don't look at me!" Devon said, stepping away. "It's all yours now."

Damn it. The talisman ring was the last thing he needed, today of all days.

Chase looked back toward the road. The carriage was still in sight, caught in the drive between an old coach and a landau. Herberts was shouting deprecations to an elderly driver who appeared to be deaf, as well as slow. Holding the ring in his fist, Chase vaulted over the railing and ran.

But just as he reached the carriage, the landau moved. Herberts whipped the horses to life. They took off at breakneck speed and were soon dashing down the drive, weaving precariously and taking the corner into the street at an astounding pace.

Chase watched until the carriage was out of sight, the ring warm in his palm. Damn it, what was he supposed to do now? He hadn't planned on returning to his lodgings until . . . he frowned, his throat tight. Perhaps never.

Shoulders slumped, he looked down at the ring, the strange runes gleaming in the light.

"Bloody hell. I suppose I'm stuck with you." He held the ring at eye level and gave it a fierce scowl. "Just don't get any ideas; I wasn't made for marriage and it will be a cold day in hell before I am."

That said, he shoved the ring into his pocket and made his way to his phaeton.

2 GG
m
L
Ef  CO

52
64/55
538770
531-4158